Book Title: SAPPHIRE - The Eternal Love

Written and Illustrated by

Kemal B. Caymaz - Copyright © 2023

Translated by Esat Ulusol

Edited by Ceren Karanar – Suna Rızalar

Cover Design by Raif Kızıl

ISBN: 9798865462583

November 2023

SAPPHIRE

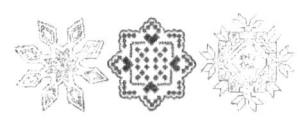

Kemal Behcet Caymaz

BOOK ONE

The Eternal Love

Translated by Esat Ulusol

KEMAL BEHCET CAYMAZ was born in 1989, in the coastal city of Kyrenia in North Cyprus. His elementary and secondary educations were at Girne American Elementary School and Girne American College. In 2003 he attended Nicosia Anatolian High School of Fine Arts and started studying art. During this time his passion for writing has began. He wrote several stories for the school magazine. In 2007 he graduated from high school moving on to the Near East University Faculty of Fine Arts and Design - Department of Plastic Arts. In 2011, he graduated from the university in painting and elective ceramic majors as well as opening his first solo exhibition 'Once Upon A Time' (Bir Varmış Bir Yokmuş). The Once Upon A Time series was exhibited at the United Nations building in the Buffer Zone where the Cyprus talks take place. In 2014, he was awarded the Artist of the Year award in the Young Artists Painting Competition of the TRNC. Later he represented the North Cyprus at the 17th Türksoy Festival meeting the Artists in Sheiki, Azerbaijan. Commencing in 2014, he wrote and illustrated the first book of the SAPPHIRE series "The Promised Time" it being published by Dante Publishing in 2016 as the first fantasy novel set in Cyprus. He successfully completed his post graduate studies in 2017 at Mimar Sinan Fine Arts University on painting major at Nedret Sekban Atelier with his thesis on "Different Child Images in Painting from the 20th Century to the Present". In the same year he received an honourable mention in the Young Artists Painting Competition of TRNC Ministry of Education and Culture, Directorate of Culture Department. A year later in 2018 he was awarded with his series called "Artık Yeter" (It's enough) by the Directorate of Culture of the TRNC Ministry of Education and Culture, dedicated to the children who passed away. Sapphire "The Promised Time" and "The Eternal Love" Turkish edition published by Işık Kitabevi in 2020. He was awarded "Fantasy Novel Incentive Award" in the Ali Nesim Literature Awards. He worked as an instructor in the Plastic Arts Department of the American University of Cyprus between in 2018-2022. He is a member of Mediterranean European Art Association (EMAA) and also a member of Association of Paper Artists of Cyprus and Fantasy and Science Fiction Association (FABISAD). He has participated in many national and international exhibitions and seminars and he is currently working as an art teacher in schools affiliated with the Department of General Secondary Education in TRNC Ministry of National Education.

ESAT ULUSOL was born in London, United Kingdom in 1995. After completing his Bachelor's Degree with high honors in Translation and Interpreting at the Near East University, he received a Master's Degree education on English Language and Linguistics at the University of Westminster. Following a Formation at the Teacher Academy, he is now working as a Translator / Interpreter / Consultant and English Language Lecturer. He translated Colours in Blackness by Tammy Dunning in 2018, Tek Kanatlı Bir Kuş by Yaşar Kemal in 2019 **and** Safir Yegane Aşk by Kemal Behçet Caymaz in 2023.

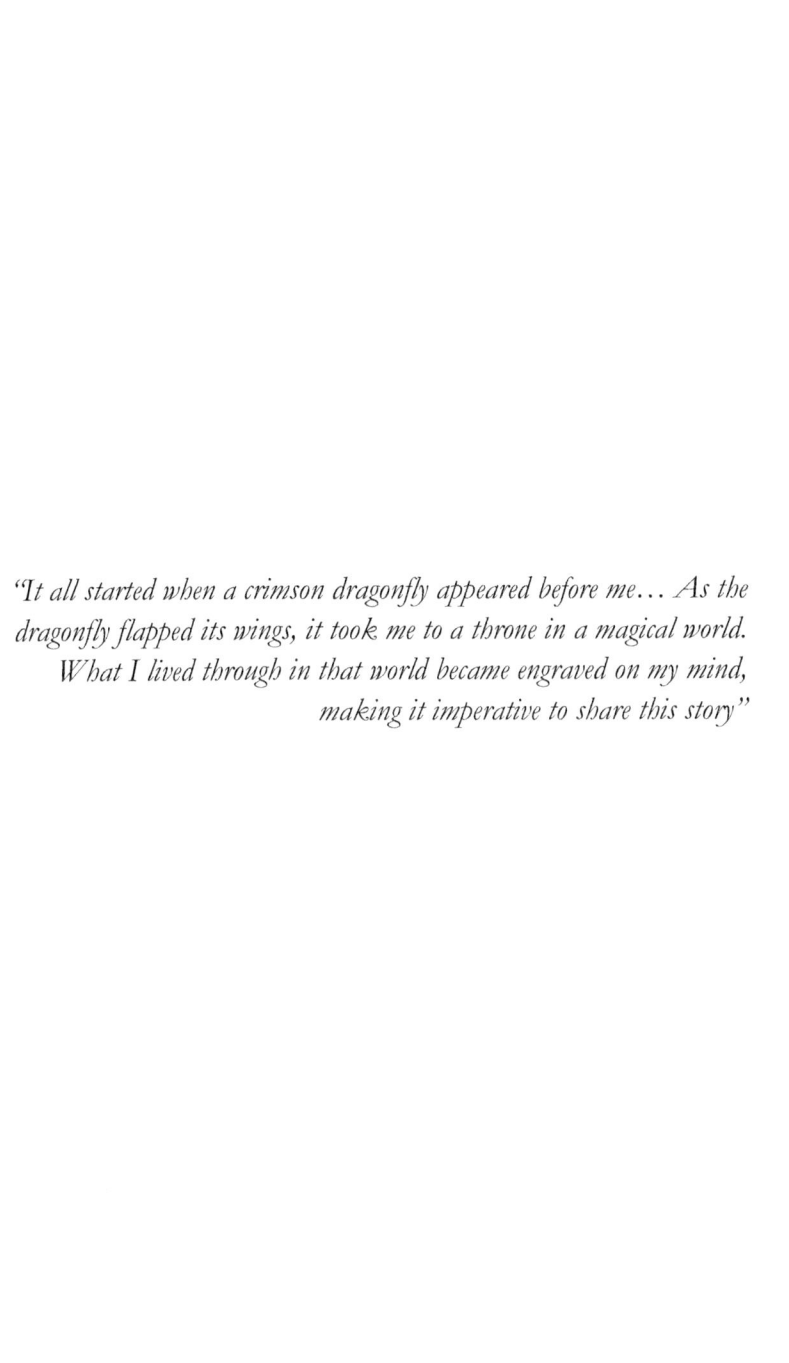

"It all started when a crimson dragonfly appeared before me… As the dragonfly flapped its wings, it took me to a throne in a magical world. What I lived through in that world became engraved on my mind, making it imperative to share this story"

BOOK TWO

The Eternal Love

To someone:

Even if a thousand years pass and we are born again, I know that we will meet once more. And I will fall in love with you again.

> "Alas, that Love, so gentle in his view,
> Should be so tyrannous and rough in proof!"
>
> **William Shakespeare**
> **Romeo and Juliet**
> **Act 1, Scene 1**

> "O love, come
> Kill me every day.
> Then give birth to me every day again
> Do not spare me your compassion and your intimacy.
> Burn me in your sunlight, hide me in the moonlight."
>
> **Suleiman The Magnificent**

INDEX

PROLOGUE: 17
CHAPTER I: Love Means Sorrow 35
CHAPTER II: The Clatter..47
CHAPTER III: Hidden Maneuver 67
CHAPTER IV: The Demons of the Great White House 91
CHAPTER V: Ball Gowns Get Bloodstained 115
CHAPTER VI: A Winged Boy 147
CHAPTER VII: "Lovers" and "Pains" 171
CHAPTER VIII: A Strange Dragonfly 199
CHAPTER IX: Vasili and Vasilia 229
CHAPTER X: Poison and Objection 247
CHAPTER XI: The Judas Tree 281
CHAPTER XII: Reuniting..307
CHAPTER XIII: Birthday Surprise 327
CHAPTER XIV: The First to Fall 347
CHAPTER XV: The Secret 373
CHAPTER XVI: A Cozy Friend's House 391
CHAPTER XVII: Little Stranger 411
CHAPTER XVIII: The Black Medosh Tulips of Saint Hilarion ...433

Preface

Part of me wants those calm brown eyes.

Part of me wants Defne's irresistible passion.

Why do we always chase after the impossible?

Those brown eyes are right next to me now.

But Defne is far away.

PROLOGUE

A **silver pocket** watch gleamed in the blue room where it had been thrown. The boy who had found the watch in a shabby brass box was now in a deep sleep. The dragonfly embroidery of the watch slightly flapped its wings, and a graceful inscription appeared on the embossed surface of the watch:

> *"Old time, even if you do the most atrocious evil,*
> *my lover shall ever live young in our love."*

Then the minute hand of the pocket watch lightly trembled as it, and the boy's dreams, both went back thousands of years in time.

It was a beautiful sunset. The sky was dominated by hues of pink and orange. The holy kingdom castle shone with splendour on the majestic mountain. Colourful dragonflies were dancing over the lake where the roaring waterfall spilled.

The altar, adorned with white lilies and tulle, stood right in front of the lake. This was a royal wedding. The Prince of the Kingdom of the Morningstar and the princess of the Anisoptera Kingdom[1] would be bound together forever.

On all the tables spread along the meadow, stood gleaming gold candlesticks and a plentiful bounty of food and Commandaria[2]. All five kingdoms, who were allied with the Kingdom of the Morningstar, were invited to the wedding. In attendance were the Kings, Queens, Princes and Princesses of Dragoria[3], the Kingdom of the Faraway Land[4], the Kingdom of Troodos[5], the Kingdom of AquaMarine[6]

---

[1] *Anisoptera: Kingdom of Fairies reigning in the Morningstar.*
[2] *Commandaria: A sweet wine unique to Cyprus, it is known as one of the oldest wines in the world.*
[3] *Dragoria: A kingdom on the plains of Mesarya, east of the Kingdom of the Morningstar. It is rumored that the men of the people in this kingdom can turn into dragons.*
[4] *Kingdom of the Faraway Land: The kingdom far, far west of the Kingdom of the Morningstar. It draws its power from the cycle of the moon.*
[5] *Kingdom of Troodos: Kingdom of virgin female warriors located south of the Kingdom of the Morningstar.*
[6] *Kingdom of AquaMarine: The Kingdom of the sea people, located in the depths of the ocean.*

and the Kingdom of Soli[7].

As the fairies played a golden harp, the guests watched the groom in admiration. Seçkin was the groom and he was standing in front of the guests and the altar with a sense of nobility.

But as he stood there, he still wasn't feeling exactly like his normal self. He was a prince, he was strong, and he was blessed with an impeccable beauty. He wore clothes adorned with gold Lefkara embroidery[8]. To the guests, he looked almost like a marble statue, it was only because of his slight movements that they could know for sure that he was human. With the blink of his silver-blue eyes Seçkin started to forget everything he knew about his identity, and accepted his life as the prince.

Prince Sapphire

Prince Sapphire was watching the beautiful Princess of Fairies approaching the altar on a white stag with huge

---

[7] *Kingdom of Soli: The Kingdom located in the North East of the Kingdom of the Morningstar. Their females can turn into swans.*
[8] *Lefkara Embroidery (Lefkaritika): A type of embroidery unique to Cyprus. Different geometric motifs are embroidered with white and green (ecru).*

golden antlers. A sapphire necklace, an heirloom from his mother, sparkled brightly around her neck.

Her white and light pink hued wedding dress was embroidered in an gold Lefkara design. The skirts of her dress were decorated with poppy flowers. Her delicate tulle-like wings, which the prince could not bear to touch, looked even more spectacular today. Two white peacocks walked in front of the Princess and next to her, she was accompanied down the aisle by her father, the King of Fairies. The King was hopping around with glee, kindly greeting the guests as he passed by them.

Behind the white deer, crimson medosh tulips[9], were sprouting across the meadow.

Princess Lal's[10] grace, who was on the enchanted stag, illuminated the guests that were seated on rows. As she passed by them, the jinn, fairies, Sons of Adam and

---

[9] *Medosh Tulip: Cyprus tulip (Tulipa cypria), a tulip species from the Liliaceae family, native to the island of Cyprus. It is known as the Medosh tulip among the Turkish Cypriot people.*
[10] *Lal: (Ruby) A precious stone consisting of corundum. The colour varieties range from deep crimson or purple to pale rose.*

Daughters of Eve who were gathered there, watched her in unison with bated breath.

Esmeralde, Princess of Dragoria, sighed deeply as she watched Princess Lal with envy. The Prince and Princess of the Faraway Land, Okalper and Mel, who were good friends of Prince Sapphire were having fun and making jokes at the expense of the prince from afar. Prince Sapphire, was doing his best to avoid their gaze and trying very hard not to laugh too.

In front of the altar, right next to the prince, stood an old Saint dressed in white. He had a thin face and an arched nose. The tiredness of the long life that had been bestowed upon him could be seen in his eyes.

"I wish your mother could have seen these days too." said the old Saint, his eyes starting to water.

He smiled wryly. "Dear Hilarion… I'm sure she's watching us from somewhere" The prince comforted him as his eyes also started to mist.

Saint Hilarion nodded, smiling as he watched the Princess approach.

When Princess Lal and her father approached the altar, the King placed a kiss on her daughter's forehead and delivered her to her one and only true love. With a small puffing sound and several tiny sparkly flashes, the white stag with gold antlers transformed into a flock of dragonflies and flew off to join the rest of the dragonflies still hovering over the lake.

Prince Sapphire held the Princess's hand tightly. He couldn't take his eyes off her. "You're so beautiful," he said as he looked into her green eyes. Saint Hilarion began to speak in an almost melodic tone:

"Dear guests!" he called. "We are gathered here today to bless the union of these two faithful souls."

"You… the beautiful Princess of the Fairy Land, will you take an oath that you will accept Sapphire, the Only Begotten Son of the Supreme Creator, the noble and powerful Prince of the Kingdom of the Morningstar, as your husband, and that you will love and be faithful to him for the rest of your life?"

"I swear…forever…" said the Princess, looking lovingly into the eyes of her Prince.

"You… the Only Begotten Son of the Supreme Creator, the noble and powerful Prince of the Kingdom of the Morningstar, do you swear in the presence of the Morningstar that you will accept Lal, the beautiful Princess of Anisoptera, as your wife and that you will love and protect her all your life?"

A single tear flickered in the Princess's bright green eyes. The Prince wiped the tear with his finger and turned it into a sapphire lily which he handed to the Princess.

"Forever… I swear."

"And in the presence of our holy Morningstar, I pronounce you husband and wife. May the Almighty The Supreme Creator protect you."

"May the Almighty The Supreme Creator protect you!" the guests repeated in unison.

"You may now kiss the bride!" said Saint Hilarion.

That day, the Morningstar shone bright in the sky like never before. A few of its beams of light reached the earth, shining on the bride and groom. The Prince immediately pressed his lips against the Princess's. The taste of her sweet lips made the Prince's head spin. The guests stood up and applauded enthusiastically. The dragonflies which were hovering over the lake transformed into delicate water nymphs and surrounded the two of them. As the water nymphs floated around the newlywed couple, bright gleams of light poured down onto their heads and, bound them together forever. Then disappeared in an instant without a trace.

At that moment, a deep red fog surrounded the meadows. The sky roared. The guests looked around anxiously, and an ugly figure with the hooves of a goat emerged from the red mist. He had huge horns on his head and a body that burned like fire. He looked around. The most menacing look was spread across his face.

"Oh…" said Hematite in a raspy voice. "Am I late?"

"What are you doing here, Devil!" the Fairy King immediately roared in anger. Not a trace of his previously friendly demeanour was left on his face.

"Calm down, my King." the Fairy Queen tried to placate him. "He can't do anything while the Guardians are here!"

Hematite ignored them and began to walk straight towards Prince Sapphire and Princess Lal. Okalper, Prince of the Faraway Land, and Raphider, Prince of Dragoria, broke through the crowd and ran in front Prince Sapphire attempting to act as a shield before him. They looked as though they might lunge at Hematite at any moment. The commander of the Guardians who stood next to Artemis, the Queen of the Kingdom of Troodos, drew her arrow and firmly took her guard against Hematite.

Amethyst

Prince Sapphire touched the sapphire gem adorned on the sword which hung on his waist. The sword glowed blue at his touch.

"Sapphire... My only adversary, the Only Begotten Son of that fool who is called the Supreme Creator..." whispered Hematite, stretching his neck towards the prince and grinning. "So, the fairies finally relented and let you marry their daughter! Bravo!"

Then he cast a mocking glance at the Fairy King and the Queen.

"It brought tears to my eyes to see this happy family joining. After all, we're kind of related now, right?"

"Get out of here, Hematite!" shouted a brown-haired lad who suddenly rushed before the prince.

The boy was handsome. But his deep brown eyes looked sad. There was a beauty mark on his cheek which was shaped like a star. Amethyst looked like he was going to protect Prince Sapphire with his life.

Hematite gave the lad a disdainful glance.

"Get out of my way, doorman!" said the Son of Satan. "How quickly did you forget the plots you were conspiring?" Hematite whispered in his ear.

It was as if time stood still.

Amethyst's pupils rapidly contracted. Suddenly, he found that he had gone back in time to years and years ago… "My Prince…"

The Prince lifted his head and his gaze met Amethyst's deep brown eyes. He took a deep breath and noticed the air smelt like a mixture of must and orange blossom.

"Amethyst..." said Sapphire tenderly, "whenever my heart is weighed down, I find you right here with me. You know me very well…"

"You've been very sad lately, Prince." said Amethyst. "What's the matter?"

Prince Sapphire sighed deeply.

"It is the endless feeling of loneliness of a child who has grown up without the presence of a mother and father."

"But you are not alone, my prince." exclaimed Amethyst. "I am here for you… I love you and it pains me deeply to see you like this." Prince Sapphire smiled.

"I love you too, Amethyst." he said sincerely. "You are my only friend who has been with me since I was a child."

The sky, illuminated by the full moon, seemed clearer than ever before. The Morningstar was glistening at the earth from among thousands of stars.

The kingdom's garden of Eden was adorned with lilies. The great waterfall was pouring majestically into the clear lake.

"I've been seeing you quite sad lately too, Amethyst." said the prince.

A chilling wind whistled past the two young men. Amethyst's brown hair, which fell down to his thin chin, fluttered slightly. He averted his eyes from Prince Sapphire and turned away sadly.

"I am afraid of losing you." Prince Sapphire said in a tearful voice.

A few drops of tears fell from Amethyst's eyes.

"Why are you crying?" asked Prince Sapphire.

"One day you will fall in love." sobbed the young man in pain.

Prince Sapphire stared at him in horror.

"And you will forget me…"

"Amethyst… What are you talking about?" whispered the prince. A lump formed in his throat. "No matter what happens, I will never leave you."

Amethyst lifted his head from the ground and looked into the Prince's eyes again. He took out a dagger from the sheath on his waist.

"If your love is going to fade away from my ever-growing love, then cut out and throw away this heart of mine," cried the Amethyst.

As the wind swept between them once again, Amethyst dropped his dagger into Prince Sapphire's palm. He turned and walked dejectedly towards the great full moon.

"Amethyst wait… Where are you going?" cried the prince after him… "Amethysssssst!"

Young man blinked and suddenly Hematite's ugly face appeared before him. He was at the wedding again. He broke out in a cold sweat.

"Are you hiding behind guards now, Prince Sapphire?" said Hematite with the joy of eliminating Amethyst.

"Get out of the way Amethyst!" said the Prince calmly.

The brown-haired lad retreated and as he did so, the ground slipped under him again and everyone disappeared once again.

Amethyst found himself in a huge dark field.

He looked around as his pupils dilated in the darkness. Two drops of tears fell from his deep brown eyes and flowed down to his pointed chin.

He walked along a dirt path with little the illumination given off by the full moon in the darkest hour of the night. With each step he took, a red mist started to form and grow thicker. Behind the mist, the outline of mountain range started to appear. The shape of these mountains was reminiscent of the five fingers on a human hand.

Amethyst stood still for a moment. He snorted; his eyes were filled with tears. He glanced at the thing he was wrapping around in his hand. His heart ached. The weight of what he caried pierced his conscience like a thorn. For a moment he hated himself. How could he do such a thing?

But he had to. He had to do it for the good of all.

Remembering this gave him strength. Amethyst started to quicken his pace on the climb up the hillside. Despite his shortness of breath, he still carried on one step at a time. The red mist rippled and slowly enveloped the young man as his steps hastened up the hillside. Before, he even realised what was happening, Amethyst found himself at the entrance to a giant cave.

As he looked into the opening of the cave, he suddenly felt goosebumps all over his body. He saw that a mouflon[11] skull was hanging near the entrance. Crows cackled wickedly

---

[11] *Mouflon: (Ovis Orientalis) wild mountain sheep in Cyprus, which is in danger of extinction / fleece.*

above him, but he paid them no attention. He gazed back down at the thing he was carrying.

He had betrayed him, and, if the plan did not work, he would be punished for his betrayal. His head would be brutally cut off and placed on a spike. The thought made his eyes well up again, but after a moment, he pulled himself together and plunged forward into the darkness of the cave.

The cave's stone walls were lined with rows of torches giving just enough light to illuminate the young man's face. With every step he took, the shadows of the flames flashed across his face and his long hair swayed down around his pointed chin.

He walked for a long while until at last he saw silhouettes moving in the depths of the cave. He didn't know if it was from excitement or fear, but his heart began to beat faster.

As he walked closer, the shadows turned into figures. Several ravens were flying over an old woman who was humming something to herself in front of a huge cauldron. A glint appeared in her dark eyes when she saw the young man.

"Come, Amethyst!" she said in a serpent-like voice.

"I have been waiting for you for a long time."

At the exact moment that Amethyst was born, fate's will was that his mother would breathe her last. Ametyst's father did not want the baby boy and left him to also face his fate. The abandoned baby Amythyst was found by Saint Hilarion, who, as fortune would have it was going on a night walk to collect sage.

Saint Hilarion had brought the baby with him to the Kingdom of the Morningstar to befriend Prince Sapphire, who himself, was just a baby. Because they were brought together so early in life, Amethyst knew Prince Sapphire for as long as he knew himself. Amethyst became Sapphire's friend, companion, and squire. But things were getting messy now.

The Witch

Amethyst hesitantly moved towards the old woman.

"It will work, won't it?" he said, his eyes full of tears, "I have never betrayed him like this. It has to work!"

The old woman looked at Amethyst and then closed her dark eyes.

"I see a girl with wings… She will come from the one who gives us light… if the day comes that she sets foot in that kingdom, the prince will no longer be the same. Blood will drip from the domes of the palace all because of the girl with wings. If our Prince meets this girl, there will be devastation!"

"It will come from the one who gives us light…" repeated the boy, clutching the thing he held in his hand. "If our prince meets this girl, there will be devastation…"

The old woman furrowed her brows.

"This is not good at all. That girl will bring damnation to you and our jasmine-scented kingdom…"

"Can you really do as you say, witch?"

The woman smiled demonically. "If you give me that thing that you carry, I will make sure that the Prince will never meet the girl with wings."

Her spider-like hands reached for what the young man was carrying. "Give it to me…"Amethyst took one last look at his hands and handed the thing that he carried all the way here to the woman.

The woman took out a bronze crown which was swaddled within the white cloth. It was adorned with azure sapphires which shone so brightly that the inside of the cave was suddenly painted with iridescent blue sparkles.

"The crown that Prince Sapphire gave away unknowingly…" the witch whispered, a wild glint danced in her eyes.

"What about the strands of hair?"

Amethyst took a small cloth bag from his pocket and handed it to the woman. The woman smiled again and a serpentine hiss escaped her lips.

Amethyst swallowed. Then his knees buckled and he collapsed to the ground with grief.

The witch threw Prince Sapphire's crown into the scalding cauldron.

The witch stirred the boiling cauldron as she muttered to herself. Then she added in the strands of hair and she stirred again. The bubbling of the cauldron abruptly stopped and a sweet, pink smoke rose out of the cauldron.

"The Eternal Love," the witch whispered. "See how sweet it smells? The prince must never smell this sweet laurel scent!"

The witch muttered to herself again. The cauldron slowly began to bubble again. After a little time, a dark shadow spread out and replaced the sweet-smelling pink smoke.

"Darkness will rise… This love will never see the light of day!"

The old woman suddenly plunged her hands into the boiling cauldron. Amethyst looked on in horror as she pulled the crown back out of the cauldron. It was now covered in a thick, black liquid and the crown which sparkled so magically just moments ago was now unrecognizable.

"This crown will darken day by day, and as each day passes, it will become increasingly impossible for Prince Sapphire's fate to bring him to the girl with the wings…"

Amethyst tried to smile through his tears.

"The spell I've placed on this crown will prevent anyone except you from seeing its true changed state."

"Thank you." whispered Amethyst in a weak voice. "For what you have done, may you have anything that your heart desires."

The woman smiled. A flame flickered across her dark eyes.

"Every spell has a price, my child. One day, that price will have to be paid."

"I am willing to pay whatever it takes." said Amethyst.

-CHAPTER I-

Love Means Sorrow

The calendar showed the month of December. The winter had been harsh that year. The rain, had been pouring non-stop for days, and it was brutally cold. The whole place was covered with a thick layer of red mist that no one had ever seen before.

It was difficult for all students to leave their houses and go to school in these weather conditions. But for one person, the situation was a little more difficult. The rain and cold were barely noticeable compared to the weight of his heavy heart.

Seçkin's heart and mind were occupied only by the fact that Defne was dating Korkut. Every time he saw them together, it was like a powerful, deadly dagger was being stabbed into his heart. It was getting more difficult with each passing day. He felt as if a piece of his body was being cut off every time.

The midterm exams were over. Seçkin was so preoccupied by his thoughts of Defne, that he barely even noticed that exams had started, let alone that they had now finished. He managed to pass most of his classes but Seçkin had a feeling that he had failed in maths. This had left Seçkin exposed to his father's disappointment, which was not well hidden.

The nightmares were getting stronger and more frequent. Even though ParuParu and BesuBesu tried to help get rid of them as quickly as possible, Seçkin was exhausted. He was always tired and the incessant headaches were increasing.

And as if Seçkin didn't have enough going on, he had now also been picked to be school captain. Everyone at the school, students and teachers alike, were watching him. Seçkin could feel the pressure from the watchful eyes of his strict father too and it was starting to get tiring.

While Seçkin was being pulled in all directions, no one but his closest friends could see the pain that he was suffering. He was unhappy. Seçkin wished he had an eraser strong enough to erase all the remains of Defne from his life. He didn't want to think about her anymore. While he wanted to forget Defne, it was very difficult given that they went to the same school.

Everywhere Seçkin looked, he was faced with seeing Defne and Korkut together. The wound that he was hoping would scab over and begin to heal, would start bleeding all over again!

The only one who was enjoying any of this was Korkut. It seemed like at every time Korkut saw Seçkin, he would suddenly either clung to Defne's lips and kiss her, or he threw his arms around to hug her tightly.

Mine, Ela, Duru and Seçil had decided to quietly declare that Defne was the enemy given the hurt she had caused Seçkin. Ayaz, on the other hand, seemed to be taking a more neutral approach. He wasn't exactly friendly with Defne and Korkut, but he didn't see them as enemy. Ayaz had been acting weird lately anyway, like he wouldn't be concerned if the world started to burn around him.

During the difficulties that Seçkin was going through, he found comfort in his friendship with Sahra. When he spent time with her, he was able to relax a little. He felt a little less burdened. But unfortunately, she seemed to be disappearing a lot lately.

It was another icy cold day. The sky was shrouded in a distressing red mist. Several ravens were cackling perched on the thin branches of the Judas tree.

Seçkin was sitting under the tree, on the concrete floor steps which elevated and housed the Atatürk bust. The wound in his heart was so painful that he didn't care about the frosty cold hitting his face. Ela, Mine and Ayaz were seated next to him. Duru and Seçil had gone to the canteen to get some snacks.

His friends never left Seçkin alone during the breaks. Because he wasn't himself lately and they were getting very worried about him. Seçkin was once more preoccupied.

"I'm so ugly. That's why she didn't like me."

"Oh, don't be silly!" said Ela. Then she immediately changed the subject.

"Anyway, what were we talking about … I read something interesting recently. Did you know that the tablecloth in Leonardo Da Vinci's "The Last Supper" is embroidered with Lefkara?"

"I don't care…" Seçkin shrugged indifferently

"There was a cover with a Lefkara stream motif on the table." Ela continued, despite Seçkin's disinterest. Seçkin sighed. Her attempts at trying to distract Seçkin were futile.

A light breeze blew through Ela's hair. The warm scent of jasmine danced in the air.

Seçkin rested his head on Ela's shoulder as he stared at the bare Judas tree. A few beady-eyed ravens perched on the tree. Ela looked at Ayaz with a silent call for help in her eyes.

"Enough is enough! Look at me!" said Ayaz suddenly angry. He took Seçkin's face in his hands. "That's not you, man! Come to your senses! What is this?"

Seçkin met Ayaz's anger and jumped to his feet. "You don't understand!" he exclaimed, shaking with anger.

Ela wanted to step in immediately, but seeing the determination in Ayaz's eyes, she decided not to intervene.

"What don't I understand, Seçkin Saral? Ok, so you liked a girl and got rejected! It happens to everyone! But not everyone turns to the living zombie that you have become!"

"You just don't understand! This is not an ordinary crush; it is something else."

"What makes it different?"

"I don't know." Seçkin said breaking down in tears and collapsing on the concrete floor next to Ela. "I can't live without her." he said to himself.

"If it takes me beating the living daylights out of you, for you to come to your senses, believe me, I'll do it! Because you really are acting like you need a beating right now."

Ela threw a confused sideways glance at Ayaz. "Stop looking at me like that!" he shouted back.

39

"Enough of this nonsense!" said Ela. "He has to face his pain. It's been like this for a month, for God's sake, a whole month!'"

As all of this was happening, Mine was leaning against the trunk of the Judas tree and seemed unusually calm. It did not go unnoticed by Ela how unusual it was for Mine not to have an opinion on a matter like this.

As Mine moved from her watchful position and moved towards Ayaz, Ela thought that this probably was not going to go well. Ela quickly shook her head to signal to Mine that she should stop whatever she was planning to do, but Mine paid no attention to Ela's pleadings.

With a determined look in her eyes, Mine grabbed Ayaz, who was still yelling at Seçkin and dragged him to the end of the fence line, away from the others.

"Let me go!" Ayaz roared.

"You let Seçkin go, you freak!" Mine hissed through her teeth.

Ayaz looked sad. "Stop calling me that!" he replied sternly.

"What the hell are you doing? Are you trying to depress him further?" Mine asked.

"I'm trying to get him to snap out of it!"

Mine's eyes twitched. "He is not like you. Seçkin is sensitive!"

"Seçkin is sensitive." Ayaz imitated Mine in an annoyed tone.

"Don't you have even a little bit emotion in you? Why do you always have to be so senseless!"

"That's enough! Typical of you girls to make a big issue out of nothing."

"Oh, come on! What about you? Don't you play girls' feelings? You love them for two days but forget about them by the third day!"

"Why are you turning the subject on me?" Ayaz stared at Mine in shock.

Mine fell silent.

Ayaz frowned. He got a little closer to Mine. They were so close now that they could feel each other's breath. "What's wrong with you, girl?" Ayaz asked.

Mine stared at Ayaz's dark eyes for a moment. Her lips were dry, her heart beat quickened. Then she suddenly withdrew, wiped the beads of sweat that had formed on her forehead, and Ayaz behind to quickly return to Seçkin and Ela.

Meanwhile, Defne walked out into to the garden where they were all sitting.

Seçkin was nervous. He wanted to avert his gaze, but he could feel himself being pulled towards her.

Mine got even more agitated when she saw Defne. "I can't stand to see this this two-faced cow anymore!"

Ela looked at Mine to once again silently communicate that Mine should back down. She didn't pay attention this time either.

"The devil inside me says that she needs a beating!"

"Mine!" said Ela deciding that her communicative glances were obviously not doing anything to change Mine's mind.

"I'm sorry, but I'm not going to sit by silently and pretend as if nothing happened. She's mocking all of us."

Seçkin's friends all agreed on one thing. They all thought Defne was a liar and she had been acting very strange lately. Seçkin sat silently and listened. He did not join their discussion.

Seçkin thought there was something strange too. The Defne he knew would never change so suddenly. But did he really know her? Or had he just romanticised his own ideal Defne in his mind?

"I can't take it anymore." said Mine, finally. "Someone needs to put her in her place."

Mine charged angrily towards Defne. "Mine stop!" Ela shouted after her.

"Liar!" Mine's voice boomed behind Defne.

Defne turned her face to Mine, astonished at what was happening.

"You two-faced, bitch!"

Defne froze.

"You think you're fooling us, you half-wit?" said Mine. Blinded by her anger. "You loved Seçkin, huh? You liar!"

While tears dropped from Defne's eyes, Seçkin, Ela and Ayaz rushed to Mine and tried to stop her.

Mine was really dangerous when she got angry.

"Seçkin did not deserve this heartbreak! None of us did!"

Then they all heard Korkut's voice from behind them. "What is going on there?" he growled.

He walked over to them and looked Seçkin up and down with his dark eyes.

"Control your friends, Saral!" he said arrogantly. "No one can intimidate my girlfriend!"

Defne

"Ha!" said Mine in a contemptuous tone.

She walked over to Korkut and gave him such a stare that he turned pale, he tried not to let on how uncomfortable this made him.

"Get the hell out of here before I kick the shit out of you"

"Enough!" Seçkin's angry voice rose in the garden. Everyone turned and looked at him. He grabbed Mine's wrist, and pulled her towards him.

"What do you think you're doing? The girl made her choice." he hissed, shooting flames from his eyes. "Please don't humiliate me!"

Mine returned Seçkin's angry gaze. "It's not about the choice she made. That she fooled us all. Should I let her make fools of us?"

"Enough Mine!" Seçkin hissed again.

"Come on, Mine," said Ela, looking sideways towards Defne and Korkut. "The air around here seems to be deteriorating."

Seçkin and Defne made eye contact for a brief moment. But Defne quickly averted her green eyes away from him.

"Watch yourself, Saral!" Korkut bellowed as Seçkin and Ela tried to calm Mine down. "You are nothing without your friends!"

Everything from that moment happened in an instant.

Mine shook off Seçkin and Ela's arms from her shoulders and punched Korkut straight in the face.

Korkut was surprised too surprised to do anything. After a few seconds, he gently wiped the blood from his lips and forced himself to put on his usual sly expression. A crooked smile appeared on his face.

"Wow," Korkut said, raising his eyebrows. "Looks like I underestimated you, blondie!" he forced a grin.

Then he turned towards Seçkin. "But we shouldn't be too surprised, right? A weak person like Seçkin only feels safe around people like you!"

Seçkin rushed at Korkut, but Ayaz managed to hold him back.

"Drop it, Seçkin. He's not worth it! Let him drown in his own filth." said Ayaz.

Duru and Seçil, who were just now making their way back from the canteen, saw what was happening and immediately rushed over too.

"What's going on, abi[12]?" Seçil cried out to Seçkin.

"You stay there, princess!" Ela warned her.

Seçkin once again took a sneaking glance at Defne. She was trembling, hiding behind Korkut.

"Get the hell out, Korkut!" growled Mine. "Go on, get out of our sight!"

Korkut grabbed Defne's hand and grinned. He hit Seçkin on the shoulder and entered the school building.

A strong icy wind blew, once again tossing girls' hair around. Seçkin and Ayaz tried to gather themselves. The mirror particles that had been hiding on all of them for months rose to the sky in a mass of air. It reached the clear sky with the sun shining behind the red clouds and with interlocking flashes, flew towards the Morningstar.

---

[12] *Abi: A term of endearment meaning 'Older Brother'.*

-CHAPTER ll-

The Clatter

When Ela had managed to calm everyone down, they began to feel the cold in their bones.

"Can't we just go inside now?" Seçil whined, her teeth chattering.

Seçkin embraced his sister and tried to warm her. Then they all agreed with Seçil and walked towards the canteen for a hot drink.

When they entered through the canteen door, they saw Defne and Korkut again. They were sitting at the table directly opposite the door. Mine couldn't help but chuckle at the sight of Korkut pressing an ice bag to his lips. Seçkin couldn't bear to see them anymore. But just as he turned to leave the canteen, Ela stopped him.

"Don't!" Ela grabbed his wrist and pulled Seçkin back. Seçkin forced smile on his face and acted as though the sight of Defne and Korkut didn't bother him.

Mine couldn't help but giggle, staring obviously at Korkut's swollen lip. Seçil sat next to her brother and snuggled into his side.

"I love you so much, Abi." she whispered. "Forget about her."

"I have already given up!" said Seçkin. Then he turned to Ela, Ayaz, Duru and Mine.

"I wish we hadn't come here…"

Mine frowned. "Why? Make yourself comfortable! If anyone should be bothered, it's them."

Seçil pulled out of her brother's embrace and stood up. "I'm going to get something to drink. Abi, would you like some tea?" she asked sweetly.

Seçkin shook his head.

"What about ayran[13]?"

Seçkin shook his head again.

"Coke?"

Seçkin once again said that he didn't want anything.

Seçil started to get annoyed. "And what about poison?" she said sarcastically. "Ugh... I'm going to kill myself in the end!" Seçil rolled her eyes and walked towards the canteen counter.

"She's right, come on!" exclaimed Ela. "Life was not meant to be lived in such mourning!"

"Especially, for a girl like that!" Duru said in support.

But Seçkin had hardly heard their words of encouragement. He was now watching Defne, who took the ice pack from Korkut's hand and pressed it to his lips.

"Who am I talking to!" Ela pinched Seçkin's leg.

"Ah!" Seçkin jumped, the plastic table lifted for a moment over the four of them and fell back down.

Defne and Korkut looked toward them only for a brief moment until they met Mine's eyes, they immediately looked away.

"Are you crazy?" Seçkin roared at Ela. She shrugged. "Yes! I am a maniac who has made it her mission to help you snap out of it!"

---

[13] *Ayran: A traditional savoury Turkish drink made from yogurt and often containing mint. It is served cold.*

As laughter rose from the table, Seçkin again looked towards Defne and Korkut. She continued to press the ice bag to Korkut's face. Mine had really done some damage.

Seçkin sighed. Then his eyes widened suddenly. Korkut slowly moved in towards Defne's lips.

"No way!" squealed Seçkin. "I am going!"

"Calm down, she's just helping him with the wound" whispered Ela.

"Oh really? Look at that, birdbrain!" Ayaz replied immediately, pointing behind Ela.

Ela turned to look at Defne and Korkut. Her eyes opened wide. She was shocked by what she saw. Pressing her hand to her mouth, she let out a faint exclamation of surprise.

"They're kissing!" she said in disgust.

Seçkin immediately jumped to his feet.

"Where are you going?" Ela asked.

But Seçkin could not hear her. He inhaled quickly through his nose. Anger darkened his eyes.

Seçkin's friends watched him for a moment. Then, when Seçkin finally sat back down, they all took a breath of relief. But that relief was short lived. Suddenly, Seçkin jumped on Korkut and slammed him down with a punch straight to his face and knocked him to the ground. Seçkin grabbed his throat and started banging his head on the marble floor.

"Seçkin don't!"

"Seçkinnnnnnnn!"

There were screaming voices all around him. Some were calling for help, some were trying to calm Seçkin down. But he didn't mind the sounds at all. For now, his only thought was to kill Korkut. He truly wanted him to die as he held Korkut's head between his hands and slammed his head into the ground. He choked him with all his might. Even though his hands were drenched with sweat and his vision was starting to fog up, Seçkin was truly happy to see the fear on Korkut's face.

Then some images appeared in Seçkin's mind. A silhouette of a curly-haired boy walking on a dirt path at full moon. A cave under a huge majestic mountain. Ugly red shapes burning on the walls of the cave. Seçkin was startled as these images quickly flashed through his mind. Then a strong pair of hands grabbed him from behind and pulled him back.

"Seçkin stop! Have you lost your mind?" cried Burak. He took the boy in his arms and tried to contain him. "Calm down, Seçkin…"

Other students in the canteen tried to help Korkut up from the ground. But he had passed out and blood was pouring out of his nose.

As Seçkin's vision slowly started clear back up, the first thing he saw was Seçil crying in fear. He had horrified his sister once again.

Then he looked at all the other students that were around him. It wasn't just Seçil, everyone seemed horrified.

He tried several times to free himself from Burak's arms, but it was only in vain. Burak was very strong.

He took a deep breath and breathed in Burak's mix of musty and orange blossom scent.

Seçkin wasn't feeling well. His head was starting to spin. Not long after, he found himself once again in a great darkness.

The full moon was shining. Seçkin was dressed in white. There was someone next to him. Defne, with her green eyes and her long brown hair flowing down to her waist. She was also dressed in white. She was holding his hand tightly. Neither of them spoke. They just looked at each other and smiled sweetly, climbing a majestic mountain that rose like five fingers on a hand.

Then in the blink of an eye, they found themselves at the top of the mountain. They set out to watch what was happening below.

A piece of the moon broke off and fell into the sea. The sky darkened partially. A terrible commotion suddenly broke out.

"This is a doomsday omen!" a man's voice boomed from below. Others shouted in agreement.

Then another man said "this is a sign! A new era will begin! The same thing happened years ago before the war of Seventy-Four[14]."

---

[14] *1974: The Cyprus Peace Operation is launched by the Turkish Armed Forces in Cyprus on July 20, 1974.*

As Seçkin and Defne watched on in horror, something invisible began to flutter on the top of the mountain. A gust of wind blew. Malicious laughter broke out on all sides. Not long after, Korkut appeared out of the mists.

"Korkut?" Defne whispered, squinting at him.

"Hello, my beautiful!"

Defne smiled. He suddenly let go of Seçkin's hand and walked towards Korkut. Korkut stroked her beautiful face and placed a kiss on her lips.

Seçkin suddenly weakened. He could no longer resist the strong wind blowing on the summit and drifted into the cliff.

He narrowly avoided fall over the cliff by grabbing a boulder buried in the ground. He held on with all his might. But his hands were tense. Then Korkut reappeared.

The irises of his eyes lit up in a blaze, and his laugh echoed across the sky.

Korkut ruthlessly stepped on Seçkin's hands and tried to unbalance him.

Seçkin resisted and held on as best as he could. Just then, Defne appeared behind Korkut with her flaming irises and she grinned as she stepped on Seçkin's hands.

It was more than Seçkin could bear. He let go of the rock and hurled down the majestic mountain...

As soon as Seçkin opened his eyes, he attempted to squeeze his fingers, but he couldn't do it. His hands were covered with a sharp pain that stretched from his fingers to his wrist. His eyes scanned the room.

He was in his father's room.

Why was he sleeping in his father's room?

Then he noticed that a pair of eyes stood over him and was looking at him sullenly.

"You do get really scary when you get angry, Seçkin!"

"Sahra?" groaned Seçkin. His head was in her lap.

"What happened?"

"Nothing good, Seçkin." Sahra paused and gestured with a slight nod to the angry man standing in the doorway.

Seçkin stood up in surprise. "Your father is so angry!" Sahra whispered in his ear.

"Finally, you're awake!" said Berk Saral's angry voice from the doorway. Berk Saral swiftly approached Seçkin and slapped him.

"Hocam, don't!" squeaked Sahra.

Seçkin slumped into the chair in his father's room in shock. He was so pale.

"How could you attack one of my students? How could you be so thoughtless?" Berk Saral shouted as he grabbed his son's collar. "It wasn't enough that your grades are dropping, now you have started beating people? Idiot!"

Then Bahar Saral burst into the room.

"Don't!" she cried to her husband as her eyes filled with tears. She stepped in between her husband and her son. "Look, he's so scared already!"

"Get out of the way! You're the one who spoiled him!"

"Da-ad... what did I do?" Seçkin whined. He was in shock.

"Shut up!" yelled the man. "'What did I do?', he says! You are not my son!"

Seçkin couldn't remember what had happened, but there was a great darkness in his mind.

"That boy you beat is in the hospital right now! Everyone is afraid that he might have brain trauma!"

"The boy I beat up?" asked Seçkin dumbly.

"Yes, Korkut! What am I supposed to say to that child's family? You are going to put an end to my career as a principal after all these years!" Then he grabbed Seçkin by the collar again and pulled him towards himself.

"Talk!"

Seçkin couldn't take it anymore and as tears started to pour from his eyes, he forcibly escaped from his father's grip. He ran from the room, and without even looking at the faces of his friends who were waiting for him in the hallway.

The sky was pierced. It was pouring with rain. He was struggling to breathe. His chest rising and falling rapidly.

After a while, his feet could no longer support his body and he fell under the Judas tree and sobbed.

Then he looked up and for a brief moment he saw a short-haired man staring at him from outside the garden gate. When he wiped his tears and looked again, he didn't see anyone. Then he felt a hand grab his shoulder. He turned back.

It was Ayaz. Ela, Mine and Duru were next to him. Seçkin looked at them with fearful eyes and cried out.

"What is the matter with me?"

Ela knelt down next to Seçkin and hugged him tightly. The sky roared. Some ravens that were sitting on the branches of the Judas took flight and soared into the sky.

When Sahra went out to the garden, she watched how Seçkin, Ela, Mine, Duru and Ayaz were clamped together under the rain. She took a deep sigh.

"Poor kid…" she whispered to herself.

"It's been a while." said a voice behind her, "You've got the right time this time."

Sahra turned back and smiled as soon as she saw those deep eyes.

"Yes, this time I got it right. Do you remember?"

Burak sighed.

"Since the day I was born again in this world. This is how the Supreme Creator punished me." he said. "I was condemned to be born and grow up with this guilt."

His eyes shifted to Seçkin. "He always gets in trouble because of that girl."

"Their fates are tied together! There are some things you have to accept." said Sahra.

Burak frowned.

"I am sorry!" said Sahra, pursing her lips.

"I suffer a great guilt!" said Burak in sorrow.

"You must suffer." Sahra replied.

Then she too took a deep sigh and continued to watch Seçkin and his friends.

"That spell was made thousands of years ago…" said Burak.

"You mean…" Sahra held her breath.

"He resurrected with the solar eclipse." Burak finished immediately.

"Dark days are ahead. Seçkin must be kept protected."

"We've both committed major sins in the past." said Sahra in pain. " and for what?"

"For the sake of love." Burak lowered his head.

"Yes, for the sake of love…" she sighed.

"Good morning, Prince Sapphire!" cried Amethyst as he opened the curtains of the stone room. The prince groaned sluggishly as he squirmed in bed.

"You're never going to give up, are you?" he stretched. "Every single day…"

Amethyst smiled.

"Yes, my prince. I'll be the same way every single day."

Then the prince came to his senses. "Didn't you leave me?"

Amethyst smiled. The prince smiled back.

"You're back." he said excitedly as the prince sat up in bed.

A deep sadness appeared in Amethyst's eyes.

"I'm behaving no better than a doorman," said.

The prince frowned.

"Be assured, my dear friend, you are more than a doorman." he said jumping out of bed and hugging Amethyst tightly. He inhaled that musty and orange blossom scent through his nose.

Amethyst just stood there. His face turned red in an instant.

"My prince…" he gasped. "You are naked!"

Prince Sapphire's flawless abs, resembling a statue of white marble, shimmered in sunlight as he shyly stepped backwards.

"Sorry… I was excited to see you. I was so afraid of never seeing you again."

"Don't worry about it." said Amethyst. He picked up a satin tunic from the bed and threw it over the prince. "We have a lot of work to do today." he said.

Then Amethyst looked at the crown beside the bed, he was twisted with guilt. A dark mist descended around the radiant blue stones.

"You have to prepare immediately. You have a meeting with the Supreme Council of Elders." said Amethyst.

Then he looked at the prince and smiled.

"I am happy to be back with you." said Amethyst and he rushed out of the room.

As Amethyst walked down the corridor, his heart twisted with the pangs of betrayal. He opened the huge oak door and stepped out onto the porticoed balcony. He leaned against the railing and watched the lake, where the cascading waterfall fell in the sweet sunlight. He took a deep breath. His insides ached with the guilt of betrayal, and the lake gleamed with enthusiasm in spite of him.

Then he felt someone's presence behind him. He looked over his shoulder. A tiny little man approached him. He had long ears and bulging blue eyes.

"Is our prince ready?" asked KarlaKarla.

"He will be here soon." said Amethyst. "KarlaKarla, you seem to be quite troubled lately." he said hesitantly.

KarlaKarla sighed deeply.

"I have some concerns." the jinni said sadly.

"Prince Sapphire will soon turn eighteen, but I don't know if he's strong enough to handle the burden of a kingdom."

Amethyst smiled.

"He who brought light to this kingdom when it was going through dark times. I'm sure he will do just fine. Besides," Amethyst smiled, "with an experienced mentor like you, he doesn't have his back pressed to the wall."

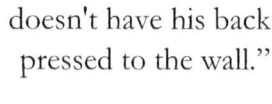

"Oh, my dear boy, how do you manage to be so kind?" said KarlaKarla squaring his shoulders proudly.

Then the Prince appeared at the oak door and stepped out into the porticoed balcony with an air of nobility. He looked enchanting in his blue jacket of silk and velvet decorated with Lefkara embroidery. On his head was a blackened bronze crown that only Amethyst could see.

"I feel sorry for myself if this headache is going to go on all day." said the Prince, groaning.

KarlaKarla curled his lip.

"Looks like you drank too much Zivania[15]last night, my prince."

"I didn't even take a sniff." said the Prince and he turned to look at Amethyst. His brown hair was blowing in the gentle breeze. His skin shone so beautifully in the sunlight that the prince couldn't take his eyes off him for a moment.

Then he caught a whiff of that sweet smell again. A mix of musty and orange blossom …

Then the prince came to himself. "We're running late for the meeting," he said suddenly walking towards the domed hall.

There was heated discussion as they entered the council hall. But, as Prince Sapphire walked towards the long table, the fervent voices suddenly stopped.

"My Prince…" said Saint Hilarion, dressed in white. He stood up from the long table and bowed to the young man. "Welcome."

But none of the other people seated at the table stood up to greet the prince.

"Looks like today is going to be pretty tough." said Prince Sapphire looking at Amethyst. Then he sat at the head of the table.

"Where are the Nephilim?"

---

[15] *Zivania: Zivania is a Cypriot pomace brandy produced from the distillation of a mixture of grape pomace and local dry wines.*

Just then, the door of the council hall opened once more, and three young women and three men with angel wings entered the hall.

"We apologize for our delay, my prince." said the strongest of the angel-winged men.

"We were hunting Goncoloz.[16]"

"Welcome, Vermeil," said Prince Sapphire. "Are the dark spirits attempting to infiltrate the kingdom again?" he asked uneasily.

"Hematite is attempting to raise an army of dark creatures, my prince." said another man with angel wings.

"Hematite will never give up." said KarlaKarla. "He yearns to avenge his father."

"He will if he continues like this!" exclaimed an older son of Adam in anger.

The prince froze. But he soon recovered. "Why do you think so, sir?" he asked. "It is obvious from your attitude that you are not satisfied with something."

"Forgive me, but I don't think you are mature enough to rule this kingdom yet."

---

[16] *Goncoloz: (Koncoloz), the creature in stories told to scare children in Cyprus. The same creature is described as an evil jinni in folk tales in the Eastern Black Sea Region.*

"A woman creates a mature man." said another voice from the table. It could be none other than a jinni as old and stocky as KarlaKarla.

"Our prince should get married as soon as possible!"

Once again, the Prince was left in shock. He made eye contact with Amethyst for a moment. He saw the young man's pupils contract. He swallowed. Then he turned his gaze back to the people sitting at the table.

"I don't understand?" he asked, frowning.

"There is nothing incomprehensible in that, my prince," said Saint Hilarion in a soothing voice. "You turn eighteen in a year. You are already of marriage age."

The prince immediately looked at KarlaKarla. "Say something immediately KarlaKarla."

But the old jinni lowered his head. "Perhaps they are right, my prince."

"But KarlaKarla…" said the young man. "I'm not in love yet." Then he took a breath. He breathed in the musty and orange blossom scent coming towards him. He trembled. He looked again into Amethyst's deep brown eyes.

He quickly came to himself again. A torrent of rage filled him.

"I will not marry without love!" he said loudly.

His breathing tightened. It seemed that his patience would soon run out.

"How many kings do you think have married in love, High Prince?" asked KarlaKarla. "To strengthen their kingdom, they often took the princesses of the nearby kingdoms as wives."

"Yes! The poor ones were sold for the fate of kingdoms!" said the Prince with disgust.

"I suggest holding a masquerade ball and inviting the princesses of the kingdoms with whom we are allied." said the Count. "Raise your hand if you are in agreement." he turned to the room.

Prince Sapphire, Amethyst, theNephilim, KarlaKarla, and St. Hilarion looked at each other as the majority of the crowd in the hall immediately raised their hands.

"It was unanimously adopted." said the Count with pleasure.

"NO!" Prince Sapphire sprang to his feet angrily. "I would never marry someone I am not in love with!"

"Is Prince Sapphire opposing the Supreme Council's decision? What rudeness!" said the Count angrily.

"Prince Sapphire, please take your seat!" said KarlaKarla concerned.

The Prince grit his teeth in anger.

"If this marriage issue comes up again, I will behead you all, Supreme Creator, as my witness!"

The crowd in the huge council hall cried out in unison. No one had ever seen the prince so angry before. A wave of surprise and fear filled everyone's eyes.

"We're not going to go back on our decision." said the Count with determination. "Prince Sapphire has proven once again that he is still a reckless teenager." said the stocky jinni on the table.

"He must be matured by a woman!"

"Never!" roared Prince Sapphire again. "I will never marry someone I am not in love with!"

-CHAPTER III-
Hidden Manoeuvre

Seçkin was suspended from school for a week by the decision of the disciplinary board. His father still hadn't recovered after this incident. He couldn't remember ever experiencing such embarrassment in all his life. His son attacked a student at his school, smashing the boy's nose and mouth. Poor Korkut was hospitalized with suspected brain trauma. Fortunately, it turned out there was no problem with his brain, but the same could not be said for his broken nose.

Seçkin had locked himself in his room all this week. He didn't talk much to anyone at home. He still couldn't remember how he had beaten Korkut. When he searched his mind, he could see nothing for the alleged time it happened. It was as if there was someone else inside him.

Seçil did not visit Seçkin's room very often. She was very angry with her brother. She just couldn't accept that he got into trouble for a worthless girl.

His friends were like the intelligence department. They were constantly calling with reports on Korkut's progress. They were trying to keep Seçkin company as often as they could.

Korkut was fine. He returned to school two days after the incident. But Seçkin was still feeling like a monster.

Every time Mine called Seçkin, she kept saying the same thing.

"That gusbo[17] has such a woody head that if you hit his head to the ground a hundred times, nothing would happen to him."

According to Mine, Korkut deserved it. He should have been thankful that he had escaped Seçkin's wrath with only a broken nose.

Ela crossed her arms and disapproved of Mine's attitude in horror, the way she does quite often. Yes, Korkut's actions

---

[17] *Gusbo: Meaning 'Pickaxe' in Cypriot Dialect used to insult useless people.*

were not acceptable, but it was not wise for Seçkin to attack him like that.

ParuParu and BesuBesu had not been around for days. It had been quite some time since Seçkin had last seen them. He had grown accustomed to those strange creatures, and without them he felt very lonely.

Sitting in his room, Seçkin was constantly examining that silver pocket watch. It had a dragonfly pattern on the cover. When he first found it, he was so certain that he saw an inscription on the back, but he never saw that inscription again.

He spent the rest of his days sleeping. He just wanted to sleep all the time. To sleep and maybe never wake up…

"Seçkin… Seçkin… Seçkin, come on, son!"

"Mom, a little more please"

"I'm going to go and wake Seçil now. Start getting dressed by the time I get back!"

"I don't even have the energy to get out of bed!" Seçkin thought. With difficulty, he heaved his duvet off of himself.

"I think what my mother said is true. I should sleep less. As a person sleeps, he weakens."

Seçkin stood up. A thousand and one thoughts raced through his mind as he walked towards the wardrobe.

"I can hear what Ela is going to say."

Look at you Seçkin… Your eyes are swollen from sleeping. Look at that beautiful face of yours!

Seçkin was stunned the moment he looked in the mirror. His face… It wasn't there! The chocolate brown eyes, which were the same as his mother's were not there. Neither was his furrowed eyebrows nor his high cheekbones…

His flawless face was missing. It was like a flat piece of marble that a sculptor had not yet begun to carve.

"What happened to me? Where did my face go?" he cried.

He heard his mother's voice in the hallway as his hands and feet began to tremble.

"Seçkin, are you ready?"

"Soon mom!" He yelled out. "Damn it! She shouldn't see me like this!" he said this time to himself.

Seçkin immediately headed to his desk.

"Where are my paints? I have to draw my face again!"

He picked up a few coloured markers from the desk.

He looked in the mirror and tried sketch his face. But his hands were shaking so much that it was almost impossible. His heart was pounding harder with every passing second.

"Damn, I can't do it!"

Seçkin fell to his knees in despair. He was crying, but he had no eyes so that the tears could not flow.

He threw the marker he was holding into the full-length mirror in anger. The mirror cracked and scattered like a thin spider web in an instant.

Seçkin stared at his half-drawn face in the broken mirror. "This is not me" he groaned hopelessly.

"Damn it! Who am I? I cannot recognize myself!"

"Seçkin... Seçkin... Come on, son!"

Seçkin jumped out of bed screaming. He was drenched in sweat. He took a deep breath when he realized that it was all just another nightmare.

Bahar Saral gloomily patted her son's shoulder.

"Are you okay, son?"

Seçkin did not speak. He rubbed his eyes.

"How am I going to save you from these nightmares? I've never felt so helpless." She groaned.

It made him sad to see his mother like this. "I'm fine, don't worry mom!" he said and hugged his mother tightly.

Bahar Saral loved her son so deeply. What would she do if she knew that one day, he would need to fight Satan to awaken a fallen kingdom?

When Seçkin returned to school, his friends greeted him enthusiastically. As soon as Ela saw him, "Your eyes are swollen from sleeping, handsome!" she said and hugged him tightly.

Some people, especially Korkut, were not very happy about Seçkin's return. After the incident, the students at the school divided into two groups: Seçkin supporters and Korkut supporters.

Supporters of Seçkin had his back. Korkut's supporters thought that Seçkin had lost his mind. They saw him as a dangerous lunatic. Some even wanted to have him removed as the school captain.

There had been some developments while he was away from school. The basement, which had used as a warehouse for years *(and was previously used as a morgue when the school was a hospital)* was organized as a sculpture workshop. Özden Atakol organized a meeting with the teachers and students of the painting department and together they decided to hold an exhibition there to celebrate.

An exhibition called "Lines in Candlelight" would display the works that the students created over a week.

Also, a drama teacher had started at the school and had begun to teach tenth and eleventh grade illustrators. Unfortunately for Seçkin, twelfth graders were exempted from drama classes as well as sculpture classes because they had to prepare for the University Selection Exam.

When Seçkin met the new drama teacher Özlem Karam, he was devastated by the fact that he would not take drama lessons again. Because Özlem Karam was a very sweet woman with a wonderful tone to her voice. Seçkin attended eleventh grade drama classes several times and watched a small production they prepared for the "Lines by Candlelight" exhibition.

After a week of preparation, the day of the exhibition had come. Seçkin was lost in the tumult of this exhibition preparation. Özden Atakol was always on the go, never getting tired while ticking off various things that needed to be done.

Finally, the pictures were hung along the corridor. Özden Atakol stood in the middle of the corridor and looked at the walls adorned with the students' work.

"Very nice." she said with a satisfied expression.

Everything was almost ready, all that remained was to arrange the candles under the pictures.

The students brought the candles picked out carefully for each artwork and began to line them up in the long corridor of the basement.

While Seçkin and Ela were placing their candles under their own pictures, Özden Atakol called the two of them and gave each of them a piece of paper.

"You two will make the opening speech, dears." she said in a kindly, but authoritative tone.

Seçkin's shoulders slumped instantly. For a moment, he looked at his mother and Derin Zade with a helpless expression.

They both shrugged back to him as if to say, "You have no choice."

"But I... in front of everyone... How?" he mumbled at last.

Özden Atakol shrugged.

"No use complaining. It is already decided."

Seçkin bent his head, sighed, and began to arrange his candles again.

Then he looked at Ela. She was fervently saying something to Mert. Then they both disappeared down the corridor.

"Seçkin, can you help me? My pictures don't stick well to the wall." said a voice from behind him. It was Damla. Seçkin helped her stick the pictures on the wall.

Özden Atakol's voice suddenly echoed in the corridor.

"What do you mean you won't come? If you don't come, I'll tear up your pictures and throw them away, Melek!" her voice rang in anger.

Damla looked at Seçkin and whispered, Melek will not come to the exhibition again."

"I have no idea why she is doing that." he whispered in a surprised voice.

Damla shrugged. "Me neither."

Melek had not participated in any exhibitions at the school since her first year of school. She would bring and place her pictures and then disappear. Sometimes she didn't even want to exhibit her paintings. No one could understand why she was like this, but it drove Özden Atakol into the brink of madness.

"She's not coming?" Derin Zade asked the angry Özden Atakol, "No!" she muttered back. "I have never seen such a fine arts student in my life. She has no excitement."

Then she turned to Seçkin as if to channel her anger. "Seçkin Saral, have you practiced your speech?" Seçkin was startled.

"Not yet, hocam. I am going to find Ela and we will get started." he said.

Then he hurried from the basement and entered the school. While climbing the worn marble stairs, Seçkin collided with Şeyda and Havva, who were running around gathering up some last-minute items for the exhibition.

"Seçkin watch out!" Şeyda squeaked. Her cheeks flushed.

"Sorry," said Seçkin. "Have you seen Ela?"

They both shook their heads. As Seçkin kept walking, he saw a few more students and he asked them if they had seen Ela as well.

But no one had seen her. Seçkin couldn't understand it. Ela would never leave him in such a situation and disappear.

They needed to deliver the opening speech to the "Lines in Candlelight" Exhibition and they should have been preparing at that very moment. But she was nowhere to be found.

When he got to the first floor, he decided to look in the classroom. Maybe he'd find her sitting in class, researching a lecture topic she was obsessed with.

He entered the damp-smelling corridor. Memduh Kemal was showing the black-bound notebook in his hand to some students and threatening them again. Memduh Kemal glanced sideways at Seçkin as he passed them. Seçkin's lips tightened. He had goosebumps.

He arrived at the classroom. He pushed the green door of the room open, but the classroom was empty. Then he turned back again and headed for the exit to the second floor. He could hear the faint voices of two people arguing just a few steps up. The voices were rising and falling.

Seçkin soon realized that the voices belonged to Ela and Mert. But why would they be arguing?

Seçkin frowned. He couldn't understand what they were saying, but whatever they were fighting about, it was quite heated.

Seçkin went up a few more. They both fell silent. Then Mert appeared and slammed into a surprised Seçkin begore disappearing into the first-floor corridor.

Seçkin was tempted for just a moment to follow Mert. But he raced up the steps instead. Ela was sitting on the steps, crying out loud.

Seçkin couldn't make sense of anything. It was the first time he had seen Ela like this. He had never seen her cry before. It was thundering outside now. When Ela lifted her head, she noticed Seçkin's presence. She quickly wiped her eyes and sniffed several times.

"Ela?" asked Seçkin. "What happened? Why are you crying?" he crouched in front of her.

Ela pushed the papers she was holding towards Seçkin and said, "I can't memorize the speech we're going to make. I got very nervous." She tried to lie, but Seçkin could see through it.

Seçkin nodded and sat next to Ela.

"I heard you … and Mert, you were arguing." said Seçkin hesitantly.

She leaned her head on his shoulder and sighed deeply.

"Why were you arguing?" he asked.

"He asked me out." said Ela.

Seçkin smiled in surprise.

"What? Well, this is great Ela!" said Seçkin. Then he began to speak with excitedly. "I like Mert... He is a gentleman... And very good looking..."

"But… I rejected him." Ela interrupted.

"Why? Is it because of the University Selection Exam?"

Ela didn't say anything. She just took a deep sigh.

"Don't be silly, Ela!" snorted Seçkin.

"I have to pass that exam! My mother couldn't go to university, even though she wanted to. She expects a lot from me."

There was silence between them for a while.

"It must be so hard…" Ela muttered at last.

"Seeing the one you love with someone else…"

"I don't understand." Seçkin looked stunned.

"I'm talking about Defne." Ela replied.

"Don't deny it. I know you're still in love with her."

Seçkin smiled sadly. "Oh right! I forgot you're a psychic."

"This has nothing to do with being psychic. I see how you still look at her, Seçkin." said Ela. Then she looked up and smiled at him. "And you've carved her name on your desk." Seçkin also smiled. His cheeks flushed.

"I took my chance with love. I have suffered the most." Seçkin said, suddenly saddened.

"Oh Seçkin… my handsome idiot friend… if love was easy, what would it mean anyway?" Ela said then patted his shoulder.

"You are a good guy, Seçkin Saral. One day Defne will know your worth."

"Maybe…" Seçkin shrugged. "What can you do, it's life."

Ela hugged Seçkin tightly. He inhaled the scent of jasmine in her hair.

They sat in silence for a while. Neither spoke.

It wasn't long before their silence was broken by a laugh. Korkut walked around the corner with his broken nose. Seçkin met his eyes. As soon as Korkut saw Seçkin, a sly smile appeared on his face. Then he grabbed Defne by the waist and hugged her. Seçkin frowned in anger. Korkut was even more delighted when he saw this.

"Come on my love, let's get out of here." he said to Defne.

Seçkin looked to Ela and rolled his eyes. Ela turned livid with anger.

Suddenly, Ela grabbed Seçkin by his shirt and clung to his lips. Defne saw this and kept walking straight ahead like a robot. Korkut's mouth fell open in astonishment. After a moment's hesitation, Defne and Korkut disappeared up the stairs hand in hand.

When Ela pulled herself back from Seçkin's lips, she saw the frozen expression on his face. She turned red with embarrassment.

"This… what …what was that?" Seçkin asked. So surprised that the words barely escaped his lips.

"I just couldn't bear to see him show off to you any longer," Ela muttered quickly.

"Sorry Seçkin… well… I didn't want your first kiss to be like this." said Ela.

"I was planning on marrying the first person I kissed." Seçkin said with a crooked smile on his face, "I guess life isn't like it is in fairy tales."

"Oh, silly!" she smiled at him. "Obviously, from now on, I am your girlfriend!"

"What?" Seçkin froze.

Actually, in the first year of school, most people suited Ela and Seçkin to each other and said that they should go out. But neither of them had ever thought of the other in that way.

There was such a pure friendship between them. This would never change.

Ela was Seçkin's best friend. She was the precious one who always wanted to be by his side.

"What do you mean?" Seçkin asked, his eyes wide.

Ela rolled her eyes.

"We will spread a rumour at school. And since Korkut saw us kiss, we won't have to make much of an effort ourselves."

"Shame on you, Ela. Do you mean to call him a gossip?" he asked.

Ela rolled her eyes and smiled.

"I have never seen anyone like him in my life. A true stirrer."

Seçkin burst into laughter.

"Look!" said Ela, suddenly getting serious again. "This will be our hidden manoeuvre. Let's see how Defne will react to this. Also, Korkut will see that you are not suffering from love, and he will leave us alone."

Seçkin attempted to act indifferent.

"But I'm not suffering from love anyway!" he said smugly.

After that, Ela's lips twitched. She rolled a wad of paper in her hand and hit Seçkin on the head.

For a moment, he was shaken, as if he was not sure where he had come from. Then he admitted, "Okay… Okay… I'm suffering from love."

Ela threw her head back and burst into laughter. "Stupid!"

She looked at Seçkin with admiration and sighed.

"Oh, my Seçkin... No matter how much your heart bleeds, you put aside your own troubles and make those around you laugh."

She rested her head on his shoulder once again.

"You are a friend like no other."

Then she thought for a while. "This secret will remain just between the two of us, Okay, Seçkin? Neither Mine nor Duru nor Ayaz. We won't even tell them it's not real."

Seçkin thought for a while. He was mostly comfortable with the plan, but there was one problem.

"And what about Mert?" Seçkin asked.

Ela didn't say anything. Her eyes were filled with sadness.

The sky rumbled again as the two of them sat on the steps together.

Mert appeared on the steps leading to the second floor. As he passed the two of them, breathing through his nose, he made eye contact with Ela for a moment and immediately turned his head in anger and continued on his way.

Ela's cheeks were wet with tears again. She hugged Seçkin tighter.

After a while Seçkin jumped to his feet. "Oh my God," he said to Ela, "Özden Hoca is waiting for us!"

They both quickly got up and went down to the basement. The exhibition was almost open. But neither Seçkin nor Ela could rehearse what they were going to say in their opening speech.

"You're finally here!" she snapped at them. "Where did you two disappear to?"

"We were rehearsing the speech upstairs," Ela lied.

Seçkin gave her a sideways glance, then started helping his other friends, lighting candles along the corridor.

Mine took Ela by the arm and looked at her face carefully. "Just a minute! Look at me… Have you been crying?"

"It must be from the damp smell in the basement. My eyes are itching terribly. I guess it was an allergy." she replied wishing deeply that Mine would believe her.

Mine didn't seem to notice the lie. She turned her attention to fixing the pictures which were starting to come away from the wall.

Duru came in with her usual excitement. "Everyone has started to gather. Are you ready?" her voice echoed in the gloomy candlelit corridor.

The students finished their work one by one and went upstairs. Under a roaring grey sky, they mingled with a group of teachers, students, and some families of students.

Seçkin and Ela took their places for the opening speech. With each passing second, Seçkin's heart pounded with excitement.

How was he going to deliver this speech? Ela tried to calm him down by holding his hand to relieve his nerves. Korkut, who was watching them from afar was pointing towards Seçkin and Ela and saying something to his friends.

Ela was right. "Korkut has already started to work." she whispered in Seçkin's ear.

They both smiled.

Afterwards, everything happened so quickly that Seçkin couldn't absorb it all.

With Özden Atakol's nod of approval, they started the opening speech. They both delivered their speech expertly. The principal of the school, Berk Saral, cut the ribbon with the teachers of the painting department and formalised the opening of the exhibition. Can, Havva, Şeyda and Ferhun staged a short production they prepared with their drama teacher. Sahra played the reed flute and provided the background music. Then the exhibition began. While walking through the exhibition some students kept staring at Seçkin and Ela and whispering. This did not go unnoticed by Mine, Ayaz and Duru.

"Why are they looking at you like that and whispering?" Duru asked in an inquisitive tone.

Ela shrugged. Seçkin smiled.

"There's something going on with these two! They've been acting strange since they got here." said Mine.

Ayaz grabbed Seçkin by the collar and pulled him towards himself.

"Speak up!"

Then Bade and Meryem appeared next to them. Both of their faces lit with joy.

"Congratulations," said Bade. "So, you finally decided to listen to us and start going out!" Meryem followed her with "Haven't we been saying this since the first day we saw you."

Mine, Duru and Ayaz froze with their mouths wide open.

"Stop touching my boyfriend, Ayaz!" exclaimed Ela.

She pulled Seçkin from Ayaz's grip and straightened his clothes. Then she turned to Bade and Meryem.

"Thanks a lot girls. And if you'll excuse us, we need to resolve a friend crisis." she said, pointing to Mine Duru and Ayaz, who were still frozen and waiting for an explanation.

Bade and Meryem nodded, smiled, and left.

Ela turned towards her friends and took Seçkin's hand. Seçkin's cheeks reddened.

"We're going out," she said.

"WHAT!" cried Duru. Ayaz let out a strong laugh. His voice resounded in the gloomy corridor so strongly that the visitors of the exhibition turned to look at them for a moment.

Mine was still like a sculpture.

"I can't believe this. Seçkin is in love with Defne!" she said all of a sudden.

"Is what I heard true?" asked a fairy-like voice from behind them. Seçil looked from Seçkin to Ela.

"Yes, princess, your brother and I are going out." said Ela as she hugged the little girl lovingly.

Seçil laughed in admiration. "Wow!"

Seçkin looked at Mine, Duru and Ayaz. This seemed to come as a shock to them.

"There is something not right!" said Mine, "Seçkin is in love with Defne! How could he go out with you?" she said, looking at Ela again, "No deal!"

Ela smiled.

"That's what you think." she said beaming with pride that she was dating Seçkin Saral.

"Who is Defne? That girl is no match for me!"

She then cast a sideways glance at Seçkin. This was the first time Seçkin had seen Ela like this. This girl could be dangerous when she gets mad. In fact, she was a lot like Mine in that way. You never knew what she might do.

"How nice!" squeaked Duru. Then she thought for a moment. "In that case, should we call you yenge[18] or should we call Seçkin enişte [19]?" she asked naively.

They all burst into laughter.

"So, dumb!" Mine snapped at her. "Look at the nonsense you think of!"

Then she narrowed his eyes again. "There's something not quite right with this situation!"

※ ※

"Maybe they're right." said Prince Sapphire sadly. "Perhaps I am not mature enough to rule a kingdom, Amethyst."

"I don't think so, my prince." said the young man.

The full moon shone above them in all its glory. But the Garden of Eden was gloomier that night than it had ever

---

[18] *Yenge: A term of endearment for a woman who has married into a family. Typically, what one would call their uncle's wife.*
[19] *Eniste: A term of endearment for a man who has married into a family. Typically, what one would call their Aunty's husband.*

been before. Not a single branch moved. It was as if the jasmines and lilies, even the cascading waterfall, shared in the prince's unhappiness. So much so that even the sky was covered with relentless despair.

The prince sighed deeply. His headache was getting worse with each passing day.

"I haven't been feeling well lately." said the prince.

"There's a strong anger in my head that I can't make sense of and I can't control."

"If you're talking about what happened in the council hall today, let's face it, it was a little too much." smiled Amethyst.

"They're all crazy." said the Prince, "They're going to force me into marriage."

Amethyst lowered his head in despair.

"That's what I was afraid of, my prince." he muttered, lips drooping.

The prince approached the young man and grabbed his shoulders.

"Believe me, nothing like that will happen." he said in a soothing voice. "I would never marry someone I am not in love with!"

Amethyst looked at the prince and smiled. The prince smiled back at him. The prince's eyes were fixed on Amethyst's deep brown eyes.

Amethyst was a very handsome young man. The prince sighed. The scent of musk and orange blossom filled the air once again. "I wish I could marry you Amethyst," said the prince suddenly.

Amethyst froze. His heart began to pound.

"What? I don't understand."

The prince quickly fixed his words. He didn't even understand what he was saying.

"Well… you are the only person who has been with me since I was a kid. You know everything." said the prince, trying to correct what he had said. "If only you were a girl."

Amethyst frowned.

"Good thing you're with me, Amethyst." said the prince, looking affectionately at the young man. "I love you very much. Whatever happens, that's the only thing that won't change."

"And what are your plans for that masquerade ball, my prince?" Amethyst asked. Prince Sapphire felt like he was going to suffocate. He loosened the collar of his shirt.

"Do you think my whole destiny will be changed by a masquerade ball?" asked the prince. "Do you think I would give up that easily?"

"Then what will you do, my prince?" the young man asked curiously.

The prince smiled.

"If they start to pressure me too much, I'll fake my death."

As the moon appeared and disappeared back among the clouds, the two young men looked at each other and burst into laughter…

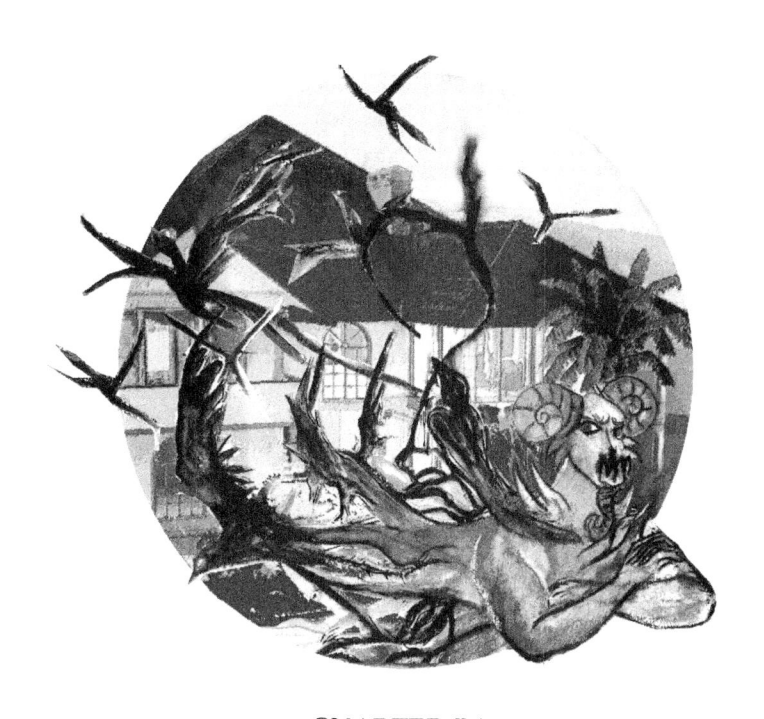

-CHAPTER IV-

The Demons of the Great White House

From that day on, the news about Seçkin and Ela dating spread widely across the school. It was exactly as they expected. Korkut did a good job in sharing the news around. While the news came as a surprise to some of the students, Bade and Meryem were thrilled because they had said from the very beginning that Seçkin and Ela should be together.

After their initial surprise, Ayaz and Duru seemed to finally come to terms with the news. But the same couldn't be said for Mine. She was the only one who couldn't be convinced, she knew both Seçkin and Ela well quite well.

Mine recalled how in the early years of their friendship, she had also suggested that Seçkin and Ela should consider dating. She was a little hurt when they laughed and told her there was no chance.

Now they were dating. It was a joke!

Whenever they came across Defne and Korkut, Ela would surprise Seçkin with her advances. She would cling to Seçkin's lips in an almost fit of rage just to annoy Korkut.

Korkut seemed to be visibly angry whenever he saw Seçkin and Ela kissing. He didn't like that Seçkin seemed to be over Defne and no longer suffering from the idea of losing her. He seemed happy and in love. There was nothing left for Korkut's to show-off.

Strangely though, Defne did not seem to be bothered at all. No matter what Seçkin and Ela did, they couldn't incite a response from Defne. In fact, Seçkin couldn't even be sure she was alive. This didn't seem to be the old Defne that he knew. Her green, fairy-like eyes were dulled.

"I bet Korkut will try to pick up Ela soon," Ayaz said happily one day.

"Ughhh... God forbid, Ayaz!" Ela shuddered.

"How did his ego got so deflated in just a few days?" Ayaz asked with a mischievous smile.

They were on break for recess and the day was shrouded in a reddish mist. The rain was starting to drizzle again.

Seçkin and Ela were sitting where the rain could not reach them. Ela was feeding Seçkin the tahini buns she made herself.

"I have to feed my man. He's so skinny," she teased, bursting into laughter.

Then Mert came out into the garden, but he ran back inside quickly as soon as he saw Seçkin and Ela.

Seçkin felt like the buns were stuck in his throat. He was so upset about Mert that he couldn't enjoy the buns. Mert was a good friend of Seçkin. They always had great conversation, if you exclude all the times Mert tried to 'educate' others on how-to pick-up girls. But since he heard that Seçkin and Ela were dating, he seemed to become more hostile. Seçkin thought it wasn't fair too. He knew that Mert cared for Ela deeply.

Seçkin noticed that Ela's eyes filled with tears whenever she saw Mert. No matter how hard she tried to hide it, she was madly in love with Mert. But in her selflessness, she had put her friend first and denied love for herself.

Seçkin could barely contain his guilt. He tried to tell Mert the truth several times, but Ela stopped him.

Seçkin wondered how much longer he could hold out. He knew what that pain was like. He didn't want to inflict the same pain that he experienced with Defne on either Ela or Mert. To make matters worse, Ela's love for Mert was not unrequited like Seçkin's for Defne. Ela and Mert both loved each other. Seçkin felt like he could give up on this ridiculous game at any moment so that they Ela and Mert could be together. "We must end this game!" Seçkin whispered in Ela's ear.

Ela, committed to their new story, ignored him. She turned to look at Ayaz, who was sparring with Can.

"We have to finish now!" Seçkin insisted. Ela frowned.

"How many times do I have to tell you? Never give up!"

"Oh my god, Ela!" snorted Seçkin

A cold wind blew between the two of them.

"I'm afraid you might fall in love with me!" he finally said in a low voice, trying to reduce the tension.

It seemed to work. Ela's face, which was tense with anger, now softened. "Well, you should pray for that to happen. Where else will you find a charming girl like me?" she replied.

They both burst into laughter.

"Hey you!" Ayaz snapped, just a few meters away. "Stop playing!"

"What happened? Are you jealous?" Can teased him.

"Hey! I'll break your mouth and nose!"

Then, Mine appeared at the gate with a big birthday cake in her hand, and Duru threw herself into the garden behind her and started singing excitedly.

"Happy birthday Ayaz! Happy birthday Ayaz!"

"Oh no! What's the date today?" Ela asked, looking at Seçkin in horror.

"December twenty-four!" said Seçkin. He bit his lips.

"We forgot Ayaz's birthday!"

"But Mine didn't forget!" said Ela, her eyes shining. "She's been very concerned about Ayaz lately."

Seçkin smiled. He was aware of that too. The crew's hot-headed tomboy seemed to be losing her heart to Ayaz.

"Let's go to them!"

When Ayaz saw the cake in Mine's hand, he swallowed in surprise and blew out the candles in one breath.

His eyes filled with tears for a very brief moment. He hugged and kissed all his friends. And to stop himself from getting emotional, he decided to tease Mine and stir her up a bit.

The class bell rang and they all started to climb the stairs for the lesson in the workshop while eating their slices of cake…

After school, Seçkin didn't want to go study with the others. So, he made an excuse and ditched Ela and Duru. After seeing them out, he sat under the judas tree and waited. There was a meeting at the school, which meant that his parents would be late.

He took out the silver pocket watch from his pocket and started playing with it. He had been carrying it with him for a while. He had a strong feeling that that dragonfly on the watch would bring him luck.

While sitting in the garden, something caught his eye. There on the concrete floor was a lone cello. Its owner was nowhere to be seen, but Seçkin knew who it belonged to. His heart started beating fast. Defne was just here not long ago probably waiting for her mother.

Seçkin put the watch in his pocket and got up from the yellow bench and walked over to the cello. He took out his phone and opened the contacts. While he was debating with himself whether or not he should call her, the school's garden gate creaked and Defne began to walk towards him with her fairy-like beauty.

Seçkin stared at her with admiration.

"I was just looking for you." he mumbled, his voice only slightly higher than a whisper.

Defne did not speak. Her cheeks flushed as she grasped the handle of the cello case lying on the floor. They briefly made eye contact. Then she turned around and walked away again. Seçkin felt that his already wounded heart started to bleed again. He watched after Defne, who walking away with complete indifference…

When Seçkin came home, he called out to his grandmother and grandfather and went to his room. He was feeling down about what had happened today. "Who even is Defne?" he thought to himself She did not even thank Seçkin for minding her cello.

Seçkin wondered where he went wrong. He fell in love with her. Was that his wrongdoing?

Seçkin threw himself on the bed. He stared blankly at the ceiling for a moment. He felt like he was on fire. This love was hurting him more and more each passing day. The rain that had started earlier had now moved in and was beating hard against his window. Seçkin knew that it would take him a long time to heal from this pain.

Day by day, Seçkin's anger towards Korkut was growing. He had a hard time restraining himself from attacking him again. Seçkin had unconsciously attacked him weeks ago, but now consciously wanted to do it. But his father would not take pity on Seçkin again.

While Seçkin was contemplating this, someone knocked gently three times on his door.

"Come in!" Seçkin called out.

The door opened slowly and Özdemir Bey stuck his head into the room and smiled under his moustache.

"Can I come in, boy?"

Seçkin jumped to his feet and opened the room door wide. "Come in grandpa."

"It's been a long time since I chatted with my grandson." said Özdemir Bey as he entered the room.

Seçkin smiled. Özdemir Bey looked out at the magnificent sea view then took a seat in the chair next to window and watched as the heavy rain continued to fall. The orange lights of the town were reflected in the sky.

A gust of wind blew outside and the leaves of the great palm tree swayed.

"Wow… What a storm! We are experiencing the most severe winter in recent years." Özdemir Bey sighed.

Seçkin looked out the window. The lilies and roses in the garden had shed their flowers. Their leaves were stressed from being tossed around by the storm.

"So… Son?" Özdemir Bey asked. "You seem to be pretty unhappy lately. You used to tell me everything. Tell me who is this girl who has upset my grandson?"

Seçkin looked at his grandfather for a moment in surprise.

"Whoever it is, it doesn't matter anymore, grandpa."

Özdemir Bey smiled.

"Oh, to be young and to have that first taste of love…" he sighed.

"You've always been an emotional kid anyway. Never let those whose heart is dark with evil bring you down, son."

Seçkin's eyes filled with tears, but then he smiled. He watched the olive tree on which he had once built a treehouse. It stood firm against the storm.

"You know, grandpa? I wish I had no weakness and could resist the storm like this olive tree."

Özdemir Bey smiled sweetly.

"Who is stronger on a stormy day, son? The olive tree or the reed?"

He looked at the tree again.

"The olive tree is stronger, Grandpa."

Özdemir Bey's eyes sparkled. He was sure that this would be his grandson's answer.

"I gave my grandfather the same answer when I was your age. For years, I stood upright like an olive tree against difficulties. But the day came when my heart couldn't take it anymore. After I got sick, I realized that this was the wrong way to think. The olive tree withstands the storm, yes, but inside it rots. In the end, it is destroyed. But not the reeds. They look weak, but their gentle bending from one side to the other helps them to stay intact and not collapse. So be a reed! Even if you bend down to the ground, you just get right back up. The reed is truly strong." said Özdemir Bey.

Seçkin smiled.

"Yes, keep on smiling – exactly like that!" Özdemir Bey smiled. "Stop wandering around so sadly all the time, you're depressing me."

Seçkin was in his room… the room was shrouded in a strange crimson mist. The soothing blue walls of the room had taken on a damp grey hue. An iron bed stood in the middle of the room. For a moment, Seçkin thought the iron bed reminded him of the bed in the workshop, but this thought slipped from his mind almost as quickly as it had arrived. The silence in the room was making him sad. As he lay the iron bed, he pressed the duvet against him and started trembling.

In the great silence of the partially empty room, Seçkin heard a faint sound. It was a creeping, crawling, slithering sound. He felt like there was something else in the room. But what could it be?

Lying under the duvet, Seçkin started to hear a hissing sound. His heart leaped as he realised what the thing, he was feeling in the room was. Seçkin slowly poked his head out of the covers and looked at the ground.

There was a giant snake in the room. On its head was a black crown. Seçkin's heart jumped again and his hair stood on end. He leapt out of the bed onto the icy, dusty floor. But the cold didn't bother him anymore. He hardly felt the coldness of the floors on his bare feet as he walked toward the snake. The snake hissed madly, and threw itself under the iron bed. Seçkin also leaned under the bed. He had an unexplained desire to catch the snake. As he stretched out his hand towards the snake, it crawled out from under the bed over the wall cabinet. While it did this, Seçkin noticed that the snake was shrinking somehow.

He managed to leap at the snake and suddenly grab it. Both Seçkin and the snake remained motionless for a while. Then he heard another loud hissing sound in the room. The snake started struggling in Seçkin's arms, it turned into a black crow and attempted to escape by flapping its wings, but it was unsuccessful. Then the crow turned into a mosquito and slipped out of Seçkin's hands.

Seçkin tried to catch the fly by clapping his hands together, but it was in vain.

The black crown that the snake was wearing fell to the ground. Seçkin's gaze fell on the crown. It was covered in blood. Though initially Seçkin didn't understand where the blood had come from, he soon realised it was his own blood. He was bitten by the snake.

Suddenly, Seçkin shot awake and opened his eyes. ParuParu and BesuBesu were there. They were back. They had come to his aid again, just as they did every time, he faced a bad nightmare.

They both looked at Seçkin's face with concern.

"Are you okay, High Lord?" asked ParuParu in a whispering tone.

Seçkin immediately lowered his head under the bed to see if the snake was there. There were no signs of a snake. But as Seçkin bent down under the bed, a few drops of blood dripped onto the floor. His nose was bleeding again. With the anxious glances of the two jinn watching him, Seçkin jumped out of bed and ran to the sink in the bathroom. He washed the blood dripping from his nose, noticing that sun was starting to come up now. He left the bathroom, exhausted, and returned to his room.

"The great white house is filled with demons. It can't go on like this anymore!" said ParuParu. "The infidels are trying to break into your dreams and wither you inside!"

"What can we do, sir?" BesuBesu asked. She was sitting next to Seçkin, holding the boy's hand tightly with her bony hands.

"What we should have done all along, my darling!" said ParuParu, his eyes gleaming. "We forgot to make a protection talisman for the house!"

"A protection talisman?" Seçkin asked curiously. "Like rock salt or something?"

ParuParu shook his head.

"No, Sir…"

"Then how will you do it?" the boy asked, his big brown eyes grew even bigger.

"With your blood, sir!" replied ParuParu wisely. "We will enchant your blood and smear it along the entrance of the house!"

"My blood?" Seçkin was horrified.

"Yes, High Master. Your blood is precious, if you only knew what it could do." said ParuParu.

"Yes, my blood is precious ParuParu and it is barely enough even for me."

The jinni smiled. He snapped his fingers. A golden light flashed. A silver dagger and a small glass bottle appeared out of nowhere in ParuParu's hand.

"Is it going to hurt a lot?" ' Seçkin asked hesitantly.

BesuBesu patted the Seçkin shoulder.

"Don't worry. It will only be a tiny sting. Just a few drops will do the trick."

Seçkin closed his eyes and extended his wrist to ParuParu.

The jinni swept the silver dagger swept over Seçkin wrist and his eyes gleamed gold.

Seçkin's blood dripped into the little glass bottle.

"The great white house will be cleansed ..." the jinni smiled.

The first light of a new day was illuminating Nicosia. The dark clouds had dissipated. The storm was over. It seemed like the day would bring a brilliant new start for everyone. Everyone that is, except for one person...

Seçkin was no longer the lively and cheerful person that he used to be. He still suffered from his love pain. The great darkness in his heart was growing day by day.

As soon as Seçkin set foot in the school, the class bell rang.

Bzzzzzzzzzzzzzzzzz!

"They have to be sadists to call the students to class with this bell in the morning." Mine muttered, covering her ears in anger.

"I think our assistant principal is a sadist anyway!" said Ela. She pointed to Memduh Kemal, who was waving and threatening several seventh graders with his black-bound notebook.

"Is it true, Ela, that the Cyprus History test is today?" Seçkin asked, panting, catching up behind them.

"Yes." said Ela. Then her eyes opened wide. "Don't tell me that you haven't studied!"

Seçkin raised his eyebrows, he had not studied.

"Come on, Seçkin, it would be good if you started to focus on your lessons now." said Ela patronizingly.

Mine nodded as well. "I agree. Forget about that hypocrite."

By the time they got to the classroom, the teacher had already started to take attendance.

Ela shyly stuck her head through classroom doorway and politely cleared her throat.

"Ahem… Ahem… Can we come in, hocam?

The history teacher was a caring young lady. "Of course. The students are the benefactors of the school, even if they do come late. I won't keep you out, especially when there's an oral test." said the history teacher.

"Oral test? But last week you said that it would be a writing test!" Duru said immediately.

The history teacher got up from her desk and walked over to Duru. "I lied, Duru! Don't trust the history teachers too much!"

Seçkin smiled. "I thought it was the math teachers you couldn't trust." he said shyly.

"Why are you complaining? Are your powers not working?" said Ela.

"What are you talking about?" Mine interrupted.

"Duru can guess the questions!" said Ela mocking in disbelief.

"Nonsense!" Mine rolled her eyes.

"Duru had passed all the oral tests with this extraordinary talent." She teased.

Duru frowned.

"Don't say another word." she immediately snapped, covering Ela's mouth with her hand. Ela bit Duru's hand. Duru's scream echoed throughout the corridor.

"What is going on there?" the history teacher asked, looking up from the book she was leafing through.

Duru jumped to her feet, raised her hand in the air and screeched.

"Hocam! Ela bit my hand!"

The history teacher chuckled. "Ohh so you raised your hand, Duru! Well-done, I was looking for volunteers for the oral test."

Duru turned red.

Seçkin let out a sigh of relief. He didn't study for the exam. He might have had a chance if he could copy answers in a written test, but he would not be able to pass an oral test.

"Well, let's see, now you're going to prove that extraordinary power of yours." said Ela, barely suppressing her burst of laughter.

"Shut your mouth! I haven't studied! I only know a little about the British period." said Duru, wiping the cold sweat from her forehead. "Please let the question be about the British period! Please, please, please…" she prayed, closing her eyes and clasping her hands together.

"Hmm… Let's see…" said the history teacher as she rummaged through the book.

"Duru Boran… Can you tell me about the education of Turkish Cypriots during the British period?"

Duru's eyes widened.

"My God… thank you… thank you," she whispered to herself. She then took a sideways glance at Ela and smiled confidently.

"There was predominantly religious education. In addition, lessons based on Turkish Nationalism were given."

"Well done, Duru. See, it wasn't worth your fear at all."

She took a sigh of relief and sat down. She winked at Ela, who was staring at her in surprise.

"What's up babe? Do you believe it now?"

"How do you do this?" Ela said, her mouth hanging open. "It is unfair!"

"It's a secret," Duru said. "Not everyone in the class needs to know."

If there was a subject that Duru knew, the teachers would always ask about it in oral exams. She didn't understand how that could happen either, but it always seemed to happen.

Others slowly got up to take the test. After Duru, it was Ela, then Sahra, then Mine, then Ayaz. As Ayaz sat down, he was cursing while wiping off the beads of sweat from his forehead. Seçkin's prayers were answered. The class bell rang just before it was time for his turn, and the students rushed out of the classroom.

"Saved by the bell," Seçkin exhaled.

It was time for their independent painting research now. "Who would go to the workshop and paint now, when there is fresh air outside?"

"I would!" exclaimed Ela immediately.

"You cannot be serious!" Seçkin said with a grimace.

"I promised Derin Hoca that I will finish the painting I started this week!" she said, shrugging her shoulders.

"I kind of need to do some work too!" said Mine, "I have a lot of work to catch up on."

"I will work too!" said Duru.

Whenever one of these three decided to do something, the others would follow. They were like dominoes.

"Fine, you guys can work!" said Seçkin disappointed, "I'm going down to the garden."

Leaving the girls behind, he descended the stairs a little sad about having to go alone. He purchased his favourite packet of pink crisps from the canteen and went out to the garden. There was nobody around.

"Where has Ayaz gone?" Seçkin wondered. "He must be sitting upstairs with Can talking about BMX bikes." he said to himself.

Seçkin walked over and sat under the judas tree. He began to devour the crisps. The crows on the judas tree began to caw loudly and flap their wings. Seçkin started to get irritated. He jumped to his feet and threw the packet of crisps at the crows.

"Damn crows! I'm sick of you!"

"What anger is this!" said a familiar soft voice. Seçkin's heart started pounding as he closed his eyes and took a deep breath and turned around.

There stood Burak. Seçkin hadn't seen him in a long time. He had shaved his hair short. He looked very handsome.

"You haven't changed at all since the last time I saw you! You're going get in a lot of trouble one day because of your anger!" said Burak.

"Hello Burak." Seçkin said, frowning, Burak approached the boy and looked at Seçkin's face and smiled sweetly.

"I wonder when your face will smile again." said Burak, looking at Seçkin with admiration.

Seçkin couldn't help himself and smiled.

"Yes, like that…" said Burak.

There was a brief silence.

"Um… can I ask you something?" said Seçkin.

"Of course. you can ask me anything." Burak smiled.

"What you said about Defne… How did you know?"

"That she is unreliable?"

Seçkin lowered his face.

"Instinct" Burak said with a shrug.

There was another brief silence.

"You're one of them too, aren't you?" Seçkin frowned.

"Them?"

"You told me that I'm rather popular even in a world I haven't visited yet" Seçkin reminded him.

"You look so cute in this pink tee, Seçkin." Burak said, as if he wanted to change the subject immediately.

Seçkin was a little afraid of Burak. He turned around wanting to walk away. But Burak pulled him in from his arm.

"Stop, Seçkin!" said the boy, frowning. "I've been waiting for you for millennia!"

Seçkin just stared at the boy.

"Millennia?" said Seçkin, his eyes starting to fill "So, you are one of them!"

Seçkin analysed the brown eyes under Burak's furrowed brows. No sea could be as deep as Burak's eyes. "Who are you?" he asked as his heartbeat quickened.

"I can't tell you that right now," Burak grumbled. "But please listen to me. You're so confused, you don't know what you're doing, Seçkin. Let me help you."

"What am I doing?" Seçkin asked.

"Tell me… is it true that you are dating Ela?"

"Yeah, so what?"

"I know you don't love her." said Burak.

"I love her." the Seçkin replied through gritted teeth.

Burak shook his head. "You are lying, Seçkin! You are fooling yourself"

"What am I supposed to do, Burak?" Seçkin asked, finally giving up.

Seçkin sighed, tears in his eyes. He couldn't stand it anymore. He was more afraid than he had ever been before. He knew he was in love with Defne. But why was he so confused whenever he saw Burak? Why did he feel such a strong sense of attachment towards him?

Burak didn't say anything.

"I see…" Seçkin finally breathed, "It would be better if we were friends from afar."

"If you were wiser, you would know that self-deception is worse!"

"Enough, Burak!" Seçkin immediately turned to walk away.

"Are you afraid to hear the truth?" Burak shouted after him.

Tears streamed from Burak's eyes as Seçkin walked away. Burak was losing himself again in the remorse that he has suffered since the day he was born...

***

The days were all bleeding into one and New Year's was fast approaching. While the students who already had a date were wondering what they should wear to the masquerade ball, those who did not yet have dates were wondering who might a good suitor to accompany them.

Seçkin didn't care about the school ball at all. While, he was still mourning for Defne, he also could not stop thinking about Burak. It had been days since Seçkin saw him and he wanted to see him again.

Seçkin was thoroughly confused. Had he been in love with him for millennia? Millennia... Burak was one of them, this was an indisputable fact. But should he tell ParuParu? Or... what if they're not on the same side? Could Burak be a bad person?

"It's best not to say anything to anyone for a while," thought Seçkin.

While Defne did not even look at Seçkin, Burak valued him, loved him.

Seçkin had these overwhelming feelings for Burak that he couldn't identify. He had accepted his feelings. But he wasn't in love with Burak. He was in love with Defne.

The school council had begun preparations for the ball. Ela hung elegant wreaths of pine leaves on the stair handrails. Seçkin, with Ayaz's help, had brought in a huge Christmas tree to decorate the school hall. Meanwhile, Mine and Duru took out ornaments and started to decorate the Christmas tree. New Year's Eve was slowly taking over the school.

"Of course, we're going to the ball together." whispered Ela as she wrapped the trinket she was holding around the tree. "Like every year!"

Seçkin and Ela were going to the ball together. That's the way it should be. They were lovers, and lovers go to the ball together.

Duru was going to go with Bora. Only Mine and Ayaz remained dateless. It was not yet clear who would accompany them.

"Well, why don't you two go together…" Duru said to Mine.

"Never!" growled Mine as she hung a few ornamental balls on the Christmas tree.

"I don't get you." Duru rolled her eyes. "Do you want him to be snatched up by the cheeky strange girl?"

"I don't care!" said Mine a little defensively. "He is free to go to the ball with whoever he pleases!"

Then, when Ayaz entered the hall with even more ornaments, Mine put down the decorations she was holding and walked towards Ayaz angrily.

"Go on, invite the cheeky strange girl to go to the ball with you." Ayaz's eyes opened wide; he couldn't make sense of what was going on.

"I... I thought we'd go together?" he said trying to understand what was happening.

Mine's cheeks turned red.

"What makes you think I would accept that?" Mine said trying to sound indifferent.

"Because I know you well." said Ayaz, shrugging.

Mine looked at him and frowned. Ayaz bit his lip in fear.

"If you know me that well, why are you always annoying me?" Mine asked at last.

Ayaz took a deep breath and smiled.

"Because I like to annoy you. It's an excuse to be close to you."

"Okay…" said Mine a little more content. "But I have a condition!"

"What is it?"

"You'll not do any perversion."

"We'll see." Ayaz said with a smile. Then he started to hang the colourful lamps he had brought for lighting.

Mine swayed slightly on the spot and watched Ayaz for a short while. Seçkin, Ela and Duru exchanges glances surprised about what they had just witnessed.

"My god! Is this the same cold Mine that we all know?" whispered Ela.

"Yes. But her coldness dissolves in the face of love." said Seçkin.

"They seem to belong to each other. I never thought it would happen." said Duru.

When the tree was decorated, Özden Atakol gathered all the students of the painting department to the workshop to draw the traditional New Year's raffle as they do every year. They would all take turns drawing out a name from the raffle bag.

While Derin Zade was shaking raffle the bag with a smile, Seçkin looked around him with concern, praying that he would not draw the name of the cheeky strange girl.

When Ela read the name on the paper she drew, her eyes lit up and she gave a small shout of joy. Mine frowned as soon as she drew her paper. She wanted to draw again, but Özden Atakol did not allow it.

Duru was rather indifferent when she drew her paper from the raffle bag. Ayaz however did not have the same response. As soon as he read the name written on his paper, he left the workshop at once. "Fuck!" his voice boomed as he stormed off.

When it was Seçkin's turn, he stood up from the stool he was sitting on and, in spite of his pounding heart, plunged his hand into the bag. A smile appeared on his face as he opened the small piece of paper and read the name written on it. After months of torment, life had finally been kind to him. Thank goodness it wasn't the cheeky strange girl …

-CHAPTER V-
Ball Gowns Get Bloodstained

Spectacular crystal chandeliers, harp tunes, and masked princesses... The glass-domed ballroom shone brightly under the stars. The elegant decorations mesmerised those who saw it. Snow was falling inside the hall from the enchanted ceiling.

The Sons of Adam, Daughters of Eve, and the jinn were sipping their commandaria wine in groups, while keeping their watchful gazes on Prince Sapphire. Each one of them was wondering which princess the prince would like among those invited.

The prince, sitting on his throne, was watching everything with a deep expression of hopelessness. He had a strong headache. But what was a headache compared to the emotional turmoil he was experiencing? As the princesses of the surrounding kingdoms introduced themselves one by one, the prince was getting more distressed with each passing second. He didn't like any princesses, who seemed to him to be little more than dolls adorned with ornaments.

Amethyst stood beside the price as usual. He looked just as unhappy; his deep brown eyes were filled with sorrow. As the princesses glided gracefully past the prince, a broad-shouldered man appeared among them. He cleared the crowd and passed through the masked princesses, dancing with delight.

He approached the prince. As soon as the prince saw him, his face lit up with an irresistible smile. The man took off his black mask. He was as handsome as Prince Sapphire. He was brunette. It was obvious that he came from a noble family. He looked at the prince with his slightly parted front teeth and smiled sweetly.

"Okalper!" said Prince Sapphire in surprise. "I didn't know you were coming."

"Prince Sapphire!" Prince Okalper smiled happily. He held out one of the two wine glasses he was holding.

Prince Sapphire stood up, took the glass and hung it up. Then he embraced the man longingly.

"Welcome, Prince of the Faraway Land." he said, his eyes full of tears.

"I needed you so much…It's been a long time."

"I didn't believe it when my father told me, but it's true." said Prince Okalper.

"These nutcases really organized a masquerade ball to get you married, huh?"

"Unfortunately, it is true." said Prince Sapphire, frowning.

"You can't do such a thing, brother!" said Prince Okalper anxiously drinking his wine.

"You are a lover. You can't be forced into marriage like that."

"One of the rare moments when Prince Okalper is right..." said a soft voice from nearby.

Prince Okalper

Amethyst approached the two princes and stood between them.

"Welcome, my prince." Amethyst said with displeasure. It was clear that he wasn't happy to see Okalper.

"Hello, Amethyst." said Prince Okalper indifferently. "You have not changed at all. You still get this strange look on your face whenever you see me."

Then he turned to Prince Sapphire again and smiled.

"Do you remember when we played by the lake, Sapphire?" he said sarcastically, "Amethyst couldn't share you with me. He was always fighting."

"He was jealous." Prince Sapphire rolled his eyes.

Amethyst also smiled.

"You haven't changed either, my prince. You're still childish." he said as if he was upset.

"Amethyst!" said Prince Sapphire, as if to warn him. The Prince looked at Okalper and smiled shyly.

"My fiancée, Mel was looking forward to meeting you." said Prince Okalper. "I have told her a lot about you. But unfortunately, she had to stay and sort out a last-minute mess in the kingdom. She sends her love. You will surely meet one day."

"You've written to me dozens of times. You never mentioned your engagement." said Prince Sapphire in surprise.

"I was going to surprise you, chief." said Prince Okalper.

"She's a real adventurer... She's very brave." He hesitated for a moment. "A little dominant."

Prince Sapphire laughed.

"I'm sure she has to be a little dominant to control you." he said happily.

While they were chatting, Saint Hilarion suddenly appeared beside them.

"My Prince, may I present to you Esmeralda, Princess of Dragoria," said Hilarion.

"Oh yeah." said Prince Sapphire rather indifferently. "Welcome, Princess Esmeralda..."

"Hello my Prince." the princess bowed gracefully. She took off her mask. She was a stunning brunette beauty.

Her curly hair fell over her shoulder. "It is an honour to meet you."

"Me too." said Prince Sapphire. "Please have a drink and enjoy the ball."

Then he fell into conversation with Prince Okalper again. Saint Hilarion sighed deeply and mingled with the princess in despair with the crowd.

"Well..." said Prince Okalper. "You're not going to be sitting here all night, are you? No matter what concerns you have, when you are at a party, you should enjoy it, brother."

And before Prince Sapphire even had a chance to respond, Prince Okalper handed the wine glasses to Amethyst, grabbed Prince Sapphire by the arm and pushed him into the dance floor among the masked princesses. Everyone on the dance floor applauded with delight. Amethyst put the wine glasses aside angrily, folded his arms and snorted.

Princess Esmeralda

"Where did this troublemaker come from again!" he muttered to himself.

The two princes began to dance with the princesses. Prince Okalper was working the room, going from dancing with one princess to another in rapid succession. He always knew how to have a good time. Prince Sapphire also surrendered himself to the princesses. Oh Okalper! This man's happiness and delight were contagious.

The two princes danced for a while under the watch of Amethyst's fiery eyes. Prince Sapphire's crown caught Amethyst's attention for a moment. It was no longer glowing. The stones on it were so dark that Prince Sapphire seemed to be carrying a rusty tin on his head. Seeing this, Amethyst became even more uneasy. As he continued to watch the prince, the prince was starting to look worse with every passing second.

Prince Sapphire suddenly stopped in his tracks. Beads of sweat gathered on his forehead. Then a pain struck his head so intensely that he let out a bitter cry. Prince Sapphire collapsed to the ground before everyone in attendance. He tore at his clothes frantically. Wounds began to spontaneously open on his body.

"Prince Sapphire!" cried Amethyst. He immediately ran to the prince. "What's going on?"

Prince Sapphire cried out in pain.

"Amethyst, I am dying!"

Nephilim appeared as everyone watched on in fear. They carried the prince on their backs and lifted him from the ground.

KarlaKarla and St. Hilarion broke through the crowd and ran to the prince.

"What's going on, KarlaKarla?" Prince Okalper's eyes widened.

The place had turned into a bloodbath in an instant.

"The Prince has been poisoned!" said KarlaKarla fearfully.

"Quickly, get him out of the hall! Hurry!"

The snow, which after many years had silently fallen and covered everything, had surprised everyone in Cyprus. When Seçkin woke up that morning, he swallowed in amazement at this new white world. He had never seen anything like this before. In the past, every time it snowed, it would come with the rain and it would melt as soon as it hit the ground. Only the high hills would be covered in snow. In Cyprus, the most snow would fall on the Troodos Mountains in the South of Cyprus, the Greek Cypriot side. Turkish Cypriots who wanted to see snow would travel to Troodos. It was like this every year. But this year's solar eclipse started to upset all the balances, as they said. To tell the truth, it was good. Because the New Year's celebrations would be beautiful with snow.

Seçkin wore a purple-coloured shirt that he bought specially for the New Year's Eve ball, then put on a sweet bow tie and straightened his collar. Then he combed his hair, which was scattered in all directions, and tidied himself up. He looked at his reflection in the mirror with admiration. He still looked perfect. He always dressed well. It was a habit he developed because of his upbringing. His grandfather always said, "One who has been brought up in a good family should always dress accordingly."

The family always had a noble presence. For as long as he could remember, whenever Seçkin's family went anywhere all eyes would turn and gaze at them with admiration. And, to be perfectly honest, he enjoyed it.

Seçkin felt the shirt fit snugly on him. His body was looking more perfect with each passing day. His six pack was noticeable now. It was incredible. To get into shape like this without going to the gym! He would have laughed if anyone had told him that. But as time passed, things started to make sense. According to ParuParu, there would come a day when he would have to go to war with the Devil and his son. And when that day came, Seçkin needed to be strong. He needed to be the Savior of the Kingdom of the Morningstar.

A strong pain stabbed in his stomach as Seçkin remembered this bitter truth. He stepped away from the mirror and slumped into the chair in his room. There was going to be a war. He knew how bad war could be, he had heard many recounts of the Cyprus war of 1974 from his family. And to top it off, he would be facing off with supernatural beings, not just humans. Every time he thought about this, he felt deeply uneasy.

How could he contend with the Devil? He covered his face with his hands. The burden of this bitter truth was crushing his soul. It had been months since ParuParu had appeared before him, but he still had not found any trace of the prince and princess. And he didn't know how to find them, which was another problem in itself. If Seçkin could find the prince, maybe he could gather some courage from him.

His gaze fell on the useless pocket watch on his nightstand. He took it in his hand and turned it over.

As he grappled with the thoughts in his mind, a "Snap" sounded in his room. He excitedly lifted his head and saw the opaque smoke.

"ParuParu! BesuBesu!" his voice rang excitedly.

"Hello, High Master!" said ParuParu. He and BesuBesu bowed low to the ground and greeted Seçkin.

"You look very handsome, High Master!" said BesuBesu. She blinked her eyelashes and looked at Seçkin in admiration.

"Thank you, BesuBesu." Seçkin smiled shyly.

"You look tired," he said to them. "Where have you been?"

"Everywhere!" smiled ParuParu. "I took my wife for a ride!"

BesuBesu hit ParuParu's arm. "No time for jokes, sir!" BesuBesu scolded him lightly. Then she turned to Seçkin.

"We're looking for the Fallen Guardians."

"Fallen Guardians?" asked Seçkin. "The guardians of the prince and princess?"

Yes, ParuParu nodded. "Nephilim!"

At this moment, the baby PihiPihi, who had been sleeping in BesuBesu's lap, started to cry.

Seçkin walked over to BesuBesu and patted PihiPihi's head tenderly. The baby jinni fixed his big bright blue eyes on Seçkin and eagerly extended his hands towards him.

"Would you like to hold him, sir?" ' BesuBesu asked.

Seçkin hesitated for a moment, then nodded in agreement.

He took the baby in his arms. Even if the jinni was many times stronger than himself, he was still an innocent baby.

As Seçkin held the baby, faint flicker of a memory flashed in his mind. He felt as though he had experienced a similar moment before. The silhouette of a long-haired girl holding a baby in her arms came to his mind. But this moment did not last long. While he watched the baby jinni, PihiPihi soon fell peacefully asleep.

"He has been grumpier than ever today." said BesuBesu. "When a faithful jinni child becomes this grumpy, it is never a good sign."

"Today, be more careful than ever, High Master!" said ParuParu, "Dark days are ahead. No place is safe anymore!"

While Seçkin nodded approvingly, he heard Seçil's voice from the corridor.

"Are you ready, Abi?"

The jinni instantly vanished with a "Snap!"

When Seçkin arrived at the school, no one of his own crew was around. The snow-covered school garden was dazzling. Seçil left her brother and walked to her classmates with a shiny gift package in her hands. Seçkin passed by the many eyes that were watching him and proceeded towards the school building. A few students were sitting on the footstep of the entrance door, trying to guess what gifts each of them had brought. After greeting the students sitting in the doorway, he went inside. He climbed the worn steps decorated with wreaths, and arrived the twelfth-grade painting workshop. He stood in the open doorway and took a look at what was going on inside.

Ela and Duru were there. Can was with them. Duru was standing in front of a mirror, trying to attach a train of fuchsia tulle fabric to her dress, and Ela was helping her. Can looked at the two of them and burst into laughter. He found this train-attaching debacle quite funny.

"Good morning!" Seçkin said after watching his friends for a while.

"Good morning, my love!" Ela replied sweetly. She put the tulle in Duru's hand and excitedly walked over to Seçkin and kissed him on the cheek. Then she looked him up and down and nodded in admiration.

"Your bow tie is so sweet. You look so handsome!"

He smiled shyly.

"You are very beautiful too."

It wasn't something he said out of politeness. It was true. Ela was really beautiful. She had gathered her into an elegant bun. She was wearing a purple mini dress with a tulle tail that fluttered down to her heels. Even though she and Seçkin hadn't discussed it at all, they were dressed in harmoniously. Just as they had for the last three years!

"We're matching again!" exclaimed Ela.

Duru waved her hand as if to say "Here we go".

"They're matching again. No wonder they ended up together!" she grumbled.

Seçkin smiled.

"And again, you tied tulle together and made your own dress."

Duru excitedly looked away from the mirror and turned to Seçkin. She was graceful in her turn as though she were putting on a little show.

"I used my mother's old curtain tulle this time. How does it look?"

"In one word, wonderful!" said Seçkin.

Duru always sewed her own clothes for special school events. And they weren't just basic outfits, they were quite elegant. She would gather up leftover tulle she found around, put them together and turn into a princess.

Then Seçkin shook hands with Can and greeted him, before slumping down into the worn-down leather armchair. "Have Mine and Ayaz come yet?" he asked.

"They haven't arrived yet!" exclaimed Can. "Our phoenix will be reborn today!" he said and burst into laughter.

"How is he going to be reborn?" Seçkin asked in surprise.

"What are you not understanding? said Can happily "He's going to be all suited up!".

Seçkin smiled.

"I hope he doesn't do anything wrong by Mine!"

"Mine can run circles around him, don't you worry!" said Ela.

"Ughh!" Duru said in frustration, still in front of the mirror. She was struggling to attach the tulle rolls to her waist.

"Why don't you come help, instead of just standing there!" Duru said at last, looking at Ela.

Ela rolled her eyes and walked over to Duru.

Not long after, Mine appeared in the workshop. Without greeting anyone, she dropped her bags on the floor and slumped into one of the empty seats, sadly.

She was wearing a sweater and jeans and her hair was tied up in messy ponytail.

"What happened, Mine?" asked Seçkin, puzzled.

"Nothing!" she said, but her face told a different story.

"Why aren't you dressed?" asked Ela in shock, struggling with Duru's tulle train.

"Do I look naked to you?" she snapped.

Seçkin and Can looked at each other in surprise.

"You know perfectly well that I didn't mean it like that!" she rolled her eyes. "Why didn't you wear that lace dress we bought?"

Mine let out a sigh. She immediately covered her face with her hands and burst into tears.

"I'm so ugly!"

Everyone was in shock. Mine was crying? She never cried!

"Whoa!" exclaimed Seçkin. He jumped to his feet and knelt in front of Mine. "Don't talk nonsense! You're not ugly, Mine."

"You're re lying!"

"She's not lying!" Can chimed in, raising his eyebrows.

"If you were ugly, would Ayaz fall madly in love with you?"

They all stared at Can in disbelief. They almost swallowed their tongues in surprise.

"Did he tell you that?" Mine asked, tears shining in her eyes.

Can nodded his head, instantly regretting revealing this information.

"But don't let him know that I told you." he said with fearful eyes. "He'll kill me if he finds out."

Mine smiled.

"Come on, Mine, get up!" said Ela, "Let's get you dressed up."

"I feel like everyone will laugh at me in that dress." whined Mine.

"Nonsense!" said Duru. "You just trust us and don't worry about the rest. Right, Ela?"

"Yes, now that we have fixed Duru's train, dressing you will be a piece of cake," said Ela.

Mine wiped the tears from her cheeks and smiled.

The girls then kicked Seçkin and Can out of the workshop so they could continue to get ready. Mine surrendered herself Mine and Duru's care to get her ready.

Seçkin and Can went down the worn stairs together and entered the canteen. Seçil was there with her classmates.

They were opening the presents that they had exchanged. A sparkle appeared in her eyes when she saw her brother. She happily waved a musical jewellery box that she had just unwrapped and showed it to Seçkin.

"When should we exchange our gifts?" Can asked Seçkin.

He shrugged. Ayaz still hadn't shown up.

"I guess we'll do it after Ayaz gets here."

"Where the hell is he, anyway?" whined Can.

"Abi!" Seçil called. She excitedly took the hand of her classmates, Ata and Mete, and came over to Seçkin.

"What's up?" Seçkin asked, raising his eyebrows.

"Ata and Mete will both accompany me to the ball this year!" Seçil said, blushing, "I promised to dance with both of them."

While Seçil was leaving the canteen, and entering the ballroom, with two handsome boys on her arm, Seçkin and Can looked at each other and had to restrain from laughing.

"Your sister turned out to be flirtier than you, Seçkin!" Can said with a mischievous smile.

"A real Cazzude[20]" said Seçkin, shaking his head.

Meanwhile, the ballroom door opened again and Bora rushed out. He was going to perform at the ball and they were busy setting up the instruments.

"Hello, Seçkin. Where is Duru?" he asked as soon as Bora saw Seçkin.

"They are getting ready in the workshop." replied Seçkin. "You know how girls are, they take forever to get ready!"

Bora smiled.

"Do you need anything?" Seçkin asked. "Maybe we can help."

---

[20] *Cazzude: A word that Seçkin created to refer to his sister as a witch.*

"Thanks, Seçkin, but everything is ready. You guys already got most things ready days ago. We're just tuning the instruments now."

Bora winked at them and went back to the ballroom.

While Seçkin and Can were standing in the hall watching people pass by, Ayaz finally arrived.

"Good morning, guys!" he called out from behind them.

Seçkin and Can turned towards his voice.

With his jet-black shirt, rubber suspenders, and short hair combed to the side, Ayaz looked like a gentleman from the fifties.

"Where have you been, man!" Seçkin scolded him.

Can looked over his glasses and hit Seçkin's arm with his elbow. "I told you he would be reborn!" he said mockingly. "You look so handsome, Phoenix!"

Ayaz was livid. He walked over to Can with fire in his eyes.

"Look at me, you idiot... I'll break your mouth and nose!"

Can laughed even more.

While they were arguing, Defne appeared.

She was stunning. She looked almost like a fairy. Her curly auburn hair cascaded down to her waist. She was wearing a purple dress too. Her beauty outshone anyone else who passed by her. Seçkin couldn't take his eyes off her.

"She looks gorgeous!" said Ayaz.

"Yeah, absolutely." said Seçkin, in a trance.

When Seçkin finally pulled his eyes away from Defne and looked at Ayaz, he realised that Ayaz wasn't looking at Defne. He was looking to the top of the stairs. Seçkin followed his gaze to see what Ayaz was looking at.

It was Mine. She was wearing a short, red, lace dress.

Mine had let down her blonde hair to fall down past her shoulders. Ever since Seçkin had known her, she had always kept it tied back. She had transformed from a hot-headed tomboy into a beautiful lady. She descended down the worn marble steps gracefully. "Wow!" Can whistled as Mine came down the stairs.

Ayaz, on the other hand, seemed to have lost his voice. With his mouth wide open, he watched this beautiful lady approached sweetly towards him.

When Mine reached them, Ayaz gently took her hand, kissed it and said "You look beautiful".

Mine's cheeks turned red and she looked at Ayaz and giggled shyly. "You can close your mouth!" she said playfully.

Behind Mine, Ela and Duru also came down the stairs.

"Everyone in the workshop! They are waiting for us to exchange presents." said Ela. "We have to go back upstairs."

Mine linker her arm into Ayaz's. Ela and Seçkin hugged each other and then started to climb the stairs.

"Well, what about me?" Duru asked with a hint of jealousy. "My boyfriend is busy tuning instruments in the ballroom."

They all burst into laughter.

"I am at your service lady, for the time being." said Can. Duru immediately took the boy's arm and, like a princess, began to climb up the worn steps with the others.

There was a sweet excitement in the twelfth-grade painting workshop. Students of the painting department from all grades were sitting on stools lined up in the shape of a crescent moon, thinking about the New Year presents they would shortly receive.
The shiny gift packages held by the students were sparkled brightly and their radiant colours reflected off the pale walls of the workshop. Mine had just coldly given her present to the cheeky strange girl and had sat down again. When the cheeky strange girl eagerly called Ela's name, Ela got up and, just as coldly as Mine, shook hands with her and took her gift.

After hearing that the cheeky strange girl was going to attend the ball with Mert, Ela was mad. If their teacher wasn't watching them, instead of fake smiling, Ela would have hit the girl over the head with the gift. She should be thankful that Özden Atakol was sitting there and smiling sweetly at them.

"Yes, my dear Ela!" Derin Zade called out. "Who are you giving your gift to?"

Ela's eyes gleamed as she watched at her friends sitting on stools. Seçkin's heart began to race. Then Ela fixed her gaze on Duru and Seçkin was disappointed.

"Ah!" Duru jumped up excitedly "Oh is it me? Is it me?" She clapped her hands together excitedly.

Ela smiled seriously and said "Sit down, Duru! It's not you!"

Everyone in the workshop burst into laughter, Duru collapsed back onto the stool. She was clearly disappointed.

Ela once again scanned the people lined up on their stools, and finally, "Seçkin!" she exclaimed.

Applause filled the workshop. Seçkin stood up in surprise and walked over to Ela. While winking at him, Ela placed a sweet kiss on his cheek and handed a gift to her so-called lover.

"I was really curious about this gift that Duru missed out on!" Bahar Saral said, "Open it, Seçkin!"

The workshop started chanting, "Open it! Open it! Open it!".

"You're being too polite, son, tear it up!" Özden Atakol insisted while Seçkin was attempting to open the gift package with care.

Seçkin did as his art teacher said and tore up the package. He took out an intricately woven dreamcatcher object which had delicate bird feathers suspended beneath two intersecting circles.

"What is it?" Özden Atakol asked. Seçkin himself was trying to work that out.

"It's a dreamcatcher!" said Ela happily.

"Dreamcatcher?" Seçkin asked, raising his eyebrows.

"Yes," said Ela, "You told me you haven't been sleeping well because of the nightmares you have been having! So, I decided to get you this. According to Native American belief, if you hang this over the top of your bed, good dreams will filter through the net in the middle of those circles and flow through the feathers to you. Bad dreams, on the other hand, get lost because they do not know the way."

"Fabulous, Ela!" said Özden Atakol while Bahar Saral and Seçkin examined the dreamcatcher.

"I hope it works," said Ela hugging Seçkin warmly.

Seçkin's gift was to Derin Zade. He gifted her an oil painting work called "The Forbidden Apple". Derin Zade, on the other hand, had drawn Ayaz's name in the New Year's draw and gave him a set of gloves, a beret and a scarf that she had knitted herself.

Finally, only Ayaz was left to give his gift. Before he could even call her name, Duru jumped up and embraced him.

"I had a hard time finding a gift for you," Ayaz admitted. "Hope you like it, babe!"

He handed Duru a small package. Duru opened the package excitedly and took out a silver necklace with an Angel pendant.

Duru clapped her hands with delight and gave the necklace to Ayaz asking him to put it around her neck.

This year's gift giving ceremony came to an end without incident.

When Seçkin and his friends went downstairs, there was a crowd forming in front of the ballroom door.

A lanky boy stood in front of the door, "No entry without a partner!" he kept repeating.

Duru reached into her bag and took out some colourful masquerade masks.

"Guys, don't forget your masks. It's a masquerade ball!" she said cheerfully and handed a mask to each of her friends.

"Duru, these are amazing!" said Ela admiringly, putting on a gold-coloured mask decorated with feathers. Then she took Seçkin by the hand and entered the ballroom.

The ballroom was dimly lit with colourful lights creating a disco like atmosphere. Students in the school choir took their places, ready to kick off the event under the leadership of Ayhatun Yıldız.

Ayhatun Yıldız hit the ground with her heel three times. And the choir began to sing.

A dark, melancholic song filled the ballroom.

> *"Over the hills…Was a forest…Over the hills…*
>
> *Was a forest… There all creatures lived pleased."*

Everyone, including the students singing the song, shuddered. It was obvious that they were not happy with the choice of song. On such a beautiful day, this song seemed so out of place.

*"Arrived a hunter…Cruel he was… Hunted them one by one…
And deforested"*

Ela leaned in close to Seçkin's ear and whispered, "No one understands what's happening to Ayhatun Hoca." she said anxiously.

"She's been so moody lately! She acts as if she no longer belongs to this world."

"No sunshine…No rain…No one ever seen the cruel's end..."

Seçkin took a deep sigh. An unpleasant feeling weighed him down.

"Won't someone put an end to this torture?" said Mine's voice from nearby. She took Ayaz by the arm and came to join Seçkin and Ela. The two of them seemed to understand each other surprisingly well.

Ayaz took two glasses filled with sweet Commandaria from the table and gave one to Mine, while sloshing down the other glass.

"Hey! Take it easy!" Seçkin exclaimed. "You'll be drunk in no time if you drink like that!"

"From this?" Ayaz asked. "This is just grape juice, you know!"

"Oh, Ayaz! Please be careful! It was already hard enough to get the school administration to approve the wine," said Ela.

"Okay, I got it!" Ayaz grumbled.

As Mine took a sip from her wine, Ela leaned in and giggled. "You know, Mine, men only give this wine to the girl they're in love with."

Then the choir finished their song and Bora and his band took the stage. Burak was playing the drums. He hit the drums for a count of three and the band started playing a lively, heart-warming song.

Seçkin met Burak's eyes for a moment. Had he treated him badly that day? Thinking about it broke his heart. He was connected to Burak somehow. It hurt to know that he was hurting him.

"Come on, let's dance!" Ela's voice rang out. She grabbed Seçkin, who was eating a plateful of golifa[21], by the arm, led him into the midst of the masked student groups to start dancing.

While Seçkin was awkwardly accompanying her, he saw Korkut standing in the darkness for a moment watching them. Then he looked around.

Defne wasn't dancing with him. She was sitting down and having a drink with some girlfriends. Duru was right in front of the stage where Bora was playing the bass guitar and dancing while she watched him.

Mine and Ayaz were chatting happily and sipping their drinks.

---

[21] *Golifa: It is a sweet food commonly made for New Year's Eve in Cyprus. It is made by mixing wheat, almonds, pomegranate, raisins and sesame. Golifa, which is distributed to neighbours as an offering in Greek Cypriots, is made in Northern Cyprus for a new year to be abundant and fruitful.*

Seçil was dancing sweetly with her two companions. She was coming out of one's arm and taking the other's arm. She was almost like a little princess.

Seçkin closed his eyes and took a deep breath. Then, a thought lit up his mind. Sahra! Where was she? He hadn't seen her yet today.

He looked back to where he had seen Korkut. Korkut was gone.

Seçkin asked for Ela's permission and left the ballroom. His ears were ringing from the loud music.

He saw Havva and Şeyda, who were standing in the entrance hallway chatting and laughing. Şeyda looked at Seçkin with admiration as he greeted them and passed by.

Seçkin stepped out to the snow-covered garden. The pristine landscape dazzled him for a short time, but soon his eyes adjusted and he looked into the garden.

Sahra was there.

She was sitting alone under the judas tree, looking around in a contemplative manner as she always did.

Seçkin walked over to her.

"Sahra?"

Sahra stared at the boy's face vacantly for a while, and then smiled.

"Hi Seçkin!"

"Why are you sitting here alone in this cold?" asked Seçkin.

"I'm not cold! The Sahara breeze warms me!" said the girl.

"Yes. I forgot that." Seçkin muttered to himself.

"Did you say something?" said Sahra.

"Why didn't you go to the ball?" Seçkin changed the subject. Sahra smiled.

"Actually, to tell the truth, I couldn't find a date to go with." said Sahra, "I guess men don't find me very attractive."

As soon as Seçkin heard this, his heart broke. He looked Sahra up and down. Her Cleopatra style haircut did not look bad at all. But her haunting glances were a bit off-putting. The high-shouldered sequined orange dress, which looked like something from the eighties, wasn't helping either. But despite everything, Sahra was a young girl and every young girl wanted to feel special.

Seçkin jumped to his feet and extended his hand to her. "From now on, I'm your date, young lady!" he said with a mischievous smile.

A glint appeared in Sahra's pale eyes and she took Seçkin's hand.

"Well, what about Ela, wouldn't she be upset by this?"

"No! Of course, she wouldn't." Seçkin said and took the girl by the arm and led her to the school building.

Two big crows, which had been perching on the judas tree and watching them for a while, cawed and took flight.

When Seçkin and Sahra entered the ballroom together, couples were dancing to a romantic song that was playing.

"Where have you been, Seçkin?" asked Ela. She appeared right next to him as soon as she saw him.

"I was just chatting with Sahra outside." said Seçkin.

"Hello Ela, how are you?" Sahra greeted her sweetly.

"Hello, my dear Sahra…" Ela replied, raising her eyebrow at Seçkin, trying to understand what was going on.

"You missed the big event!" Ela said excitedly, "Ayaz confessed his love to Mine."

"Ahh! Really?" said Sahra, her cheeks red and giggling.

Ela nodded happily.

"It was about time!" said Seçkin. Then he looked around trying to spot Mine and Ayaz. They were in the middle of the dance floor, dancing closely together.

"When were you planning to dance with me?" asked Ela playfully, clasping her hands and tilting her nose in the air.

Seçkin smiled, "I promised another beautiful lady before you. Will you dance with me, Sahra?"

Sahra's pale cheeks flushed again, and she reached out her hand to Seçkin and shyly walked with him to the dance floor.

Ela stared at them in disbelief with her mouth open. Then she nodded and smiled fondly at Seçkin. This boy was one of a kind. While Ela was watching them, her gaze drifted to the cheeky strange girl who was dancing with Mert.

Ela's lips tightened in anger and her eyes filled with tears. "Damn you!" she thought bitterly. Then, all of a sudden, Ela felt a sharp stabbing pain in her head.

There was an explosion and the windows of the hall shattered. Dozens of crows flew in and attacked the students. Screams rose up from around the hall. Terrified students tried to escape from the ballroom.

Amid the chaos, Seçkin looked for Seçil anxiously in the crowd. Ayaz got hold of a crow that was attacking Mine, and thew it against the wall by its wings. Mine fainted and collapsed into Ayaz's arms.

Seçkin was still running around in terror, looking for Seçil. Finally, he found her under a table, kicking a crow that had been attacking her. Seçkin kicked the crow in anger and pulled his sister out from under the table, hugging her tightly. Thankfully she wasn't hurt.

While Seçkin was shielding Seçil against the monstrous crows, he reached down and grabbed Ela's arm. She was kneeling on the ground, still struggling with the stabbing pain in her head. He led them out of the ballroom. Ela's arm was slit, and blood was seeping onto her dress.

A girl's cry erupted from the marble staircase. An eighth-grade girl, drenched with sweat, ran down the steps in horror.

"Ayhatun Hoca!" she said with a trembling voice. "Ayhatun Hoca is lying in blood in the first-floor hallway!"

Seçkin and Ela stared at each other in horror. Sahra immediately rushed up the staircase.

"Sahra, wait for me!" Seçkin shouted after her.

"Abi, don't go!" Seçil said, trembling with fear.

"Duru! Bora!" Seçkin called out. "Take Seçil and Ela to the garden."

Duru and Bora nodded and grabbing the two girls and heading for the exit. Seçil stared after her brother in fear and burst into tears.

Seçkin ran after Sahra. Then Burak, who saw Seçkin climbing the stairs, followed after them.

When they reached the upper floor, they were confronted with a horrifying sight. Ayhatun Yıldız was lying at the end of the corridor under the big window. Her wrists had been slit, and blood was oozing down the corridor. Seçkin immediately rushed to Ayhatun Yıldız's side. Sahra crouched next to Seçkin and checked Ayhatun Yıldız for a pulse.

"She's dead!" Sahra said mournfully, her voice trembling.

Then a red smoke emerged from behind Ayhatun Yıldız and transformed into an inscription which was floating by her head.

"Sahra, what's going on?" Seçkin asked, scared.

"Don't be afraid Seçkin!" Burak immediately reassured him as he patted Seçkin on the back.

Sahra seemed to enter a trance-like state as she examined the inscriptions formed from the smoke.

"It is written in Arabic!" she said at last, her eyes narrowing into thin lines.

"You know Arabic! What does it say?" Seçkin asked.

"I sacrificed myself for the King of Hell!" She translated.

"What?" Seçkin gasped. He looked like he might die from fright.

After a while, as the inscription disappeared, Seçkin felt the warm liquid flowing out from his nose.

"Your nose is bleeding!" said Burak, wiping the blood from his nose.

Seçkin pushed Burak away, tears flowing from his eyes.

Berk Saral's voice rose from the end of the corridor. Seçkin's father was racing towards them with a group of teachers next to him. His mother and Derin Zade were with them. Duru and Bora were following them.

They had just found out what had happened from the girl who was screaming at the top of the marble stairs earlier.

"Ayhatun!" cried Berk Saral in horror. "What happened to her?"

"Seçkin!" cried Bahar Saral immediately. "Quick, come to me!"

With his feet barely able to carry him, Seçkin walked over to his mother in tears. His nose was still bleeding and his wrists were stained with blood from wiping his nose.

"What does all this mean?" cried Berk Saral angrily. "Did you do this, Sahra?"

Sahra looked at the headmaster's face fearfully.

"No!" cried Seçkin, breathing heavily. "Sahra and I… We came to see what was going on! Then Burak came after us."

"Why is your nose bleeding?" Bahar Saral asked in horror.

"I don't know!" he said in tears.

"The woman obviously committed suicide!" said Memduh Kemal, "She's been acting so strangely lately!"

While everyone was trying to understand what had happened, Seçkin, with tears in his eyes, walked over to Duru and Bora. Just then, he heard a 'Snap'.

Seçkin's heart started to race even more. He looked around in a panic.

"ParuParu?" he whispered as he walked away from his friends.

"It's me, High Master!" said the jinni's voice.

Seçkin looked around, but ParuParu was nowhere to be seen.

"Don't bother looking, High Master, you won't be able to see me!" said ParuParu, "I am invisible!"

"ParuParu, what's going on?" Seçkin asked as tears fell down his face.

"Your teacher sacrificed herself for the Devil, High Master! If this continues, Azazel will soon be resurrected …"

Seçkin felt nauseous. It was the first time he felt the reality of the fact that he was going to have to encounter the Devil. Suddenly he felt weak at the knees, and he was scared to death…

-CHAPTER VI-

A Winged Boy

A smile...

Defne was smiling and Seçkin couldn't stop watching her.

"Abi, if you keep looking at that girl, I'll go and tear her hair out!" Seçil grumbled. She was sitting next to the boy and she was furious.

Seçkin pursed his lips.

"Okay… I'm not looking!"

After a while, his eyes went back to Defne's side.

"Abi, you're looking again!" squeaked Seçil.

"Oh Seçil! Leave me alone!"

"You are dating Ela abla now, abi… Or have you forgotten? So, stop staring at this girl!" said the young girl angrily.

Everywhere was covered with a ghostly crimson mist again. People were used to this by now. Cyprus was having a strange winter. The snow melted quickly.

It had been weeks since Ayhatun Yıldız's death, but she was not forgotten as quickly as the melting snow. It wasn't raining. The sun was not shining. Teachers and students were still mourning her death. A new choir teacher had come to the school. But she wasn't a lively, fun person like her. Her place could never be filled.

The school building was pale. It stood like a ghost in the fog. The building too seemed to mourn the passing of the jovial, elusive choirmaster it had said goodbye to weeks ago.

The death of Ayhatun Yıldız was also widely covered in the press. Some believed it was suicide, while others claimed that Ayhatun Yıldız was a murder victim. Families who believed that the incident was a murder began to worry about the safety of the school. There were even those who took their children off the school.

Everyone was talking about the Nicosia Anatolian Fine Arts High School no longer being a safe school. This shook the school building deeply. But despite everything that was going on, it was stubbornly trying to stand there with its weak foundations.

"Is your gaze betraying me again?" asked Ela's voice from nearby. The girl came out of the school building and smiled mischievously. She sat between Seçkin and Seçil with a pink package of Lays in her hand. "Anyone want some bug crisps?"

"Me!" Seçil said in a fairy-like voice. She dipped her hand into the package, took the prawn cocktail crisps and popped it into her mouth. "I love these crisps!" she said with a full smile.

"How's your arm, Ela?" Seçkin asked.

"I'm going to have the stitches removed today." she said.

She, too, had survived the crows attack on Prom Day with three stitches on her arm.

"Forget about me, you look a little pale, Seçkin." said Ela.

"I have a headache. I couldn't get any sleep last night." Seçkin pursed his lips.

"I thought your headaches were gone, abi." Seçil exclaimed immediately. "I think we should tell my mom."

"No, Seçil. It doesn't always hurt." he lied.

"Do you know? Ata's family, who is in the seventh grade, came to take their son off the school." said Ela, sullenly.

"Ata's leaving too?" Seçil immediately jumped to her feet and her eyes widened, "Abi, not Ata, too!"

Seçkin and Ela looked at each other and smiled.

"Looks like someone has a crush on Ata!" said Ela.

Seçil sat down next to her abi and her cheeks turned red.

"He is my classmate!" she replied immediately, squirming shyly. "We are only three people in the class anyway! I hope Ata does not go, abi!"

Meanwhile some people nearby were shouting.

"How could you do this to me?" Mine's voice rang from nearby.

Seçkin, Ela and Seçil looked in the direction the voice came from.

"What's going on?" Seçil asked with frightened eyes.

Mine and Ayaz were standing in the doorway of the school building, arguing. The students passing by were looking at the two of them in surprise.

"They are fighting!" said Ela in horror.

"How fast!" Seçkin wondered, his eyebrows raised. "Haven't they just started dating last week?"

Ela shook her head.

"It was clear from the beginning that this would happen. They're both crazy."

They locked their gazes on Mine and Ayaz in curiosity. Then Mine started to cry.

"Do you think we should go near them?" Seçkin asked hesitantly. "It seems like the situation is a little serious!"

Seçkin and Ela, jumped out of their seats before Seçil's astonished looks and ran to the new couples' side who were arguing fiercely.

"What is going on in here?" she asked, looking at them in surprise.

"I should have realized I couldn't trust him!" she sobbed as soon as she saw Ela. "All men are the same!" She snuggled into Ela's side and sobbed.

Mine started to dress and act girly, lately. She started to wear her school uniform skirt since after the New Year's Eve ball. She was doing her hair even more carefully. And now, when her heart was broken, she would hug a friend and easily burst into tears.

"What did you do to the girl, Ayaz?" Ela asked immediately, her eyes blazing.

"Nothing!" Ayaz shrugged.

"What nothing How can it be nothing?" growled Mine. She came out of Ela's arms in anger.

"That bitch! She was holding your hand when I entered the classroom!"

"Who is she talking about?" Seçkin asked Ayaz. He was trying to understand what was going on.

"Cheeky strange girl!" growled Mine. "After Mert, she is wagging her tail to Ayaz now."

Seçkin and Ela's eyes met for a moment. Ela's lips tightened in anger.

She remembered how angry and heartbroken she was when she saw the cheeky strange girl in Mert's arms at the New Year's Eve ball. No one could understand Mine better than her.

"Shame on you, Ayaz!" Ela grimaced.

"Ela! At least you don't do this!" Seçkin said, trying to calm the atmosphere.

"No one is wagging their tails at me!" Ayaz finally growled, full of anger. "And even if she is, I don't see anyone else but you, don't you understand!"

He approached her and tried to hold her hand, but Mine quickly backed away.

"Don't you ever touch me again, freak!" cried Mine, in tears.

Thus, it all happened at that moment. Ayaz suddenly raised his hand and slapped Mine so hard that everyone froze.

Seçil, who watched them from the garden, immediately screamed. Seçkin and Ela just stared, not knowing what to do.

"Never say that to me again!" Ayaz shouted in a daze.

Seçkin, Ela and Mine stood there for a while and looked at Ayaz with eyes full of fear. No one had ever seen him like this before.

152

Ayaz looked at his hands, sighed with regret, and ran down the stairs in tears.

"Ayaz!" "Wait!" Seçkin called after him after a short wobble.

"Leave me alone!" cried Ayaz's tearful voice.

Ayaz ran through the worn marble steps two steps at a time and raced down to the first-floor corridor. Then he opened the creaking door of the men's room and stepped inside.

Seçkin followed him into the corridor, but slowed his pace as he came to the end of the corridor. Ayhatun Yıldız's bloody corpse that had been lying there weeks ago came to his mind. He still could smell her blood. He felt nauseous for a moment, then shook his head to forget what had happened, and immediately followed Ayaz into the bathroom. The door, with rusty hinges, closed by itself with a chilling creak.

Ayaz was leaning against the sink, he seemed that he lost his control. He turned on the faucet and washed his face with vigorous movements. Then he started punching the sink in a fit of anger. He was crying. This was the first time Seçkin had seen him like this amongst all those years he had known him. He was always callous and mischievous. But now, contrary to what he had thought all these years, he was not devoid of emotion.

"Calm down Ayaz!" Seçkin patted his friend on the shoulder sadly.

"Leave me alone!" Ayaz roared again. He opened his hands. "How could I hit her?" he said regretfully.

Seçkin lowered his head to the ground and sighed in sadness. Mine would never forgive that slap; he knew it.

"You became the victim of a moment of anger." said Seçkin. "You know that Mine is a wounded girl. Her father left her mother when she was a child and ran off with another woman. Her mother has been drinking non-stop since then. This is why she can't trust men!"

"I know!" said Ayaz. "But I swear to you, I didn't do anything to hurt her, Seçkin! I would never. You know Deniz, she gets too intimate to everyone. But my eyes see no one but Mine!"

Seçkin believed in Ayaz. He saw that honesty in his eyes. It was so obvious that he had been wronged while he was bitterly crying there with his head bowed, it made his heart sink.

"Mine is right. I'm a freak!" Ayaz finally said in grief.

"Don't be silly Ayaz!" Seçkin snapped at him. "What kind of talk is that!"

"I am a freak!" said Ayaz like crazy. "I will show you!"

Ayaz brought his trembling fingers to the buttons of his shirt. Seçkin was trying to understand what he was doing. While watching his friend, he once again saw how much the feeling of not being able to express himself with the resentment of being wronged hurt him. This made him very sad. Although he had a previous record of hitting on girls, Ayaz had not cheated on Mine as he said.

He was sure of it.

Ayaz took off his shirt and threw it aside. He wore a corset under his shirt. Seçkin wondered why he was wearing that corset, but he didn't ask. Ayaz took it off and his perfect body was revealed. He had a six-pack. It was obvious that he was involved in sports. But Seçkin could not see anything strange in this. There was nothing wrong with the boy's body.

Ayaz looked crazy. It was like he had gone mental.

"Are you ready?" he asked through his teeth. He closed his eyes tightly and turned his back.

Seçkin was horrified at what he saw. He swallowed hard and let out a small exclamation of surprise. It is not known how many minutes he stared at Ayaz, but after a short time he could not stand it any longer and fell to his knees.

Ayaz had an inverted V-shaped slit in his ribs, and two small wings like an angel were growing out of that slit. There were wounds on the wings that were about to heal. It was as if someone had tried to cut it and failed.

"I tried to cut them! Repeatedly!" cried Ayaz in despair. "But I couldn't stand the pain. It's like cutting my flesh!"

His feet could not carry Ayaz any longer, and he fell to his knees in embarrassment and burst into sobs.

Outside, a thunderclap cracked the sky.

So that's why Ayaz's back was constantly hurting. Because of these wings, he didn't take off his top when he was modelling in the design classes.

"What a great shame!" whined Ayaz.

Seçkin and Ayaz just stood there for a while, looking at each other with blank eyes. Neither of them spoke.

Seçkin remembered the guards ParuParu had told him about. The guards that were the ascendants of humans and angels that had wings of an angel, in the leadership of Prince of the Kingdom of the Morningstar.

Nephilim! Ayaz was one of them. This was obvious.

Seçkin immediately jumped to his feet. "This is not a shame!" he said, her eyes gleaming with hope.

"What?" whined Ayaz. "What's normal about this, tell me?"

Seçkin frowned.

"Pull yourself together! I'll introduce you to someone…"

After school, Ayaz got into the black Mercedes with Seçkin. Seçkin told his parents that Ayaz was going to stay with them that night. They did not object either. In such cases, it wouldn't be a problem anyway. Seçkin was free to bring his friends to his home.

When they got home, Seçkin casually greeted his grandmother and grandfather, and went straight to his room followed by Ayaz. As they both entered the blue bedroom, Seçkin closed the door and turned the key and locked it.

"Why did you lock the door?" Ayaz asked in surprise. "Who are you going to introduce me to? Come on man, isn't this mystery too much?"

"I'm going to rape you!" said Seçkin with a mischievous smile.

"I knew!" Ayaz smiled. "I knew from day one that you liked me!"

Seçkin shook his head and smiled, then,

"Paru Paru!" he called out.

Ayaz looked around in surprise.

"ParuParu? What is it?"

"Wait a little bit." he said, smiling. It was obvious how amused he was by this situation.

Not long after, a 'Snap' sound was heard in the room, and the tiny jinni appeared in the opaque smoke.

"Oh fuck!" said Ayaz, jumping back in fright. "What is this?"

"Did you summon me, my High Master?" asked Paru Paru devotedly.

"Is this thing an alien?" Ayaz asked, his heart beating with fear.

ParuParu frowned. He folded his arms. He lifted his chin as if in movement.

"I am not an alien!"

"He's a jinni!" said Seçkin. Then he smiled. "A faithful ambassador jinni!"

"A what jinni?" Ayaz asked in disbelief.

"He is a good immigrant jinni!" Seçkin replied to him. Then he sighed with delight. The day he met ParuParu, he had the same reaction as Ayaz. Every time he thought of this incident, he burst into laughter.

He looked at ParuParu, who was watching Seçkin and Ayaz curiously.

"I think I found one of the guards, my dear friend!"

An excited glint appeared in ParuParu's eyes.

He grinned to his ears, showing his teeth. He walked over to Ayaz and looked at him from head to toe.

Then a second "Snap!" voice was heard again in the room and BesuBesu appeared in the smoke.

"Is what I heard is true?" she said excitedly as she emerged from the opaque smoke.

Ayaz turned pale once again.

"Man, what kind of world are you in?" he asked in horror. Then his knees went empty and he slumped on the armchair in the room.

"Did his wings grow out?" Paru Paru asked while still examining the boy.

Seçkin nodded.

"But how can this happen?" said BesuBesu. "Guardians don't get wings before they're eighteen!"

"Ayaz turned nineteen on the twenty-fourth of December." Seçkin informed. "He's a year older than me!"

"Show them!" ParuParu commanded.

"What?" asked Ayaz.

"What do you mean by what! Show me your wings!" said ParuParu excitedly. "You bewildered guard master!"

"Yes sir!" Ayaz grumbled, grinding his teeth at ParuParu.

Seçkin watched this son of Adam and the jinni, who were quarrelling with each other. How well they were getting along!

Ayaz got up. He took off his shirt and turned around and spread his thin angelic wings.

ParuParu and BesuBesu's eyes filled with a great gleam of joy. Not long after, BesuBesu's smile quickly faded like the winter sun.

"Why are your wings injured?" she asked as she examined them.

Ayaz didn't say anything. He just lowered his head and sighed in regret.

"Did you try to cut them off?" snorted Paru Paru.

Ayaz slowly nodded his head.

"What a great sin!" groaned BesuBesu. "They are a gift from your previous life!"

"Enough!" Ayaz finally exasperated. "Are you going to start telling me about what the hell is going on here, or should I walk away?"

ParuParu and BesuBesu stared at the boy's face in surprise. How angry this son of Adam was?

"Please sit down, young man!" ParuParu pointed to the armchair.

Ayaz did as he said, albeit with a grunt, and slumped on the seat.

ParuParu and BesuBesu started telling the boy the whole story. But they could not convince Ayaz. He stubbornly refused to admit it. Just like Seçkin did months ago.

"So now I'm one of the three male guards guarding the prince?" he asked for almost the tenth time. Then, as he did each time, "This is sheer nonsense!" he growled again.

ParuParu and BesuBesu looked at each other in shock and gulped. Indeed, this young man seemed incurable. He was a total rebel.

"I was born as a result of the relationship of a human being and an angel, huh!"

"In a previous life… Yes." said Seçkin

"Nonsense!" Ayaz foamed with rage again.

"When you say that, remember that you have wings, Ayaz!" Seçkin warned him at last. Hesitantly, he pointed to the boy's angelic wings.

"Don't worry, I can't forget even though I want to! Because their weight on my back won't allow it!" said the boy.

Ayaz closed his eyes. His lips twitched in disbelief. But no matter how much he said he didn't believe it, deep down he knew it was true. The proof of everything was those skinny angel wings that were starting to grow on his back…

Seçkin was walking through a huge church that seemed to have no end. Everywhere was navy blue. There was a divine gloom all around. He felt like he couldn't breathe for a while. This gloom was pressing down on his throat again. He looked at the ceiling. He saw thousands of stars shining behind the church's cross-vaulted roof. He felt a little better when he saw them. Fortunately, the church had a glass dome on its ceiling. The stars were visible.

The boy's breathing soon improved. He continued walking slowly through the huge space. At last, a majestic gothic rose window appeared before him. Beams of light glinted through the tinted stained-glass windows. The red, green, purple and blue of the stained glass were reflected around. He continued to walk nonstop.

A rotten wooden cube appeared in front of him. On the cube there was an hourglass. He felt something vibrating in his pocket. He dug his hand into his pocket and pulled out a silver pocket watch. The watch was not working.

Seçkin walked again and left the cube behind. He could hear bell sounds. As he got closer to the rose window, he saw a sarcophagus there just below the window. A baby was crying on the sarcophagus.

Seçkin immediately took a few steps towards the baby. But he was blocked by three male silhouettes with angel wings.

He paused where he was. The baby was silent. The bells rang again, and a beam of light from the rose window illuminated one of the three silhouettes that were standing side by side.

It was Ayaz. His perfect body was bare and his wings were majestic.

"You found me!" he said in a muffled voice. "And what about the rest?"

Seçkin swallowed with a pale face. He stared at the silhouettes standing on both sides of Ayaz.

"Time is running out! The trumpet will sound very soon!"

Seçkin immediately turned around. He drifted with the speed of light to the hourglass he had just left behind. The last grain of sand was about to fall. And he, too, fell like the others, amid Seçkin's sorrowful gaze.

Meanwhile, something like a whistling sound echoed around. Then a laughter resonated and some kind of jester danced and somersaulted coming near Seçkin. He had no face and had the body of a woman.

While the chilling laughter echoed in the enormous church, she handed a red apple to Seçkin.

Ayaz hissed.

"Do not eat from the tree of the knowledge of good and evil! Because the day you eat from it, you will surely die!" he said in a muffled voice.

Seçkin did not listen to him. He looked at the apple with a great appetite. Normally, he didn't like to eat apples. But now he wanted that apple so badly that he couldn't resist it.

Seçkin took a bite from the apple. The jester burst into laughter as Ayaz and the other two silhouettes immediately disappeared with a puff sound. The baby on the sarcophagus began to cry again.

Seçkin gasped. He dropped the apple. The apple rolled and stood under the jester's feet. The jester's faceless head suddenly turned into the face of a creature with flaming eyes.

"You are weak, Seçkin Saral… You are too weak!" said a malignant voice echoing in the church.

Seçkin could not resist any longer, so he fell at the feet of the jester and was thrown into a huge dark void… Seçkin was startled. Trembling, he opened his eyes. He was covered in sweat. The dream catcher that Ela had given him was hanging over his top. He watched it for a while. It didn't work. He was having nightmares again.

He got up in bed. His head felt like it was going to burst again.

Ayaz was snoring in the bed they had prepared for him on the floor. Seçkin had offered to give him his bed, but he had arrogantly opposed the boy. "Sleeping in bed is for sissies like you. I'll sleep on the floor." he said as he prepared the bed on the floor.

This situation bothered Seçkin, but as far as he could see, Ayaz seemed at ease.

He got up from the bed. He tiptoed out of the room not to wake Ayaz. Rubbing his eyes, he descended the stairs. He headed for the kitchen, but the light in the living room caught his attention. He slowly made his way to the living room. The television was also on. Seçil was sitting there like a little owl, staring at the TV with bloodshot eyes.

The news on television was about the incessant suicide incidents in Cyprus.

"Seçil?" Seçkin called out.

Seçil jumped in her seat in fear.

"Oh abi! You scared me!" she said, taking a deep breath with fearful eyes. Then she opened her mouth wide and yawned.

"Why didn't you sleep? It's almost daylight." Seçkin asked. Confused, he looked at his sister.

Seçil pursed her lips.

"I could not sleep!" she said, exhausted.

Seçkin sighed in concern.

"Why?" asked. He sat next to her and stroked her hair.

Seçil rested her head on her brother's shoulder and took a deep breath.

"Abi, look, everyone is committing suicide... It's weird, don't you think?"

"Yes." Seçkin said with a knot in his throat. Azazel came to his mind.

Neither of them spoke for a while. But both were terrified by what had happened recently.

"Do you know? I think my father convinced Ata's family. My friend will not leave the school!"

"This is great news, shorty!" he smiled.

"Abi, shall we sleep here tonight?" the little girl asked at last.

Seçkin looked at her affectionately and nodded. After a while, the two fell asleep in front of the TV...

Screams... loud bawling...

Prince Sapphire was in agony. A deep darkness had descended on the night. While the stone walls of the palace groaned from the cries of the prince, his friends were gathered in front of his door in a mournful wait. So much so that Amethyst was crouching in front of the Prince's door, hysterically covering his ears with each new cry.

"It's not poison. A powerful spell was cast through his crown." said Saint Hilarion's voice from nearby.

"So much so that we should be thankful that the Prince is even alive."

"O Supreme Creator, spare our prince to us." said KarlaKarla.

"But how can this happen?" said Prince Okalper angrily. "Who dares to touch the Prince's crown?"

Then his glance met with Amethyst's. He rushed over to him and grabbed the young man's collar and lifted him off the ground.

"Tell me, Amethyst, how could they enchant Prince Sapphire's crown by snatching it from the palace? "How could you not notice such a thing?" Prince Okalper hissed through his gaping teeth.

Amethyst sobbed in grief.

"Prince Okalper, please come to your senses!" said KarlaKarla, stepping between the two of them.

"As you can see, Amethyst is just as sad as you are."

"Just because he's sad doesn't change the fact that the Prince is on his deathbed." said Prince Okalper, letting go of Amethyst.

"Prince Okalper is right." said Amethyst through tears. Then he paused for a moment. "I should have been more careful."

"If something happens to Sapphire, I'll take your head with my own hands!" said Prince Okalper.

"If that happens, you won't be needed." said Amethyst. "I'm going to kill myself anyway."

Then a young man with angel wings appeared from the end of the corridor. He was tall with broad shoulders and majestic wings. But he looked exhausted.

"Vermeil…" said KarlaKarla. "Any progress?"

"The spell on the crown is not breaking!" said Vermeil. "It was so powerfully enchanted that we, Nephilim, had to use every last drop of our strength, but it was futile."

"It must be Hematite's work!" said KarlaKarla. "He somehow managed to infiltrate the palace."

"This is the work of someone inside the palace, not outside!" said Prince Okalper. Then his eyes met Amethyst's eyes once more.

Amethyst averted his eyes.

Then Prince Sapphire cried out again in pain.

Amethyst also covered his ears with pain.

"You must put a stop to this, Saint Hilarion!" cried Prince Okalper.

Saint Hilarion thought for a moment.

"There is a way…" said the old Saint. "But it is too dangerous"

"What is it, my Saint?" asked Prince Okalper.

"The Everlasting Flower." said Saint Hilarion, "Its essence dispels even the darkest spells."

"Let them prepare the horses immediately! We have no time to lose." said Prince Okalper.

"Relax, my prince..." said Saint Hilarion, "The Everlasting Flower is found only in Anisoptera."

"My prince," said KarlaKarla quickly. "It's the Fairy Kingdom..."

"The Kingdom of the Morningstar is forbidden to the fairies! They can't see each other…" said Saint Hilarion.

"Azazel once committed a great massacre in the Fairy Kingdom. Thus, he cursed our Fairy Kingdom and the Supreme Creator forbade these Kingdoms from meeting with each other." said KarlaKarla.

Prince Okalper was momentarily shaken. Then he recovered immediately.

"No matter what... I'll go there if that's the only way to save Prince Sapphire." he said boldly.

"Then you must take the Nephilim with you," said Saint Hilarion.

"The Nephilim are not that powerful right now. As they tried to break the spell on the crown, they became weaker.

They need to rest." said the angel-winged man. "But I will accompany our prince."

"Thanks, Vermeil." said Prince Okalper.

"The mouflon that pulled Azazel out of this planet's atmosphere is still alive." said KarlaKarla. "I suggest you to travel with it."

"Then let them prepare the mouflon," said Prince Okalper.

"You are embarking on a very dangerous job. May the Supreme Creator protect you," said Saint Hilarion.

"Actually, we are stronger than Azazel. He was alone. Next to me will be a young man with angel wings." said Prince Okalper. "Let's see if you're strong enough to break the atmosphere."

The angel-winged man gave a wry smile.

"Have no doubt."

"This is the most cursed night I have ever had!" groaned KarlaKarla sadly. "I hope the new day shines its light on us."

Then the door to Prince Sapphire's room opened. "Prince Okalper!" called the gate guards.

"Prince Sapphire wants to see you."

Amethyst's heart was broken. He didn't expect this. His eyes filled with tears as he stared after Prince Okalper. Prince Sapphire… The only person he loved since childhood… Instead of him, he was calling Okalper to his side.

With this deep ache in his heart, the young man walked down the corridor and disappeared. No one even noticed his absence.

Prince Okalper got up as swift as an arrow and entered Prince Sapphire's room.

"Okal-per…" groaned Prince Sapphire from his bed. "Come closer..."

Prince Okalper just stared at his childhood friend. His heart started beating faster with each step.

Was this Prince Sapphire? That beautiful young man who resembled a white marble statue… It was not him anymore. His skin was bruised. There were deep wounds on his body. His silvery-blue eyes turned bloodshot.

"My prince…" said Okalper, his eyes filled with tears.

"I swear I will take the head of whoever did this to you with my own hands."

"I-want-you-to-promise-me." said Prince Sapphire, speaking with difficulty.

"If-something-happens-to-me... This Kingdom is under your custody."

Prince Okalper smiled tearfully.

"Unfortunately, I will not accept this. I already have a kingdom far away. Thus, you need to get better!" he said, "There is a flower that will save you from this spell, brother. We'll be on our way in a little while. I'll find it and bring it to you."

Prince Sapphire smiled vaguely through tears.

"Be-careful." he whispered. Then his eyes widened again and he began to scream.

Prince Okalper rushed back from the room immediately. Leaving behind Prince Sapphire's cries that made shook the palace, he immediately hit the road with the winged Angel...

-CHAPTER VII-

"Lovers" and "Pains"

    What a beautiful sunset...

The sky shines pink and gold... Seçkin sighed deeply. He was sitting on the yellow bench in the high school garden with fences on both sides. The bench was thoroughly worn-out. It was just like his soul rotting from deep inside. While he was resisting the strong pain in his head, the fallen leaves of the Judas tree were floating on the ground. As the ravens perched on the bare branches of the tree screeched madly, he felt the presence of someone beside him. It smelled like a mix of must and orange blossom. Seçkin opened his eyes as he inhaled that beautiful scent. His gaze met those deep brown eyes.

"Burak?" he smiled. Something warm flowed into his heart.

"Seçkin…" Burak's voice whispered. "You have really pretty hair!" said Burak, suddenly, "It falls on your face when you lower your head. "This scene seemed very familiar to Seçkin for a moment. He felt as if he had experienced a moment like this before.

Seçkin did not speak. He stared at the weak branches of the Judas tree and wondered when it would be full of flowers.

Then he felt something vibrating in his pocket. He immediately dug his hand into his pocket. He pulled out a silver pocket watch. It wasn't working. His fingers rubbed the dragonfly relief.

"I love you Seçkin!" said Burak at last. With his beautiful, soothing voice.

Seçkin smiled.

"Me too," he said, looking affectionately at the boy.

Burak smiled too. He slowly approached the boy. While his scent tickled Seçkin's insides, Burak immediately kiss the boy's lips.

Then everything changed in an instant. They suddenly found themselves in front of the huge Full Moon. They were in the cloistered courtyard of the kingdom.

Seçkin stepped back. But he was no longer himself. He was a prince, but there was great grief in him.

"My prince…" said Amethyst.

Prince Sapphire did not speak.

"I'm sorry, my prince!" said Amethyst, pulling a silver dagger from his pocket.

"Cut out this heart of mine." said the young man, handing the dagger to the Prince.

The Prince took the dagger. He pierced Amethyst's heart with tears. Amethyst felt nothing. He just stood there and let his heart separate from his body. Then he smiled.

"Nooooo!"

Seçkin woke up startled. He was out of breath. He tried to move his hands as he took a deep breath, but he was cramped all over.

Where did this dream come from? This shouldn't have happened. This was wrong. He couldn't betray Defne.

His head was aching like it was going to burst, again. He started to sob as he just sat on the bed. He had never been so confused in his life. His whole balance was upset now. He couldn't put a name to his feelings for Burak. Was it love? It couldn't be. Because he was in love with Defne. He was sure of that. He couldn't get that boy out of his mind. He had a strange attachment to him. He literally felt like he couldn't live without seeing him.

Seçkin was still trembling as ParuParu and BesuBesu immediately appeared in the room with a "Snap" sound.

"What did you see, High Master?" asked ParuParu immediately with concern.

"I don't remember ParuParu!" he lied. He was ashamed. He didn't want to tell them about Burak.

He stood up. It was dawn outside. As he looked out the window, he could hear the sound of azan. The dogs were also howling with the prayer.

The days were passing so quickly It had already been a week since Ayaz's incident. Sooner or later, he would meet Satan. It was inevitable. While he didn't want to think about it, he knew that with each passing second, he was one step closer to that day. When he thought of this, he felt as if his throat was being squeezed by a huge callused hand.

While he was going through these, the red smoke that had recently hit the window of the blue room and failed to get in rose back into the sky. Smoke danced in the air and crossed the vast forests. It passed over the high hills and infiltrated a cavern in an enormous mountain towering in the shape of five huge fingers.

The torches on the veiny flashing walls of the cave filled themselves with fire.

"Forgive us, the forgiving king of the infidels, but we are no longer able to enter the child's dreams!" whispered the voice from the red smoke.

"It must be the faithfuls! So, they found the boy." said the muffled voice in the cave.

A great gust of wind rose up around him, like the flapping of a crow's wings. A few ravens from the cave rushed out desperately. The red smoke also gradually turned into the silhouette of a creature.

"Yes. That miserable jinni called ParuParu does not leave the boy alone for a moment." said Hematite. "He has made some kind of talisman that prevents us from entering the room! But they cannot avoid the effects of magic. The child will melt emotionally day by day…"

"ParuParu? Who is he?" asked the voice from the walls of the cave.

"KarlaKarla's grandson, sir."

"KarlaKarla… I remember him. He used to be my most loyal friend…" said the hoarse voice.

"Thousands of years ago, when his son joined us, he on the other hand, showed great resistance to us." said Hematite, grimacing contemptuously.

"I took great pleasure in separating his head from his body!"

"Then it will not be difficult for you, my dear son, to separate the head of that wretched ParuParu from his body." the muffled voice within the walls of the cave ordered.

Hematite's brows furrowed. His lips tightened.

"Forgive me, but this will not be easy. Because the jinni lives in the boy's room. As I said, a kind of protection talisman is made for the house. I've never seen anything like this before."

"He must have used the boy's blood! The child's blood is precious in every way!" said the voice.

Hematite swallowed. The truth that he was afraid to express suddenly spilled out of his mouth:

"We are not strong enough to overcome that power yet. Unless the child's blood is shed in the holy land, we will not be able to become fully strong."

Hematite shifted his gaze to the ground. His shoulders slumped with the weight of this bitter truth he had voiced.

There was silence in the great cave for a while.

"Then keep making sacrifices for me until that day comes, my dear son…" the voice said after a while.

Hematite nodded. The sound of his hooves echoed in the huge cavern, and after a while it turned into smoke and flew out of the cave with the ravens...

The next day started as usual. Seçkin woke up in the morning, got ready while huffing and puffing and came to school. Cursed the ringing bell and entered the class with his friends. After literature and mathematics classes, the bell rang again, but this time when they heard it, instead of sighing, they took a deep breath and they were off to the recess. There were only a few weeks left for the semester break. Exams were approaching. But they were all so desperate that no one even thought about the exams.

The rain had just stopped and the smell of wet soil was pervading. In that terrible calmness after the rain, the students were fidgeting around like puppets in the garden of the school.

Seçkin and his sister were sitting on the bench under the Judas tree. Seçil was staring at the crows perched on the tired, weak branches of the tree and humming a rhyme to herself.

"The crow said 'caw'. Crow said, 'Come out and look at this branch...[22] "

Mine and Duru, on the other hand, were sitting on the steps of the Atatürk bust and chatting again.

While Seçkin watched them, he thought that they were definitely talking about Ayaz.

Then Ela appeared. Leaving the school building, she moved her hair out of her eyes, dispersed in the light breeze. She split Seçkin and Seçil and sat on the bench between them angrily.

"I can't believe!" she said, frowning, crossing her arms over her chest.

"What happened?" Seçkin asked curiously.

"Özden Hoca! She has decided to do the file review tomorrow!" she replied to Seçkin.

"But there is one more week until the exams!" Seçkin objected immediately. "Besides, most of my work is incomplete!"

Ela took a deep breath.

"Mine too!"

"Yours too?" he asked in surprise. His eyes were wide open.

---

[22] *A rhyme in Turkish language "Karga, karga gak dedi, çık şu dala bak dedi."*

"Do not look at me like that! You know how it has been lately.

I haven't been very efficient."

Seçkin put his arm around Ela's shoulder. He filled his lungs with that jasmine scent.

"We both made a big mistake!" Seçkin whispered in Ela's ear. "We must end this game now!"

Ela did not look at Seçkin and gave no indication that she had heard him. She smiled lovingly at Seçil, who was watching the two of them with admiration, and stroked her cheek.

"Why don't you come to the cram school anymore?" she asked, trying to change the subject quickly.

Seçkin shrugged.

"I don't want to. I guess I'll disenroll."

Seçil's eyes widened.

"Abi, my father would never allow this!"

"Are you out of your mind?" Ela got angry immediately.

"How will you prepare for the University Selection Exam?"

Seçkin shrugged again.

While Ela and Seçil looked at each other and sighed with concern, Ayaz went out to the garden with a lot of chocolate and crisps packets in his hand.

"Catch it!" he said as he tossed a pink packet of Lays into Seçkin's lap.

"Ayaz! What's going on?" Ela asked. "Are you going to eat all of these?"

"Yes," Ayaz nodded frantically. "I ate so much today, I'm not even full!"

There was a commotion on the Judas tree. The ravens soared into the sky, squealing.

"What the hell happened to them!" cried Ela.

Seçkin saw a hooded figure watching them through the garden gate. But as soon as the boy looked at it, it suddenly turned around and disappeared.

Then his eye fell on the black crow's feather that was floating from the sky and descending to the ground.

A black feather fell on Seçil's lap. The little girl took it and began to examine it.

"I hate these crows! Whatever the hell they came from!" said Seçkin.

"Who knows what more bad luck they will bring upon us!"

"Let go of that thing right now, honey!" said Ela to Seçil when she noticed the feather she was playing with, while she looked at the feather as if it was carrying a disease.

Seçkin grabbed the feather from her sister's hand and immediately threw it to the ground. Then he kissed Seçil, who looked at him with a confused expression, on the cheek and hugged her. Seçil immediately relaxed in her brother's arms.

"Anyway…" Ela sighed after a short pause.

"I'm going to go out to the workshop and do some work. See you later."

Ela got up from the worn-out bench. She lowered her head helplessly. She entered the school building with her shoulders slumped under the pressure of her recent experiences.

While her heart belonged to Mert, not being able to be with him and not being able to hug him was hurting her more and more every day.

Maybe Seçkin was right. They made a big mistake by starting this game. But would she be happier if she let her dear friend who was like a brother to her, crushed by Korkut? Of course not! She had done the right thing.

As the girl, wearily, climbed the steps of the stairs, pessimistic thoughts flowed through her mind, one after another. It was best to devote herself to her lessons, as she always did to forget her pain.

As she climbed the stairs to the third floor, a warm hand held her wrist. She was startled.

Her eyes met with Mert's. Ela stood still. The tears in her eyes wet her cheeks. In the blink of an eye, she found herself in Mert's arms and her lips met his soft lips.

"I am really sorry!" said Ela, out of breath, as she pulled back from Mert's kiss with difficulty.

"Everything with Seçkin was a planned game against Korkut and Defne."

He stroked the girl's hair. The girl's jasmine scent was making the boy's head spin. He felt as if he would go mad with joy at what he had heard.

"My heart belongs only to you!" said Ela and kissed the boy's lips again. He started kissing her like crazy. Thankfully the students were in class and the third-floor stairs weren't used much at this hour. Otherwise, if both of them were caught in this state, they would immediately be a gossip topic.

But the moment Ela withdrew from those sweet lips, she was shocked. Korkut stood there with his broken nose, a few steps down, watching them. He had a nasty smile mixed with a triumphant gleam on his face. Ela was horrified, but it was too late. She lowered her head and bit her lips regretfully. She had ruined the whole plan.

Despite all their efforts, Seçkin and Ela's plots were in vain. Those at school had learned that the two of them were not dating.

Mine had been saying the same thing for days as soon as she learned the truth.

"I knew it from the very beginning that there was something in this situation!"

Worse still, everyone was talking about the fact that those two had planned this to make Defne jealous. Every time he met Seçkin, Korkut had a nasty smile on his face. It was as if he wasn't the person who had lowered his head when he had met him only a few weeks ago. He was crushing him with those filthy black eyes. That's why Ela was consuming herself all the time.

"How could I do that!" she said with tearful greed. "If I had restrained my feelings even a little bit, we wouldn't strengthen the sneaky Korkut's hand!"

There was short time left for the half term break. Soon there were going to have Examining Works of Art exam with Derin Zade, but they were sitting in the garden, lamenting to their bad luck in the cold winter breeze.

"I told you from the start that it wasn't a good idea." Seçkin said with a shrug.

Ela sighed sadly.

"Yes, you did!"

After a short silence, "It's all because of you!" she said to Mert, having it out on him. "You came and kissed me!"

Mert spread his hands to both sides and just stared at Ela.

"How could I know that you were making plans? You didn't say anything!"

"If you knew me a little bit, you would understand that!" Ela snapped.

"My eyes have never seen anyone but you!"

"Please don't start again!" whimpered Seçkin, looking at them exhaustedly. "It is what it is! I've seen enough people that suffered from love lately. At least you two should be happy."

All three of them had their eyes on Mine and Ayaz. Mine was under the Judas tree, talking to Duru unhappily. Ayaz was somewhere close to them. He was sitting on the steps in front of the Atatürk bust with Can. They were still not talking each other. But Seçkin could see how the two of them secretly looked at each other. They seemed to be trying very hard not to talk to each other.

"I really feel bad for them!" said Ela.

Seçkin sighed, too.

"Me too!" he said unhappily. "But in this case, Ayaz was indeed innocent!"

Just then Seçkin saw Burak walking around the garden. He didn't come to school very often anymore. As soon as Seçkin saw him, his heart broke again. He was being unfair to him. The boy's only fault was to care about Seçkin. He thought about talking to him, but he remembered the dream he had. That dream in which he kissed him. He hated that he was so confused. For a while… They stared at each other briefly. Burak's brown eyes that looked sad, followed Seçkin. But when Seçkin got embarrassed and turned his gaze back to his friends, the boy sighed deeply and disappeared into the school building.

Before long, they started the Examining Works of Art Exam. Silence reigned in that huge twelfth-grade workshop like never before. On the exam paper in front of Seçkin there was "What the Water Gave Me?" work of Mexican surrealist painter Frida Kahlo".

Derin Zade asked each of them to comment on an artist from different art movements without sparing no effort. Seçkin studied the picture with exquisite care. Then he clicked on his pen and started to write a few sentences. Water had given Frida a life full of pain. A broken spinal cord, the longing to have a child and the betrayal of her relatives!

And what did it give to Seçkin?

A crooked smile appeared on his face.

"It gave me a life to meet Satan! Some kind of sacrifice," he thought. Then he whispered to himself.

"So, my life isn't much brighter than yours, Frida."

"What?" said Ela, sitting at the next table, as she got drowsy of writing.

"Nothing!" Seçkin waved his hand at her. Then leaned and glanced at the girl's paper. Ela had filled the paper again, as she always did. In fact, she would get an extra page if there was such an opportunity. But Derin Zade said they should only write one page.

Seçkin would never be as smart and hardworking as her. He knew. Ela wasn't human, it was like she was a dragon.

Then he looked at Ayaz, who was shaking his head in despair. Unlike Ela, he had not written a single thing on his paper. Seçkin could never be as indifferent as Ayaz. He was somewhere between Ela and Ayaz. And he was happy about it.

He involuntarily smiled while watching Ayaz's desperate effort for a while. Every time he thought of the fact that Ayaz was one of the fallen guards, the same smile appeared on his face. Maybe he wasn't good in his studies, but one day he would be by his side in their battle against Satan. He would definitely kick ass. Seçkin saw this potential in him.

Then the recess bell rang. And Mine covered her ears and muttered to herself.

"I hate this sound."

As Derin Zade got up from the tattered leather sofa, "Exam time is up. You can go out, my dears!" she said in her sweet affectionate voice. Then she collected the exam papers and headed for the door and went out into the corridor.

Seçkin watched Derin Zade walking away along the corridor. After Ayhatun Yıldız's death, she was acting strangely, too. He had also recently seen her whispering with Sahra.

Ayaz immediately jumped out of his seat. He opened the huge workshop window. The wind whipped the green cypress and eucalyptus trees. Ayaz's hair fluttered with the infiltrating cold breeze. Then he stretched and took a deep breath.

"Why did you leave your paper empty?" asked Seçkin unpleasantly.

Ayaz looked at him over his shoulder.

"Because I'm not in the mood for any exams."

"But," Seçkin tried to speak, but Ayaz immediately raised his hand as if he wanted to silence him.

Seçkin lowered his head down. He left Ayaz who was lost in thought behind and took Ela with him while going out of the workshop. Seeing Ayaz like this made him really sad.

When they entered the third-floor corridor, they encountered Derin Zade.

Derin Zade looked at him and smiled sweetly.

"Seçkin!" the woman called in a polite tone. "Can I talk to you a little bit?"

"Of course, Hocam." Seçkin replied in surprise.

"Alone." said Derin Zade.

The boy glanced at Ela and followed the woman. They walked down the corridor. Finally, they entered the eleventh-class painting workshop. Derin Zade gracefully closed the door of the workshop.

There was no one else in the workshop but the two of them.

Derin Zade pulled out a stool in the middle of the workshop and settled in there. Then she looked at Seçkin, who was watching her curiously, and politely motioned for him to sit across.

Seçkin did what the woman said and sat down. The woman cleared her throat kindly, while Seçkin was waiting in anticipation.

"I've been seeing you pretty upset lately. I am aware of your feelings towards Defne. You are suffering from great love pain."

Seçkin's cheeks blushed. For a moment, this icy workshop felt very hot to him.

"Don't lower your head, my dear boy. I didn't say that to embarrass you." Derin Zade smiled sweetly.

"I also heard that you started to dislike yourself. You are not ugly, Seçkin."

Seçkin was even more embarrassed.

"Can't you see how handsome you are, for God's sake, my dear boy?"

"Hocam… Well… I just…" the boy cringed.

"Do you know? There is another heart that beats for you in this school."

Seçkin almost swallowed his tongue in surprise. Yes! He had heard that there were many girls at school who liked him before, but who could be so infatuated with his love in order to tell this to Derin Zade?

Seçkin immediately thought of Ela. He didn't know why he thought of her in the first place. It was even funny that he thought of her first. The girl had been going crazy for Mert for months. And they finally started dating. Maybe it had been in his subconscious, because people around him were shipping for them for years.

"Who do you think this girl could be?" asked the woman.

Seçkin swallowed hard. He shook his head as if he had no idea.

"Şeyda!" said Derin Zade, out of the blue.

Seçkin could not comprehend it for a moment.

"Who?" he asked, while his forehead wrinkled.

"Şeyda, my dear son!"

Oh my God, was that elusive half-witted girl in love with Seçkin?

Seçkin thought for a while. In fact, at last year's New Year's ball, she had swindled him and given him a red heart-shaped pillow with the words "My first and only love" written on it. She supposedly bought that gift for someone else, but when that person didn't come to the ball, she got angry and gave it to Seçkin. But no one other than Seçkin had believed it. Seçkin was very naive. He believed her immediately. In fact, Mine said to him, "This girl is in love with you, boy!", but Seçkin did not dwell on this event. But Mine was right again.

"I should have understood that…" Seçkin muttered to himself.

"Şeyda is a very sweet girl. How will you respond to this situation?" asked Derin Zade. She was more like an excited high school girl rather than a teacher.

"Well… umm… Şeyda is like a sister to me. So, it's impossible for me to reciprocate to her feelings."

Derin Zade's eyes shone as these words spilled from Seçkin's mouth.

"I was pretty sure you were going to tell me that." said the woman. "Oh, my dear boy, what a kind young man you are."

A faint smile appeared on Seçkin's lips as his cheeks blushed.

"Oh my God, first Burak and now Şeyda…" he thought to himself. "How fortunate I am."

"I see that you are very saddened by these recent events. Defne may have rejected you, but as you can see, there are other hearts around that are beating for you. Feel it and know what a colourful personality you have." Seçkin shyly looked at Derin Zade. The woman's warm eyes that looked with love got teary, and she sincerely embraced him.

"Fight for your love! Defne will surely understand your worth one day."

※ ※

"Hahahaha… What did you say? Şeyda is in love with you?"

Ayaz was laughing like crazy.

Ela and Duru couldn't believe what they heard with their eyes wide open, while Mine was side eying Ayaz.

"Will you stop laughing!" Seçkin said, avoiding Ayaz's eyes.

"Sorry, but I'll laugh about it all day whenever I remember it."

Mine and Ayaz were standing so close to each other for the first time in a long time.

"Who told you that?" asked Ela.

" Derin Hoca." he said, pouting.

"Was that the reason you talked in the workshop today?" asked Ela.

Seçkin nodded.

"Uh…huh…"

Ayaz let out another laugh.

"Hahahahaha…"

"I figured it out after that New Year's present she gave you last year! Do you remember what I told you?" said Mine at once, triumphantly.

He nodded his head.

"I remember!"

"I was thinking… Actually, she is a pretty girl!" said Ela with a mischievous smile.

"Yeah right!" said Ayaz, mockingly.

"She is pretty, but it's a matter of intelligence," Seçkin said.

"She's not exactly the level-headed type!"

"Oh, does Defne seem level-headed to you?" Mine grumbled, making a face.

"Mine is right. If Defne was a level-headed person, she wouldn't have dated that idiot called Korkut anyway." Duru confirmed Mine.

"Stop talking about it, not going to happen, okay?" Seçkin finally snapped.

At that moment, Seçkin saw someone watching them between the iron railings of the garden walls. It was a short-haired person in a green coat. It was unclear whether it was a boy or a girl. He had seen this person before. When their eyes met, that person turned its back and quickly disappeared from sight.

"Who was that girl? A new fan or something?" Ayaz asked.

"Girl? Do you think it was a girl? It looked like a boy to me." said Ela.

"I don't know, Ayaz. But I saw it several times in the same place." said Seçkin.

"Who are you talking about?" asked Duru.

"There was a girl in a green coat just outside staring at us. I guess she is from Science High School." said Ayaz.

"Seçkin Saral's fame reach all the way to Science High School!" Duru smiled.

Seçkin's face got red.

"I don't want to study at all for tomorrow's math test." Seçkin said suddenly as his head fell on Ela's shoulder.

"Oh, the baby's head fell off again!" Mine complained. "Boy, lighten up a bit!"

"We will go to the cram school to study." said Ela, "Aren't you coming again?"

Seçkin shook his head.

"I don't want to."

"I don't understand how your father doesn't get involved in this situation," Duru said. Then she opened her eyes and asked.

"Doesn't he know?"

"The papers are coming home announcing my recent absence. Do you think it's possible that he doesn't know about it, Duru dear?" he said, rolling his eyes. "But he never makes a sound about it. Isn't it very strange?"

"What did you give to the man? How can Berk Saral, who makes a fuss about everything, not speak up about this?" Ayaz asked.

"I think he is waiting for the University Selection Exam. Especially if I can't pass the exam, I will be killed by inches." Seçkin said with a shrug.

"Well, how do you plan to pass that exam if you are not going to the cram school, handsome?" asked Ela.

"Ok! Okay, you are putting too much pressure on the boy, huh! All he needs right now is some alcohol. He will drink and relax and then study for the exam." said Ayaz.

"Aww… Shall we go to the Witch's Cauldron before the cram school?" Duru asked eagerly. Atelier Witch's Cauldron Cafe has been the favourite gathering spot of Seçkin and his friends lately.

Its owner was once a teacher at the Fine Arts High School. After her retirement, she restored an old Nicosia house in the Arabaahmet area and turned it into a atelier-cafe full of fantastic items.

"Yes. It's not a bad idea, actually. I have been yearning for some apple tea!" said Ela.

"Then let's hang out there for a while!" Duru suggested with childlike joy.

Then the five friends gathered under the pale January sun to go to the Atölye Cadı Kazanı Cafe…[23]

ParuParu paced back and forth in the blue bedroom while it was Twilight.

PihiPihi was falling asleep on Seçkin's lap. She was sucking her tiny bony thumb while fiddling with the thumb nail of the boy. She hadn't changed much, despite the months that had passed by since Seçkin met her. She had just grown a little. Jinni were growing slower compared to humans. BesuBesu mentioned this during a conversation they had at night.

It had been half an hour since Seçkin had given up on the math equations he had spent the night on and threw the books on the floor. He glanced at them from the corner of his eye and frowned. Then he continued rocking PihiPihi.

BesuBesu was sitting next to Seçkin and she was going through an old album with the photos of the boy's infancy and she kept muttering, "Our High Master is so cute! How sweet is our High Master!".

A photo caught Seçkin's attention. He was about two years old. He and his mother were playing on the quilt they had

---

[23] *Atölye Cadı Kazanı Café (Atelier Witch's Cauldron Cafe: Cypriot Artist Nilgün Güney's Atelier Cafe in Arabahmet, Nicosia – Walled City.*

laid on the floor. The colourful little cars were lined up symmetrically as always.

He studied the frilly dress of his mother. It was very similar to the dress that BesuBesu had been wearing since they met. In fact, it was exactly the same.

Seçkin just stared at BesuBesu's face.

"Why are you looking at me like that, High Master?" the female jinni asked when she felt the boy's gaze on her.

This dress had seemed so familiar to him from the first time he saw it. But he was sure now.

"Well… BesuBesu, that dress is a bit familiar don't you think?" Seçkin asked, pointing to the photograph.

BesuBesu smiled.

"Yes, this is that dress." said BesuBesu, frowning.

"These belong to your mother, High Master. We smuggled them out of your mother's closet months ago when we moved here."

He examined the red corduroy trousers that ParuParu was wearing. It belonged to Seçkin. It was the trousers that he wore very fondly in his childhood.

"ParuParu!" he smiled. "I think those pants were my favourite pants from my childhood!"

ParuParu smiled shyly. He tilted his head and swayed where he was.

"Why did you feel the need to do such a thing, didn't you have clothes?" the boy asked.

"The Supreme Creator has cursed all jinni because of the infidels.

That's why we can't have anything new. We can only wear old clothes belonging to the owners of the house we live in." replied BesuBesu.

Seçkin felt a pang of grief. His mother always kept old clothes. It was good that they came handy now.

"So, what happens if you buy and wear something new?"

"First, it stings like thorns in our skin. And then it catches fire on us!" BesuBesu replied, opening her eyes wide.

"I am so sorry about this, BesuBesu!" said Seçkin, stroking the female jinni's back.

"Don't be upset. At least we don't walk around naked like infidels! What a shame!" the female jinni shrugged. Then she got buried in the photo album again.

"So, what do you eat and drink?" Seçkin asked suddenly. This was a thing that always bothered him, but he always forgot to ask.

"These, sir!" said BesuBesu. She took out a gold bracelet from her pocket and handed it to Seçkin.

"But this is my mother's bracelet." said Seçkin in horror.

"She was looking for this bracelet like crazy."

Then the boy gasped.

"Are you eating gold?"

BesuBesu nodded.

"This is another curse of ours, my lord!" said BesuBesu.

"But when the Kingdom of Morningstar awakens, we will be able to feed on normal food like before!"

Seçkin thought for a moment.

"Well, isn't it hard to find gold every day, BesuBesu?"

BesuBesu smiled.

"We don't eat every day! A bracelet like this will last us three months!"

Then Seçkin's eyes shifted to ParuParu, who paced around. Then he couldn't stand it any longer.

"Enough is enough, ParuParu!" said Seçkin wearily. "Can you stop wandering around and tell me what you're thinking?"

ParuParu paused. He looked at Seçkin with his big blue eyes and sat down on the carpet in front of the boy.

"Oh, High Master!"

Seçkin rolled his eyes.

"How many times do I have to tell you? I don't like it when you call me High Master!"

He looked at the cute jinni with the straw-coloured beard and smiled fondly.

"Call me Seçkin! Only Seçkin!"

"Oh, Seçkin Master!"

Seçkin chuckled. But that was a short-lived moment as ParuParu grimaced.

"What's going on ParuParu?" he asked, with eyes filled with fear.

ParuParu let out a deep breath with strong despair.

"I've been thinking about this red smoke for a while. You know the smoke that disturbs you in your sleep…"

"The protection talisman cast on the house will keep him away for a while, but the Infidels are everywhere! They're probably increasing more and more!

ParuParu suddenly got serious. "What happened to your teacher is obvious as you know. The sons of Adam are in great danger! In order for Satan to become stronger, they are brainwashed and driven to suicide by the infidel jinni. That way, Azazel gets stronger."

This was true, the news of suicide in the newspaper was increasing day by day.

"We must act quickly and find the other Nephilim. The Supreme Creator forbid, I hope we will act before the infidels so that they do not seize and brainwash them."

Seçkin nodded. He wondered if the remaining Nephilim were also among his friends. Who knew, maybe they were, or maybe they were waiting on the other side of the world for the day that they would meet...

-CHAPTER VIII-
A Strange Dragonfly

The stars in the endless galaxy were shining. Prince Okalper was advancing relentlessly towards the Morningstar on the back of the winged old mouflon with the enormous Nephilim beside him. They had already successfully pierced through the atmosphere. They travelled over the hills and far away, but they still could not reach Anisoptera. They were very tired and felt like days had passed. But the hope of healing Prince Sapphire as they travelled across the vast galaxy gave them strength.

"You know, Vermeil?" Prince Okalper said.

"Once I had a very bad fight with Sapphire because of Amethyst. So much so that it turned into a fistfight. I was furious and wanted to kill him. But when I saw him lying in that bed, I felt such a pain in my heart that I realized I would feel very lonely without his presence, let alone killing him… Even though we are far from each other, knowing his presence somewhere gives me strength. He's really like my flesh and bone."

"Prince Sapphire's presence gives all of us strength, my prince." said Vermeil.

"I don't know for how long we've been traveling. Days may have passed… Maybe… We lost him." said Prince Okalper in despair.

"If so, you would feel it, my prince." said Vermeil.

"We would both feel it."

Prince Okalper suddenly rose between the wings of the old mouflon and reached for the shining star on the horizon.

"Look at that, Vermeil! We're getting close, my man!" he pointed excitedly to the orange planet.

They got closer and closer with every passing second, eventually finding themselves entering the planet's atmosphere. Prince Okalper felt that he could not breathe for a moment. The planet was very hot. The Prince's breathing also got better as he descended towards the ground.

"The Morningstar…" said Vermeil with admiration, "the majestic planet that illuminates our Kingdom…"

"It really is more beautiful than I've ever imagined." said Prince Okalper.

They both landed on the planet. Prince Okalper staggered for a moment as he jumped off and landed on the ground from the mouflon.

"Finally!" said Prince Okalper, as he stretched his neck. "There is nothing like stepping on the ground."

Vermeil smiled.

"How are we going to find this Everlasting Flower, my prince?" he asked later.

"Ah!" Prince Okalper remembered. He took a scroll from his pocket. "Saint Hilarion gave me a drawing of it."

They both stared, not knowing what to do under the red sky. A huge palace gleamed on the horizon, surrounded by trees with pink flowers. It was reminiscent of the shape of a beehive.

"We have to find the flower and get out of here at once before we get caught." said Prince Okalper. Then he patted the head of the old mouflon.

"You wait here, my strong friend."

Mouflon grunted and squatted down and fell asleep.

"My man is very tired," said Prince Okalper, smiling.

Then they entered a path with Century plants lined up one after another. They were walking and looking in hopes of finding the flower.

"There are so many Century plants." said Prince Okalper.

"Fairies are known for their great patience, and Century plants are patient trees, my prince." said Vermeil.

"There is no other existence as patient as they are."

After walking for a while, a huge lake appeared before them. Colourful dragonflies were flying over it.

"Look at those flies, chief!" said Okalper, fascinated.

"They have such beautiful colours."

Dragonflies approached the two men and surrounded them. Prince Okalper and Vermeil relaxed to the enchanting melody in their ears. Then, after a blink of an eye, they stared at the spears pointed at them.

"Who are you?" asked a soldier with dragonfly wings.

"What are you doing in our Kingdom?" asked another.

Prince Okalper looked at Vermeil with fearful eyes. Then he gathered his strength immediately. He squared his shoulders and lifted his head up.

"I'm Okalper. I am the Prince of the Faraway Land." he said, pulling off his shirt sleeves and pointing to a tattoo of the cycle of the moon on his arm.

"I've come to see your King."

"Who are you then?" they asked to Vermeil.

Vermeil gulped. He didn't know what to say.

"He is my aide." said Prince Okalper at once.

Vermeil smiled, as if he was insulted.

"Aide!" he muttered to himself.

The soldiers lowered their spears.

"We have come here to discuss a matter with your King." said Prince Okalper.

Then a trumpet sound was heard, and the soldiers stepped aside in two long lines.

"Long live our King Asparagus and Queen Laverna!" they shouted in unison.

"What is going on here?" asked King Asparagus.

He had a round face and tulle-like wings. At first glance, he gave the impression of a kind-hearted man, but behind his eyes you could see that he was short-tempered. He was shorter than the queen.

King Asparagus

"Strangers…" Queen Laverna groaned.

She was a beautiful woman. She had a pomegranate-like flower bud on her head.

"Who is that angel-winged man? He reminded me of the one who did the massacre years ago."

"I am Prince Okalper," said the prince. "We have come from the Earth to speak to you, King Asparagus."

"Our intention is not war!" said Vermeil.

"I am listening…" said King Asparagus.

Prince Okalper and Vermeil looked at each other.

"We came here to save someone we love so much." said Prince Okalper. "He was enchanted. And he needs the Everlasting Flower to heal."

"Nothing here can be taken to Earth!" said King Asparagus immediately, "Not even a single stone. This is the rule of the Supreme Creator!"

"But King Asparagus…" said Prince Okalper. "If we do not get the flower, the Son of the Supreme Creator will die!"

Queen Laverna

"Wait a second…" Queen Laverna squinted her eyes and approached Prince Okalper.

"In your eyes I see the Kingdom on Earth. His kingdom, which was cursed by Anisoptera many years ago…"

"We came here for Prince Sapphire." admitted Prince Okalper.

"He is not well!"

"Prince Sapphire is none of our business. We have nothing to give to that kingdom where the murderers live!" said Queen Laverna.

"He is the Son of the Supreme Creator! Besides, murderers don't live in that Kingdom!" said Vermeil immediately, "You can't blame Prince Sapphire for Azazel's sin."

"How dare you!" said Queen Laverna.

"My King!" cried one of the soldiers. "There's a mouflon here!"

"A mouflon?" cried Queen Laverna.

"They came here with the Devil's creature!"

"Soldiers!" roared King Asparagus "Throw these men in to the dungeon right away!"

"No!" said Prince Okalper. "I am the Prince of the Faraway Land, you cannot do that."

"The laws of the Earth Kingdoms are invalid here." said King Asparagus. "You have trespassed Anisoptera."

"But our Prince will die! He is the Son of the Supreme Creator!" cried Vermeil again.

"So that's how the Supreme Creator saw fit." said Queen Laverna.

"No! He can be saved if we bring the flower." said Prince Okalper

"Please… Fairies can't be that cruel! Please give us the flower! I promise you we will never come to this kingdom again."

"Nothing from Anisoptera can be taken to Earth!" King Asparagus repeated sharply. "This is the rule of the Supreme Creator."

"NO!" cried Prince Okalper, his throat tearing. Both struggled to escape from the soldiers, but it was in vain.

Invisible chains bound Vermeil by both hands and feet like an animal. Prince Okalper was detained with an invisible chain around his neck.

"Let go of us!" cried Prince Okalper. But these cries were futile. No one could break these chains.

They were taken to the palace, where there were trees with pink flowers all around. They were thrown into the dungeon...

Days passed. One day King Asparagus summoned the two young men before him.

"Do you still insist on staying here?" asked King Asparagus.

"I'm not going anywhere without the flower." said Prince Okalper.

Behind the throne of the King and Queen were four more thrones. There were three beautiful princesses with dragonfly wings sitting on the thrones, and a ten-year-old prince. The older girls seemed quite uninterested in the subject, but the brunette princess in a red dress was listening with great attention.

"I spared your life!" said King Asparagus, "For I do not want to go to war with the King of the Faraway Land. But if you insist on not leaving here, I can assure you that you will be subjected to all kinds of torture."

"I don't care!" said Prince Okalper. "I will endure any torture for Prince Sapphire."

"Likewise, I'm not leaving until I save our prince." said the man with angel wings.

"What a strange love…" Queen Laverna whispered to her husband. "They really love their prince."

"I've never seen anything like this before," said King Asparagus. "I am quite curious about the prince of that kingdom on earth."

"Maybe they're right, huh Asparagus?" said Queen Laverna. "Maybe the prince is not like the Devil."

"Whatever it is, the rule of the Supreme Creator cannot be broken, my Queen," said King Asparagus.

For a brief moment, Prince Okalper's eyes met with the princess in the red dress sitting behind King Asparagus' throne. There was a deep sadness in her green eyes. It was as if they were carrying the same sadness.

"Soldiers!" called King Asparagus.

"Take those two stubborn goats back to the dungeon. No food or water! Maybe they will come to their senses!"

The soldier fairies did as the Fairy King said. They dragged Prince Okalper and Vermeil back to the dungeon.

Days turned into nights; nights turned into days. One night, a scarlet-coloured dragonfly escaped the soldiers and entered the dungeon. It flew over the dark stairs and eventually transformed into a body with dragonfly wings.

Her face could not be seen through the hooded cloak she was wearing.

"Prince Okalper," she called in the dark dungeon. The prince was startled. He immediately opened his eyes and rose from the hay on which he was sleeping.

"Who are you?" asked Prince Okalper.

"This is not important. I'm just someone who shares the same sadness as you." said a fairy from under the hood.

"I came to help you."

"My prince, this may be a trap," said Vermeil hesitantly.

"You can count on me," said the silhouette, and pulled a flower from her pocket. It had hairy leaves and was purple.

"Everlasting Flower," said Prince Okalper excitedly.

"Yes." said the silhouette, "Your prince is a good man, you must save him."

She snapped her fingers and the gates of the iron bars opened. The flower, too, flew up in mauve gleams and landed in Prince Okalper's palm.

"Hurry, and leave the planet while I distract the soldiers."

"What about the mouflon?" asked Prince Okalper.

"The mouflon is where you left it." said the silhouette.

"I'll reward you if you tell us who you are." said Prince Okalper. He made a sudden move towards the silhouette.

The silhouette receded immediately. But the green eyes under the hood gleamed for a moment.

"I cannot do this." said the silhouette, "Save your prince! That will be the biggest reward for me."

"My Prince, let's hurry!" said Vermeil.

"Go on!" said the silhouette. Then it quickly turned into a scarlet dragonfly and flew around the soldiers, distracting them.

Prince Okalper and Vermeil also rushed out of the dungeon at full speed under the red sky. Meanwhile, the fairy soldiers became aware of the fugitives who had fled. They shoot their arrows. There was complete pandemonium. The angel-winged man threw the prince on his back and flapped his wings, leaving behind the fairy soldiers who attacked with arrows from behind. They passed through the century trees and came near the old mouflon that was waiting for them.

Prince Okalper jumped on the mouflon.

"Come on, old friend, one last effort!" cried Prince Okalper, "Gee ho!"

The mouflon flapped its wings and soared into the sky as fast as it could. Leaving the fairy soldiers behind, the Prince of the Faraway Land and angel-winged man pierced through the atmosphere of Morningstar with the Everlasting Flower…

Report cards have been received and the semester break had started. Ela was top of the class again. Seçkin's report card, on the other hand, was fair enough, if you don't count the four he got from the mathematics. But that four... It was enough of a reason for his father to grouch until the end of the holiday.

Considering his recent condition, he should be thankful that he only got low grade at math. He didn't feel like doing anything. He was in some kind of depression. Fortunately, he had Ela. She helped him cheat in the exams. But Seçkin had to beat around the bush in order to persuade her to do so.

After all that had happened, the fact that Seçkin's mind was still dwelled on Defne was driving Ela crazy. The schemes they played were of no use either. Seçkin was upset. He was not interested in his studies at all. When lessons were on the table, Ela turned into a dragon.

After receiving his report card, Seçkin left the classroom and immediately ran into the garden. While Ayaz was mumbling curses to himself about his teachers because of the low grades in his report card, Seçkin searched for Defne for a while.

Most students had already left school with the excitement of the holidays. An unsettling calmness reigned around. It had rained. The smell of wet soil was all around.

"Bro, who am I talking to!" Ayaz got angry at last.

Seçkin got startled.

"Did you say something?" he asked drowsily.

"I am talking about going somewhere and getting some booze!"

Seçkin shrugged.

"It is possible!" said the boy, still looking around.

"Don't look for nothing." said Ayaz. "She's already gone with her boyfriend!"

"Who?" Seçkin asked, ignoring him.

"Get out of there! We both know that you were looking to see that girl called Defne again." Ayaz grumbled. "Your mind is still hung up on her!"

Seçkin ignored him. He walked slowly across the wet concrete floor and sat desperately at one of the wooden picnic tables. Ayaz sat next to the boy.

"I heard that Mine is crying almost every day," Seçkin said.

Ayaz's face darkened.

"Really? Still?" he asked stupidly.

"Come on Ayaz, it hasn't even been a month!" exclaimed Seçkin. "You two are in love with each other, man. Put an end to this resentment now!"

"Fuck off! Love huh?" Ayaz grumbled, "Mine was a cookie for me. Just like the ones before!"

Then Defne came out of the school building with her report card and an unhappy face. She walked wearily in the garden under the curious gazes of Ayaz and Seçkin, and sat down under the Judas tree, on the wooden bench with chipping yellow paint, and put her head in between her hands. She was in deep thought.

"It looks like your girl has failed some of her courses, too!" Ayaz grinned.

"It serves her right. This was doomed to happen after all those bill and coos with Korkut."

"Wander where her boyfriend is?" Seçkin asked curiously.

"He will come and behave impudently soon, don't worry!"

But Korkut did not come. Instead, Ela, Mine and Duru and came out of the school building to the garden giggling and walked over to Seçkin and Ayaz and settle around the table nicely.

"Are you watching Defne again?" Duru asked with a mischievous smile.

"Yes! In this situation, we will always be watching from afar!" Ayaz rolled his eyes. "If this girl had done the same thing to me, I would have carved her eyes out as soon as she looked at me!"

Mine slightly averted her eyes and hissed at this but Ayaz ignored her.

"Finally, you will be Şeyda's, Seçkin!" Duru joked.

"God forbid!" said Ela, immediately pulling her ear and knocking on the table.

"Is she crying?" Mine asked while carefully examining Defne.

"Is she crying?" Seçkin sprang to his feet immediately. "I wonder whether you should go and ask her how she is?"

"I rather die!" Mine hissed as she crossed her arms and settled more into her seat.

"I'll go," said Duru, "She looks really sad. Poor girl!"

"I agree." said Ela.

Both got up from the table and walked towards Defne, while curious gazes followed them. Seçkin, Ayaz and Mine started to watch what was going on with curiosity.

Defne was talking about something while crying. Duru was comforting her and stroking her shoulder. Ela, on the other hand, was examining the girl's report card and was covering her mouth with her hand. When they both finally returned, Ela shook her head in despair.

"Korkut has deranged the girl! Poor thing!"

"She has nine low grades!" said Duru in horror.

"Nine?" Seçkin gulped.

"Let her be worse!" Mine said as she crossed her arms.

"Don't say that, it's a sin!" said Duru, pouting her lips.

"She should have spent less time with that idiot named Korkut and studied a little more. I don't feel sorry for her at all!" Mine hissed, looking at Duru with fiery eyes.

Seçkin didn't say anything. He got up from the table and approached Defne. Ela, Mine, Duru and Ayaz stared at him with their mouths wide open.

"Defne?" Seçkin muttered, looking at the girl with timid eyes. The girl's teary eyes met with the boy's. It was the first time in a long while that they were this close.

"Defne, are you okay?" Seçkin asked hesitantly. His heartbeat was accelerating.

"It's none of your business!" said Defne, snuffling.

Then she lowered her head again.

Seçkin took a deep sigh. He couldn't understand why she was suddenly so hostile towards him.

"Are you still going to stand there and stare stupidly at me?" Defne asked with her head down.

A few crows came and perched on the branches of the Judas tree. They started to caw.

"Why are you treating me like this?" Seçkin asked.

"It's like you suddenly became someone else! Were your feelings for me all a lie?"

Defne slowly lifted her head from the ground. She looked at Seçkin for a while with hateful eyes. She then stood up from her seat and approached as close to the boy's nose. While Seçkin was watching her, he thought of the puppets with blank eyes in the puppet theatre.

"Yes, everything I said was a lie!" said Defne in a coldly. "I've had enough of both Korkut and you!"

Among the horrified looks of his friends, Seçkin was so enraged that for a moment his hand went up. Ela immediately closed her eyes and screamed. The boy looked at Defne ignominiously for a while with anger in his eyes. He wanted to give her a big slap and shake her like crazy to wake her up. He wanted to purify whatever the black spirit was inside her with that slap. But he didn't.

He squeezed his hand tightly, trapping all his anger there. He clenched so tightly that his fingernails bled his palms.

When the boy regained his consciousness, he found his friends near him. Defne, on the other hand, got into the earth-coloured car that came to pick her up and left the school garden with her secrets…

Seçkin got up early in the morning. He tossed and turned in his bed for a while, accompanied by the light beams that filtered through his window and flowed into his room. He couldn't stop thinking about Defne. Oh, Defne how angry he was at her. He hardly contained himself not to slap her beautiful face. He was glad that he didn't slap her. He was horrified every time he thought of this. There was a strange anger lurking inside of him. But no matter how angry he was at her; he still couldn't help but think about her and not worry about her.

Who knows how bad her father had scolded her when he saw those low grades. He knew from his own father how insufferable they were in such situations. Berk Saral turned his face away from him, even though he only got one low grade in mathematics. If he had low grades from nine courses, he would probably have disowned him.

"Oh Defne!" he whispered to himself. When everything was so good, why did she suddenly start dating Korkut? Seçkin still couldn't make sense of this sudden change. It felt like he was going crazy every time he thought of it.

He slowly sat up in bed. He picked up the silver pocket watch that was on the nightstand and began to study it absentmindedly, turning it over in his hand. He could have sworn that he saw a writing on the back the day he found it. But the back of it was now immaculate. Maybe he was wrong. Maybe it was a momentary illusion…

Who did this watch belong to? He had intended to ask his mother about this several times, but gave up immediately. Because Bahar Saral would scold her son for opening that forbidden box. No matter how hard he tried, Seçkin could never convince her mother that the box had fallen in front of him and revealed all her privacy.

He looked at the sun shining behind the white tulle curtains. The grey clouds that surrounded the sky yesterday had dissipated. There was no uncanny crimson mist around. It was a beautiful day like never before in a long time.

He got out of bed and got dressed. He walked out of his room and down the stairs. His grandmother had already prepared breakfast. Everyone was at the breakfast table.

"Good morning!" rang the boy's velvet voice.

Everyone at the table greeted him warmly.

"First Seçil, now you! I am surprised, honestly!" said Bahar Saral, looking at her son with eyes wide open.

"Why?" Seçkin asked.

"Because I thought I wouldn't be able to get you out of your beds today but you woke up early in the morning."

Seçkin didn't say anything. He just smiled. He looked at his father. He still hadn't looked at him since yesterday. It was obvious that he wanted to make him feel guilty because of that treacherous grade of four.

Seçkin took his gaze from his father and took the cheesy puff pastry her grandmother had just taken out of the oven and popped them into his mouth. Thankfully, the February half-term break had come and he was having his breakfast comfortably. He couldn't explain how much he missed doing this. Especially the cheese puff pastries.

"Mmm… Yummy…" Seçkin groaned as he ate them. "Grandma, you know this business!" he complimented the sweet woman.

Nazikter Hanım smiled shyly. "Enjoy it, my prince."

"Grandmother?" Seçil called out, chewing with her mouth full. "Shall we do gullirigya[21] today?"

21 | Gullirigya: A dessert unique to Cyprus. The dough is spiral-shaped and cooked in boiling carob molasses.

"Gullirigya?" asked Nazikter Hanım. "Where did that come from, princess?"

"It has been a long time since I had it. I'm craving for it!" said Seçil "Please! Please!"

"I want that too." sighed Seçkin longingly.

Seçkin also loved gullirigya. Small spiral-shaped dough cooked in boiling molasses was the dessert of his childhood.

"Shall we? I couldn't decide." said Nazikter Hanım, looking at her daughter with indecisive eyes. "Can we find dough at this hour?"

"I'll go get dough, mom!" said Berk Saral, frowning, taking a sip from his tea.

"Well then!" said Nazikter Hanım with a nervous smile. "Let's make it!"

Seçkin sat lazily in front of the TV for a few hours after breakfast. The smell of molasses boiling on the stove surrounded the whole house. His mother and grandmother had prepared the dough and started to shape it. Seçil was playing with the small piece of dough that was given to her after grumbling so much.

Seçkin was watching his sister and smiling mischievously.

"You are doing it wrong, Seçil!"

"My gullirikya will be in the form of a star, not a spiral, abi!" Seçil snapped right away.

Time hung heavy on his hands. Seçkin was starting to get bored at home. He stuck his head out the window. It was indeed a beautiful February day. Sun was shining. The sky was glowing in blue. Mountain tulips bloomed on the hill next to their house. The hill was adorned with their purple and white colours among the bushes. A visit to the grove on the hill would not be bad. Seçkin hadn't been there for a long time. He used to go there often with Seçil to collect wild blackberries when he was little. Were the blackberries ready to be picked?

Seçkin took a few of the desserts and popped them into his mouth. He left his grandmother, who still put the dough in molasses, with her mother, who shaped the dough, and ran out of the house without being seen by Seçil. He needed to be alone so badly that he was praying that Seçil would not notice and tag along.

When he got out into the garden, a lizard climbing on the wall of the house jumped in front of him and startled him for a moment, but then he ignored it and kept on walking. If your home is in a mountainous region, you can often encounter lizards walking on the walls. Seçkin was used to this.

He climbed the slope and made his way towards the grove on the hill. He passed by the meadow he had dreamed months ago. The whole place was like his dream about solar eclipse. It was adorned with lush meadows and mountain tulips.

He remembered the crimson mist that surrounded him on that beautiful day. A gloomy feeling filled him for a moment. He quickened his steps and walked away.

When he arrived at the grove, he was filled with peace, as he always did when he came here. There were cypress and pine trees growing one after another around the long meadow, happy flying birds and wild blackberry bushes… Everyone seemed to welcome him with joy. Pollens were flying around and butterflies were flapping their wings as if they were enchanted.

Seçkin took a deep breath of pleasure and sat in the shade of a rather tall pine tree and looked around deeply.

As he filled his lungs with fresh pine air, a fiery-red dragonfly appeared out of nowhere in the grove. It flapped its wings and flew away.

"hop hop hop…"

The dragonfly flew around the grove, then landed on the branch of the pine tree that the boy was sitting under and watched the boy.

When Seçkin looked up at the sky, he saw the dragonfly above him. His eyes widened and he stared at it in amazement. Because it was way bigger than normal. It was about the size of his hand. Its colour was perfectly radiant. He had never seen anything like this before.

He stood up and moved closer to it. Now they were standing nose to nose. Going this close to a normal dragonfly, would make it fly away. At least, that was what Seçkin had encountered so far. But this one seemed to just stand there and stare at the boy.

Seçkin swung his hand to make it fly, but nothing happened. There was no movement. For a few moments they both stared at each other.

Finally, Seçkin's patience ran out. He took a stick and tried to strike the creature, but he couldn't do it and furiously threw the stick to the ground.

"How dare you! So, you were going to hit me with that?" a voice came from the grove. The sound was mesmerizing.

Seçkin looked at the grove, and there was no one around. But the voice he heard came from quite close. It was very clear and understandable. As the boy looked around in amazement, the fiery red dragonfly took wings from the branch it had landed on. He moved closer to Seçkin, dancing in the air.

"I was the one talking to you!" said the dragonfly as it sprinkled away its sparkles.

Seçkin was completely stunned.

"Whoa!"

The boy turned pale. His mouth opened in surprise. This could never be true. It was unreal. It was a hallucination.

Yep, his imagination was definitely playing tricks on him. Then he thought of ParuParu and BesuBesu. The dragonfly standing in front of him was just as real as they were.

"You can hear me, right?" asked the dragonfly.

Seçkin shook his head stupidly.

"Who are you?" he finally asked curiously.

Suddenly, a blinding light shone out of the dragonfly. Among the thousands of dust particles, the light grew bigger and bigger, and it took on a form, finally transforming into a woman with graceful slender wings.

"I am Laverna, Queen of Anisoptera!" said the woman in a noble and charming voice.

"Queen Laverna…" repeated Seçkin.

She was a beautiful woman. She had a pomegranate-like flower bud on her head, and pollens were flying around it. Her skin was radiant with fiery-red shimmers that covered her entire body, starting from her cheekbones. But there was a strange sadness in her eyes. It was as if they were carrying the shadow of an entire century.

"I am very sorry." Seçkin said, "Please forgive me!"

The Fairy Queen bowed slightly and smiled.

"The Great Promised One! What an honour to stand before you!"

"Please don't bow!" said Seçkin. "You are a queen; I must bow before you."

The boy did what he said. He kneeled before Queen Laverna and greeted her.

Queen Laverna swallowed in surprise, and soon her eyes filled with tears.

"What a kind lad you are!" she said, looking lovingly at Seçkin.

With a sudden flick of her wrist, she waved her hand, and two of the little mushrooms in the meadow snorted and grew in an instant.

"Please sit down!" said the Fairy Queen, pointing at the mushrooms to Seçkin. "I want to have a little chat with you."

Seçkin did as she said and sat down. After watching each other in silence for a while, Queen Laverna was the first to break the silence.

"Have you met the faithfuls?"

Seçkin nodded his head.

"Yes. ParuParu and BesuBesu appeared months ago."

"So, your guide was ParuParu... I knew his family. His grandfather was our High Prince's most loyal friend." said the woman, closing her eyes in grief for a moment.

"Did you find out what happened to our Ally Kingdom?"

"I know some things, but ParuParu and BesuBesuda don't remember much. Prince Sapphire and Princess Lal. I know Azazel, who lost everything for his greed… the wicked Hematite who followed in his father's footsteps!"

In an instant, her eyes filled with tears. She groaned "Oh Lal!".

"You…" Seçkin swallowed. "You are Princess Lal's mother, right?

Queen Laverna said nothing. She just nodded her head.

"What about the other fairies?" Seçkin asked, looking around excitedly, "Are they here too?"

Again, the woman didn't say anything, she just shook her head bitterly.

"The jinni's may have had their memories erased, but I remember what happened that night. Hematite attacked our kingdom at the birth ceremony of Prince Sapphire and Princess Lal's baby. The prince and princess were also killed that night. Right after the death of the prince and princess, the fairies came together and used all of their power. They sealed the Son of Satan next to his father and cast a spell to bring the prince and princess back into existence centuries later. They spent all their life buds for them. And finally…" the woman paused. She sighed in grief.

"Finally…" repeated Seçkin.

"They turned into black medosh tulips and took root in to the earth… They never returned to Anisoptera. When judgment day comes, the Promised will awaken the prince and princess again. Then the fairies will regain their strength and wake up."

"And you?"

"I too turn into a tulip at night, but I am freed with the dawn." replied the Fairy Queen.

"Centuries later, when Satan and his followers are freed by an eclipse, the Supreme Creator promised that the light of the Promised will begin to shine, too. He then appointed one from each of the three races of the Kingdom. These three guides would one day find the Promised One and prevent the Infidels from seizing him. As far as I understand, this task was given to ParuParu, one of the faithful jinni. And from fairies to me! For centuries we have struggled to find you… Thank God you are finally here!"

"What about the sons of Adam? Who is my guide amongst them?" he asked suddenly.

"Has the son of Adam not appeared before you yet?" asked the Fairy Queen in amazement.

Seçkin shook his head.

"May the Supreme Creator bless… Great Promised, believe it or not, I don't know!"

For a while neither of them spoke. They watched the butterflies flying through the enchanting grove, the lilac tulips swaying in the breeze.

"Queen Laverna…" Seçkin murmured at last…

"Will there really be a war?" he asked with fearful eyes.

"Last time, there was." said the Fairy Queen. Then she sighed for a few seconds.

"The Supreme Creator said to us exactly this:

With the solar eclipse, the Son of Satan will be released. The trumpet will sound. The nine kingdoms will come together and the final war will begin…" Laverna lowered her head and sighed in sorrow.

"Hematite was released with the solar eclipse. And Azazel is still lurking somewhere."

Seçkin swallowed in fear.

"People are committing suicide one after another." said Seçkin.

"Azazel is definitely behind these deaths." said Queen Laverna.

"I am afraid, ma'am. I still haven't found any sign of the prince and princess. I don't even know how to find them. Let alone that, ParuParu and BesuBesu don't know much either."

"The time…" said Queen Laverna, "When the time comes, their light will shine as bright as yours did. But fear not, Great Promised…"

The woman frowned.

"Fear makes you kneel and cloud the mind. When you face Satan, he will try to weaken you by using your fears. Resist him with your courage."

"But I am not strong, my Queen!" Seçkin said in a low voice, "I am not strong enough to stand against a creature with supernatural powers called Azazel!"

Queen Laverna frowned.

"That is how it seems to you! You have been promised by the Supreme Creator. If you weren't strong enough, you wouldn't be given this mission."

Then she smiled.

"I believe it... I believe that you will save us all. Please, you believe it too!"

Seçkin nodded hesitantly. Then Seçil's voice was heard nearby.

"Abi..."

"I have to go!" said Laverna quickly, "I'll always be near you!"

In a blink of an eye, the Fairy Queen transformed into a dragonfly with a bright light and soared into the sky.

The mushrooms on which Seçkin was sitting on throw the boy off and shrank as they grunted. With the pain of his coccyx hitting the floor, he suddenly found himself on the ground.

"Where are you abi, for God's sake?" Seçil asked with a resentful tone, crossing her arms. "What are you doing sitting on those wet meadows?"

"I've fallen Seçil!" Seçkin grumbled, "I'll get up if you help me!"

"Oops... I'm coming to help you right away, my dear abi!" the girl's voice rang hastily. She grabbed the boy by the arm and lifted him up. "Are you okay abi?"

Seçkin nodded and hugged her and they walked towards their home.

As the two were walking away from the grove, Seçkin could bet on it that the Fairy Queen was still watching him from somewhere…

-CHAPTER IX-
Vasili and Vasilia

"Snap"

Seçkin was hopelessly slumped on the armchair in his room, buried in the magazine he was holding, when ParuParu and BesuBesu suddenly appeared before him.

"I was wondering when you'll be back." the boy muttered, drowsily. "I called you so many times, didn't you hear??"

"Unfortunately, we did not hear, High Master!" said ParuParu sadly.

"What happened to you?" Seçkin asked.

"PihiPihi is not sleeping again!" said BesuBesu with a life-weary tone.

It was really hard to be a mother even for a jinni.

Seçkin opened his mouth wide and yawned. While he threw the magazine he was reading to a corner, the following headline stood out:

"Omen of Doomsday: Red fog in the air is driving people to commit suicide!"

PihiPihi was squealing.

"I hope my family isasleep." he said as he hurried past the jinni and headed for the door. "We will get caught one day!"

He slowly opened the door. He poked his head into the hallway to check if there was any noise coming from his family on the ground floor.

There was no sound.

Half an hour ago, the last member of his family had gone upstairs to sleep.

Seçkin turned his gaze to the bedroom doors lined up along the corridor. The bedroom doors of her parents, Seçil, and his grandparents were all closed.

Probably everyone was asleep.

He pulled his head back into his room and slowly closed the door behind him.

Seçkin embraced PihiPihi, whose big blue eyes had turned red from crying. PihiPihi sniffed and watched Seçkin for a while. Then she started playing with the boy's thumb and closed her eyes peacefully.

"She feels so peaceful in your lap. How do you achieve this?" BesuBesu asked, watching Seçkin with some admiration and jealousy.

"I don't know…" answered Seçkin.

Then he took a deep sigh.

"You know, I met the Fairy Queen today." Seçkin said as he sat on the couch with PihiPihi on his lap.

ParuParu and BesuBesu stared at each other with wide eyes.

"The Fairy Queen? Queen Laverna?" they both asked, their mouths wide open.

"Yes," he nodded.

"But we were told she was dead." said ParuParu.

"Even though she turns into a tulip at night, she's alive!"

"Praise the Supreme Creator!" groaned BesuBesu.

"Well, what did she tell you?"

"There has been a war, ParuParu. Hematite and his army attacked Morningstar. The prince and princess were also killed in that war. That is why the Supreme Creator separated the sons of Adam from the jinni and condemned you to live in another dimension."

"Now everything is falling into place. We were all exiled because of the heretic jinni." said the jinni with tears in his eyes.

"And what about the fairies, what happened to them?" BesuBesu asked.

"They used all of their power to make the prince and princess reborn after thousands of years. Eventually, they turned into tulips and took roots in the ground."

"So, they too are waiting for the day when the trumpet will sound somewhere." murmured ParuParu.

"ParuParu, did you know that I also have a guide from the sons of Adam who is seeking me?" Seçkin asked immediately.

ParuParu scratched his head and swallowed guiltily.

"Emm…Well… I think I knew, High Master." murmured ParuParu.

"Why didn't you tell me then?" Seçkin asked as he handed PihiPihi, who had fallen asleep in his arms, to BesuBesu.

ParuParu lowered his head. He swayed where he was and sighed for a while. Then he looked at Seçkin with tearful eyes, begging for forgiveness.

"Because if I told you that a son of Adam was also looking for you, you would trust him more than you trust me. After all, he is one of your kind, and I am a jinni."

Seçkin did not speak for a while. He turned to the window and watched the town lights twinkling under the starry sky. ParuParu might have been right. He could trust a human more than he could trust a jinni. But in all that time, ParuParu had been more than a guide for him. He was a true friend to him.

"I should have known about this regardless, ParuParu." he said at last. Looking at ParuParu's reflection on the glass. He saw that the jinni's deep blue eyes were tearing quite a bit.

Then he turned and walked over to him and patted the heartbroken jinni on the shoulder.

"You are my most trusted mentor. And you are even more than that. You and BesuBesu and PihiPihi are my friends that I never want to lose."

He smiled at the jinni with loving eyes.

"So never hide anything from me no matter what, okay?"

ParuParu stared at Seçkin barely containing his tears. Then he couldn't take it any longer and a few tears rolled down his cheeks from his huge blue eyes.

"I am sorry!" he sobbed, hugging Seçkin tightly. "I promise I will never hide anything from you again!"

"Do you know who he is, then?"

"No, Master, unfortunately I don't know!"

This half-term break was so boring. Yes, it was really boring, indeed. Seçkin was spending most of his days in front of the television. Because his father had cancelled all holiday activities due to that four on his report card.

Although Seçil rebelled against this, this was a bad apples excuse situation.

"It's all because of you, bro!" Seçil said as she crossed her arms and pouted while looking at the television. "Now we sit here and pensively watch TV while we could have been skiing in Troodos!"

"What can I do, Seçil?" Seçkin asked, drowsily.

"You could have cared about your studies instead of chasing after that wretch girl." the little girl snapped right away.

While commenting on an elderly couple seeing each other for the first time, Nazikter Hanım, who was peeling fruit for her grandchildren, looked at Seçil's attitude with a highly steely look, but Seçil did not even care.

"I am having a lousy vacation because of you!" she groaned again.

"Shhh!" Nazikter Hanım warned her granddaughter with a shocked expression again.

"Seçil, treat your brother with respect! I don't want any disrespectful behaviour!"

Seçil jumped up from the chair. As she passed Seçkin, she hissed angrily and stuck out her tongue. Then, muttering to herself, she climbed the stairs to the upstairs.

"A real Cazzude!" Seçkin muttered Seçil's nickname, shaking his head.

The weather was bad again today. A ghostly wind howling was coming from outside.

Seçkin took a deep breath and put his head between his hands.

"Seçkin?" said Nazikter Hanım, "Don't be discouraged, my prince! You will increase your grade the next term."

"I'm sick of everyone blaming me, Grandma. No one cares about how I feel!" he said hopelessly. "Let Seçkin be successful in his courses and get high grades. This will make everyone happy! But they don't even ask how I am!"

Seçkin also got up from the sofa and headed for the door, amid the sad gazes of Nazikter Hanım. The door creaked open and the boy got out to the balcony. He watched the rose bushes and lily leaves and trees swaying in the wild wind. They were pretty weakened. Seçkin closed his eyes for a while. He took a deep breath, his hair swaying in the blowing wind, and filled his lungs with air. His loved ones were constantly sticking a sharp knife into him and turning that knife and bleeding the wound that couldn't be scabbed.

Then he heard his grandfather's voice in the wind.

"Let's carry those boxes too, son-in-law!"

He looked in the direction the voice came from. His father and grandfather were carrying things into the little shed next to the house.

"Look at these, how many I once made!" said Özdemir Bey with admiration.

Seçkin went down to the garden and walked towards the little shed, stopping in the doorway of the old wooden door. He took a glance inside.

There were frames of various shapes hung on the walls. They were decorated with seashells and colourful mother-of-pearl sands.

As soon as Seçkin saw these frames, he immediately remembered. They were hung on the walls of the house where he lived.

Bahar Saral always mentioned that her father decorated them in his youth.

"Grandpa?" the boy called from the doorway.

Özdemir Bey turned to his grandson as he was placing the jars filled with seashells on the shelves, which he took out of dusty wooden boxes. Then he smiled.

"Seçkin, come, my son! Come and see what I made when I was young!"

Seçkin entered the shed as he felt his father's gaze on him.

Within a few hours, they had succeeded in giving the place an atelier atmosphere.

"Do you see this? We did it together with your grandmother." Özdemir Bey showed a heart-shaped frame decorated with purple mother-of-pearls.

"There are so many seashells!" said Seçkin in astonishment.

"These belonged to a Greek friend of mine. He passed away a long time ago. May he rest in peace. He made a will to his wife. He said give all the materials to Özdemir. The day I went to offer my condolences, his wife fulfilled the man's will. She is a good woman!"

Özdemir Bey sighed longingly.

"Oh Christo! How well we were getting along. This war has brought the two communities apart for nothing. Because of the damned meddlesomeness of the ones in charge of the government!"

The sadness in his grandfather's eyes brought ParuParu to Seçkin's mind. He too had lost his family, friends, and home because of the malicious Hematite. ParuParu was just like the immigrant Cypriot People.

But how could one yearn for something he didn't quite remember? ParuParu was a baby in swaddle when he was exiled from the Kingdom of the Morningstar. But he was yearning. That was the sense of belonging. Everyone was happy where they belonged.

Seçkin also took a deep sigh. No matter what, he would save his friend from this torment. He would reawaken the Fallen Kingdom and bring ParuParu back to his home from which he had said goodbye to, when he was a little baby.

Seçkin shook his head, to get rid of these thoughts.

He walked over to a shelf, lined with jars of multi-coloured mother-of-pearl sand and studied them carefully.

"I get bored of sitting at home all day." said Özdemir Bey.

"It will be good for me to get back to this hobby."

Do you want to help me, son?" he asked. Then he smiled at Seçkin with an excited expression.

Seçkin swallowed hardly, looking at his father, who was watching him with keen eyes. He was punished. He was under some sort of house arrest. But the shed was within the confines of the house, which had become a cute workshop. In other word, once he accepted this offer, Berk Saral could not object in any way.

Seçkin nodded slightly, barely ignoring his father. His father sighed heavily and threw himself into the garden in defeat. Özdemir Bey, on the other hand, put an apron in his grandson's hand and showed him the desk with a childlike excitement.

"Come here…" said the old man excitedly. "First of all, you're going to glue the glass that the photo will go into." He took the heart-shaped hardboard and glued it to the glass.

"Now I'm leaving this to dry," whispered Özdemir Bey, under the curious gaze of his grandson. "After it dries, you can start gluing seashells on it. Finally, we're going to sprinkle the board with mother-of-pearl sand to cover it!"

While the Sun was setting and the Moon was showing its face, and the darkness was getting brighter with dawn, this vicious circle was repeating itself every new day, and Seçkin Saral was completely stuck in the frame atelier. Maybe it was an escape. It was an escape from his father's pointless attitude, from thinking about Defne, from worrying about Burak, avoiding Seçil's sarcastic words. One way or another, it worked.

Seçkin had made many frames with this passion. He was working until midnight. However, when he started to feel dizzy from the glue smell in the atelier, he gave up and went to his room and jumped on the bed. It continued like this for weeks.

He was still working in the atelier a few days before the end of the semester break.

"Abi!" Seçil's voice called. She opened the door and immediately entered eagerly.

"Abi, get ready quickly, father will take us to "Şirin Yalı" to eat fish for dinner!"

"Şirin Yalı" was the oldest fish restaurant in Karşıyaka. Its owner was an old man. He was also a relative of Özdemir Bey. As far as Seçkin could remember his father would take the guests who came to visit them to Şirin Yalı. Seçkin loved that place's squid. The squid he ate there was not like any others.

"Abi, get up!" Seçil grumbled. "You'll get high from the glue smell in here!"

"Oh Seçil, you didn't get off my tail, huh!"

"Didn't get off your tail?" Seçil opened her eyes immediately. "Abi, you've been working like crazy here for two weeks! Nobody came and said anything to you. School is starting tomorrow! I got depressed from sitting at home!"

Seçkin took a deep sigh. His sister was right. He had her housebound, too, because of the four he got from math. Seçkin put the purple mother-of-pearl sand jar he was holding on the table. He yawned and stretched. Click and Snaps came from his spine. Then he looked at his sister and smiled.

"Tag along, Cazzude! We're going to eat fish!"

"Seçil, stop throwing those things into the sea!" Berk Saral roared while he sloshed down the glass full of raki he was holding.

Seçil was throwing fried squid into the sea from the balcony.

"But dad, look how the fishes eat!" said the little girl in admiration.

"Well, the big fish eats the little fish!" snorted Berk Saral.

"The important thing is to have power! One has to work well for that!"

He took a glance at Seçkin, then turned his gaze back to the sea.

Seçkin could no longer tolerate this sarcasm. He didn't say anything either, but anger was evident in his eyes.

Bahar Saral, on the other hand, was tired of standing between father and son all the time.

"My dear husband… I think you drank too much!" said Bahar Saral, snatching the glass from the man's hand and drinking it all. "This is like poison! I don't understand how you drink!"

"Coke is the best!" Seçil raised his glass.

Nazikter Hanım stepped in immediately.

"That is also very harmful, my princess!"

"Well, what are we going to drink then? Everything is harmful! You can't drink ayran at the fish restaurant's either, grandma!" Seçil said angrily, at last.

"Leave my angoni[24] alone!" said Özdemir Bey. "Let's throw caution to the wind!"

---

[24] *Angoni: Greek origin word meaning "grandchild" used in Cypriot Turkish.*

"God forbid!" said Nazikter Hanım with concern, "Don't forget your heart condition, Özdemir Bey!"

"Don't start again, woman!" the old man grumbled. While Nazikter Hanım was staring at her husband in shock, who became rude for a moment, the man began to sing a song in Greek. Everyone at the table burst into laughter.

"Siko horepso kukli mu

Na se do na se haro

Çiftetelli turkiko

Şinanay yavrum, şinanay nay"

While Özdemir Bey was singing with pleasure, Seçkin started to remove the bones of the grilled sea bream that had just arrived. On the other hand, he was eating tahini with lemon from the appetizer plates on the table. Every now and then he would watch the sparkling sea, contemplate, and then get back to listening to his family.

He missed his friends so much. What were Ela and Mert doing? Surely, they had spent the whole holiday together. They must have compensated the pain for all the troubles they had faced. What about Ayaz? His arms and feet were definitely covered in bruises again. Because he used to go to steep terrain and ride his BMX on every holiday. According to Seçkin, the reason why Ayaz became more attached to the bike was that he did not want to think about Mine. No matter how much he denied it, Ayaz loved Mine very much and was in pain. How could Seçkin reconcile them? It wouldn't be bad if both of them put their stubbornness aside.

Then Defne and Burak came to his mind. His stomach knotted. Have Defne and Korkut met during the half-term? What about Burak? Would he continue to come to school? He missed seeing those deep eyes so much. No matter how much he denied it, he had a strange love for him.

As all this passed through his mind, Seçkin watched the deep blue sea. On this February day, the sea was shining brightly, despite the crimson mist.

"Oh Vasilia…[25]" Özdemir Bey sighed as he finished his song and filled his lungs with the smell of the salty sea. "My beautiful Karşıyaka…"

Karşıyaka… This beautiful town was once a small Greek village called "Vasilia". It was named after two brothers who were separated from each other. Until 1974, Turks were minority. After the war, many Turks immigrated here. The village grew and developed over time and became a popular seaside town.

Özdemir Bey returned to his grandchildren.

"Do you two know how this place got its name?"

---

[25] *Vasilia: It is the Greek name of Karşıyaka Village. Karşıyaka, which was established under one of the high hills at the end point of the northern slope of the Beşparmak Mountains to the west of the town of Lapta, is a settlement with unique characteristics with its location between the mountain and the sea and its natural texture.*

They both looked at their grandfather blankly and shook their heads.

The man smiled under his moustache and cleared his throat.

"There was a very wealthy French Count who lived in Jerusalem centuries ago. The man had a beautiful wife and two children. His son's name was Vasili, and his daughter's name was Vasilia. Then the Count died in the battle in Jerusalem. After that the woman came here with her two children. As soon as they set foot on our land, they planted the Amelanchier saplings they brought with them from their old farm."

Özdemir Bey took a sip from his raki and continued.

"As the time went by, they became a family that produced and sold and regained their wealth. The family's son, Vasili, was sent to France to receive a good education. But his mother did not hear from him for a long time. The woman finally went to the king and said that she had not heard from her son. The king knew long ago what had happened to the boy. Vasili was killed in France and thrown into a stream."

"Shame on them," groaned Nazikter Hanım with her eyes filled with tears. "God bless our children."

Bahar Saral also looked at her children who were watching their grandparents with curiosity and sighed sadly.

"Amin."

"When the mother, who learned of Vasili's death, told this to her daughter, the girl was devastated by what happened to her brother. Their house was in a very high place. It was almost like an eagle's nest. Then Vasilia could not stand the pain of losing her brother and threw herself from the top.

Their mother, who was in pain, named this place "Vasilia" in order to keep the memory of her children, whom she lost at a young age. She also had a monastery built here, which was a feudal lordship at that time, where a hundred nuns could be trained, and she planted wild pear trees around it."

"A very tragic story." sighed Seçkin.

"Is that monastery the one which is over there, grandpa?" Seçil excitedly pointed to the Sina Monastery at the foot of the mountain.

"Yes, princess." said Özdemir Bey, nodding.

"Sina Monastery."

Seçil's eyes sparkled.

"Wow…"

"Actually, the main reason why I am telling you this story…" Özdemir Bey looked into the eyes of the little girl.

"Is Seçil's attitude towards his older brother lately…" he waved a finger at his granddaughter in a jokingly scolding expression.

"I see that you treat your brother pretty badly, princess. Let Vasilia's great love for her brother set an example for you. You shouldn't hurt your brother for small things!"

"But grandfather, I love my brother so much!" Seçil immediately defend herself.

"I'm just a little angry that he didn't study because of that girl, that's all!"

Then she snuggled into Seçkin's side and embraced him lovingly.

"My dear abi! I love you very much." she said cutely.

Seçkin took a deep sigh and shook his head, smiling. Then he hugged the little girl with love.

"Yes!" said Özdemir Bey, smiling under his moustache. "This is how I always want see you!"

While everyone at the table was watching this beautiful brother and sister with love, Seçkin turned his gaze back to the sea. The sea rippled and foamed. The boy thought he saw something on the cliffs across him. It was a person with a strange shining crown on his head. But his body was of a fish. Waving his tail on the cliffs for a moment, he glanced at the boy and disappeared into the bright sea.

Seçkin just gaped at the cliffs with his mouth wide open.

"Did you see that too?" he shouted excitedly to those at the table.

"Did we see what?" Bahar Saral asked, looking blankly in the direction her son was pointing.

"There is nothing there, abi." Seçil said in shock. Seçkin gulped in bewilderment. Then he didn't make a sound.

After jinni and fairies, now he had seen a mermaid.

Everything fantastic, whose existence could not be proven in the real world until today, was now appearing in front of the boy one by one. So, what was next?

-CHAPTER X-

Poison and Objection

The half-term break was over. Seçkin had had the most mediocre break ever. If it weren't for the frame workshop, he would have definitely died from boredom. He could not meet with his friends during the break because of house arrest. He had texted with Ayaz on the internet for a few nights and talked to Ela on the phone. He had no idea what Mine and Duru were doing. The useless duo. He would deal with them soon.

Defne... the first and only love he could not have... He wondered what she was doing? He missed him so much. He even missed watching her from afar...

When he came to school, Ayaz was in the garden sitting under the judas tree, having a snack. Seçkin immediately ran to the boy and greeted him. Then he sat down on the bench and took a deep sigh.

"So, Berk Saral sentenced you for house arrest, huh!" said Ayaz. "What a father! Do you think we should abduct him and give him a lesson?"

He pursed his lips and smiled. Then his eye fell on the boy's elbow. Ayaz had a huge scar on his elbow. Obviously, there was another BMX accident.

"Don't be silly, man! He can waste us all by himself!"

"You must break the chains against your father now! Man, you will turn eighteen soon!"

Seçkin shrugged. Desperately, opening his hands.

Ayaz shook his head in despair.

"I'm wasting my breath!"

There was a brief silence between them.

"I almost forgot! Touch my back!" Ayaz broke the silence excitedly.

"What happened?" Seçkin asked immediately with fear.

"Man, touch it!"

Seçkin swallowed in amazement. He felt the boy's back, then immediately pulled his hands back in horror.

"They are not here!" he said, his voice trembling. "Did you cut them off?"

Ayaz immediately burst out laughing.

"I was pretty sure you were going to say that!" he said, laughing like crazy.

"I didn't of course! Last night, that crappy jinni came to visit me. I told him that my wings were starting to grow and that I am now having trouble hiding them. And he gave me this potion."

Ayaz took a small glass bottle with a deep blue liquid from his shirt pocket and shook it before Seçkin's eyes.

The blue liquid flashed gold for a moment.

"Great!" Seçkin said, "Now you will be able to take off your top and be a model for us in pattern lessons!"

Ayaz's hopes dashed. He made a face.

"So, you linked this event to your pattern class! Berk Saral has brainwashed you well, my friend.

A cool wind blew and a few crows came and landed on the Judas tree.

"These again!" Seçkin grimaced. "We could never get rid of these devils."

"I have a present for them!" Ayaz said with a sly smile. He took a sling from his pocket, grabbed a stone from the ground, and threw it at the crows.

The crows screeched and took wings from the tree.

"That's it!" Ayaz gritted his teeth. "Now they have something to be scared of!"

"Do you know? ParuParu is telling the truth. They're definitely spying on us and informing their master." said Seçkin.

"To hell with their master!" said Ayaz.

"Still no sign of the prince and princess?" he asked later.

Seçkin shook his head sadly.

"No! According to ParuParu, when the time comes, I will somehow find myself with them."

"We went to eat fish yesterday." said Seçkin.

"Well…?"

"I think I saw a mermaid in the sea, Ayaz!"

Ayaz stared pale at the boy's face.

"A mermaid?" he whispered.

"Why not? We have jinni friends named ParuParu and BesuBesu!" Seçkin folded his arms.

"Jinni could exist; they are also mentioned in the Qur'an. But a Mermaid… I don't know!"

"Oh, I almost forgot! I also met Queen Laverna!" Seçkin exclaimed, Ayaz immediately frowned.

"Queen Laverna? Who is she?"

"She's the Fairy Queen… Princess Lal's Mother." said Seçkin.

"Well? What did she tell you?" the boy asked immediately in curiosity.

Seçkin took a deep sigh.

"That I also had a mentor among the sons of Adam…"

"Yeah… Well, I always showed you the right way." the boy bragged.

"Stop kidding!" Seçkin smiled.

"Okay okay… Who is it? Someone familiar?"

Seçkin suddenly thought of Burak. He didn't even know why he thought of him at that moment. Maybe it was because he missed him so much. He looked around. He wished to see him.

"I don't know…" he said, then, as he stared at the ground, thinking, he remembered the thing in his pocket. He put his hand there. He took out his silver pocket watch embossed with a dragonfly and began to turn it around in his hand.

"What a beautiful watch." said Ayaz, looking at the watch with admiration.

"I found it months ago." said Seçkin.

"And who does it belong to?"

"I don't know. It was in my mother's wardrobe."

"Are you rummaging through your mother's wardrobe? What were you looking for in there, pantyhose?"

"I was looking for a pillow, you idiot! Pillow!" Seçkin frowned. He looked at the boy with a threatening look.

"Okay, okay, I was kidding. Don't be mad!" Ayaz said immediately.

"What an anger!"

"The first night I found this watch, there were strange letters on the back of it. But after then, I didn't see anything again."

Ela entered the school grounds holding Mert's hand. Both had smiles on their faces. They looked like they had a good half-term break.

"Seçkin!" ' Ela's voice rang out. He let go of Mert's hand and immediately ran to the boy. She pulled the boy up from his seat and hugged him tightly.

"I miss you a lot! My dear Seçkin!"

Ela hugged him so tightly that the boy's bones cracked.

"Ela okay… you broke my bones!" Seçkin whined.

"You are so nanemolla[26]!" she pushed him back.

"What a love!" snorted Mert with childlike envy.

"This bond between you makes me jealous!"

"Well, anyone who is with Seçkin, has to accept being the fellow-wife!" Ayaz joked.

"Ugh, don't be jealous!" Ela said, hitting her boyfriend's shoulder.

---

[26] *Nanemolla: In Cypriot Turkish, it is a word used for people who are sensitive and coy.*

"Haven't Mine and Duru arrived yet?" she asked later.

"They haven't!" said Seçkin.

Ela sighed.

"Let's see what your situation will be?" she asked, turning to Ayaz.

"Our situation?" asked Ayaz, pretending as if he didn't understand.

"She's talking about Mine and you!" said Seçkin.

Ayaz shrugged.

"I'm not going back to that tomboy when there are so many beautiful chicks around!" Ayaz said immediately, raising his chin in arrogance.

"We know that what you are saying is not your true thoughts!" said Seçkin immediately. After a short mournful glance with Ela.

Ayaz sighed deeply.

"I'm sure it's better for both of us this way."

While they were brooding in grief, a brown-coloured car drove into the schoolyard. It slowly approached the square where Atatürk's bust was located. Then it stopped with its brakes squeaking. One of its back doors opened. Defne set foot in the school with all her beauty.

As soon as Seçkin saw her, his heart began to beat like crazy. It had been a long time since he had experienced this feeling. Because every time he met her in the last few months, he had been caught in a great flood of anger. But now… His heart was pounding again. Like the day he saw her for the first time…

The minute hand of the pocket watch in the boy's hand trembled slowly. An elegant writing appeared on the back of it. But Seçkin did not even notice the writing because he was lost in Defne's green eyes.

"She had cut her hair!" said Ela. "She got jealous and got bangs like mine."

"Yes…" said Seçkin, stupidly.

"Behave yourself!" Ayaz finally slapped the boy on the neck.

He pulled Seçkin away from those green eyes.

Defne also disappeared after walking into the school building.

"Ugh Ayaz, you ripped my neck out!" said Seçkin, rubbing his neck painfully.

"You still drool over her!" Ayaz grumbled.

"Well!" said Ela, "That's what love is."

Seçkin took a deep breath and glanced at the pocket watch he was holding.

"What a beautiful pocket watch! Are there dragonflies on it?" rang Ela. "Who gave it to you?"

Seçkin smiled.

"I found it in my mother's wardrobe." Seçkin replied while stroking the watch.

"In your mother's wardrobe?" Ela asked sullenly.

Seçkin rolled his eyes. Then he looked at Ayaz and sighed.

"Why is everyone surprised by this? I opened my mother's wardrobe to get a pillow and this watch came out of a box that almost dropped on my head!" exclaimed Seçkin in a low voice.

"Okay, what are you getting angry about!" said Ela in horror.

"You are so angry these days!"

Then Mine and Duru also arrived at school.

"Did you see that boy on the bus looking at you?" Duru shouted in front of everyone as soon as she arrived.

"Don't be silly!" whined Mine, embarrassed.

"I am being real!" Duru insisted while looking at Ayaz with a sideway glance.

Ayaz's face darkened with jealousy.

"Oh, I can't take it right now!" said Mine at last. Then she disappeared headlong into the school building.

"You see, right?" hissed Ayaz through his teeth.

Seçkin, Ela, Mert and Duru smiled while giving each other meaningful glances.

"If I were you…" Duru said, "I would put an end to this resentment. Or someone else will take Mine!"

Ayaz got even more angry. He jumped up from the bench that had chipped paint on and walked towards Duru.

"Look at me, halayık[27]!! Don't make me break those twig legs!"

Then he caught sight of the boy in the green coat, who was watching them behind the railings. He had short hair and chubby cheeks.

"Same kid again!"

In the end, he couldn't take it any longer.

"Hey you! Look here! Why are you spying on us?" shouted Ayaz.

Seçkin followed him as he briskly walked towards the railing, leaving the others behind.

Mysterious Boy

At that very moment, the crows that fled the Judas tree appeared again. They squeaked close. They flapped their wings and surrounded Ayaz and Seçkin like a whirlpool.

Then a huge gufi snake[28] appeared and hissed, targeting Seçkin.

---

[27] *Halayık: A brunette girl in Cypriot Turkish*

[28] *Gufi Snake: The Greek name of the snake, which is called the deaf snake in Cyprus. In addition, Cleopatra requested this special snake from Cyprus to kill herself. It's one of the snakes that has the most powerful venom in the world.*

"A snake!" cried Ela.

Mine was leaving the canteen with a green packet of crisps when she heard Ela's scream.

Then came more screams from the garden.

Everyone started running around like crazy. Teachers and students rushed into the garden in terror from all around.

"Ayaz!" said a tenth-grade boy, "A huge gufi snake attacked Ayaz."

Mine's heart started beating like crazy. She stood still. For a while she didn't know what to do. What the hell was that kid saying? What snake? Ayaz… Mine slowly walked down the corridor. When she came under the red sky, she faced the painful truth.

Ayaz was on the ground in the meadow behind the Atatürk bust. Because he was stung by the snake thrown in front of Seçkin. And what a sting! His face was covered in blood.

His head was in Seçkin's lap. The boy's hands were shaking. "It's because of me!" Seçkin sobbed. "He will die of poison!"

Duru, Ela and Mert were standing beside them. Their faces were like chalk. Teachers and students were running around. Someone was calling an ambulance.

Mine was frozen. It was like she was in shock. As she slowly approached Ayaz, her feet could not carry her. Finally, she collapsed next to Ayaz and Seçkin.

"Ayazzzz!" she gave a heart wrenching cry.

"Ayaz… Don't die!"

Seçkin and Ela stared at each other with tears in their eyes. Ela immediately hugged Mert's neck and sobbed.

Ayaz opened his eyes vaguely.

"Mine…" he groaned as he reached her with his hand, "Don't be afraid, my love!"

"He is alive!" Mine smiled, a mad happiness in her eyes.

Mine held the boy's hand tightly. "Thank God!" she groaned.

The clock had struck midnight a while ago. Two winged silhouettes suddenly passed in front of the full moon as it was shining brightly over the magnificent palace. The silhouettes got lower and lower. And Prince Okalper on the old mouflon and the angel-winged man landed in the cloistered courtyard of the palace. Prince Okalper hurriedly jumped off the old mouflon and rushed to the oak door into the long corridor. Vermeil followed him. With great excitement mixed with fear in their hearts, they quickened their steps and approached Prince Sapphire's bedroom. But there was no one around.

"Where is everybody?" asked Vermeil with eyes filled with fear.

"Supreme Creator, protect Sapphire…" said Prince Okalper.

His heart pounding with fear, he opened the door of the room. Vermeil couldn't dare to go inside. The knees of that huge strong man were trembling.

Prince Okalper walked in sorrow. The colours of the stained glass of the rose window reflected in the room, the tulle curtains fluttered in the gentle wind. The young man approached the bed with a feeling of grief. Prince Sapphire was there. He was lying on his bed with a divine beauty. The wounds were closed, but his scars were barely noticeable. A girl was sitting next to him. Her back was turned. She was praying for him, clutching the prince's hand.

"Is he dead?" Okalper whispered with difficulty through his dry lips. He fell to his knees and began to sob. The girl turned back. She had a round face and brown hair.

"Okalper!" she said as her eyes filled with tears, "Thanks to the Supreme Creator."

"Mel…" said Prince Okalper in tears.

"My love…"

Then he looked at Sapphire again.

"Is he dead?" he asked again, "Is my brother dead, Mel?"

Princess Mel got up from the bed and walked over to the young man. She grabbed him by the shoulders and lifted him off the ground.

"Calm down Okalper!" said Princess Mel. "Thank The Supreme Creator! Prince Sapphire is alive. Saint Hilarion puts him to sleep with gufi snake venom to lessen his suffering."

"We brought the flower!" said Prince Okalper, immediately hysterical. Then someone entered the room.

"Our Prince is back!" said KarlaKarla, entering the bedroom with Vermeil.

"We were starting to lose hope."

"The flower is here," said Prince Okalper, pulling the magenta-coloured Everlasting Flower from his pocket.

"Tell St Hilarion. We must break the spell as soon as possible."

Then Amethyst appeared. Leaning against the edge of the door, he looked at what was going on.

"Prince Sapphire's personal Chief of Chamber graced us with his appearance." said Okalper, sarcastically. Then he approached the young man and looked at him and snorted. "Where the hell were you instead of standing by the side of your prince?"

"Okalper don't." Princess Mel interrupted.

"Amethyst was pretty tired, so I let him. I wanted to pray for the prince."

"It has been exactly one month. Where were you, my prince?" said Amethyst in disgust.

"You fool!" said Prince Okalper, raising his hand angrily, but Princess Mel stopped him.

"Come to yourself! What you are doing in front of Prince Sapphire's sickbed is a great disgrace."

Princess Mel pushed these two young men out of the bedroom. Then Saint Hilarion also appeared at the end of the corridor, rushing towards him, holding something draped in a black cloth in his hand.

"Welcome, Prince Okalper." he said when he reached the threshold of the room. "May the Supreme Creator protect you"

Hilarion entered the bedroom. He approached the bed. Prince Okalper and Princess Mel followed him.

He uncovered the thing that was wrapped in his hand. So much so that those who saw the crown that appeared were left in horror. The crown that was once beautiful with a blue sparkle had now turned into an astonishingly black tin. Prince Sapphire's blood was dripping from it.

"Supreme Creator, the almighty," said Princess Mel, closing her eyes and hugging Prince Okalper. "I've never seen anything this horrible in my life."

Saint Hilarion put the crown on Prince Sapphire's head before the fearful eyes of everyone present, and as soon as he put the crown on, the prince's eyes opened wide and his irises blazed like fire. The old man immediately took a golden potion out of his pocket. He threw the Everlasting Flower into it. The golden potion instantly turned purple. Hilarion approached Prince Sapphire, lying motionless in shock, and made the prince drink the potion. An azure light flashed. The dark spirit that had entered the prince's body lifted with a terrifying cry. The blinding blue light washed and cleansed every part of the prince's body. The darkness on the crown also disappeared. The blackened and rotting stones began to glow blue again.

The prince coughed several times. Then he opened his eyes.

Those silvery blue eyes illuminated the spirits of those present.

"Prince Sapphire!" said Saint Hilarion. "Are you okay?"

"Sapphire..." Prince Okalper called.

My prince..." Amethyst said in tears.

The prince did not speak. He just looked around...

They were in the hospital... The huge gufi snake had bitten Ayaz from several places. Precautions were taken against poison. But the scar on his face was bad. He had been in surgery for two hours.

Mine was crouching in front of the operating room door, swinging back and forth. She looked like she was freaking out. Berk Saral was constantly walking around.

"Gufi snakes are very poisonous, aren't they, hocam?" Ela asked as she sat on a black leather bench and rubbed her eyes.

"Yes, but thankfully they neutralized the poison." said Berk Saral.

Seçkin was standing there staring blankly at what was going on. Those white fluorescents and the smell of the hospital was making him feel dizzy.

For a moment, the boy felt as if he was going to pass out.

"Seçkin!" Mert held him. He immediately lend his friend his shoulder. Seçkin walked with Mert's help and sat next to Ela.

"Are you okay, Seçkin?" she asked, taking his hand.

"Your hands are cold again."

"I am good." Seçkin said, "I'm getting worse from the hospital smell!"

That was true. Every time Seçkin came to the hospital, bad memories came to his mind. He was poisoned by broad beans when he was only five years old. He had been in the hospital for days, drawing blood. Those were hard days…

Then, Seçkin suddenly heard a familiar voice.

"Snap!"

"ParuParu?" he whispered in a low voice.

He immediately looked around.

"High Master, I am here!" whispered ParuParu, "But don't look, you can't see me!"

"What are you doing here, ParuParu?" Seçkin whispered vaguely.

"I came to tell you! I went into Ayaz's surgery. I made him drink a potion against the poison of the heretics. There is nothing to be afraid of! Only…"

Seçkin held his breath.

"Only what ParuParu?"

"There will be a large scar on his face." said ParuParu's voice.

Seçkin's eyes filled with tears. "It's because of me!" he groaned.

"Don't say that, Seçkin," Ela patted her friend on the shoulder.

A 'snap' sound was heard again in the hallway.

"Why did it take so long?" whined Mine, tearfully.

Ela got up from her seat and walked towards her friend. She knelt down next to her and hugged her tightly.

"Don't be afraid… He'll get over it!"

Then the door of the operating room swung open and the doctor in white coat came out.

"Do not worry!" he said in his comforting voice, "The surgery went very well. However, there will be a scar on his face for the rest of his life."

"Thank God!" she groaned; eyes full of tears.

"The scar doesn't matter, what's important is that he is alive."

Before long, they took Ayaz out on a stretcher. He was asleep.

Seçkin felt as if he had a proud smile on his face as he looked at him. Our young guard was already saving lives. He would also stand against the Devil and his army when it was time.

While they were taking Ayaz to the room, the last thing Şeçkin saw was Mine's eyes, which lit up with joy. Then he felt that warm discharge from his nose. His eyes darkened and he collapsed onto the cool marble…

"My prince!" a thick man's voice called out, and Prince Sapphire looked up from nearby. His eyes met with the angel-winged man.

"Vermeil?"

"How do you feel?"

The prince did not speak.

Days passed, but Prince Sapphire still couldn't get up from his sickbed. That day he called everyone in the kingdom next to him.

Prince Okalper and Princess Mel were standing beside him. The five Nephilim, led by Amethyst, Saint Hilarion, KarlaKarla, and Vermeil, were also there.

When everyone had gathered around him, he spread his hands wide and sat up on the bed. He tilted his head slightly, and the light streaming through the window made his face shine with divine beauty.

"One of you betrayed me." said Prince Sapphire sadly.

"The grief of this fact is preventing me from healing."

"Our prince…" said KarlaKarla as his eyes filled with tears.

"Who can do that when everyone loves you so much?"

"Only a royal can touch the crown, KarlaKarla," said Prince Sapphire.

"I knew that from day one." said Prince Okalper angrily. "Whoever he is, I swear I'll take his head with my own hands."

"No. I don't want to know who did this." said Prince Sapphire.

Everyone froze.

"But Sapphire…" protested Okalper.

"Do not object!" said Prince Sapphire. "I don't want to know who did this. When the day comes, he will burn with enough remorse. That will be the only major punishment for him."

Amethyst lowered his head sadly. He struggled not to burst into tears. Because of this hopeless love he fell into, he had betrayed his prince, albeit unintentionally.

"You know, my prince. You are the best prince I have ever seen." said Vermeil, looking admiringly at the prince's face. "I don't think I can live a day without seeing your face, let alone betraying you."

"I owe you and Prince Okalper a life-debt now, Vermeil." said Prince Sapphire. "You both took great risk to save me."

"We couldn't live in a world without you, my prince," said Vermeil. "So, get well soon."

"I am tired…" said Prince Sapphire, "especially… This betrayal has made me greatly weakened." he continued angrily.

"Prince Okalper will represent me in the Kingdom of Morningstar until I get through this period…"

Prince Okalper stared in amazement, like everyone else who was staring at each other.

"But Sapphire…" he whispered. "You cannot do this."

"That wouldn't be wise, my prince. If Hematite finds out about this, he will attack the Kingdom." said KarlaKarla.

"I am not leaving my kingdom!" said Prince Sapphire. "Hematite won't dare to come as long as I'm here."

"As you order, my prince." said KarlaKarla.

"You can leave now." said Prince Sapphire firmly.

"Leave me alone with Prince Okalper and Princess Mel…"

When Seçkin opened his eyes, the first thing he saw was fluorescent light glowing on the ceiling. The bright white light dazzled his eyes. He rubbed them right away.

"Seçkin?" called Berk Saral.

"Dad?" Seçkin said, barely moving his lips. "What happened to me?"

"You couldn't stand the hospital smell any longer!" said the man, smiling in a mocking tone.

"You still look like that five-year-old."

Seçkin immediately stood up from where he was lying.

"Ayaz?"

"Ayaz is fine… He just regained consciousness." said the man, reassuring his son.

Then the door to the room creaked. Ela poked her head into the room.

"Sir, the doctor wants to see you!" said the girl in a tired voice.

"I'm coming," said Berk Saral. He winked at his son and left the room.

"Ela…" Seçkin groaned.

"Handsome… How are you?" asked Ela. He walked over to Seçkin. She gripped the boy's hand tightly.

"I want to see Ayaz!" said Seçkin.

"Seçkin, you should sleep a little longer!" said Ela, "Your blood pressure is very low."

"I'm fine Ela!" the boy grumbled. He frowned.

"Okay, don't look at me like that!"

Ela helped her friend to get up. Seçkin stood up with the support of the girl. He stood for a while, waiting for the dizziness to pass. Fortunately, that didn't last long. Then he slowly walked out of the room.

They moved along the corridor. They passed Berk Saral, who was talking to the doctor.

They headed for the door opposite the chair where Duru and Bora were sitting.

Seçkin opened the door. Ayaz was lying there. He was awake but looked exhausted. Mine was sitting next to him, stroking the head of his only love.

"Ayaz…" Seçkin called out.

"Aha!" said Ayaz, "You finally woke up! What jealousy, man! You're struggling to keep the attention."

The boy's voice was lighter than it had ever been.

Seçkin didn't say anything. He walked over to his friend and looked at him for a long time. His face was bandaged. Because of him, Ayaz would live with this scar on his face for the rest of his life. This was unfair. He had to be in Ayaz's place. He was the target. Then he burst into tears.

"Your face!" Seçkin groaned while touching the boy's bandage.

"I am sorry!" sobbed the boy. He started to cry, sighing.

"Don't cry like a girl, my man…" said Ayaz in surprise.

"I'm sure I feel more handsome with the scar on my face."

Then he looked deeply at his friend. How much he loved Seçkin. He had never noticed this before. Moreover, it's not just that. Ela, Duru… What about Mine? Would he ever leave her hand again? Has he ever loved or been loved like this before? He grew up without a family.

His mind flashed back to the days when he would shiver alone on cold winter nights in the corners of the orphanage. But he wasn't alone anymore. His family was there for him and he would never let them go...

The days chased each other. Spring has come.

Jasmines have bloomed in the Kingdom of the Morningstar. Everywhere was filled with the scent of jasmine. Prince Sapphire started to feel better day by day.

During this period, Prince Okalper and Princess Mel were duly fulfilling their duties in the Kingdom of the Morningstar.

Prince Okalper handled the administrative decisions regarding the kingdom with great success, despite all the reactions of the Supreme Council of Elders. Princess Mel, on the other hand, was responsible for the inner peace of the kingdom. She wandered among the people. She established good relations with them. Both of them visited Prince Sapphire at every opportunity and consulted with him about their decisions.

Prince Okalper could not stand it long and managed to get his childhood friend out of bed and took him hunting. They were hunting as they did in their childhood, resting by the river, going crazy and diving into the lake. Princess Mel, on the other hand, was constantly checking the prince's medicines and feeding him with her own hands. Their bond of friendship had grown stronger. Everyone in the kingdom was content. But there was someone who didn't want to see these two troublemakers from a distant land any more.

Amethyst was starting to feel more and more alone. Because Prince Sapphire was getting further and further away from him every day.

While Prince Sapphire and Prince Okalper were taking a breath by the lake on a day when they were out hunting again, the sun was shining overhead and the lake was sparkling sweetly.

"Someone helped us in Anisoptera, Sapphire. If it weren't for her, neither of us would be here now." said Prince Okalper.

"I'm very curious as to who she is." said Prince Sapphire.

"I don't know, but it was someone who knew you well." sighed Prince Okalper. "She had lush eyes. And her smell… She smelled like bay leaves."

"Green eyes…" Prince Sapphire repeated. "I wish we could find out who she is. "I would reward her."

"She told me to save my Prince and that would be my only reward." Prince Okalper recalled.

"How strange…" said Prince Sapphire, frowning. Then Vermeil appeared. He flew closer with his majestic wings and landed between the two princes. He had a roll of parchment in his hand.

"There is a letter to Prince Okalper." said the angel-winged man.

Prince Okalper received the letter. He opened the roll. The sparkle in his eyes quickly faded like a winter sun.

"Who did it come from?" asked Prince Sapphire curiously.

"My father…" swallowed Prince Okalper. "My father got very sick."

He handed the letter to Prince Sapphire.

"We need to hit the road tonight, brother." said Prince Okalper sadly.

"Vermeil, tell them to prepare the carriages." said Prince Sapphire.

"Okalper and Mel are returning to the Faraway Land."

"Sure, my prince." said Vermeil then flapped his wings and soared into the sky.

That afternoon was spent preparing Prince Okalper and Princess Mel for the journey.

"I don't feel comfortable leaving you, Sapphire." said Prince Okalper. "You are still not fully healed."

"I am good. Really." Prince Sapphire tried to convince him.

"Don't forget to take your medicine, Prince. Please don't feel distaste and eat, please. You are regaining your strength." said Princess Mel.

"Thank you both so much for everything."

Prince Sapphire hugged Okalper and Mel affectionately.

"We'll be back as soon as my father gets better." said Prince Okalper. "In the spring, the Kingdom of the Morningstar is more beautiful."

"The gates of this kingdom are always open to you, brother." said Prince Sapphire.

Okalper and Mel got into the carriage. When the coachman said "Gee ho!", the horses reared up and the Prince and Princess of the Faraway Lands took off in their chariots pulled by winged unicorns, soaring into the sky…

Two weeks later, Ayaz returned to school. Mine did not leave Ayaz's side for a moment during this two-week period.

They were both smiling when they came to school with their one and only love.

Everyone went to Ayaz and embraced him. The boy's face now had a line-shaped scar that started from the top of his nose and extended to his left cheek. But that didn't matter. It gave him a different aura.

Sahra gave him a gold bracelet as a token of his heroism.

"In our culture heroes are rewarded!" she said in a dreamy voice. Then she pulled him and kissed his scar.

Even though Mine was livid with jealousy, Sahra hugged her and softened her.

When they entered Özden Atakol's class, the painting teachers asked them to paint murals on the walls of the workshop this semester.

As they worked feverishly in the workshop, the green wooden door got politely knocked three times.

"Yes!" the old woman called out over her glittering glasses.

The door opened slowly and Özlem Karam greeted everyone with her voice coming from the diaphragm.

"Hello! Sorry to interrupt your lesson, hocam!"

"Oh Özlem… Come inside, please!" said Özden Atakol sincerely.

"Thank you, hocam I have an announcement for the students…" The Woman said politely.

"I have wanted to establish a theatre club at school since I came to school. The principal approved this idea. I want you all to audition this afternoon."

At that moment, very different reactions were heard from the class. While some people's faces lit up with excitement, others slapped their foreheads. There were even those who exaggerated and hid under the tables.

"There is no escape!" said Özden Atakol. "Everyone will attend the auditions, otherwise you won't be able to pass my course!"

"But hocam! This is unfair!" Ela said quickly.

Seçkin looked at Ela and smiled.

"Don't look at me like that, Seçkin!" said Ela, "Acting is not for me!"

In the afternoon they gathered in the great hall.

The three-person jury included Memduh Kemal, Özlem Karam and literature teacher Halit İnce.

When it was Seçkin's turn to stand in front of them, his heart seemed as if it was going to stop with excitement. He pulled out one of the A4 papers turned upside down on the table and read the tirade there:

"The uninjured mocks the wound. Stop! What is that light filtering through the window? Yes, it's the east, and Juliet is the sun! Rise, beautiful sun, Kill that jealous moon!"

While there were meaningful glances at the jury table, Seçkin turned and walked out of the hall.

"How was it?" Ela asked, adding "I screwed up! I told you I have no talent." immediately.

Seçkin shrugged.

"I don't know… I guess it went well."

"I guess mine was good too!" said Ayaz.

"Really?" Seçkin asked.

He couldn't imagine Ayaz on stage.

"Great!"

"Why are you grinning so stupidly?" Ayaz grumbled.

"I would be honoured to be on stage with you, sir!" Seçkin teased him.

"Shut up you henpecked!"

They entered the canteen while they were talking to each other, laughing and having fun. Defne was there. She was chatting and laughing with some girls.

While the others settled at a table, Seçkin and Ela walked to the sales section and thought about what to eat. Crisps, waffles and cokes! They almost got whatever they had seen and sat down at the table.

"Whoa! Are you out of famine?" Ayaz grumbled

"We are hungry, man! I spent too much energy in the auditions, I need to be fed!" said Seçkin with a mischievous smile.

While they were eating their snacks with great appetite, Defne got up from the table next to them and walked out of the canteen.

As always, Seçkin stared after her.

The hours chased after each other. They kept running from lesson to lesson that day.

When Seçkin came out of the life-consuming math class, he saw the crowd gathering in front of the board in the first-floor hall. The students passing by were looking at him and whispering as he walked towards it in curiosity.

As he approached the bulletin board, he split the crowd and reached the A4 paper pinned there. The results of the elections were announced. The following was written on the paper:

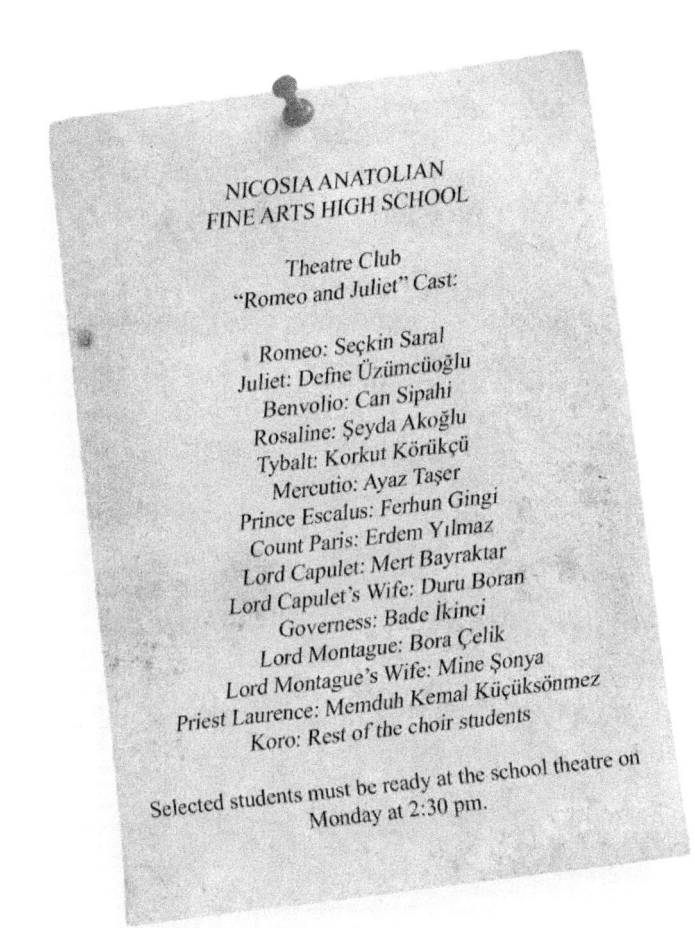

> **NICOSIA ANATOLIAN FINE ARTS HIGH SCHOOL**
>
> Theatre Club
> "Romeo and Juliet" Cast:
>
> Romeo: Seçkin Saral
> Juliet: Defne Üzümcüoğlu
> Benvolio: Can Sipahi
> Rosaline: Şeyda Akoğlu
> Tybalt: Korkut Körükçü
> Mercutio: Ayaz Taşer
> Prince Escalus: Ferhun Gingi
> Count Paris: Erdem Yılmaz
> Lord Capulet: Mert Bayraktar
> Lord Capulet's Wife: Duru Boran
> Governess: Bade İkinci
> Lord Montague: Bora Çelik
> Lord Montague's Wife: Mine Şonya
> Priest Laurence: Memduh Kemal Küçüksönmez
> Koro: Rest of the choir students
>
> Selected students must be ready at the school theatre on Monday at 2:30 pm.

Seçkin still couldn't believe what he was seeing. He read the list once again… And once again…

Erdem put his hand on the boy's shoulder and said, "Congratulations Seçkin. You got the lead role!" He could only come to himself when he heard this.

"Thank you, Erdem, you have been chosen too, congratulations…"

"Thanks," said the boy. "Did you see that the assistant principal is also going to play the priest? That man is so funny!"

Seçkin smiled.

Erdem winked at him and started walking down the stairs.

Just then, shouts rose from the administration corridor.

"I object, sir!" a boy's raucous voice roared. "I object to this list!"

It was Korkut who shouted.

"Defne… She can't play the lead role with Seçkin!"

"Come on, Korkut!" replied Memduh Kemal's voice.

"We are not going to change the jury's decision just because one student does not want it!"

"That's right Korkut. Please be reasonable!" said Özlem Karam's voice.

Seçkin moved away from the board and approached the administration.

"You…" said Korkut through his teeth when he saw the boy. "Don't be too happy! You will never fool my lover!"

He angrily walked towards Seçkin.

"What are you saying, you idiot!" Seçkin grumbled contemptuously.

Ela, Mine, Duru and Ayaz suddenly appeared behind Seçkin.

"What's happening here? What is he yelling for?" Ayaz asked.

"Whoa! Look at this! Seçkin and Defne will be playing the lead roles!" Duru groaned with a childlike excitement.

"Really? Let me see! Am I on the list?" Ela asked excitedly as she rushed towards the board.

"Boomer! I already knew that I wouldn't be selected!"

"I object! Defne will not be a part of this play!" said Korkut, in a hissy fit.

"Let Defne decide this if you please, Korkut!" said Özlem Karam with her gentle voice coming from the diaphragm.

"Yes, Defne, what do you say?"

Everyone froze at that moment. As Seçkin's heartbeat accelerated, they waited to hear the words that would come from Defne's lips.

Defne looked at Korkut for a brief moment and then at Seçkin.

"I want to play!" she finally said while averting her eyes from Korkut.

Korkut just stared at the girl, his eyes sparkling with fire. This is how this fanfare came to an end.

-CHAPTER XI-

The Judas Tree

That night, the sky was adorned with stars. In the cloistered courtyard of the magnificent palace, a young man stood alone, watching the lake where the majestic waterfall spilled. He had deep brown eyes. Tears wet his cheeks. The pain of his mistake pierced his conscience like a needle.

How had he become so blind? How had he fallen into Hematite's trap? He almost killed the prince with his own hands.

While the moon was reflecting on the huge lake, two unicorns approached the lake and drank water.

"Amethyst?" said someone nearby.

Amethyst turned around.

Prince Sapphire was there in all his majesty and nobility like a marble statue.

"My prince…" the young man whispered as he wiped away his tears.

"Why are you crying?" asked Prince Sapphire.

Amethyst lowered his head.

"Maybe because you left me all alone."

Prince Sapphire smiled. He approached the young man. He put his hands on the stone balustrades and sighed deeply. He closed his eyes and listened to the sound of the majestic waterfall. Then he opened his eyes.

"I know we haven't been spending much time lately." said the Prince, looking at the young man. "And it's like you want to tell me something."

Amethyst's tears started to fall like beads. He sobbed and hugged Prince Sapphire's neck.

"I was so afraid something was going to happen to you, my prince."

He sighed and cried.

"Amethyst…" said Prince Sapphire as he stood still, "Okay, don't cry anymore. Look, I'm fine."

"I swear I would never do anything to hurt you on purpose, my prince…"

"I know, Amethyst…" said Prince Sapphire, pulling him back and wiping his tears. "You are one of the few people I trust in this life."

"Isn't another one Prince Okalper?" he said in jealousy.

Prince Sapphire smiled.

"Both of you are heirlooms from my childhood, Amethyst. You became the family of a child who grew up without a mother and father. I can never choose between the two of you."

Then he smiled.

"Wipe your tears now. You became watery-eyed so much huh."

Prince Sapphire patted the young man's shoulder, turned around, and opened the great oak door and disappeared.

Amethyst looked at the full moon and cried out in pain.

The young man cried…

Hours passed while he cried…

While he was crying, the Sun and the Moon rose and set one after another…

Days and years passed while he cried...

After a blink of an eye, Amethyst found himself at the wedding again… Prince Sapphire and Princess Lal were married. The girl the sorceress once said... She was now Prince Sapphire's wife. Then he looked at Hematite. He had reminded him of his pain of past mistakes with a single sentence in his ear.

Amethyst turned pale.

"Move back Amethyst!" said Prince Sapphire calmly.

Amethyst moved back. He walked behind the prince as he frowned at Hematite.

"Here I am!" said the Prince. Seeing Hematite disgusted him.

"Why did you come? I don't remember inviting you to my wedding."

Hematite pursed his lips and gave the prince a disdainful look.

"Tisk tisk… I honestly couldn't find this behaviour appropriate for a gentle prince like you." He beat the air with his hand.

"I wanted to be with you on your happiest day. That is all! Also, don't I have the right to come and go here whenever I want? Let's not forget that my father once ruled this kingdom. He was the First King of this place"

"Yes! He was a king who was with his daughter and caused her to give birth to a freak like you." Angel-winged man burst out from behind the guests. "Your father was such a scumbag that he even had a child with his own daughter!"

"How dare you!" growled Hematite's voice. All of a sudden, his eyes burned with anger. Hematite finally let out a soft, high-pitched laugh as the guests huddled together in fear. You filthy half-breed!"

The angel-winged man's face darkened with anger. He tried to leap at Hematite, but the prince blocked him with a stern look.

"Calm down, Vermeil! We are not rude to our guests." he said, then looked at Hematite with a disdainful look.

"Even if they are rude enough to come uninvited to a royal wedding!"

Vermeil spat on the ground in disgust.

Hematite snorted. "You and your rabble are guests here." he said contemptuously, looking into the prince's face. "And the day will come when I will retrieve this kingdom that is my right from you."

"He will retrieve, he said, haha!" said Prince Okalper from nearby.

"Dude, you couldn't even retrieve the woman you love! You imprisoned the poor woman underground and devastated her!"

Hematite's eyes twitched. With an animal-like growl, he grabbed Prince Okalper's throat.

"Don't you ever say that again, Prince of the Faraway Land!" he hissed through his teeth

"Slow down, Hematite!" Raphider, Prince of Dragoria, threw him back.

"You filthy beast!" Hematite hissed at the brunet man.

"One day I will destroy that filthy dragon kingdom of yours too!"

"Do your best, hairy hoof!" mocked Prince Raphider.

"Enough!" roared Prince Sapphire.

"You still don't understand, do you? You are by no means the heir to this kingdom, Hematite! Azazel lost all his rights over the kingdom the day he got into sin while ruling this place… So did you!"

Hematite hissed indifferently.

"But don't say that. He only killed a few fairies. There were so many of them that they couldn't even tell who was alive and who was dead!"

In an instant, the faces of the fairies that were there darkened. Their anger reflected in their eyes like a volcano ready to erupt. The darkness of death appeared in those radiant green eyes. The meadow was shaded by dark clouds. In an instant, a state of silent mourning reigned over this enchanting wedding.

"Get out of here, Hematite!" said Princess Lal as her eyes filled with tears.

"Aww… Beautiful princess… How beautiful and innocent you are…"

Hematite tried to wipe the princess's tears with his long finger, but the prince quickly drew his sword and struck the Devil's hand.

Hematite desperately withdrew his hand and stared at the young man's face bitterly.

"I assure you that I'll cut it next time!" the prince growled, his brows knitted with threat.

"Sapphire…" Hematite gritted. "One day the truth will surely find its place."

"Yes, justice always prevails, Hematite!" Princess Lal interrupted. "No one should doubt it!"

Hematite's eyes narrowed cruelly, and a strained smile appeared on his lips.

"I swear that one day this kingdom will be mine! I will make it happen even if it is the last thing I do!"

As his voice echoed across the sky, he swung his cloak and turned into a red smoke and disappeared in an instant…

The gossip was all around the school. Everyone was talking about Seçkin and Defne playing the lead roles in the "Romeo and Juliet" play that was going to be staged by the Theatre club.

No matter how much Korkut objected to this situation, he got a good scolding from the assistant principal and was silenced. He was also on the black list. Memduh Kemal took a great pleasure in writing the boy's name on the blacklist, in the manner of a referee showing a yellow card.

Seçkin, on the other hand, was looking forward to the afternoons. In the play rehearsals, he was looking into Defne's eyes and trying to impress her. But it was futile. Defne was still as cold as ice in spite of the sweet weather that was starting to warm…

On a day by the end of March, they were at play rehearsal again.

"Have not saints lips, and holy palmers too?" Seçkin read the paper in his hand.

"Ay, pilgrim, lips that they must use in prayer." said Defne coldly.

"O, then, dear saint, let lips do what hands do; They pray, grant thou, lest faith turn to despair." "Saints do not move, though grant for prayers' sake." said Defne.

"Then move not, while my prayer's effect I take." Seçkin eagerly made a move to kiss Defne, but the girl quickly stepped back and hit the boy's head with the rolled-up paper.

"Hey what did you do that for?" the boy got angry at last.

"Stay away from me!" said Defne.

Özlem Karam sighed deeply again. Defne was doing the same thing every time. This girl was a problem for the play. She approached the two of them as she frowned and prepared to give her gentle voice an angry tone.

"What happened again guys?"

"He tried to kiss me!" said Defne, crossing her arms and raising her chin.

"My dear Defne, but that's what has to be done according to the play!" said the drama teacher in a weary voice. Then she took another deep breath and clapped her hands.

"Okay, we're repeating the scene!"

"Saints do not move, though grant for prayers' sake." Defne read gruffly again.

"Then move not, while my prayer's effect I take." Seçkin got very close to the girl. They were breathing each other's breath now. Defne's breath was so sweet that Seçkin felt dizzy for a moment. Then, just as he was about to kiss her, she pulled back again.

"Did you think you were going to use the play as an excuse for kissing me!" said Defne, crossing her arms again and raising her chin arrogantly.

Seçkin's barya,[29] who was watching them a short distance away, was quite bored.

"This girl is an idiot!" said Mine. While shaking her head disapprovingly.

"Exactly!" muttered Ela, "Look at her attitude! Where would you find someone like Seçkin!"

"That's what some people do when they find it." sighed Duru.

---

[29] *Barya: Baria. Greek word used in Cypriot Turkish. Meaning group of friends, close friends.*

The three of them were sitting side by side, resting. Ela was not selected for the play, but she was in the stage preparation branch. She was frequently there watching the rehearsals and spending time with her friends.

"I don't want to kiss Seçkin!" Defne said, "My boyfriend doesn't want it either!"

"Screw your boyfriend!" Seçkin grinned. "I'm not keen on kissing you either!"

"I swear she's a complete idiot!" said Mine again, slapping her forehead.

"What is going on? Isn't she kissing again?" said Ayaz, who had just arrived in the hall, smiling mischievously.

All three girls shook their heads wearily.

"The girl is right! Her boyfriend is jealous!" Ayaz shrugged.

"Oh…" Ela rolled her eyes. "If I had a boyfriend like Korkut... I'd be sure to betray him every day"

"Look at his face, it's like God smashed it from the side!" said Duru.

Ayaz smiled.

"I don't know about God, but Seçkin smashed it very well!" said the boy.

All four of them turned and looked at Korkut, who was leaning against the window and was watching Defne and Seçkin in anger. His broken nose was illuminated by the sunlight. His brows were furrowed and he had a crazy look in his eyes. He looked like an angry bull.

Meanwhile Özlem Karam's voice echoed in the huge hall.

"Ok! That's enough for today!" the woman said angrily.

"My dear Defne, I hope you pull yourself together by tomorrow!"

While Defne was looking at this polite drama teacher's face with embarrassment and leaving the hall with Korkut, Seçkin gave the two of them strange looks and shook his head. Then he walked over to his friends and sat down between the girls.

"God is testing me!" he said, drooping his lips wearily.

"You know, sometimes I wonder what's wrong with this girl! The more I spend time with her, the more I think about it now."

"Believe me, we've been questioning this for months, man…" Ayaz said immediately.

"But Defne was not like that, Ayaz! There is a huge difference between Defne, whom I knew before, and now!" said Seçkin.

"For God's sake, the girl isn't even smiling anymore. She's like a statue!"

Ela wrapped her arm around Seçkin's neck and rested her head on his shoulder.

"Forget it, Seçkin! Trust me, it's not worth worrying about for an unstable girl."

Seçkin scowled in grief.

"Yes…" he said weary, "She's totally unbalanced…"

"Lal?" murmured Prince Sapphire in his bed.

But no one answered.

The young man, lying on his face with his eyes closed somewhere between asleep and awake, reached his arm to his side.

No one was there.

Prince Sapphire immediately opened his eyes and sat up in bed.

The colourful sunlight that hit the stained-glass window in the room reflected on his body. The young man stretched and got up from the bed, which was surrounded by white tulles.

He put on something and left the room. The corridor was empty. He moved on in surprise and opened the oak door. As the sunlight dazzled his eyes, he looked out into the cloistered courtyard.

Vermeil and Amethyst were there. They were joking and laughing with each other as the sun shone sweetly on them.

Seeing their prince, they immediately got up and saluted him.

"Good morning my prince!" said Vermeil.

"Good morning."

The prince greeted them, then asked curiously.

"Do you know where Princess Lal is?"

Vermeil and the Nephilim exchanged expressive glances and smiled.

"The princess is over there." said Vermeil.

At that, Amethyst frowned.

"Who knows what else we'll see." he muttered displeased.

The Prince looked in the direction Vermeil was pointing. There was a huge tree in front of the balustrades. Princess Lal was also there under the tree. Next to her were a female Nephilim with angel wings, all gathered around this huge tree watching the dragonflies flying over it. Colourful sparkles were pouring from the dragonflies, and pink flowers were blossoming on the tree.

Prince Sapphire moved closer to them as he tried to understand what was going on in amazement.

"Sapphire!" rang Princess Lal's voice. She came right up to him and gave him a kiss on the cheek.

"What's going on princess? Where did this tree come from?" asked the prince.

"Isn't it beautiful?" Lal replied.

"Yes, very beautiful." said the prince, smiling, "But where did it come from?"

"I had it brought from the Morningstar, my prince." said Princess Lal.

"We just got married, did you already miss your home?" asked Prince Sapphire. "Are you unhappy here?"

"No, my prince!" said Princess Lal quickly. Then she took the young man's hands. "I am happier with you than I have ever been. You are now both my family and my home." Then her eyes misted.

"I just wanted something in our kingdom that belonged to where I came from. But if you don't like it, I'll tell the fairies to remove it immediately."

Prince Sapphire stroked the cheek of his one and only love, then smiled.

"I loved it." said the young man, looking into those green eyes with admiration. Then he folded his arms and lifted his chin arrogantly.

"So, you left me alone in our bed this morning because of this tree. Tell me, what is the name of this beautiful tree?"

Princess Lal took the head of her only love in her hands and began to playfully kiss the young man's cheeks. Then, "Judas Tree, my prince…" Princess Lal replied happily… "The symbol of our love."

※ ※ ※

As the days went by quickly, April came. The almond trees were filled with white and pink blossoms. Small seasonal flowers took their place in the gardens of the houses. Even the school's dysfunctional, worn granite pond had lovely colourful petunias planted around it. But the crimson mist that had surrounded the whole winter still continued. This was not normal.

Fog aside, there was something else missing on this spring day. Every time Seçkin's eye got caught on that place, he could feel the lack of it growing in his soul. Normally this should not be the case. He shouldn't be standing so tired and dull on this sweet spring day. He wasn't like this. But that was it; damn it was. There was definitely something amiss.

There was another feverish work that day in the twelfth-grade painting workshop. Seçkin had already put on his blue overalls and started to paint his part of the workshop wall. However, the huge spider web he drew wasn't coming out as he wanted. On top of that, Özden Atakol's "This is not good Seçkin... This is not you!" complaints made Seçkin nervous.

"Never mind!" said Ela to Seçkin while she was painting the angel-winged Ankh[30] symbol she drew on the wall in yellow. "Again, she is not in the mood!"

Ayaz also grimaced and hissed, "Grumpy senile."

But Seçkin still felt bad. This fog was pressing down on his throat. The huge workshop was like a cage again.

"I'm going down to the garden," said the boy at last. He threw the brushes he was holding onto the table. At that moment, a great gust of wind rose from outside. When the people in the workshop looked out of the wide windows, they saw that the crows perched on the weak branches of the Judas tree suddenly took wings.

"İllak[31]!" groaned Mine.

---

[30] *Ankh: Its literal mean is "life". It is an Ancient Egyptian symbol consisting of a small circle placed on the letter "T". Also known as the "key of the Nile".*

[31] *İllak: A cry of disgust in Cypriot Turkish.*

"They haven't been around lately. They're here again!" said Seçkin.

"Looks like they've been craving slingshots again!" said Ayaz, pulling it out of his pocket.

Seçkin took a deep breath. He left everyone behind and rushed out of the workshop. When he went downstairs, piano sounds were rising from the corridor as usual. As the boy rushed down the worn-out marble steps, someone called out from behind.

"Seçkin!"

Seçkin didn't hesitate immediately. He struggled to keep his balance so as not to fall off the step. He looked over his shoulder.

It was Sahra.

"Hello, Sahra," said the boy.

"I didn't see you today." said Sahra, walking up to the boy.

"I'm going to go downstairs and sit for a while. If you're not busy, will you accompany me?"

Seçkin smiled. It was exactly what he needed right now. A good friend to chat with... Even a somewhat giddy friend!

"I would be very happy with that."

Sahra was full of joy as she took Seçkin's arm.

"You know, Seçkin. I may be a sleepwalker." she said and burst out laughing. "Last night while I was sleeping in the dorm, I opened my eyes and found myself in the hallway. Besides, my feet were freezing."

"But this is very dangerous, Sahra." said Seçkin. His eyes widened.

"Don't be sad, Seçkin. I am going to sleep in my shoes tonight."

Seçkin was stunned for a moment. Then he smiled. This girl was perfect. She would find a solution that would make her happy in every situation and she didn't worry about anything. What Seçkin wouldn't give to be like her?

When they went out into the garden, the crows were still on the branches of the Judas tree. When Seçkin and Sahra sat on the bench under the tree, they began to caw bitterly. Seçkin watched the Judas tree with sadness. The tree was still carrying the effects of the harsh winter. It was tired and leafless. The tree didn't seem to be ashamed of its leaflessness as Seçkin stared at it. Wasn't it jealous of the bougainvillea flourishing in front of it and the flowers that bloomed around it? Its species had already bloomed their flowers and started to leaf out.

As the crows cackled and groaned, Seçkin remembered the big crow that had attacked him months ago. If ParuParu had not intervened, it would have pierced his heart. He startled.

"I hate these crows," Seçkin finally said.

"Ignore them Seçkin!" Sahra shrugged.

"Ignore them so they don't achieve their goals."

Seçkin hesitated for a moment. What was this now? ParuParu said that they served Hematite, but how could Sahra know that?

"What are you trying to say?" he asked, bewildered.

Sahra chuckled.

"Forget it, Seçkin. Believe me, I don't want to spoil this beautiful moment with crows."

Seçkin smiled.

He remembered the dream he had had months ago. There was curse and peace there also, as he felt here now.

"You know Sahra? I dreamed of you months ago."

"Really? Aww... So exciting! So, what was I doing?" the girl's voice rang.

Seçkin remembered how Defne got away from him with Korkut in the fog and how Sahra gave him peace.

He smiled.

"You were comforting me, as always." said the boy. "I'm glad you're by my side, Sahra."

He rested his head on Sahra's shoulder. He could feel the coldness of her body, but he didn't care. While her body was this cold, her heart warmed his heart.

"I think I've lost hope," Seçkin muttered.

"Don't say that, Seçkin!" she frowned. "Never let a wave of despair spread through you."

"Look at me…" the girl said as she lifted the boy's head from her shoulder.

"If true love was an easy thing, we'd all have it. This is a test!"

"Ela said something similar months ago." he said, pouting his lips.

Then he sighed.

"Have you ever been in love, Sahra?" Seçkin asked.

The girl's haunted gaze went far away for a moment.

"I was, a long time ago." said the girl in her dreamy voice. "But it's been so long that I forgot what it felt like!"

"I'm sure it's best not to remember! I regret falling in love." said Seçkin.

Sahra sighed deeply.

"Defne… I mean… I don't understand how she can change that much. Or was she always like that and I saw her the way I wanted to see her?"

"Don't worry, Defne will soon be the same as before!" said Sahra.

"You said so in my dream. You said one day she would come back."

Sahra looked at the boy affectionately.

"Because that's what it's supposed to be! No matter what, no power can prevent what should happen."

Neither of them spoke for a while.

"Are you seeing Burak?" she asked, suddenly breaking the silence.

Seçkin gawked at the girl's face.

"With Burak?"

"I've seen you two chatting here a few times!" replied the girl.

Seçkin's heart suddenly started beating like crazy. Had Sahra heard and seen something? Then that dream came to mind. That dream where he kissed Burak… For a moment, Seçkin felt queasy and his eyes filled with tears. Burak… He hadn't seen him since the semester break. Although he was afraid of him, he missed him. No matter what, he felt connected to him in some way. But it wasn't love… It was something even stronger than love.

"I haven't seen him in a long time!" said Seçkin

"Love… It can suddenly blind you and cause you to do wrong things! So don't blame him!" said Sahra.

Seçkin got petrified.

"Do you know?" he asked in horror.

A warm smile appeared on Sahra's face.

"That Burak is in love with you?" she asked mischievously. "Of course, I know …"

What kind of a girl was she? How could she know about everything like that? No, Sahra wasn't human… She couldn't be.

"How do you manage to do this?" asked Seçkin. "How can you know everything?"

Sahra giggled.

"Instinct!" said the girl.

"Ela also senses things before they happen, you are way more than that!" said the boy then got silent. "Wander what Burak is doing?" he thought.

"I am afraid of Burak" he said suddenly.

Sahra smiled.

"It is not Burak that you are afraid of. You feel a kind of connection towards him… You are afraid to fall in love with him."

Seçkin looked at the girl's face in shock one more time. Then he lowered his head feeling ashamed and nodded.

"Don't be afraid Seçkin, you are not in love with him." said the girl straight away. "What you feel is not love."

"What is it then?" murmured the boy while still holding his head down.

Then Defne came out into the garden. She walked towards the Atatürk bust with a few girls and sat on the steps.

Seçkin's head rose up as the girl's scent filled the boy's nostrils with a slight breeze.

"No matter how angry you get at her, you still can't take your eyes off of her, can you?" Sahra asked Seçkin, who was looking deeply at Defne. "That is what love is… that's love that you feel for Defne." said the girl.

Defne and Seçkin's eyes met for a moment. Her shadowy eyes shone as green as before for a moment. But this was so short-lived that Seçkin didn't even notice. Then she got restless and jumped up and walked back to the school building without looking at Seçkin's face. The other girls shot menacing glances at Seçkin and followed her.

"I don't understand what's going on with them!" said Sahra, shrugging.

"Because they're Korkut's minions too!" replied Seçkin.

The school bell rang as the girl shook her head gloomily.

"Oops!" she jumped to her feet. "I have to go to class! See you later!"

After embracing Seçkin sincerely, the girl skipped into the school building.

Seçkin took a deep breath and looked up to the sky. This red mist hadn't cleared yet. It had been around for almost a year. The Devil was getting stronger somewhere. He knew that this fog was about him.

The boy's eyes fell on the Judas tree. It hurt him to see it like this.

, Its weak branches, unlike his huge body, should have blossomed now. It was time. It had even passed.

As he looked at it, Seçkin's eyes filled with tears for a moment.

"Or have you lost hope like me?" he thought.

As he was unhappy, the tree was unhappy also. There was a connection between the two of them, or at least Seçkin thought so.

The tree was tired like him. Yes… It was like Seçkin.

But now she had to answer to him. It wasn't fair for her to betray the boy like that. He would never accept this.

Seçkin closed his eyes and breathed in the fresh spring air again.

When he opened his eyes, he felt someone's presence next to him. He took a breath. It was filled with bay scent.

He looked beside him. It was a girl with auburn, wavy hair and green eyes...

It was Defne...

Seçkin just stared into Defne's shadowed emerald eyes, unable to make the slightest sense of what was going on. His heart started to beat like crazy. He tried to figure out if he was dreaming or not. He tried to analyse what he was seeing.

It wasn't a dream. Defne... She was really sitting next to him right now.

But why? How could she have come and sat next to Seçkin, ignoring that psychopath called Korkut? Was she not afraid that Korkut would see?

After all, Korkut and Seçkin were now two sworn enemies.

Defne hesitantly cast a sideways glance at Seçkin.

"I need to talk to you, Seçkin..." said the girl. Her voice was shaky.

"What about?" asked Seçkin, petrified.

She stared at Seçkin for what seemed a very long time. But nothing could be read from Defne's eyes. It was as if there was a dark shadow on her irises.

Defne sighed.

"About us." she said in an icy voice.

"There is no such thing as us!" Seçkin snapped. He shrugged.

"Yes," said Defne. She shook her head. "There is no such thing as us! But you don't understand that. I don't want to feel your gaze on me all the time."

"My gaze is not on you!" he hissed, gritting his teeth. "I have to look at you like that during play rehearsals!"

They looked at each other. Defne's eyes misted.

"I love Korkut."

They slowly started to get closer to each other.

"Ugh Seçkin... What's going on with me? Why can't I resist you?"

As their lips approached each other,

"Because..." said Seçkin. "I am an irresistible man."

Defne was so close to him that she could now hear the boy's heavy breathing.

"We can't do that... it's a sin." Defne groaned but finally surrendered to Seçkin.

When their lips met, it was as if everything had stopped and disappeared. There were only two of them. It was like they were in void. They were in a vast space that only they existed.

The same image vaguely appeared in both of their minds.

A majestic castle... A couple with a small baby in their arms... The feeling of being separated from each other for too long...

"This feeling... I once... lived in a place... It brings back memories." thought Defne. "My heart is beating like it's going to explode! I wonder if this is what they call love?"

"Warm and soft... I've felt it before... Those sweet lips." thought Seçkin.

As they kissed each other under the Judas Tree, the tree was waking up from its long hibernation. Slowly growing sprouts began to emerge from its weak branches.

After a while, the boy's cheeks were washed with Defne's tears.

Then everything happened so quickly…

Defne's forcibly pulling her lips back from Seçkin's, hugging him tightly with sobs and then getting up and running away…

Her eyes went back to normal, too. Seçkin had seen it. Those icy eyes were as green as they were on the first day.

As Seçkin gasped and stared after Defne, a voice rang in his mind.

"Thus from my lips, by thine, my sin is purged."

-CHAPTER XII-

Reuniting

"Did you kiss?"

Ela squealed so loudly that the curious eyes of the people sitting in the canteen focused on her. The preparatory class students sitting at the table next to them had already started whispering.

"Would you please be quiet? Everyone heard you!" said Seçkin, feeling uncomfortable with the curious eyes around him.

"Excuse me, but you could have knocked me over with a feather, Seçkin!" said Ela. "I wonder where she is now? "I don't know." sighed Seçkin.

Ayaz grinned. "So? How was it? Tell me." he said excitedly.

"I don't know. She got up and ran away from me afterwards. "I think she was crying." Seçkin replied.

Ayaz gently hit Seçkin's arm with his elbow.

"Oh no! I hope you're not that bad of a kisser."

"I'm sure Seçkin knows how to kiss." Ela immediately intervened.

Then she pursed her lips. "I can guess why she's crying. She sees herself as betraying Korkut."

Mine rolled her eyes.

"I think she should be glad she's come to her senses. It was inconceivable that she dated that Garavolli[32]haired guy anyway."

"So, what happens now?" asked Duru. She was looking with pure surprise on her face.

Mine did not give Seçkin a chance to say anything.

"Nothing! She has already lost her chance, darling. Just because Seçkin responded to her kiss doesn't mean he will be with her, right?

---

[32] *Garavolli: Snail, Slug in Cypriot Turkish.*

There was a deep silence at the table.

As they kept looking at each other, Seçkin looked at the others giddily and smiled.

Mine immediately frowned.

"So, what! Are you going to be with her?" she fumed immediately. Then she slapped him on the forehead. "From the expression on your face I can see that you already have come around!"

She grabbed the boy's shoulders and started shaking him.

"Come to your senses, Seçkin! I bet she went and threw herself into Korkut's arms as if nothing had happened. It's clear what she wants to do. To keep both of you in her pocket!"

"Well, let me go, Mine," the boy moaned.

"You are so cruel, Mine," said Ela.

"I am cruel, huh? You all hated her until a few hours ago."

"Yes, that's true." agreed Ela. "But now the situation has changed."

"So, there were no tongues involved?" Ayaz intervened again with an amused curiosity.

"Oh Ayaz!" Mine gave him a condescending look.

"What's the matter, darling, even we still don't kiss with tongues!"

Then Defne and Korkut appeared in front of the canteen door.

But it was like… Were they fighting?

"Leave me alone Korkut!" said Defne with her fairy voice.

"But Darling… Why?" said Korkut pathetically.

"It's over… Don't you understand?" repeated Defne.

Everyone in the canteen looked at those two in shock.

"Why…" the boy groaned, frantically rubbing his broken nose.

"Because I don't love you!" Defne replied immediately. She crossed her hands and lifted her chin up arrogantly.

"After all this time, have you come to your senses now?" snarled Korkut.

Defne laughed contemptuously at Korkut.

"I didn't know what I was doing for months! It was like I was brainwashed somehow… But yes… I finally came to my senses!"

Korkut lowered his head to the ground and hissed.

Defne made eye contact with Seçkin, who was watching those two with his friends.

"Now leave me alone!" said the girl with all her beauty. Then she looked at Seçkin and smiled with love. "Because my boyfriend can attack you at any moment!"

"Your boyfriend?" Korkut grimaced as he looked back and forth at Seçkin and Defne.

Seçkin froze along with everyone at the table.

"I love Seçkin!" said Defne. "And if you don't leave me alone, he will break your nose once again!"

"Wow!" Ayaz whistled.

Ela, Duru and Mine almost fainted from surprise.

"Come on man, get up and go near your love!" said Ayaz.

"Seçkin don't!" cried Mine. "Leave that hypocrite alone!"

When Seçkin recovered from the shock wave he entered, he ignored Mine. He got up from the table. He approached Defne and Korkut with a fatuous, arrogant walk. He wrapped his hand around Defne's waist and kissed her on the cheek. Everyone in the canteen had their mouths open.

"Leave my girlfriend alone, Korkut!" said Seçkin contemptuously.

Korkut frowned. That mad bull look that had settled on his face in recent days appeared once again.

"You two… My revenge will be great!" he growled.

"Come on Korkut, move along!" said Ayaz from the table.

"Good riddance!" said Duru.

While Korkut was shaking his finger threateningly at the lovers, he turned around angrily and began to climb the worn staircase, grumbling to himself.

"Heşaaaa! [33] Ela applauded. "Long live the true love!"

Defne's cheeks turned red and she looked down in embarrassment. Seçkin watched her with admiration. Then

---

[33] *Heşa: It is used as a shout of joy in Cyprus, like "Heyo".*

he grabbed the girl by the arm and immediately left the canteen.

They both ran into the garden. The lovers passed by the Judas tree and approached the eroded ornamental pond. Then they stopped there. They looked at each other with admiration.

"I love you so much," said Seçkin, caressing the girl's cheeks like crazy.

"Me too," said Defne. Wrapping her arms around the boy's neck.

"Forgive me! I am so ashamed of what I put you through!"

"Shhh!" Seçkin silenced her. His finger traced her red lips. "Those days are long gone now."

The girl smiled. Two large tear drops rolled down her cheeks from her eyes.

Seçkin wiped her tears. And kissed the girl's lips. While the crows were cawing above them and disappearing from sight, true love's kiss swept them both off their feet...

As the days passed, Seçkin was literally blissful. Despite all the pain he had suffered and all the disappointment he had experienced, he was happy to see that he was not wrong about Defne. He was falling more in love with Defne every day.

Defne was constantly apologizing to the boy. She still couldn't understand how she dated Korkut when she loved Seçkin. It was as if she was brainwashed for months. But Seçkin's kiss cleared all of the dark magic.

They were met with a nice surprise when they came to school the morning after the day they kissed. The Judas tree was in bloom. It was now a princess adorned with purple and pink flowers.

There were also students at school who looked at them with strange eyes. That's why they were careful not to be so close during breaks. Because Korkut and his crew were doing their best to infame the girl. They all said the same thing: While Defne was dating Korkut, she had fallen in a forbidden love affair with Seçkin.

This situation bothered both of them very much. Seçkin was trying hard not to attack that fool called Korkut again.

Seçkin and Defne may not have been seen together during breaks, but in the afternoons, after the play rehearsal, they would stay at school for a few hours, spend time together, and then go home. On those afternoons, while Defne was hugging, kissing and smelling Seçkin, a bulge appeared in the boy's trousers.

His friends also missed seeing Seçkin happy. But things didn't seem to be going well for Seçil. She had been having constant fits of jealousy ever since she found out that her brother started dating Defne. She was insulting both of them and making the world miserable. The little girl still didn't trust Defne.

The big crows with devil eyes were no longer perched on the Judas tree. They didn't even land on the schoolyard. Seçkin saw them flying over the school from time to time... But that red mist in the air still hadn't disappeared.

When the spring rain ended that day, it left behind a pale sunlight and a wet, sweet serenity. The school building was stubbornly trying to survive the years like a ghost. It was pale and tired. But the Judas tree, adorned with violet flowers, gave it some colour.

Seçkin and Defne were chatting in the garden with a distant attitude. While the sun was shining faintly overhead, Ela and Duru were sitting on the steps of the Atatürk bust, looking at the two and giggling.

Seçkin exchanged glances with Ela and Duru and asked for permission, got up by Defne's side and walked towards the girls.

"At least don't do this in front of the girl!" Seçkin said, a little angry and a little embarrassed. Duru burst out laughing.

"What happened? Are you disturbed, little bird?

"His name is lovebird now," said Ela. Then she burst out laughing.

Seçkin rolled his eyes.

"You are in love... Lalala... You are in love... Lalalala..." both girls started singing.

Defne burst out laughing from where she was sitting.

"I can't find anything to say to you." Seçkin grumbled. "Is this what I was doing when you were with your boyfriends?"

"Ummm... Let's think about it." said Duru as she raised her head and looked at the sky.

"This guy is younger than you! Also, he's a bum!" she recalled while imitating Seçkin.

Ela fainted from laughter. Seçkin turned purple with anger and walked near Defne again, making threatening signs at the two of them.

"I love these two!" said Defne.

"Yeah right!" Seçkin hissed through his teeth. "Botherers!"

Seçil went out to the garden, hopping. She smiled and looked around. As soon as she saw Seçkin and Defne hugging each other, she grimaced and walked back into the school building. Seçkin and Defne looked after the girl and sighed with sorrow.

"Seçil will never accept me!" said Defne. Then she looked down to the ground in sorrow.

Seçkin let out a bored breath.

"Believe me, she's acting like a witch as always. Otherwise, she loves you too."

Defne looked into the eyes of her one and only love and smiled.

"I hope so…"

As the bell began to ring loudly, the girl covered her ears with her hands.

"This bell is getting worse every day!" she whined.

Then, quite reluctantly, she got out of Seçkin's arms and stood up.

"I have to go to the cello lesson!"

Seçkin smiled. He took the girl's hand and kissed her.

I will wait for you here!"

"Don't you have class?"

Seçkin shook his head. "No!"

"Well, see you!"

Then Seçil appeared again and as she was hopping out into the garden with the pink packets of crisps in her arms, she encountered Defne, who was walking to the school building. Defne smiled at the girl sincerely, but Seçil ignored the girl and walked straight to her brother arrogantly.

"Your tree is blooming beautifully, isn't it, abi!" her voice rang out while handing one of the crisps packets to the boy.

"Yes…" said Seçkin with pleasure. "Finally…"

"Aww…" said the little girl, hugging the boy. "I love you so much, my dear abi!"

"I love you too, cazzude!" said the boy. "But you've been making me sad lately."

Seçkin got out of his sister's arms and moved a little away from her. Then, he could barely contain himself and put a serious expression on his face.

"Abi, what did I do to upset you?" the little girl asked dumbly.

Seçkin crossed his arms.

"For example, you treat Defne very badly!" said Seçkin arrogantly.

"Oh, that's the issue..." Seçil grumbled, immediately flashing fire from her eyes. There was no trace left of her previous cuteness.

"I don't like that girl. She literally has you wrapped around her finger!" said the little girl.

"You are wrong, Seçil. Defne loves me very much."

"Does she?" Seçil hissed through her teeth. Then she jumped up angrily. "Abi, have you forgotten what she put you through?"

She had turned into a cazzude.

"Ugh! How easily everyone forgot what happened!" cried the little girl. "But be aware that I will not forgive her, abi!"

He left Seçkin behind, who was staring at her, and ran to the school building in anger. Seçkin stared at Ela and Duru, who were still sitting on the steps of the Atatürk bust, with their mouths wide open. They were both terrified.

Seçil collided with Sahra at the door.

"Be careful princess!" Sahra caressed the little girl's cheek.

But Seçil got rid of her hand and started climbing the worn stairs without saying a single word.

Sahra went out to the garden in surprise and walked to Seçkin, who was sitting under the Judas tree with a shocked expression on her face.

"What's wrong with Seçil?" she asked in a dreamy voice.

Seçkin shrugged and then leaned his head on the shoulder of Sahra, who was sitting next to him.

"Oh Sahra!" said Seçkin hopelessly.

"What happened, Seçkin?"

"Seçil will never accept Defne."

Sahra smiled.

"Oh Seçkin, look at what you are worried about!"

"Don't laugh, Sahra…" said the boy while pursing his lips.

"Are you crazy? Seçil's anger is not towards Defne! She doesn't want to share you with anyone! If this was another girl, not Defne, the situation would still be like this. Don't worry, she will get used to it very soon!"

"Really?"

Sahra smiled again.

"Really! Do you remember what I told you when you were suffering from Defne's love pain?

Seçkin smiled.

"You said, do not be sad. She will come back to you sooner or later; your fates are connected."

"Now I say Seçil will get used to it!" said Sahra.

Seçkin wrapped his arm around Sahra's shoulder and hugged her with love.

"You are a wonderful person, Sahra. I love you very much!"

Sahra's pale cheeks turned red and she smiled.

"Oh Seçkin, I love you so much too. But be careful Defne shouldn't hear you say that to me. Otherwise, she will get jealous."

"Hey!" Ela called from the steps of the Atatürk bust.

"You are not a single guy anymore, Seçkin! Get away from Sahra! Since I can't hug you, you won't hug others either!"

Seçkin and Sahra immediately burst out laughing.

"You should go and hug your boyfriend, Ela!" Sahra smiled mischievously.

"Oh, my dear Ah… If you only knew… Today my boyfriend is going from one class to another. I haven't even seen his face yet!" Ela pursed her lips.

In the afternoon, they gathered in the big hall again and rehearsed. On one side, Korkut was looking at Seçkin and Defne, with the mad bull looks on his ugly face. On the other hand, Şeyda dreamed of being in the place of Defne, who was deeply in love with Seçkin. Even in the play, she was going to portray a girl in love with Romeo. What kind of fate was this?

When Seçkin got tired of these eyes staring at them, he would grab Defne by the arm and pull her out of the hall and into a secluded area. After being alone for a while, they returned to rehearsals. Özlem Karam was getting angry and tearing her hair out every time those two disappeared. The show was a few weeks away. Everyone was very nervous.

Ela was trying to decide on the colours of the decoration with a few students who were assisting her.

"I think a purple-dominated decor is ideal for the game. After all, this is a love tragedy," said the girl, scribbling something on the list in her hand. "Remember, we will also hang stars on the ceiling. Stars will be seen in every scene!"

"But Ela abla, how will we hang those stars?" an eighth grader asked anxiously.

"With fishing line, my girl! We will put it on the fishing line and hang it!"

Duru drew the costumes. She was taking measurements of the players and keeping notes.

"I didn't like this dress at all, Duru!" Mine grumbled. "For one thing, it makes me look so fat!"

"But this is what it should do, my dear Mine. You're Romeo's mother so you need to look plump!" said Duru wearily.

"My plump girlfriend!" Ayaz immediately mocked.

"Look at me, shut up or I'll beat you, boy!" squealed Mine.

In the afternoon, they all lay down on the grass in the garden, exhausted from work. There was almost no one left in the school other than them. Seçil was holed up in the violin classroom on the second floor, playing Vivaldi's Four Seasons. The sound of the violin leaked through the open windows and was heard by Seçkin.

"How sweetly the sun shines!" said Defne. She was lying on the ground and her head was on Seçkin's lap. Seçkin was caressing his one and only love's hair while yawning lazily. He had already recovered from what he had suffered. True love had overcome everything. As they were lazed on the grass on this beautiful afternoon, they seemed to be relieved of the tiredness of the whole year.

"How nice to see you like this!" said Ela. Looking at those two with admiration. She was sitting on the grass, embracing Mert. "You are finally together, now I won't worry even if I die!"

"You don't say!" said Ayaz. While massaging Mine's shoulders, he said, "I was exhausted of hearing Defne's name throughout the year."

Everyone except Seçkin and Defne burst into laughter.

"What's wrong with you?" asked Duru. She opened her eyes wide when she saw that her friends were not laughing.

"Oh, I'm getting angry with Korkut and his crew." Seçkin grumbled.

"They are constantly gossiping about Defne! We can't hang out comfortably at school because of them!"

"Ugh... Ignore what everyone says and live your love to the fullest!" Ela said, frowning.

"Something inside me tells me to kick his ass!" Seçkin fumed again.

"Don't worry, Seçkin!" said Ela. "Don't forget what happened last time!"

Defne sighed in exasperation.

"Ela is telling the truth, Seçkin! It's not worth getting in trouble for that bastard!"

"I'll get in trouble, if necessary, not because of that bastard, but for you!"

Exclamations of "Aww" were heard from the group.

Defne's cheeks turned red.

"What a romantic boy!" said Duru. Then she made a face at Bora and folded her arms, "Darling, why don't you tell me such things?"

Bora smiled in surprise. "We get it, Seçkin, you are a romantic! But you're making it hard for us, man!"

"Making it hard, huh?" Duru roared. "The last time you said nice things to me was when we were camping at Karpaz!". Then you stole my heart and the romance ended, right?

"At least there were romantic days with your boyfriend! "I've never heard anything," Mine reproached.

"You should be ashamed!" said Ayaz as if he was insulted.

"Don't I say nice things to you, traitor?"

Mine smiled mischievously. She spread even further into her boyfriend's arms. "It's true, you say it sometimes, I forgot!"

While they were fighting and laughing with each other under the sweetly shining sun, Sahra was watching them with admiration from the huge window of the twelfth-grade workshop. They were all together again after a long time. As the girl looked at them with a sad smile, her heart jumped for a moment. Her breathing got shortened. Her body trembled slowly.

"Please just a little more…" she muttered to herself. "I need more time."

Then she lowered her head to the ground and exhaled sorrowfully.

"I'm running out of time."

While Seçil continued to play Vivaldi's "Spring" on her violin, the days continued to pass quickly, one after the other, like a melody coming out of the violin...

"My prince!" called the brunet young man.

"Amethyst."

Prince Sapphire turned around. Amethyst and Vermeil were standing there. They were both in grief.

"The Supreme Council of Elders has gathered, my prince." said Vermeil.

The prince let out an annoyed sigh.

"Let's go then! "It is not good to keep the elders waiting."

While the moon was shining overhead, the flowering branches of the Judas tree in the garden were swaying in the gentle breeze. The sound of an owl was coming from nearby. Not much time had passed since the wedding.

"Is what is said true, my prince?"

"That the jinni living in the kingdom rejected me and the princess? Yes. It's true, Amethyst. But this is their choice, we are not going to force anyone to stay with us, right?"

Vermeil sighed angrily.

"Because of Hematite… God damn that Devil!"

"In a way, it was good… I learned who my real friends that love me are among the jinni."

Amethyst also sighed deeply.

While these words were coming out of Prince Sapphire's mouth, the old jinni with bulging blue eyes approached them. "Sapphire… My dear son… What are we going through?" asked the jinni, his eyes watering considerably. "There shouldn't have been such a rebellion after the wedding."

"Dear KarlaKarla…" Prince Sapphire took this little jinni's hand and kissed it.

"It's nice to have you with me!"

"What are you talking about?" KarlaKarla reproached. "Me and your wet nurse are always by your side! May the Supreme Creator damn those seeds of the Devil! "What did they bring to us while we were living here in peace?"

"And is it true, Mr. KarlaKarla?" asked Vermeil.

"Did your son join them?"

The jinni lowered his head in shame. His eyes watered even more. His cheeks were wet with tears.

He nodded, sadly.

"Forgive me, my prince. I couldn't raise my son strong enough!" gulped KarlaKarla. "He couldn't resist the seeds of evil that were planted inside him."

Prince Sapphire patted his little friend on the shoulder.

"Don't lower your head, KarlaKarla! Don't blame yourself for this!"

"My only sadness is that my one and only ParuParu will grow up without a father. We are old now. The thought that one day, when my wife and I pass away, he will be left alone makes me sad," said the jinni.

Prince Sapphire smiled sadly.

"ParuParu will not grow up alone… I will never leave him alone!"

-CHAPTER XIII-

Birthday Surprise

When Seçkin woke up that morning, there was no one around. It was ten o'clock in the morning. Suddenly a feeling of dread washed over him. School?

"Oh my God, I'm late for school," he thought to himself, but then he paused. "But why didn't my father wake me up?" a voice rang in his mind.

This was not a good sign at all. As he left his room and went down to the living room with his eyes half open, he tried to understand why there was this meaningless silence. When he went downstairs, there was no one around. Seçkin headed to the kitchen and opened the fridge. He took an ice-cold cherry juice and sloshed down. Then he went back to his room and fell back on the bed. He tossed and turned in bed for a while with this feeling of loneliness.

Then he straightened up. "What's the date today?" he thought to himself. Then he looked at the calendar on his desk.

The calendar pages showed May twenty-eight.

"Today is my birthday..." he muttered to himself. "I turned eighteen..."

Suddenly, a "Snap" sound was heard in the room.

"Happy birthday, High Master!" rang ParuParu's voice.

Then BesuBesu and PihiPihi appeared from the opaque smoke, and all three jinn began to sing at once:

"Happy birthday, High Master... Happy birthday, High Master!"

All three looked very funny. Especially PihiPihi, who couldn't even speak yet, was singing along to the song and clapping with her tiny hands while making strange sounds of her own.

Seçkin couldn't help but smile for a moment at this ceremony of the jinni, then sat on the edge of the bed and frowned.

"What's going on, High Master?" asked BesuBesu.

Seçkin didn't say anything. He took the phone on the nightstand and called his mother.

The phone rang but no one answered.

Seçkin sighed deeply.

"Do you know where my family is?" he asked finally.

The two jinn stared at each other with unconscious eyes.

"They left in the morning and went to school as usual." replied ParuParu.

"What about my grandmother and grandfather?"

"Oh, believe me, we have no idea, High Master!"

"You are jinni! How could you not know? the boy asked.

Then he took another deep sigh that reeked of unhappiness.

"Today is my birthday but no one remembered!" said the boy, "Even Ela didn't send a message, she never waited until the morning, she always sent it at midnight!"

Seçkin immediately laid down on the bed and pressed the pillow to his head.

"I'm so lonely!" he groaned miserably.

"And, I am supposed to have a girlfriend! Leave my birthday aside, she didn't even call to ask why I didn't go to school today."

The two jinn looked at each other with worried eyes again.

"Don't you think you worry too much about the little things?" asked ParuParu.

"This is not a small thing, ParuParu! Especially my mother and father... They struggled for eight years of their life until they made me!"

BesuBesu shook her head disapprovingly. Then she looked at her husband and made a hand sign as if to say, "This kid is crazy."

"You'd best go and take a shower, maybe you'll come to your senses, High Master!" said the jinni at last.

"I don't want to take a shower or anything. Leave me alone, I want to sleep!"

And while the jinni turned into opaque smoke, Seçkin closed his eyes. He pondered for a while in the harmoniously fluctuating darkness. There were many voices in his head. He turned from side to side for minutes. He finally gave up. He realized that he couldn't sleep. He got out of bed, grabbed a towel from his closet and headed to the shower.

He walked under the hot water with the pain of being forgotten.

He watched how the bathroom mirror got covered with steam. As the warm water flowed over him and warmed all his bones, Seçkin stood there and thought. Why didn't anyone call or text? If it had been forgotten, wouldn't it be possible for even a few people to remember it? Or were all of them on to something? When Seçkin thought about this, a smile appeared on his face.

"They are definitely planning a surprise for me..." he thought to himself.

Seçkin turned off the tap and got out of the shower with these thoughts in his mind. He dried himself and wrapped the towel around his waist and entered his room. Then he heard that voice.

"Beep beep!"

He stared at his mobile phone with excitement. There was a message. He immediately grabbed his phone and opened the message. It was a number he didn't recognize. Yes, finally someone had wished him a happy birthday:

"Happy Birthday Seçkin!"

Seçkin examined the number once again but did not recognize it. Then he decided to call. He pressed the button and the phone rang.

The call was accepted immediately.

"Hello Seçkin!"

Seçkin's heart started beating like crazy. He knew this voice. It was Burak's calm, soothing voice.

"Burak?" said the boy in surprise.

"It's me… It's been a long time since I heard your voice."

There was a short silence between them.

"Happy birthday Seçkin!" said the boy finally.

"Tha-Thank you…" Seçkin gulped. A warm feeling filled his heart.

"How did you know it was my birthday? How did you find my number?"

A sigh came from the phone.

"I will not answer these questions, Seçkin." said the boy sternly.

Seçkin rolled his eyes.

"Thank you Burak… See you." said the boy afterwards.

"Take care, Seçkin…"

"You too…"

"I love-…"

Seçkin hung up the phone and threw it on the bed. Then he looked at his reflection in the full-length mirrors of his closet.

Did he like Burak's call? He did! So why was he uncomfortable with this situation? So why couldn't he cut off his relationship with Burak altogether? Why did he feel a slight ache inside when he thought of this? What was this feeling of loyalty he felt towards Burak?

Why, why, why?

He examined his hair falling in front of him. Burak was always saying how beautiful his hair was.

Seçkin was suddenly horrified and immediately looked away from the mirrors.

He would never understand what he felt for Burak.

He got dressed. He went downstairs and entered the kitchen. His stomach was growling with hunger. He immediately opened the fridge and took out three eggs. Then cheddar cheese and milk… He also took out a pack of flour and a large deep plate from the kitchen cabinets.

Thus, Seçkin started making an omelette with the grief of loneliness that being forgotten brought upon him.

He broke the eggs, mixed them with flour, added milk, grated the cheese, cooked it and ate it.

Then he collapsed on the couch in the living room and turned on the television.

He watched… He watched… And he watched.

The clock was striking two. His brain was starting to tingle from looking at the TV. His headaches had increased lately. In the evening, his nose bled again.

Seçkin stood up from the couch, his eyes darkened for a moment, and he felt dizzy.

Then he heard the sound of the car parking. He approached the window and peered through the blinds.

His family was here. Seçil had already gotten out of the black Mercedes and ran to the front yard. Then she knocked on the door like crazy.

Seçkin went and opened the door.

"Ugh! Where have you been, abi! I'm about to pee myself!" said the little girl as she ran straight to the toilet. While Seçkin was staring after the girl, his mother appeared at the door. Then his father… They both greeted the boy and then entered.

While Berk Saral was climbing upstairs to change, Bahar Saral walked in to the kitchen.

"What did you eat, son?" the woman asked as she looked at the dishes on the counter.

"I made an omelette, mum!" said the boy, grumbling.

"Why didn't you wake me up in the morning?" he asked, standing in front of the kitchen door and frowning.

"Your father sensed that you woke up several times at night." said the woman.

"He didn't wake you up in the morning because you didn't sleep well at night.

Did you have a nightmare again?"

Seçkin shook his head. "No!"

"I wonder what I should cook today?" the woman whined as she opened the kitchen pantry and examined the legumes.

Seçkin sighed with sorrow.

"Where are my grandparents?"

"Believe me, I have no idea!" said the woman while looking at the packets of beans in her hand.

"Aren't we going to go out tonight?" the boy asked at last.

Bahar Saral stared at her son.

"Why should we go out tonight?"

"Okay…" grumbled Seçkin. "I'm going to my room!"

"What are you going to do in your room?"

"I want to sleep!" Seçkin shouted at last.

"Okay, okay, why are you yelling?" said the woman as she stared after her son.

Seçkin started to climb the stairs, grumbling to himself. He met his father halfway.

"What's going on again?" asked Berk Saral, unable to understand his son's anger.

"There's nothing wrong! Enjoy yourself!" he replied.

The boy immediately snapped at him. Then he went into his room and slammed the door.

Berk Saral shook his head and smiled. Then he continued down the steps.

Seçkin threw himself on the bed and pressed the pillow to his head.

"They just forgot… They forgot!" he groaned to himself.

Then he heard the sound of a car. But it wasn't Mercedes' sound. It was the sound of another car. He didn't get out of bed. He listened to the sounds coming from below.

Some people were running around with excitement.

Then he heard footsteps ascending the stairs.

The door to his room opened and…

"Happy birthday Seçkin! Happy birthday Seçkin!"

Seçil was standing there smiling like a fairy with a cake in her hand.

His mother was looking at her son with tears in her eyes. His father also kept smiling under his moustache.

Seçkin stood frozen for a while. Although his perception capacity faltered for a moment, his smile spread widely across his face.

"Did you think we forgot about you, silly?" Seçil's fairy voice rang out.

"Seçkin, are you going to gawk?" said his mother, "Get up and blow out the candles!"

Seçkin did what his mother said. While his cheeks were blushing in embarrassment, he jumped out of bed, bent over the cake in Seçil's hand and blew out the candles.

"Did you make a wish, abi?" the girl asked excitedly.

"Yes, I did" said Seçkin. He had a family that loved him very much. What more could he want?

"My dear boy!" his mother hugged him. Both of their eyes filled with tears.

"Happy birthday son!" said his father. Then he smiled mischievously.

"How well we deceived you!"

Then Özdemir Bey's voice was heard from downstairs.

"Seçkin! Seçkin, where are you, son?

Seçkin left the room. He ran down the stairs. Özdemir Bey and Nazikter Hanım were standing at the doorstep waiting for him.

"Happy birthday my prince!" said the plump grandmother while kissing her grandson and hugging him.

While the boy got out of the woman's lap and wiped his cheeks, "Happy birthday, son!" said Özdemir Bey. He also hugged his grandchild. "What I wouldn't give to be eighteen!"

Özdemir Bey and his wife's eyes met for a moment. While Seçkin was trying to understand what was happening, the man reached into his pocket and pulled out a car key. The key had a bull crest on it.

"What's going on?" Seçkin said while staring blankly at the key in his grandfather's hand. "This is for you!" said his grandmother

"Your eighteenth birthday present!"

"A car?" said Seçkin in astonishment.

"It's not called a car! Go and see what it is!" said Özdemir Bey.

While Seçkin's heart was pounding, he grabbed the key from his grandfather's hand and sprung out like an arrow. As the fresh spring air filled his lungs, he walked towards the private path of the house, panting... Then he saw it.

A jet-black Lamborghini...

Its paint sparkled so much that it was as if it had tens of thousands of tiny diamonds on it. Its silver rims, combined with the sunlight, dazzled Seçkin.

"Oh my God…" said Seçkin, as his knees buckled for a moment.

"My god! Is this thing mine now?

"Yes… It's yours!" said Özdemir Bey's voice behind the boy.

"Thank you very much, grandfather!" said the boy while hugging the man's neck. "It's beautiful!"

Then Seçil appeared. When she saw the car, her eyes widened in surprise and she let out a musical scream.

"Mum! Dad! Come and see this!"

They both ran into the garden and were stunned by what they saw.

"Dad… Dad, what have you done?" Bahar Saral gulped.

Özdemir Bey shrugged.

"What have I done? My grandson will be a university student soon, so I bought him a car!"

Berk Saral frowned.

"But this is too much, Dad!"

"Not at all!" said the old man while looking at his grandson with a careless love.

"Dad, come and check out inside this!" Seçkin said as he opened the car door and looked inside with admiration. Berk Saral walked towards his son with curiosity he tried not to display.

"I don't understand what's up with him. Can't I buy a car for my grandchild?" the man grumbled as he walked over to his daughter.

"But dad, when you told us, we thought you would buy something simple." said Bahar Saral. "You know, your son-in-law doesn't like showing off."

"I don't care whether he likes it or not! This car belongs to Seçkin!"

"Dad, do you see the front layout of it?" Seçkin said with admiration.

"Isn't it beautiful, abi!" Seçil squealed.

"Its manual gear though!" said Berk Saral, folding his arms and trying to look indifferent. "Seçkin can't drive a manual transmission car!"

"Oh dad! Who said I can't drive!"

"I did! Remember how you constantly stopped the car when driving the Mercedes? said the man patronizingly.

"But I'll learn when I take driving lessons!" the boy replied immediately.

While father and son were arguing with each other, Bahar Saral appeared next to them and handed Seçkin his phone.

"Ela is calling!" said the woman.

Seçkin grabbed the phone with great happiness.

"Hello, Hello Ela?"

"Happy birthday handsome!" said the girl's voice

"You thought we forgot about you, didn't you?"

"You are a traitor, Ela!" said the boy, smiling.

"What could we do, your mother forbade us! She was going to make a surprise."

Seçkin squinted at his mother. The woman waved innocently to her son.

"They did! You need to see what's in front of me right now!"

"What? What's in front of you?" said the girl's voice excitedly.

"Believe me, it cannot be described but only can be experienced!"

"Oh wait!" Ela hassled with someone across the phone, "Seçkin, I'm giving the phone to your girlfriend." She keeps nagging at me!"

"Okay, see you!" said the boy.

"Hello… Seçkin?" rang Defne's fairy voice.

"Happy birthday sweetie!"

"Thank you! Where are you?"

"We are going out for dinner. By the waaaay… We will have a special little celebration for you at the Büyük Han [34] this evening!"

"Really?" Seçkin asked as his eyes opened wide once again.

Then he heard Ayaz's voice from behind.

"Tell your boyfriend not to be late! If he is late, I'll mess him up!"

"Have you heard?" asked Defne.

"I did!" smiled Seçkin. "Then see you in the evening!"

"See you sweetie!" said Defne.

Seçkin hung up the phone and put it in his pocket,

"Mom, there is a celebration at the Büyük Han this evening!" he called out.

"Yes, I know. Your father arranged it!" said the woman while examining the car with Seçil.

---

[34] *Büyük Han: Great Inn, A historical inn located in Nicosia Walled City.*

"My father?" Seçkin was surprised. He immediately turned his head and looked at Berk Saral. The man approached his son and hugged him.

"You thought I wasn't going to do anything on my son's eighteenth birthday?" he said proudly.

"You are my one and only son!"

"Happy Birthday Prince Sapphire!"

"Long live the Prince!"

Fireworks were shining over the Holy Kingdom's castle. Everyone was lighting wishing lanterns and releasing them into the sky for their prince's eighteenth birthday. Prince Sapphire lit a balloon and made his wish, then watched the balloon slide from his hands and rise into the sky.

There were cheers and applause everywhere. There was a great festive atmosphere in the kingdom. Even the jinn, who had recently gone through a dark rebellion, seemed happy. Some lost their wives; some lost their babies to Hematite's evil army. But passing of time was erasing their pain.

"Happy birthday son!" said a hoarse voice from the portico balcony. The prince took his eyes off the commotion beneath the balcony and turned around. An old female jinni was standing there looking at him with compassion.

"NejuNeju," said the Prince. He ran and immediately hugged the female jinni.

"My dear wet nurse! How nice to see you!"

NejuNeju smiled bitterly. She had baby ParuParu in her arms.

"My dear son, you don't know how happy it makes me that you have grown up to become such a strong and handsome prince!" said the jinni.

"I lost my son to the Devil. What I only have left is the baby in my arms and you!"

"I won't tell you not to be sad... Because I know it is meaningless. Those who don't experience the pain of losing a child can't understand. But never worry about ParuParu, I will always be there for him."

"I know… You are a great prince, my dear son!" said the jinni, looking gratefully at the prince. The prince took the baby from NejuNeju's arms. ParuParu opened his eyes for a moment. A sweet smile appeared on his face as he looked at the prince for a short moment with his big blue eyes and closed his eyes.

Then the Fairy Princess appeared.

"Can I come?" she asked politely.

The prince extended his hand invitingly to his one and only love. The beautiful Princess of Fairies approached her prince with excitement and held his hand, "Look, my darling! "He's such a sweet baby, isn't he?"

Lal smiled.

"Yes… Look at this little nose!"

Several more fireworks exploded in the sky. Then Princess Lal smiled.

"I have a gift for you!"

The prince smiled too.

"I wonder what it is? Is it a fairy-made shield?

Lal shook his head. Amidst the surprised looks of the prince, she took ParuParu and handed it to NejuNeju. Then she winked at the jinni. NejuNeju nodded and smiled in agreement.

Princess Lal looked at the sky. "Do you see those two stars arranged one under the other over there, my darling?" asked the princess.

Prince Sapphire turned his gaze to the stars in the southeast.

"Yes, they are our stars, aren't they?"

"Yes…" Princess Lal confirmed with an excited smile on her face.

Then she took Prince Sapphire's hand and brought it to her belly. Something moved in the Princess's belly.

"A new star will be added there very soon!" said the princess.

The Prince's heart accelerated with excitement. He forgot to breathe for a moment.

"You mean?"

Princess Lal smiled and nodded.

"Yes darling… You will be a father soon!"The Prince wrapped the Fairy Princess in his strong arms and spun her in the air while his eyes were shining with great happiness…

"I love you… I love you… I love you…"

NejuNeju let out a tearful sigh. Her big blue eyes were filled with tears and she smiled.

"May the Supreme Creator protect you!"

"Wow!" moaned Ayaz. "I swear I am jealous of you. What the hell is that?"

"My car that I haven't been able to use yet!" sighed Seçkin. They were in the Büyük Han. They were outside examining the black Lamborghini.

"I want a grandfather like yours!" said Can immediately.

"Man, if I had a grandfather like that, I would wash his feet every day!" said Ayaz.

Ela and Defne appeared in the doorway.

"What are you doing here?" said Defne. "Come on in, everyone is asking about you, Seçkin!"

"Okay, we're coming!" said Seçkin.

"Oh…" Ela said as she looked inside the car and took a deep breath. She still couldn't get used to seeing it.

"If I had a car like this, I would definitely have a heart attack!"

Seçkin and his friends entered inside leaving the black car behind. The golden light in the stone building was warming hearts.

All of Seçkin's loved ones were sitting at a long table: His mother, father, grandmother, grandfather, Seçil, Mine, Duru, Bora, Mert. Even Sahra was there. She tied her Cleopatra like fringed hair in a ponytail and wore a floral dress.

As Seçkin watched each of them with love, he felt someone missing.

Burak…

He should have been here too. He was rude to him every time. However, Burak cared for him. He loved him.

Seçkin sighed deeply with regret. He hugged Defne and placed a kiss on her cheek. His family officially testified that the two were together that night. Although Berk Saral was in shock for a moment, it did not last long. He softened immediately with the contribution of red wine and Bahar Saral. Everyone was eating their food, drinking their wine and singing.

Seçkin felt so happy and at peace for the first time in a long while. Neither a car nor anything else expensive was important to him. The most valuable gift for him was being with his loved ones. Then he heard a familiar voice in the chaos.

"Snap"

He escaped from Defne's arms and immediately jumped to his feet.

"What happened, Seçkin?" asked Defne. Everyone stared at him in shock.

"Nothing!" said Seçkin "I left my phone in the car!"

Then he heard BesuBesu's voice.

"High Master… High Master, I am outside!"

Seçkin left everyone behind and immediately went out of Büyük Han. He stood in front of the huge wooden door and looked around, there was no one there. Then the female jinni appeared behind the opaque smoke. Her eyes were red from crying.

"BesuBesu, what is going on, what is it?" Seçkin asked, turning pale in horror. "ParuParu! Sir! My husband was attacked!"

-CHAPTER XIV-

The First to Fall

"Come on ParuParu! A little more!" said BesuBesu sadly. They were in the blue bedroom. ParuParu collapsed on the armchair there. He was covered in wounds and bruises.

"Are you okay, ParuParu?" Seçkin asked once again. His hands were still shaking. He was so used to this faithful jinni that the thought of losing him wrecked his nerves even more.

"I am fine, High Master." replied the jinni in a voice barely above a whisper.

"How did all this happen, ParuParu?" Ayaz asked while examining the swellings on the jinni's hands and feet.

"I went to the grove to speak with Queen Laverna, sir, but I could not find her. And then…"

The jinni paused. His eyes widened in horror.

"Then I saw the crows perched on the cypress tree there. After looking at me for a moment with those red beady eyes, they flew towards me, then they turned into gufi snakes and attacked me from all around."

Ayaz's lips tightened.

"I know that pain." he said while touching the wound on his face.

Seçkin patted the boy on the shoulder.

"Thanks to the Supreme Creator you told me where you were going. I'm glad I got up and followed you." said BesuBesu wearily while she was bringing the golden syrup shining in a glass bottle in her hand closer to ParuParu.

ParuParu shook his head reluctantly.

"Come on ParuParu, if you don't drink this syrup your wounds won't heal!" Seçkin whined.

"But it's disgusting!" ParuParu grimaced.

Key jingling was heard below, from the mahogany entrance door of the house. The door opened with a twist.

"SEÇKİN!" roared his father's voice.

"Abi!" Seçil called as she climbed the stairs. "Abi, where are you?"

Seçkin heard a light "Snap!" sound again as the two jinn immediately turned into smoke.

The opaque smoke had immediately dispersed in the room when Seçil rushed in in terror.

"Abi!" rang the girl's voice as she entered the room, out of breath. She looked back and forth at Seçkin and Ayaz.

"What are you two up to?"

Berk Saral appeared behind the little girl. He burst into the room in anger, frowning and crossing his arms across his chest.

"I'm waiting for an explanation!" said the man.

Berk Saral went crazy as soon as Seçkin got the news and disappeared, taking Ayaz with him. The joyful celebration was overshadowed by anger. Seçkin, on the other hand, grabbed Ayaz and came home without even looking back.

Seçkin looked at Ayaz with helpless eyes. Then he lowered his head to the ground.

"I can't tell you, dad!" he replied sullenly. 'I'm sorry!'

"How can you not tell? Seçkin Saral!" Berk Saral fumed.

"Everyone was there for you. What did you do, abandon us all and run away! You have done a great disgrace to everyone, Seçkin!"

While Seçkin's eyes were filled with tears for a moment, Ayaz intervened.

"Believe me, he had to do it, sir!" said the boy, supporting his friend.

Berk Saral did not speak. He looked at his son and Ayaz for a while.

"I don't understand what you two are up to, but if you get into trouble, don't let me see you," said the man, looking at the boys with threatening eyes. Then he slammed the door and left the room.

"Looks like we had a near miss, huh?" asked Ayaz. He sat next to Seçkin and put his arm around the boy's shoulder.

"Come on man, don't sulk!"

"I'm tired now, Ayaz! I'm tired of keeping up with everyone..."

Then the boy's phone rang.

Seçil immediately grabbed her brother's phone from the bedside table and looked at the screen.

"Defne is calling." said the little girl while grimacing and then handed the phone to Seçkin.

Seçil was still very jealous of Defne. After seeing this, Seçkin accepted the fact that his sister could not share him with any other girl. There wasn't much he could do for now except to hope that she would give up this habit as she got older.

"He... Hello?"

"Seçkin?" said Defne, with her fairy-like voice.

Defne's voice felt like medicine to Seçkin for a moment.

"Seçkin? Are you there?" called Defne from the phone.

"Yes!" said Seçkin with excitement. He winked at Seçil, who was looking at him with frowned eyebrows. Ayaz looked at the little girl and stuck out his tongue.

"Where did you go and left us like that? "What the hell were you two doing?"

Seçkin started pacing in his room, not knowing what to do. This was something he usually did when he was talking to Defne on the phone. He was trying so hard not to say the wrong thing, not to stutter, and not to go crazy with excitement. Now he didn't even have the slightest idea how to answer Defne's interrogations.

Seçil and Ayaz were also looking at the boy pacing up and down in the room.

Seçkin had always been bad at talking on the phone anyway. He had repeatedly insisted to Defne that they should communicate through messenger, but she had talked about a dozen nonsense explaining that talking on the phone was better for their relationship.

"Whatever…" said the girl, a little upset when she didn't get a response from Seçkin.

"It's obvious that you're up to something. But anyway, I won't push it... What time were we going to meet tomorrow?

Seçkin couldn't understand what his girlfriend meant for a while. But soon he remembered.

He promised to meet her in Girne[35] tomorrow. After a nice meal, they would go down to the harbour.

"Now I'm in real trouble," thought the boy. His mind began to work rapidly. He tried to carefully list the words he would use in his brain.

He laughed lightly, mirthlessly.

"Well... Darling, I think it wouldn't be bad if we postponed our meeting tomorrow." he said. His velvet voice was soothing and calm.

There was a short silence on the phone. Then Defne spoke with her fairy-like voice.

"Why?"

"I am not feeling well." said Seçkin.

This was true.

"Hmmm…" said Defne. The girl's voice lowered.

"We can go out the next day. What do you think?" the boy asked desperately.

"I don't know... We can go out if I feel good."

The emphasis in her voice clearly showed that she was retaliating against Seçkin.

"Don't do this!" muttered the boy. "You know I can't stand being away from you. I would definitely come tomorrow if I could. But I'm really not well."

---

[35] *Girne: Kyrenia / It is one of the five largest cities in Northern Cyprus. It is a coastal city.*

"Okay Seçkin. "I didn't say anything anyway." said Defne. Her voice was starting to sound better. It was soft and charming like a fairy.

"I love you so much!" said Seçkin immediately like a naughty child.

Defne sighed slightly.

"Oh Seçkin, you will never grow up, will you?" said Defne and added. "I love you too, crazy kid!"

When Seçkin hung up the phone, Ayaz looked blankly at his friend's face and applauded him.

"Your relationship has just begun and you started to ditch the girl already, man!" he said disapprovingly.

"That's true abi, why didn't you want to meet?" Seçil asked, her eyes widening in surprise. Seçkin shrugged.

"Because we have things to do with Ayaz tomorrow!"

"I still don't understand what we're doing here this early in the morning!" grumbled Ayaz as he climbed the slope, out of breath.

"Did you think I would leave those who attacked ParuParu unpunished?" Seçkin replied immediately.

The morning sun was shining sweetly overhead. The lush green grass was starting to turn yellow due to the increasing heat.

"Pull yourself together, man!" said Ayaz. "What if this is a trap?"

"I don't care! I will make those jinni regret what they did!"

"I wonder what you are going to do! Are you going to throw stones at them?

Seçkin paused. Ayaz was telling the truth. What could he do against those evil creatures? He had no special powers.

"Have you forgotten this scar on my face?" said Ayaz. "Do you want to have a matching one?"

For a moment, Seçkin seemed to give up. But then he suddenly accelerated angrily towards the grove again.

"Enough! Whatever happens, happens!"

"What the fuck! I swear to God, you have lost your mind!"

When they both entered the grove, they looked around. A few crows were perched on one of the cypress trees surrounding the grove. As soon as they saw the boys, they started cawing.

"Caw… Caw…"

"Look, there they are!" said Seçkin. While pointing at the crows.

The boy was mad with anger and walked towards the tree with fire in his eyes. He bent down, picked up a few stones and threw them at the crows.

"You fucking freaks!"

"Seçkin! Stop, man!" Ayaz stared at the boy in horror.

While the crows were cawing, they spread their wings over the tree and flew towards the boy like arrows.

"Seçkin! They're coming at us!" said Ayaz in a shaky voice. One of them began to slowly change shape.

Its eyes widened, ears protruded and got longer, ribs splayed out, and wings appeared like a veil over its protruding ribs. A heretic jinni brutally jumped on Seçkin.

"You will die!" cried the jinni in his crow-like voice.

While Ayaz took out his slingshot from his pocket and aimed at the creature, there was a sound of "Snap!" in the grove.

Heretic jinn

ParuParu and his wife came out of the opaque smoke.

A golden light flashed. It hit the creature that tried to bite Seçkin. The creature's body stiffened and fell backwards.

"How dare you attack our High Master!" chimed ParuParu.

"You filthy sinner!"

Afterwards, a fire-red dragonfly appeared out of thin air in the grove. A blinding light flashed and Queen Laverna's form appeared.

She immediately walked in front of Seçkin and took the boy under her wing.

"Get out of here, you heretic jinni!"

"Queen Laverna!" murmured ParuParu as he looked at the Queen of Fairies with admiration. The Queen blew her hand and the sparkles in her hand flew towards the heretics. The sparkles then turned into a strong wind that swept them from the grove.

Are you okay, High Master? You're not injured, are you?" asked ParuParu.

"I am good!" said Seçkin, while smearing the crazy jinni's saliva on his hands to his trousers with disgust.

"Queen Laverna!" ParuParu called out, then enchanted, "What an honour to see you!"

He and his wife approached the queen and knelt before her.

The Queen of Fairies smiled fondly.

"Is this brave faithful jinni KarlaKarla's grandson?"

ParuParu immediately nodded, grinning happily.

"I am ParuParu. This is my wife, BesuBesu ma'am!"

"It's an honour to stand in front of you, my Fairy Queen!" said BesuBesu, bowing down to the floor.

"Please stand up…" said Laverna. "I would like to chat with loyal jinni like you as soon as possible!"

The two faithful jinn stood up proudly.

While the queen touched the wound on the faithful jinni's cheek in horror, she said, "ParuParu, what are those wounds on you?" she asked.

"The heretics, my Fairy Queen... I came here yesterday to meet you and the heretics attacked me! But I am fine now!" replied ParuParu.

"Thanks to the Supreme Creator you are okay!" said the Queen.

ParuParu looked at Laverna for a long time and sighed. Then his eyes filled with tears.

"You don't know how much I prayed to see you!" said the faithful jinni while his tears wet his cheeks.

"I am so happy to see someone from where I belong."

Hot…

The weather was very hot indeed. It was this hot even in May. There was no trace left of the sweet spring. Thermometers showed forty Celsius degrees. While the situation was already like this, no one could even think about what it would be like in August.

Despite his father's objections, Seçkin attended accelerated driving lessons and received his driver's license within a week. He was finally able to drive his Lamborghini. He even took Defne out for dinner a few nights. Of course, Bahar

Saral hourly called to check whether her son was in one piece.

Although he felt like cars were coming at him and he had small panic attacks the first nights when he was driving alone, he later got used to it. He was now a fearless Lamborghini driver.

The weather was gloomy again that afternoon. A red mist was floating around like a whirlpool, and a hellish heat was added to it.

Seçkin felt like he was locked in a cage again. He was sitting on the worn-out steps, waiting for the play rehearsals to end. There were a few days left until the play. The song sung by the Romeo and Juliet chorus added to the gloom in the school. Those tones, those melodies. It was like the echoing pleas in the middle of a terrible war.

Seçkin sighed deeply in sorrow.

"This heat is not a good sign," he thought to himself. The Devil was getting stronger and stronger in his lair.

A war was coming, but he didn't know what to do as the Promised One. While the boy was struggling with these thoughts, he felt the presence of someone next to him. When he turned around, Sahra was there. She was sitting next to him, looking at him with sad eyes.

"Sahra?" Seçkin's voice murmured, looking at him with questioning eyes. "Shouldn't you be in the choir?"

Sahra closed her eyes. She looked even stranger than ever.

"My time is up." she said in a whisper. Then she opened her eyes wide. She had a distressed expression on her face. "The trumpet will sound very soon!"

"A trumpet?"

Seçkin stared blankly at the girl's face. Okay. Sahra had spoken strangely before, but this time it seemed familiar to Seçkin...

"You are one of them, too…" said the boy.

"But what's going on?"

Sahra suddenly stood up. She extended her hand to Seçkin and said, "Come with me!"

Seçkin held Sahra's hand in surprise. The girl's hands were cold as ice. It was as if the cold of the passing winter had settled into her hands.

They went up the steps together. They walked towards the first-floor corridor. Seçkin's heartbeat was getting faster with each passing second. The pessimistic song sung by the choir downstairs was also echoing in the corridor. Seçkin got chills as he walked down this corridor accompanied by this song. He still couldn't understand what was happening. Sahra looked very unhappy and stagnant. She acted as if she didn't belong to this world.

The girl stopped in the middle of the corridor. She looked at Seçkin and smiled sadly.

"It's time…"

Seçkin stiffened. A beam of light filtered through the large window at the end of the corridor and illuminated Sahra. Then another... And another... The lights increased and became blinding. Sahra turned into a white dove and flew along the corridor and disappeared.

When Seçkin opened his eyes again, he was standing in the same place, but this place looked a little different. The paint on the walls was clean and not peeling. The marble was shining brightly. Colourful pictures were carefully hung on the walls. The colour of the surroundings was like the old movies. It was dusty... The bell rang loudly...

Seçkin's heart jumped.

Students left the classroom and rushed into the corridor. It was like they were all the same. The boys had ties and jackets.

The girls wore skirts and cardigans that went down to their knees. Their uniforms were neat as a pin.

Then a girl got out of one of the classrooms into the hallway. Her skin was like silk. She had long brown hair. She was beautiful. She looked so familiar to Seçkin that he just stood there, staring at her. As the girl walked down the corridor, another girl came out of the classroom and followed her. She was plump and smiling.

"Bahar!" the plump girl called after the girl who came out first.

Seçkin suddenly froze.

"But how can this happen?" he asked himself. His heart was pounding. He was now just a few steps away from her mother's younger version. He pulled himself together and quickly followed them.

"Mum!" he called after the girls, but no one heard him. He was neither heard nor seen.

"She can't hear you." said Sahra's voice from somewhere.

"Why?" Seçkin asked helplessly.

"Because it's my memory…"

When young Bahar Saral reached to the end of the corridor, Seçkin followed her.

"She will never forgive me!" rang the girl's voice.

The plump girl next to her shrugged with a distress expression.

Seçkin could barely hear the voices of those two around the groups of students.

Bahar Başarı

"Forget about it, Bahar!" said the plump girl, looking at her friend with big, cute eyes.

"Miss Derin?" Seçkin asked himself. Oh my God, that girl was her. It was Derin Zade.

Seçkin continued walking after the two young girls. Bahar ran down the clean, shiny steps of the stairs and went into the school garden.

The schoolyard was as neat and clean as Seçkin had ever seen. The garden, which is now surrounded by weeds, was adorned with lush green grass, colourful flowers and fresh citrus trees.

After looking around in surprise for a blink of an eye, Seçkin noticed the young man standing next to a beautiful granite ornamental pool with flowing water. The moment the boy saw Bahar, his eyes sparkled. He opened his arms invitingly towards her and grinned charmingly.

As Bahar approached this handsome young man, Seçkin followed behind her. The marble of that ornamental pool, which had been dysfunctional for as long as he saw it, was now shining and filled with flowing clear water.

Derin Tayane

Seçkin sighed with envy. For a moment, the desire to live in the past rose within him. Then he carefully watched the handsome young man's behaviour.

He was his father's younger self. Seçkin looked so much like him. Derin Zade was very right. No matter how much he resembled his mother, the charisma in his stance was exactly like his father's.

"Sweetie!" young Berk Saral called to the girl.

"Sweetie?" sighed Seçkin. For a moment, his father's teenage behaviour seemed very funny to him.

"Why are you looking sad?" the boy asked. The girl pursed her lips. Young girl escaped from Berk Saral's arms and looked at the flowing ornamental pool.

"Ezgi… She will never forgive me!" murmured young Bahar Saral.

The boy frowned.

"I still can't believe this issue upsets you."

"Ezgi is right!" said the girl.

"She's not right at all. Okay, she might have feelings for me, but what's important is my feelings for her. I love you Bahar! "No one can change this."

Young Bahar Saral smiled for a moment.

"But I betrayed her. I was with you knowing that she had feelings for you. I had to resist my heart. Ezgi was my best friend. I lost her." A few drops of tears fell from the girl's eyes.

While Seçkin was trying to understand what was going on, a red mist appeared and surrounded young Bahar and Berk

Saral. A terrible howl rose in Seçkin's ear, and then the scene suddenly changed.

Suddenly, Seçkin found himself in the school corridor again. The corridor was empty and silent. Suddenly, a girl jumped out of one of the classrooms, passed through Seçkin and headed towards the girls' toilet.

"Sahra?" Seçkin whispered and followed her. The green wooden door of the girls' bathroom creaked open. Seçkin was coming here for the first time. The only difference from the men's restroom was that there were no urinals.

Ezgi

The girl took out a golden key hanging around her neck.

She looked at the key for a short moment and then angrily threw it to the ground. Then she took out a rope she had previously hidden and hung it from the ceiling, accompanied by Seçkin's meaningless gaze.

"Sahra, what are you doing?" Seçkin asked. He tried to stop her, but when he touched her, it was like he was touching smoke.

The girl neither saw nor heard him. She climbed on the toilet, put her head in the circle of the rope and released her feet.

The girl's body trembled for a short time under Seçkin's horrified gaze, and then she remained standing on the rope.

"Sahraaaa!" the boy shouted at the top of his lungs. Then the scene changed again.

Seçkin was standing in the hallway, in front of the door to the girls' bathroom.

There were old teachers and students gathered there. Young Bahar Saral was crying in the arms of her lover.

Young Berk Saral and Derin Zade were consoling him.

The toilet door creaked open and the staff took out a body covered with a white sheet on a stretcher.

"Ezgi…" sobbed young Bahar Saral with tears in her eyes.

They disappeared out of the corridor, amidst the horrified looks of teachers and students.

While Seçkin was staring after them, a few beams of light reached from the window at the end of the corridor and illuminated the boy.

A ray of light appeared again in the large window at the end of the corridor. A silhouette emerged from the bright light.

As the light began to fade, the image of Sahra appeared.

She was in a long dress with a white hood. Her eyes looked like they were enchanted. Her skin was shining as if there were thousands of crystals on it. A golden key hung around her neck.

Seçkin remembered her. This was Sahra he had seen in his dreams months ago.

"Sahra?" whispered the boy in surprise.

"It's me…" Sahra said while looking at the boy and smiling sweetly. Her eyes were not sad. They looked so vivacious. They were even shining.

"But that's not my real name. Sahra is just a character I created!

"My name in your world is Ezgi! My real name is Amber!"

"I don't understand anything you say!" said Seçkin with empty eyes.

"Once upon a time, I too lived in the Kingdom of the Morningstar… I was guarding the gate of the kingdom…"

The girl's enchanted eyes saddened.

"After that night when the Devil attacked the kingdom, the fairies spent all their strength and cast a spell. "They sent the prince, princess and their guardians back to the world to be born centuries later… But there was a warp in time and I fell into the world before everyone else."

Seçkin froze. He continued to listen to the girl, dazed.

"For years, I felt like I had a duty somewhere. I felt like there was a purpose for me being born into this world. But I didn't know how to do this… How could I know anyway… I had fallen before everyone else… What I needed to find did not even exist in the world yet… But that urge inside me always confused me. Do you understand? And then…"

"And then?" Seçkin said with great curiosity. Sahra looked at the boy with admiration and sighed deeply.

"I fell in love…" said the girl in white.

"There was a very handsome young man at school. I fell madly in love with him. But I never mentioned it. My only supporter in these difficult days was your mother. But it turns out that she was in love with that young man, too…"

"Did you fall in love with my father?" The boy's eyes opened wide.

The girl lowered her head and exhaled regretfully.

"Yes… I was thoroughly confused. One day, a carnival crew came and set up tents in the swan park for a few weeks. The carnival fortune teller paid too much attention to me. I trusted her and even became her apprentice for a while. I told her about my one and only love. She said she would help me. She was going to cast a spell that would replace Bahar's soul with mine. The moment I heard this, I got crazy excited. Just think, the body of a beautiful, perfect girl like Bahar would be mine. I followed what she said. I hung myself in the girls' bathroom. I waited for my soul to enter Bahar's body, but it didn't happen. I died. When I opened my eyes with the pain of sin, I was looking at my own hanged body. I was deceived. I had fallen for the trick of a heretic jinni. It turns out that they influenced that witch to get rid of me..."

The girl sighed deeply.

"I am Amber... the Keeper of the Kingdom of the Morningstar... I fell into this world before anyone else and lived without knowing my true identity and duty. I sinned for the sake of love. My soul is cursed. I could neither enter the gates of Heaven nor Hell... I always remained in Purgatory. I spent twenty-six years imprisoned in this corridor. This is my Purgatory... I couldn't leave the borders of this school. I waited patiently without being seen by anyone for years for the Promised One to be born."

The girl smiled.

"Thanks to the Supreme Creator, finally the Promised One stands before me. I bow respectfully before you…" And she slowly pulled her dress and bent her knees gracefully.

"Do you know why I fell in love with your father? I was born to find the Promised One. And the Promised One was his seed. I am your first guide from the sons of Adam. But the time given to me is up," said the girl sadly. Seçkin swallowed. He felt as if his throat was in knots. Sahra was a soul. She was a reflection of a memory in a half body. Ezgi was the rebirth of the first fallen protector in our world in another body.

Standing in front of him was Amber. The essence of Sahra and Ezgi… The guardian of the great gate of the Kingdom of the Morningstar… Also, the guide of the Promised One from sons of Adam…

"Will I ever see you again?" Seçkin asked as his eyes filled with tears.

"My soul was cleansed from that curse. Your love purified my soul. Now, I will go and take a deep rest next to the Supreme Creator behind the seven skies to relieve my twenty-six years of fatigue..."

"Don't go… Don't leave me!" sobbed Seçkin. The girl lovingly caressed the boy's cheek.

"One day we will meet again, Promised One."

With a shining beam of light, the girl turned into a snow-white dove and flapped her wings. Then she disappeared into the sparkling world of the window.

Seçkin felt his feet leaving the ground. He was thrown away for a moment and reappeared in front of the damp corridor with crumbling walls...

"Goodbye Sahra…" the boy said to himself.

"Farewell my friend…"

That night, Seçkin couldn't sleep. As he tossed and turned in his bed, he constantly thought of Sahra. Which was Ezgi. Which was Amber… Seçkin was still confused. How many different people can one person be?

Then he took a deep breath and then something came to his mind.

He remembered the box in which he had found the silver pocket watch months ago. When that brass box in his mother's closet fell to the floor and revealed all her privacy, Seçkin had seen some photographs. There was a brunette girl with black hair in those photos.

Could it be Sahra? Yes. It was probably her. He got out of bed and walked into the hallway. Everyone was asleep. While he was trying to figure out how to sneak into his parents' room and get that brass box without waking them up, he heard a "Snap" sound.

"Are you going somewhere, High Master?" asked the faithful jinni behind him.

"Are you following me, ParuParu?" Seçkin whispered, frowning.

"Sir, I have noticed something strange about you since you came from school today. "I feel like there's something you're not telling me." said the jinni.

A thought immediately came to Seçkin's mind.

"ParuParu you are a jinni!" said the boy as he turned to the tiny man.

The jinni shook his head in surprise.

"Yes, sir. I am a jinni!"

Seçkin smiled.

"Yes, I know that." said the boy. "ParuParu, if I ask you for something, would you do it?" he asked then. The jinni's deep blue eyes sparkled.

"Whatever you wish, High Master!"

"Good!" Seçkin nodded. "There's a brass biscuit box on top of my mother's closet! I want that box. ParuParu, bring that to me."

But before Seçkin finished speaking, ParuParu turned into an opaque smoke. After a heartbeat, he returned with the box in his hand.

"There!" said ParuParu happily while handing the box to the boy. "Here you go, sir!"

The boy's eyes sparkled with admiration.

"Oh ParuParu! You are amazing!"

The jinni shook his head sheepishly ashamedly. For a moment, his cheeks turned red.

While holding the box carefully as if he were holding a newly discovered treasure, Seçkin returned to his room and sank down on the couch.

He opened the box…

Inside were dusty photographs from the eighties.

Seçkin's prediction was correct. The girl in the photos was Sahra. Which was Ezgi. Which was Amber.

She looked so cute and full of life. Her eyes shone in a sweet sparkle rather than looking sad. The only thing she had that didn't change was her hair. She was like how Seçkin knew her. She had a strange style, black hair, straight and with bangs.

Seçkin smiled sadly as she examined the photos. His mother and Ezgi were once really good friends.

Then he took the leather-bound notebook under the photographs and unlocked it.

This was Ezgi's diary... While Seçkin was randomly turning the pages, she was writing about her deep love for Berk Saral on every page of the notebook. She was telling how this hopeless love was messing her up day by day.

Seçkin finally sighed and closed the notebook as tears welled in his eyes.

He understood her very well. Who could know the pain of hopeless love better than him? He put the notebook and photographs back and closed the lid of the brass box.

"ParuParu!" he said, amidst the curious gaze of the jinni.

"Can you take this box back to its place, please?" he asked sadly.

"I'm sorry, High Master, but I won't go anywhere before you tell me what's making you so sad!" said the faithful jinni, lifting his chin up determinedly.

Seçkin smiled woefully.

"Today I met my guide from the sons of Adam!" Seçkin said as a tear fell from his eyes and flowed down his cheeks.

"But she left me…"

-CHAPTER XV-
The Secret

As the days passed, word spread about Princess Lal's pregnancy. Joy at the news of the heir spread throughout the kingdom. The people overwhelmed the Princess with gifts. Festivities were held for days for the sole heir of the Kingdom of the Morningstar.

Ally kingdoms were invited to the Kingdom of the Morningstar for the festivities. On that beautiful spring day, there were people coming from the Faraway Land. While Prince Sapphire was watching the view that unfolded before him on the cloistered balcony, he was waiting for his childhood friends Okalper and Mel, whom he missed so much.

"My prince, they are coming!" said a brunette girl in white, running to the balcony. She was shining as if there were thousands of Crystals on her skin. "The horse carriage can be seen!"

"Let's greet them!" said Prince Sapphire excitedly.

Amber bowed her head in approval and turned into a snow white dove and flapped her wings. Then, when she reached the gate of the kingdom, she set foot on the ground again in human form.

Soon the golden carriage pulled by alicorns landed in front of the entrance gate of the palace. The carriage door opened and Okalper walked out with all his congeniality. Amber raised her wand and bowed down to the floor respectfully.

"It is an honour to see you again, my king." said Amber, dressed in white.

"Likewise, Keeper of the Great Gate of the Kingdom of the Morningstar."

Time was ticking for everyone. Okalper ascended to the throne after the death of his elderly father. He was now the King of the Faraway Land.

Queen Mel got out of the carriage with all her dignity, after him. And Prince Sapphire appeared at the door.

"Okalper…Mel…" he said eagerly while running towards them.

"Welcome to the Kingdom of Morningstar, my friends." he said and hugged them.

"Where is Princess Lal?" Queen Mel asked.

"She is waiting for you in the dining hall." said Prince Sapphire with a smile.

"Let's go!" said King Okalper. "I'm hungry as a wolf, chief!"

Thus, the three friends passed through the Garden of Eden, where the majestic waterfall flowed, and went up to the palace. When they arrived at the palace, Vermeil and the Nephilim respectfully greeted the King and Queen of the Faraway Land. Then Okalper hugged Vermeil.

"Nice to see you, my angel-winged friend." he said sincerely. And they arrived at the dining hall.

The huge oak door swung open. Under the warm golden light, the beautiful Princess Lal appeared... She was standing next to the table, which was decorated with a variety of beautiful food, with all her grace.

"We have guests from far away, my darling," said Prince Sapphire.

Princess Lal smiled and approached them. She bowed gracefully.

"Welcome, dear King and Queen of the Faraway Land. "You honoured our kingdom."

"The honour is ours, our beautiful princess," said Queen Mel.

Princess Lal's eyes met King Okalper's.

"Unbelievable!" said King Okalper excitedly.

"I should have realized it was you," he said with a smile.

"Those green eyes… They remind me of someone."

Princess Lal also smiled.

"When I first saw you at the wedding, I was suspicious, but I wasn't sure…"

While Prince Sapphire and Queen Mel were trying to understand what was happening, King Okalper knelt in front of the Princess with admiration.

"I bow in honour and respect to our brave princess who saved us from the planet of Anisoptera many years ago." said King Okalper.

Prince Sapphire sighed in admiration and surprise.

"You remember, don't you, Sapphire?" asked King Okalper.

"Many years ago, I told you about that mysterious person with green eyes."

"Yes," said Prince Sapphire as he nodded.

"That was your dear wife, brother... We all owe her our lives."

Princess Lal's eyes filled with tears.

"Oh Lal..." murmured Prince Sapphire with admiration.

"I wonder how many more times you will surprise me…"

Then he held his wife's hands and kissed them with admiration.

"How strange is this thing they call fate, that girl who took us out of the dungeon is now in front of me and she is pregnant with your baby." said King Okalper as he got up and patted Sapphire on the shoulder.

"Since my childhood, I have always watched the kingdom on earth from Anisoptera. I was so curious about that place that one day I secretly went down to earth. I saw the handsome prince of that place. I fell in love with him as soon as I saw him. But we were so convinced that the people living in this kingdom were murderers that I buried my love in my heart." said Princess Lal. "But thanks to the Supreme Creator, that handsome prince is now my husband and I am carrying his child."

"How beautiful you are…" said King Okalper. "I'm happy to have friends like you."

"Please sit down, my king," said Princess Lal. "We have prepared the most delicious meals for you."

They all sat at the table together. They chatted, joked, and ate their meals with pleasure.

"I don't know if I would be as patient as you," said Queen Mel, smiling at Princess Lal. "It must be very difficult to watch the man you love from afar for years."

Princess Lal sighed deeply and looked at her husband.

"It was nice to know about his existence, even from afar…"

"Loving someone and not being able to tell them for years… It's not for me." said Queen Mel.

"Yes, we know!" King Okalper burst out laughing.

"Do you know? Mel proposed to me at my sick father's bedside."

"If it was up to you, it would take longer, my dear king." Queen Mel shrugged.

"Your father also saw your unison before he died."

"If I had seen that Okalper was getting married in my dreams, I would not have believed it." said Prince Sapphire.

"And even before you, my dear prince." Prince Okalper smiled mischievously.

"But you see, I am becoming a father before you, my dear brother," said Prince Sapphire, raising one eyebrow mischievously.

"We have to start working on it immediately, Mel!" said King Okalper.

And laughter surrounded the hall.

"Fortunately, you will wear the King's Crown soon after you become a father, brother." said King Okalper.

"It is said that after you become king, the Supreme Creator will grant you immortality. Is it true?" Queen Mel asked.

"Yes…" said Prince Sapphire. "In the Kingdom of the Morningstar, the prince who has a baby wears the King's Crown. The King's Crown is endowed with immortality."

"Wow, chief!" said King Okalper.

Now we will have an immortal King behind us! "What wars we will fight with you!"

"I prefer peace…" Prince Sapphire smiled.

"Have you decided on what to name the baby?" Queen Mel asked excitedly.

Prince Sapphire and Princess Lal looked at each other and smiled.

"Living Being," said Prince Sapphire with delight. "It will be such a name that it will be admired by all kingdoms …"

"So, it means Living Being!" said King Okalper.

"What a beautiful soul will be born…"

While they were happily eating their food and continuing to chat, there were dark shadows lurking somewhere in the distance. So much so that this festive atmosphere in the kingdom did not seem to last for long…

Seçkin's head fell on the desk, while he was sleeping soundly. The "Good night" message that was sent by Defne at midnight was still flickering on the computer screen.

There were dozens of sketches scribbled down on papers that were now under the boy's cheek. Figures with curly hair were drawn on the papers. They were drawn from profile and resembled figures on Greek vases. They had a statuesque pallor. Some were drawn as a fairy, some as a crying clown, and some as a witch.

But the most eye-catching of these sketches was a blue sketch that had *"three apples fell from the sky"* written on it. Curly-haired mermaids and mermen were chasing three apples under the sea.

This drawing was going to be Seçkin's graduation project in art class. If Seçkin could not finish this painting within a month, Özden Atakol wouldn't let him pass the lesson. She said this to Seçkin the last time she met him, while the old woman was glaring at the boy over her glasses and shaking her finger at him threateningly. And she was right. Because Seçkin couldn't think about his file this year because he was thinking about Defne. That's why he had to finish this painting no matter what.

Seçkin was tired from working. Now he was drooling on the papers on the table, breathing open-mouthed. Time was approaching five in the morning and he was both sleeping and anxiously waiting for the footsteps that would enter his room. He was uneasy. Because every school morning, someone from his family would stand over him and act as an alarm clock. The worst part was that he was awakened in the most vivid parts of his dreams. He was always woken up just when he was about to get something he desperately wanted to have or when he was about to kiss Defne.

As with every new day, this was going to happen soon. But he's been very tired lately. It would be nice if he didn't go to school today and had a good sleep.

While the sound of a rooster crowing was heard in the neighbourhood, a tabby cat was standing next to the dogs and wagging its tail at them. The dogs finally couldn't stand it anymore and got angry. They attacked the cat brutally. The cat shuddered and squealed…

"Meowww!"

Seçkin was startled. He hit his head on the shelf above the table. He managed to open his eyes a little by force while cursing the cat outside. Lazily, he scratched the back of his neck, got up from the chair, and threw himself on the bed.

The grove was burning…

The sparrows were flying desperately to escape from the blazing hell. The grass was scorched and the purple and white tulips were withered. The smell of smoke and soot was everywhere.

Seçkin was there. He was alone. He was on his knees, watching how that piece of paradise where his childhood memories took place was disappearing. Nothing could be heard other than the sizzling sound. The cypresses, the blackberry bushes, everything was disappearing in pain. A few ravens appeared above Seçkin. They squawked and circled over the boy's head.

Then an evil laughter rose behind the flames, and he saw the scarlet dragonfly in the flames. He quickly approached Seçkin. Suddenly, a sharp light flashed and the dragonfly turned into a woman. She fell at Seçkin's feet.

"You failed, Almighty Messiah!" the woman moaned as she crawled painfully on the ground. Another figure appeared in the flames. He was of gigantic size. It had hooves and flaming horns. He approached Queen Laverna and took the Queen of Fairies with his huge hand and broke her neck…

"Queen Laverna!" the boy shouted, as if his throat was tearing.

Seçkin immediately opened his eyes. ParuParu and BesuBesu were standing there gawking at the boy's face.

"I failed, ParuParu!" said the boy, grabbing the little man by the collar.

"High Master, calm down!" said BesuBesu. "You had a nightmare!"

As Seçkin slowly regained consciousness, the boy looked around like crazy.

He was indeed in the blue bedroom.

He let go of ParuParu. He hysterically stared at his hands.

"I failed!" he groaned bitterly. Then he burst into tears. He sobbed as he wiped the warm fluid coming from his nose with his hand. He was covered in blood.

"I will not succeed!"

Seçkin looked like a ghost when he came to school in the morning. While he was waiting for his friends to arrive, he was sitting under the Judas tree and looking around with drowsy eyes. Sahra was not there anymore. He no longer had the friend that came and console him and warm him with the desert breeze. Even though a few days had passed since she left, no one but him had noticed her absence. They wouldn't even be aware of her existence anyway. Poor girl was always excluded because she was different.

Seçkin sighed in sorrow. Derin Zade set foot in the school, while he was watching around.

Recently, Derin Zade's eyes were strangely always set on the boy.

"Good morning Seçkin!" said the woman as she got out of the car and approached him happily.

"Good morning miss."

"How are you, my child?"

"I'm fine, miss." Seçkin replied.

Derin Zade smiled and nodded and entered the school.

Then Ela appeared. She greeted Seçkin and sat next to the boy. Then Ayaz came, then Mine and finally Duru. And the class bell rang. They entered the math class while Ayaz was listing curses one after another.

The weather temperature had now increased considerably. Seçkin couldn't even stand the shirt he was wearing anymore. In addition to this heat, the constant equation solving of the sullen math teacher Vildan, was now tiring the boy. He took a few sips of water, and just as he was about to surrender his soul, the classroom door knocked three times.

"Knock knock knock!"

"Yes!" "Sullen Vildan called out over her glasses. The green wooden door creaked open. The vice principal who was a shining beacon of "loveliness" appeared at the door. He was holding a bundle of white paper in his hand.

"I apologize for the interruption, miss, but I came to conduct a survey for our spring trip this year.

"Let's go to St. Hilarion Castle!" Seçkin said immediately.

Memduh Kemal smiled.

"Oh, my dear child, you are lucky that St. Hilarion Castle is also on our list!" There was a brief silence in the classroom as the man distributed the papers he was holding to the students. Seçkin examined the paper in front of him:

Alevkayası
St. Hilarion Castle
Bosphorus picnic area
Salamis Ruins

The boy immediately marked St. Hilarion's Castle and tapped Ayaz, who was still undecided, on the elbow, asking him to also mark the second option.

Ayaz grumbled and did what Seçkin said.

Seçkin smiled like a little child and hugged Ayaz with excitement.

"Okay... Don't be pushy, you freak!"

The night of the play had arrived.

Bellapais Monastery[36] was shining brightly on the slopes of Girne tonight. Its orange light illuminated the tall cypress trees. The cypresses stood like huge giants, protecting the monastery. Every time Seçkin went there, Arnold Böcklin's "Island of the Dead" paintings came to his mind.

The hall was starting to fill up. Seçkin was pacing from side to side.

"My heart feels like it's going to burst!" groaned the boy.

"Wow... It really is." said Defne while touching the boy's chest.

"Calm down darling or you'll have a heart attack!"

---

[36] *Bellapais Monastery: It is a historical monastery located in the Beylerbeyi village of Northern Cyprus. It is one of the eastern examples of Gothic architecture.*

"I can't keep calm! How will I play in front of all those people?" he finally shouted, "I have already forgotten all my lines!"

"Whoa!" sighed Mine. "You're kidding, right?"

"Don't be ridiculous, Seçkin!" said Defne.

"I told you that he would cause a problem." said Ayaz angrily.

"I know my man!"

Then the curtains opened and Seçkin suddenly found himself on the stage with Can.

"Take thou some new infection to thy eye, And the rank poison of the old will die." Can's voice rang out.

"Your plantain leaf is excellent for that." Seçkin muttered. His heart was beating like crazy.

"For what, I pray thee?"

"For your broken shin…" Seçkin threw a big punch at Can. He hit so hard because of his excitement that the boy was shocked for a moment and didn't know what to do.

"Sorry" he whispered into Can's ear.

"Why Romeo? Art thou mad?" Can's eyes opened wide.

Seçkin thought… Damn, he didn't remember.

"Well, uh! I am not mad!"

"Yes…" Can whispered while nodding his head with pleading eyes.

Seçkin closed his eyes for a brief moment. When he opened them, the words immediately appeared in his mind.

"Not mad, but bound more than a madman is: Shut up in prison, kept without my food, Whipped and tormented. Good e'en, good fellow.!"

Then the scene changed…

"These violent delights have violent ends. And in their triumph die, like fire and powder,

Which as they kiss consume…" rang the voice of Memduh Kemal on the stage as his golden tooth shone.

Afterwards, Defne and Seçkin took the stage.

"Farewell, farewell, one kiss, and I'll descend." Seçkin hugged the girl. For a moment, he saw the fairish young man sitting among the audience.

It was him… Burak… He was there too. Seçkin felt safe as ever when he looked into his deep brown eyes.

Defne sobbed.

"Art thou gone so, love, lord, ay husband, friend? I must hear from thee every day in the hour, for in a minute there are many days. O, by this count I shall be much in years. Ere I again behold my Romeo!"

Seçkin looked into the eyes of the girl and his eyes teared.

"Farewell! I will omit no opportunity, That may convey my greetings, love, to thee..."

Defne clung to the boy's hand.

"Oh, think'st thou we shall ever meet again??"

Seçkin hesitated for a moment as he took his eyes off Burak. He didn't know what to say.

"Even if thousands of years pass… We will always find each other, my love." he said immediately, trying to cover up.

Defne stared blankly at the boy's face.

Seçkin forgot most of his lines that night, but every time he forgot, he masterfully covered it up so that no one noticed it except those who were in the play. The play was a success. As the curtains closed, the entire hall stood up and applauded these talented students.

That night, at the cocktail party after the show, Seçkin met Defne's family. Ela received great praise for the decoration she prepared...

"Finally! "We got through it without any trouble, huh," sighed Mine. The event was almost over. They were sitting on the grass in the monastery's garden.

Seçkin was leaning against the trunk of a cypress tree with Defne.

He opened his mouth wide and yawned.

"I am very tired." moaned the boy as he snuggled into Defne's bosom.

Defne smiled and caressed the boy's hair.

"You did a good job! I'm still amazed," said the girl.

They all burst into laughter.

"Every time I looked at Özden Hoca, she was hitting the script of the play on her head." said Mine. She jumped to her feet and pressed her arm painfully to her forehead.

"Seçkin Saral… Seçkin Saral…" she imitated the woman.

"One way or another, no one noticed but you!" Seçkin shrugged.

There was a short silence.

"Isn't it such a beautiful night?" Ela asked while watching the sky in Mert's arms.

The full moon was shining brightly. Thousands of stars were winking at these crazy young people.

Seçkin took a deep breath and filled his lungs with the scent of this beautiful night. For the first time in months, he felt at peace.

"Abi, we are leaving!" Seçil called out.

Seçkin hugged his friends, followed Seçil, to the Mercedes, yawning. He got into the car. He leaned his head on the car seat and slept deeply until he got home.

When Seçkin opened his eyes, he was in his room. He couldn't remember at what point he got out of the car and came here. A warmth flowed from his nose and dripped onto his pillow. He straightened up immediately. His nose was bleeding again. He immediately left his room and ran to the toilet.

As he leaned over the sink, the blood flowed more and more.

"Is everything okay, High Master?" asked ParuParu's voice from within the walls.

"Yes, ParuParu!" Seçkin replied.

"Erm… Okay, then!" yawned ParuParu's voice.

Then he started snoring.

Seçkin looked at the clock, it was midnight.

He left his room.

He heard a scream saying "It is enough!"

The door to his parents' room was ajar. Seçkin got closer. His mother and father could be seen from that gap. They were both pacing and arguing heatedly. Seçkin moved a little closer to the door, which was standing ajar. There was a short silence.

Bahar Saral took a deep breath while untying the tie of her one and only love. She was a little upset with him for what he had said in the heated argument that had just taken place in their bedroom, but she didn't care when she calmed down. She could never be angry with her husband. What had they lived through up until now? After all the disappointments and all the pain, it was time to be happy with her husband and children. There shouldn't be even the slightest problem in her family.

The woman looked sadly into her husband's bottomless dark eyes and hugged him tightly. There was silence for a while. They both stood there, hugging each other tightly. They seemed to be apologizing to each other for what they had just said to each other.

Then Bahar was the first to break the silence.

"We have to keep this secret. We can't tell yet!" she said while pressing her head against her husband's chest.

Berk Saral exhaled with grief. His wife's arms around his waist tightened slightly.

"Isn't it time to reveal the truth?"

The woman pursed her lips. She escaped from her husband's arms and slowly backed away.

"Oh, come on! Is it ever the right time to reveal someone that they are adopted?"

Seçkin froze. Then his knees buckled. He was out of breath.

He didn't know what to do at that moment...

-CHAPTER XVI-

A Cozy Friend's House

Under the ink-black sky, a car pierced the darkness of the night. While the lights of the city hit the window, the black Lamborghini moved on the road as fast as lightning and passed a few cars with a masterful manoeuvre. A few large drops of tears glistened on the perfectly pale face of its driver.

He still couldn't believe what he heard. His brain was tingling. Everything was like a nightmare for him right now. His life suddenly turned upside down. Everything he had ever known to be true was suddenly cut off and turned into a poisonous reality. What was it like to live in a big lie for eighteen years?

The only thing he felt now was disappointment.

While the Lamborghini was climbing a steep road leading to the small village shining on a majestic hill, two huge cawing crows flew over the top of the car and disappeared from sight.

When the car entered the village, it passed through narrow, empty streets, took sharp turns, and finally stopped in an area that could have been the village square. The boy turned off the car engine and ran out hysterically. He filled his lungs with clean air for a while. He wanted to scream at the top of his lungs. He couldn't stand it any longer and fell on his knees and started sobbing.

As the blinding headlights of the car hit his pale face, Seçkin's face looked like it had been sculpted by a sculptor in that deep darkness. It was beautiful and perfect. He looked divine even when his tears fell down his cheeks like tiny crystals. He was glowing. But, what about his fate? Was it beautiful too? Not really, considering his current situation.

He looked up at the sky, his eyes filled with tears. Not a single star was shining tonight.

"What a damn night," he thought to himself. Then, deep down, he cursed himself for being in this situation. A treacherous voice in his head kept repeating the same thing to him.

"You are adopted!"

He looked around. He was in a neighbourhood square surrounded by stone houses. In the centre of the buildings stood a small white old church.

Seçkin was afraid. Yes! Now he was more afraid than ever. This was neither because he would face the Devil in the near future, nor because of the war that would break out. He didn't even care about these things right now. Because the fear of losing his family was beyond everything. Especially the thought of losing his mother, to whom he was bonded with a strong love… He didn't even want to think about it.

Even while he was listening to the sound of water coming from somewhere on this cloudy spring night, that treacherous voice in his mind was screaming over and over without stopping:

"Adopted… Adopted…"

Even though he didn't want to believe it and tried not to hear it, he wasn't very successful.

But what about that difficult pregnancy her mother went through? What was that?

When he thought about this, a flicker of hope appeared in Seçkin's heart. Wasn't he the expected child that his parents welcomed after eight years of struggle?

He had heard this story so many times from everyone until now, was it possible that it was a lie?

He closed his eyes. Two more large tears slipped from under his eyelids.

Seçkin put these unpleasant thoughts aside for a short moment and thought about how he would find Ela among all these houses. He wondered which of these box houses could be her house?

He left the house in such a way that he took neither his wallet nor his phone. For a brief moment, "Good thing I wasn't in pyjamas at that moment." he thought.

For a while, perhaps a long time, he sat on his knees and looked at an English house decorated with flowers. But what his eyes saw could not ease his mind.

He was adopted. While dozens of thoughts were flying around in his head, this painful truth that he could not get out of his mind was hurting him.

The joke he had been making to his sister all these years had come upon himself. God... What kind of fate was this?

Just as he was thinking about these, a silhouette appeared behind the headlights of the car. She walked elegantly towards Seçkin. Seçkin was startled when he saw her. The light of the car was shining so blindingly that he couldn't see who was approaching. Then he heard that warm voice.

"Seçkin? Oh my God... It's you!"

Ela came out of the light. She ran to Seçkin and hugged him.

Seçkin hugged her so tightly like he was an orphaned, defenceless child. Ela's jasmine scent saved him from the darkness he fell into, even if only for a while.

For a while, they both sat there, clasped together, in that dark night. While Seçkin was in tears telling him everything that had happened, Ela was shocked.

"I cannot believe this!" said the girl at last. Her mouth was wide open. "You can't be adopted, Seçkin! I mean, the treatments your mother received in Australia… Then the problems during her pregnancy… Didn't you say that she spent seven months in bed to give birth to you?"

"They just made it up, don't you see! Maybe they took me from Australia."

They stood up. They were going up a gravel road. While Ela was trying to understand what was going on, she said, "I'm glad I went out for a walk. I couldn't stay at home like crazy at this hour. So this was the reason!" she sighed.

When they came to a narrow passage with a house with blue windows and its own small ornamental pool, Ela paused.

"I wonder… Couldn't you have misunderstood?" she asked, still in disbelief.

Seçkin watched the dragonflies flying over the ornamental pool full of water lilies of that house with blue windows. How vibrant and bright the colours were. It was as if they did not belong to this world.

Then he shook his head sadly.

What he heard resurfaced in his mind.

"Is it ever the right time to reveal someone that they are adopted"

That's exactly what his mother said.

"I am not their own child… I am not!" said Seçkin. He walked and sat next to the ornamental pool and again could not control his tears. They started to flow like streams.

"For God's sake, Seçkin, stop crying! You look so much like your mother that it is impossible for you to be adopted! There is definitely something afoot here."

As Ela patted him on the back, they both became silent again.

They stood next to that ornamental pool for a while. Seçkin began to examine the village as if he wanted to get rid of that treacherous voice that started ringing in his head again. He had never been to Karmi[37] before. It was a beautiful village. It was as Ela had been telling all these years. All houses had their own well-kept gardens. Colourful flowers were everywhere There was a scent of lilac coming from somewhere. There were narrow streets and passages connecting the houses. The names of the passages were written on wooden signs where they began. These names seemed quite fantastic to Seçkin. It was like a dreamland.

Almond Passage... Plum Passage... Cherry Passage...

Ela broke the silence by saying, "The weather is cold. Shall we walk home?"

Ela jumped up and turned towards Almond Passage. Seçkin followed him on the stone path paved with pebbles in that narrow street.

"My mother will be very happy when she sees you!" she smiled with childish excitement.

Then she took a deep breath.

"If I hadn't seen you, would you have sat there all night?"

---

[37] *Karmi: Karaman Village. A village with a unique view, built on a mountain slope in the west of Kyrenia. Although most of the people living in the village are British, foreigners including Germans, French, Italians, Dutch, Swiss, Americans and Canadians follow the bohemian life.*

Seçkin didn't say anything. He glanced over at Ela. He was in a daze and really could have stayed there all night.

"Oh, my handsome! What had happened to you?"

A beautiful small stone house with a garden was slowly appearing at the end of the road. Smoke was billowing from its chimney.

Ela finally opened the gancelli[38]. It was a modest country house. Its roof was surrounded by a majestic trumpet vine, its yellow flowers hanging down from the roof. The light inside was shining golden.

Ela knocked on the decorated wooden door of the house a few times. The door swung open and a plump lady appeared in the golden light. She was wearing a floral apron and holding a large scoop in her hand.

"Ela! Where did you disappear at night, girl? It's almost past midnight." rang her warm voice. Then her eyes shifted to Seçkin.

A hesitant smile appeared on Ela's face. "Seçkin surprised us, mum!"

The woman's face lit up with a kind smile.

"Wow… Seçkin…" the woman moaned, opening her arms invitingly.

"It's nice to see you here, son!"

---

[38] *Gancelli: It means garden gate in Cypriot dialect. It occurred from Greek Cypriots saying "Gancalı Kapı" (Hooked Gate) as "Gancali" due to their accent.*

The woman hugged Seçkin and patted his back. "You're such a skinny kid." she muttered.

Then she jumped back with excitement.

"Come on, get in!" she said as she waved her hands.

The entrance of the house was to the kitchen. This was a very cute kitchen. There were floral curtains, wicker Cypriot chairs and floral cushions. Everything was in harmony with this cute village house.

When Seçkin and Ela walked in, they both smelled the delicious tarhana soup[39].

It was boiling in a big pot on the stove. And at that moment, Seçkin's stomach growled loudly.

"Looks like someone's hungry." said Ela's mother kindly.

---

[39] *Tarhana Soup: The Cypriot tarhana is made from cracked bulgur and sour yoghurt.*

Ela giggled.

Seçkin felt that his cheeks turned red from the warmth spreading across his face.

"Please sit down, Seçkin." Ela's mother said, pointing to the chairs around the table. "Make yourself comfortable, okay son?"

Then a girl with curly hair resembling a twig broom came into the kitchen.

"Who came, mum?" she asked curiously. Then her eyes got locked on Seçkin.

"Whoa! Romeo!" she squealed enthusiastically.

Derya

He walked up to Seçkin and kissed him nicely on the cheeks.

"Welcome, sweet boy." said the girl. "What an honour to see you here!"

"Hello Derya." Seçkin replied with a smile.

"Don't hit on the boy, abla[40]," said Ela, shaking her head with a mischievous smile.

Thereupon, Derya rolled her eyes and pulled the chair across Seçkin and sat there.

"Will you marry me?" Derya asked, looking at Seçkin with admiration.

"Abla!" Ela squealed, shaking her head again.

"I'm sorry, but he has a girlfriend now and he's madly in love with her!"

Derya grimaced.

"No one can compete with me!" said the girl condescendingly. Then she looked at Seçkin and winked.

Derya did this every time she saw him since they first met. She was constantly teasing him, saying, "I'll marry you..."

While they were giggling, Ülker Hanım was filling the plates and placing them in front of them with pleasure.

"Or is your girlfriend that ugly girl who played Juliet in the play that night?" asked Derya.

"She is not ugly, abla!" said Ela.

"Yeah, go on and think that! ... Anyway... You played Romeo very well. Congratulations handsome."

Seçkin made eye contact with Ela. Ela smiled.

---

[40] *Abla:* Older sister.

"What happened?" Derya was surprised.

"Actually, Seçkin has forgotten most of his lines, abla." said Ela.

"He made up most of it!"

"Well, that's a bigger success." Derya looked at him with admiration.

"He played impromptu!"

"How nice of you to come to us, Seçkin!" said Ülker Hanım. "You know, my husband is a police officer and he had a shift tonight."

Seçkin smiled.

"If you don't understand, let me translate!" Derya said knowingly. "What my mother is trying to say is that we don't have a father at home tonight and we need a man to protect us at home!"

"She's trying to figure out if you are going to stay with us tonight." Ela whispered into Seçkin's ear.

"Ela! I heard you girl!" said Ülker Hanım while putting her hand to her mouth and giggling politely.

Seçkin was distracted again. He was stirring his soup gently and playing with the hellim[41] in it.

---

[41] *Hellim: Halloumi / It is a fresh cheese with a tight texture and yellowish white colour, originating from Cyprus. It can be eaten raw or after being grilled or fried in a pan without.*

Ela cleared her throat.

"Mum, if you have permission, Seçkin will be our guest tonight."

Ülker Hanım smiled fondly.

"Of course, Ela. That would make me happy. Besides, it is quite late. It wouldn't be right for Seçkin to go out at this hour."

"Thank you very much, hocam." said Seçkin.

"There is no need to thank, my dear child." Ülker Hanım replied, waving her hand. "But your family knows about it, right?"

Seçkin's face suddenly fell. He didn't want to talk to his mother or father right now. All he wanted was to stay away from all these years of fake family life for a few days and handle the painful truth he had found out.

Ela immediately understood that Seçkin was uncomfortable with this situation and delved into the subject.

"I'll handle this." said the girl, suddenly getting up from the table and taking the phone in her hand. "Bahar Hoca would never turn me down!"

Seçkin looked at Ela with helpless eyes for a moment. He didn't want her to do this. But he didn't say anything in front of everyone.

Seçkin sighed gloomily as Ela disappeared from the kitchen with the phone in her hand. He wanted to make his parents curious. He wanted to get revenge on them for the damage he experienced from his disappointment. He was going to get revenge on them for lying to him all these years. It gave him great pleasure when he thought about how his parents were writhing in worry.

"Yes. Everything is fine! Seçkin is our guest tonight." said Ela when she came back with joy.

"Come on, let me show you the room you will be sleeping in." Seçkin was angry at Ela when he got up from the table and followed her.

"Please don't look at me like that!" Ela frowned.

"Why did you do this?" Seçkin replied.

Ela stopped in a small corridor. There were three doors facing each other. Ela opened one of the doors and before entering she looked over at Seçkin and smiled sweetly.

"Don't worry. I didn't call anyone." she whispered.

Seçkin woke up in the morning with the sound of the rooster heralding the brightness of the day. He hadn't slept this comfortably in a long time.

The small bedroom where Ela hosted him was bright with the rising sun. Its walls were green. It was a very suitable colour for a house in touch with nature. Plush toys were lined up on a cute little desk. Next to those toys was a photo of the two of them embracing each other in a silver frame. There wasn't even a photo of Mert in the room. At this moment, the strong bond of friendship between the two came into play.

Seçkin straightened up and sat on the bed. When he looked out of the window next to the bed, he saw the jasmine plants right under the window. He took a deep breath. The scent of jasmine in the bedroom filled his lungs. Everywhere smelled just like Ela.

He watched the fascinating view outside for a while. Karmi Village was like a piece of heaven with its stone houses surrounded by colourful flowers, cute little paths, and ornamental pools adorned with water lilies. It was surprising how this place managed to remain so pure while human beings brutally slaughtering nature. It looked like it was untouched by humans.

Seçkin took his eyes off the window and stood up. He looked at Ela's full-length mirror. Maybe he was in the past, but now he wasn't a skinny kid at all. His body was very muscular. He didn't understand how Ülker Hanım could find him skinny. But considering the pyjamas he was wearing, Ela's father was a giant of a man. He would undoubtedly look skinny next to him.

He headed towards the kitchen where the clattering sounds were coming from, while he was holding on tightly to his too big pyjamas, to prevent himself from falling.

Ela's mother had already woken up and started preparing breakfast. On the other hand, she was trying to polish an old cauldron.

"Good morning," her voice rang out affectionately. Her eyes sparkled. "I hope you slept well."

"Good morning, ma'am," replied Seçkin. "Yes, I slept very well. Thanks."

The woman smiled.

"Oh, my dear son! Look at you! You are really skinny!"

She immediately pointed to the table.

"Come on, sit down. I will feed you well."

Seçkin smiled. He pulled out the wicker Cyprus chair and sat down.

While Ülker Hanım was pouring the tea, she said, "You should call your family. Your mother must be very worried about you." she grumbled dissatisfiedly.

"No matter what, don't do this to her, son."

A lump formed in Seçkin's throat. He stared blankly at the woman.

"Do not look at me like that. I am Ela's mother. I can tell right away when she's lying. She said she called your family, but she didn't do that, did she?"

Seçkin lowered his head and swallowed ashamed. A feeling of regret welled up inside him. That guilty feeling, he had felt for years when misbehaving appeared again. He closed his eyes. Two large teardrops run down from under his eyelids. The kitchen door suddenly opened, while he was wiping the tears in his eyes without Ülker Hanım noticing.

In the reckless light of the fresh day, a huge figure appeared in the doorway.

While Seçkin blinked his dazzled eyes, the owner of the pyjamas entered the kitchen with his daughters.

Seçkin immediately jumped to his feet as soon as he saw them. The man was huge. He had curly brown hair and a huge belly. He was wearing a police uniform, but there was no trace of a police seriousness on his face.

"So, you're the famous Seçkin, huh?"

The man, with his huge body, approached Seçkin and sincerely extended his hand to him. "I am Yusuf! Good morning, son!"

"Good morning, sir! Pleased to meet you." Seçkin replied.

"Ohoho! Look at those hands, what a skinny kid you are!"

Ela looked at her father and rolled her eyes.

"First, my mother, and now you. You both will make the boy depressed!"

"The kid is not skinny, look at those muscles, dad!" said Derya as she immediately caressed the boy's head lovingly.

"Muscles?" the man asked with a mischievous smile. He immediately rolled up his shirt sleeve and clenched his fist. The man's biceps swelled like two small hills.

"That's what you call muscles, girl!"

Seçkin stared at the man's biceps in surprise.

"Enough of the show! Let's have breakfast, everyone!" rang Ülker Hanım's voice.

They all pulled out their wicker Cypriot chairs and sat at the breakfast table.

"Tell me Seçkin, do you like our village?" asked Ela's father.

"We haven't had the chance to show him around the village yet, dad!" Ela said immediately.

"Then go out for a tour of the village after breakfast! I'm sure you have never seen such a beautiful place in your life!"

After breakfast, Ela took Seçkin by the arm and immediately took him out of the house with the excuse of showing him around the village. But she looked like she was planning something. At night, she tossed and turned in bed, unable to sleep. Seçkin must have misunderstood something. The situation they were in seemed unreal to her. Seçkin was definitely Berk Saral's and Bahar Saral's child, this was an indisputable fact.

Seçkin, Ela and Derya wandered around Karmi Village all day long. They climbed mountains together… They rode bicycles… They ate halloumi pastry with molasses.

In the evening, when Derya said that she was very tired and ran home, Seçkin and Ela went down the stairs of the church and started to wander around the lower neighbourhoods.

"You should call them!" said Ela, leaning against a dysfunctional, old red telephone box with her hands crossed across her chest.

Seçkin didn't say anything. He too wanted to call his family now, but he was also afraid.

"What if I didn't misunderstand what I heard? What if I'm really adopted?

Ela shook her head, weary.

"This is impossible, Seçkin... You are the child that has been awaited for eight years!

Seçkin shook his head gloomily.

"Maybe their efforts came to nothing and then they adopted me in Australia."

"I would never believe that!" Ela said with a know it all attitude.

Seçkin sat on the steps of a shabby building and took a deep breath.

Then a message came to Ela's phone.

"What have you been doing with that phone since the morning?" he asked, looking at Ela, who was constantly texting someone.

Ela hesitated for a moment. "I'm sending a message to Mert!"

Seçkin took another deep sigh of despair.

"I wonder what Defne is doing?" the boy whined.

"You didn't call her either, did you, stupid boy!"

"No, I didn't call!"

"Oh… Seçkin, you are going to kill me!" Ela said in anger. "You're going to screw up your whole life because of one stupid misunderstanding!"

"What misunderstanding? It's not a misunderstanding! I heard it with my own ears!" Seçkin jumped up angrily.

"Behave yourself! You're scaring me by doing this!"

"I'm the one who's afraid of people! Because they are stabbing in the back!" the boy shouted, with all his anger.

Suddenly he heard a familiar voice.

"Seçkin!" The boy paused.

It was his mother's voice.

Seçkin turned his head towards the direction of the voice. He saw that his mother and father were there. As his eyes opened wide, he immediately looked at Ela. Ela swallowed guiltily.

"So you were texting them! Traitor!"

"Ela did the right thing!" Berk Saral said in an authoritative voice as he approached his son.

Bahar Saral ran in tears and hugged her son tightly.

"You made us worried sick! Thank God!"

Seçkin looked at Ela once again with an angry gaze.

"You are a traitor, Ela!"

"Please don't say that to me! Because there is a big misunderstanding, Seçkin!" Ela said, her eyes filling with tears.

"Ela is right!" said Berk Saral.

"Come…" said Bahar Saral. "Come, let's sit here for a while!"

Seçkin looked at his mother. How much she had collapsed in one night. Her eyes were so red from crying. He did as his mother said and sat on the steps of the stairs.

"You adopted me, didn't you? You are going to say this!"

His mother sobbed in grief as she held his hands tightly.

His father knelt in front of his son and caressed his face.

"You are my child!" moaned Bahar Saral.

"I thank God every day that I have a son like you." said Berk Saral. "What a beautiful and different child you are!"

"Is it ever the right time to reveal someone that they are adopted?"

This line rang in Seçkin's mind once again.

"I heard you!" sobbed Seçkin. "You were talking about telling me the truth!"

"We weren't talking about you, Seçkin." said Berk Saral, bowing his head to the ground in sorrow.

As Ela watched this family drama in tears, she felt that she could not bear it any longer.

Apparently, neither Berk Saral nor Bahar Saral could express this hidden truth. They even avoided hearing about it themselves. They couldn't accept it.

But Ela couldn't take it anymore and cried out in tears.

"Seçkin!" she said tearfully.

"You are not the adopted one! "It's...Seçil!"

-CHAPTER XVII-
Little Stranger

It could be understood that the day was very special, even if no one said it. The snow was falling heavily. The wet air sparkled sweetly. There was a golden light outside. And the snowdrops in the garden of the kingdom bloomed with divine beauty

Nine months had passed and the time had come for the "Living Being". The baby would be born and the being would come to life in a body. The baby would be the only grandchild of the Supreme Creator. The baby would bring beauty to the entire kingdom. The "Living Being" was fortunately born with such characteristics.

But the baby's fate was shaping up in such a way that no one had even the slightest idea about it. It would be a very special baby not only for the kingdom, but for all the Realms. And it was time.

Queen Mel and Queen Laverna took the men out and closed the bedroom door.

Saint Hilarion, King Asparagus, KarlaKarla, Amethyst, King Okalper, Vermeil and Nephilim…Everyone was there and they shared Prince Sapphire's excitement.

Princess Lal screamed as golden rays of sunlight hit the corridor.

Prince Sapphire covered his ears. He paced in front of the bedroom door for a while.

"Sapphire…" King Okalper said finally.

"Calm down now, brother."

"Why hasn't the baby been born yet?" Prince Sapphire asked excitedly.

Saint Hilarion smiled. "Not everyone is as hasty as you, my prince.

"The Living Being is coming slowly!" chuckled King Asparagus.

Prince Sapphire's gaze was fixed on the burning candlesticks. He looked at the melting candles. The minutes passed as the candle melted and the bedroom door finally opened.

The Prince stared after her as NejuNeju left the room with the bloody sheets in her hands and ran out of sight. Then, when he stretched his neck and looked into the room, he saw Queen Laverna approaching with the baby in her arms, through the snow-white tulles hanging in the room.

Prince Sapphire's heart pounded like crazy and he just stared at the baby.

"You have a daughter, Prince Sapphire…" said Queen Laverna. She handed the baby into the prince's arms.

The baby wiggled with joy, reaching her hands towards him.

Her face was pale and had rosy cheeks like her mother. She was divinely beautiful. She had silvery green eyes that looked very intelligent for a baby. As a princess should be; She was simply a perfect baby.

Princess Toga

Prince Sapphire's silvery blue eyes became misty. It didn't take long before Prince Sapphire burst into tears.

"What about Lal?" he asked then "Can I see her?"

Queen Laverna nodded, her eyes filled with tears.

Prince Sapphire entered the room, inhaling his daughter's bay scent.

Princess Lal was lying on the bed decorated with white tulle. She looked tired but fine.

"My darling…" said Prince Sapphire as he clung to her lips.

"Thanks to you, I became the happiest man in the world."

Princess also smiled with tears in her eyes.

"Thank you…" said Prince Sapphire.

"Thank you for giving me such a beautiful baby."

He handed the baby into her mother's arms and turned to his friends who were waiting there with excitement. He wiped his tears and smiled.

"The Living Being was born. Long live Princess Toya!"

"Long live Princess Toya!" everyone there repeated.

Silence reigned over the big white house among the hills in Karşıyaka… But this was not surprising. Because the people of the town knew not much about the Sarals who lived in the big white house at the foot of the mountain. The reason of this went back twelve years earlier.

Berk Saral and Bahar Saral took their five-year-old son and went to Paris to visit Özdemir Bey and Nazikter Hanım, at the end of that summer Bahar Saral returned to the island with another baby in her arms. With a baby girl…

No one believed that Bahar Saral was pregnant when she went to Paris, and the rumour that she adopted little Seçil spread among the residents of Karşıyaka.

Since then, the Sarals have not talked or met with the people there much. They were always terrified that their little daughter might one day learn the truth from someone.

For this reason, instead of sending her and Seçkin to a primary school in the town, they sent them to the American Primary School in Girne. They prevented them from being friends with the kids in town. As time passed, they began to be remembered by the townspeople as the arrogant family who lived in the big white house on the hill.

Berk Saral used to take his beautiful daughter to the park every weekend. While Seçil was cycling in the park, he would play backgammon with a few of his friends and chat for a while. While all this was happening, he always managed to ignore the people who were secretly watching him for years.

Bahar Saral, who went grocery shopping with little Seçil, often heard women whispering to each other with their envious looks. She would politely turn away anyone who wanted to have a chat with her, and she would finish her shopping and leave the market immediately.

Everyone had been in a state of curiosity for twelve years. Was this little girl with silvery-gold hair adopted from Paris? There was never anyone brave enough to ask this question. But they always worried that this might have happened. But Seçkin's misunderstanding of everything caused this big secret to come to the fore again within the family.

Yes, little Seçil was adopted by the Saral family years ago. Seçkin was only five years old at that time.

They went to visit the Notre Dame Cathedral on a sunny Paris day. While Bahar Saral was examining the engravings of the magnificent gothic building, the little naughty Seçkin suddenly disappeared.

When they found the boy, he was standing by a lake.

But he wasn't alone. There was a baby there with him, left in a cradle by the lake.

Seçkin vaguely remembered the day he first saw his sister. But where he was and how it happened, everything in his mind was very vague. The only thing he remembered was the baby's surprised look on her face when he lifted the iridescent pink tulle of the crib.

The baby seemed alarmingly small to him. While the boy was watching her, she suddenly opened her green eyes and reached out her arms towards her brother with an irresistible smile on her face. It was as if she wanted him to always be with her, she would feel safe this way. Seçkin Saral understood at that moment. His sister would need his support and trust throughout life. He would protect her from all evil.

And thus, twelve years passed...

After the incident, Seçkin returned home. He was lying on the couch in the living room with his head on his grandmother's lap. His mother, father and grandfather were sitting in the living room, staring blankly at the television.

Seçil was not at home. She was at the private piano lesson she was going once a week.

Nobody was talking to each other. There was a complete silence in the hall.

"Are you going to tell her?" Seçkin asked finally. Nobody said anything.

"So, who is her family? Hasn't anyone appeared in all these years?

Bahar Saral shook her head.

"Well, wasn't there any note?" Seçkin asked again.

"There was only an old silver pocket watch…" said Bahar Saral.

"There was an old pocket watch with a dragonfly embossed on it."

"A silver pocket watch…" Seçkin repeated. The boy unbuttoned his shirt and took off the pocket watch from around his neck.

"Is this the pocket watch, mum?" Seçkin asked.

Bahar Saral stared at the boy with a look of horror on her face.

"How did you find that?" the woman asked.

"Months ago, while I was looking for a pillow in your closet, a box fell on me. "It was out of the box." said Seçkin. Bahar Saral sighed deeply.

"We corresponded with the old Priest of Notre Dame for twelve years. So far, no one has been looking for the girl. According to what he said, there won't be anyone. He insistently says that this is where Seçil belongs."

"Why would he say something like that?" Seçkin asked dumbly. "What does it mean that she belongs here?"

Again no one spoke.

"This is so weird!" whined Seçkin. "It's really weird!"

"Son, can you be quiet for a while!" said Berk Saral angrily at last.

"We're thinking about what we should do here!"

"Yes, you think in a dead silence!"

"God forbid, my prince, what kind of saying is that?" Nazikter Hanım said while pulling her earlobes.

"But it is." Seçkin grumbled while making a face.

"What do you expect us to do, my boy?" said Bahar Saral helplessly.

"I'm waiting for you to come to your senses. Do you think we can fix anything by sitting here silently? Seçkin replied dissatisfied. "We need to talk."

"Seçkin is right!" said Özdemir Bey from under his twitching moustache.

"We have to make a decision. We will either tell Seçil the whole truth, or we will draw a curtain over this truth and continue our lives as we have done until today."

"I think there is no need for this!" Nazikter Hanım's voice trembled. "She is too young to know this truth. When everything in her life is in order and she is successful in her studies, why should we tell her these things and confuse her for no reason? She may not be able to handle this!"

"Actually, my grandmother is right!" said Seçkin. "I almost went crazy when I thought that I was adopted!"

"Aww… My handsome prince!" said Nazikter Hanım while caressing her grandchild's hair.

"I also think Seçil is still too young to learn this!" said Bahar Saral as tears accumulated in her eyes.

"I will never tell this before she marries! I think this is the best decision we can make." said Berk Saral.

"Now that you know, will you be able to keep this secret with us, son?"

Seçkin lifted his head from his grandmother's lap.

"Didn't you say that secrets always alienate the people we care about, grandpa?" said Seçkin unhappily.

"There are some secrets that protect those we love, son." said his grandfather.

Seçkin nodded in agreement. He didn't even want to think about the thought of losing Seçil. Maybe they were constantly fighting with each other, but he couldn't live without her. You know, if you have to give your life for someone and you give it without hesitation, but Seçkin could have given his life for his sister without even thinking. She may not be biological, but she was Seçkin's only sister. She was his Cazzude.

"Yes," said the boy finally, "I will keep this secret…"

The summer heat was getting worse. Seçkin was sitting under the shade of the Judas tree that had lush green leaves and watched Seçil running around with Bert and Ernie.

It was a week before final exams started, and he still hadn't finished the final project he started for art class. He worked very meticulously and slowly. He was a perfectionist. No matter what he did, it had to be perfect. Otherwise, it was unacceptable.

He sighed deeply. As he continued to watch Seçil, a voice appeared in his mind.

"The place where Seçil belongs is the Saral Family."

Why would a Priest insistently say such a thing about a little strange girl?

He couldn't make sense of this. He had an urge to go to Paris.

ParuParu and BesuBesu had not been seen around for a week.

Whenever he needed them, they always disappeared.

Then Sahra came to his mind. He missed her so much. If he told her what happened, she would know what to do for sure. After all, she was a holy person who guided him. But she wasn't there either. She was gone.

"Oh, how nice! "I have no one left to ask for advice." thought the boy.

Then, when Ela and Defne stepped into the garden, these thoughts left his mind.

"You won't believe what happened!" Ela said as she immediately handed the pink Lays package in her hand to the boy.

"What happened?" Seçkin asked, his heart jumping. He looked from Ela to Defne.

Ela took a deep breath.

"Hale abla broke the Aphrodite bust while cleaning the workshop!" she said in horror.

"Is that the bust that Ferhun worked on all the time?" Seçkin exclaimed immediately.

"Yes." Ela pouted her lips and said, "That beautiful bust."

"How bad! Ferhun must have been very upset." Seçkin said while pursing his lips.

"He is crying!" said Ela.

"That janitor's butt is so huge; I'm not surprised at all!" said Defne suddenly.

Seçkin smiled. He squeezed Defne's cheek and kissed her neck.

"Look... Look... Look... Does it suit you to talk like that, sweet thing..." he muttered while caressing the girl's cheek.

The girl's cheeks turned red and she giggled.

"By the way, we have another news for you!" said Ela and Seçkin's heart jumped again.

"Don't be afraid!" Ela said as she soothed him. "This is good news!"

Seçkin took a deep breath.

"Voting results are out. We are going to St. Hilarion Castle for a school trip!" said Defne.

"Tell the truth! Really?" Seçkin asked. His eyes sparkled with joy.

Ela and Defne smiled and nodded.

"The best news I have received lately!" said Seçkin. "I wonder about that place so much!"

He sighed deeply. Then he turned his gaze to his sister. His eyes became sad again.

Defne didn't know anything. That's why she didn't notice Seçkin's sorrowful looks. But Ela knew.

She put her arm around the boy's shoulder and placed a kiss on his cheek.

"Why are you kissing me in front of my girlfriend?" Seçkin whined shyly.

"I'm not jealous!" said Defne as she kissed the boy's other cheek.

Seçkin burst out laughing.

"What a lucky man I am!" smiled the boy.

Seçil saw what was happening and ran to her brother with sweet jealousy and jumped into the boy's arms.

"Abi, I love you the most!" she squealed sweetly.

Seçkin placed a sweet kiss on his sister's cheek. "I love you too, Cazzude!" he said and hugged her tightly with his quite strengthened arms.

Then Ayaz, Mine and Duru went out to the garden.

"What a blissful family!" said Duru immediately.

"But I see a big family tragedy," Mine immediately said. "The drama of a handsome young man ruined between his two vixen sisters-in-law and his girlfriend."

"You are so lucky when it comes to girls!" Ayaz patted the boy on the shoulder.

"Of course! "I don't want you to criticize my harem..." boasted Seçkin.

Mine took a deep breath.

"Enjoy this garden, guys. After a few weeks, it will be a memory for all of us."

Their smiles were overshadowed. Everyone was demoralized.

"Wow!" said Ela. "It seems like just yesterday when I came here."

"Exactly," said Seçkin.

"Do you remember your first friend, Seçkin?" Then Ela smiled mischievously.

Seçkin grimaced.

"Come on Ela! Shush!"

Ela immediately burst out laughing.

"Defne, do you know that when Seçkin first came to school, he was hanging with the cheeky strange girl?"

"Oh really!" Defne's eyes opened wide with surprise.

"Yes, I remember that too." said Duru.

"We were always sighing and complaining about what this handsome man could be doing with that girl!"

"We always thought you would go out with her!" said Mine.

"Whoa!" Seçkin was shocked.

Defne grumbled. She lifted his chin up resentfully.

"It's good to know these, Mr. Seçkin! So you were very tasteless before me!"

Ela, Mine, Duru, Ayaz and Seçil burst into laughter.

"Ugh… Why are you trying to humiliate me in front of my girlfriend?"

The boy whined.

"Okay, don't be hard on the guy, otherwise he will cry!" said Ayaz.

"Joking apart, I will miss you all so much!" said Seçkin.

His eyes filled with tears as he looked at his friends.

Ayaz's lips trembled for a moment.

"Duh, are we going somewhere? We're just graduating… I'm already fed up with this place!"

"We will take the University Selection Exam in a few weeks, and perhaps each of us will start university in separate cities. Some of us will go to Turkey." Seçkin pouted his lips.

"I wish!" said Ayaz. "I wish I could win Turkey and get rid of you. After four years, I've had enough. Look at him, he's a crazy kid who can't get rid of!"

"Ugh!" Seçkin crossed his arms resentfully.

"So my boyfriend will leave me in a few weeks!" said Defne, her shoulders slumped in resentment.

"Shhh!" Seçkin caressed Defne's cheek.

"Don't be ridiculous, I won't leave you!"

"And Seçil is here. You won't be alone at school!"

Defne exchanged glances with Seçil and smiled at her.

Eventually the two started to get along well. Maybe Seçil still couldn't share her brother, but at least she wasn't rude to Defne like she was in the beginning.

"Yes, she is my sweet princess!" said Defne.

"Oh, that's enough sentimentality!" said Ela. "I am bored."

"Let's promise each other!" said Seçkin.

"No matter what happens, wherever we go, let this bond between us never be broken!"

"Promise," said Ela.

"Promise," said Mine, clenching her fist.

"Promise," said Duru, with dimples appearing on his face.

"Promise!" said Defne, kissing the boy on the cheek.

"Promise," said Seçil while embracing her brother with love.

Then they all turned and looked at Ayaz expectantly. Ayaz grumbled with an attitude as if he did not care about any of them.

"Don't expect me to promise, I'm tired of you!"

They all stared straight at his face.

"Don't look at me like that!"

They looked...

"Don't look!"

And they looked...

"Okay... I promise! My god!"

While the sun was burning brightly overhead, a light wind blew and passed between them, tying them tightly to each other like an invisible rope.

Just ahead of them, in front of the entrance gate of the school, Korkut was watching them secretly with his pitch-black eyes.

He understood...

No power could break this bond between them...

Seçil Saral woke up at night covered in sweat from fear, as she had been for a year.

While the full moon was shining brightly in the sky, clouds were slipping in front of it like ghosts.

The little girl sat up in bed, out of breath. Even though she tried to move her legs, she could not succeed because her legs were stiff with fear. Lately, she felt like there were eyes wandering around the walls, watching her.

While shedding a cold sweat, she gathered her courage and jumped out of bed. When her bare feet stepped on the cool marble, she felt a chill for a moment and hurried out of her room. The corridor light was not on. But it was illuminated by the light from Seçkin's room. As Seçil ran to her brother's room, her heart was beating like a drum.

The girl slowly opened her brother's bedroom door and entered the blue room.

The boy was sleeping. Seçil stood next to him for a while and watched her brother. When Seçkin felt the shadow of the girl on him, he immediately opened his eyes and sat up in bed in horror. Then he stared blankly at his sister's face, who was looking at him with fearful eyes.

"You scared the hell out of me, Seçil!" he said as he threw his head back onto the pillow.

Seçil didn't say anything and sat on the edge of the bed in lumberly.

"Abi…" she said sadly. "I had very scary dreams again. Can I sleep with you again tonight?"

"Again?" said the boy, staring at his sister.

Seçkin was now confused about what to do in this situation. What was happening to this child?

"This is the third time, Seçil. "Aren't you still going to tell me what you saw in your dreams?"

Seçil shook her head in sorrow.

The boy sighed sadly

"Come on!"

Seçil smiled. She laid down next to her brother and hugged him tightly. While stroking the little girl's hair, Seçkin thought about how long this situation would last.

"Abi…" said the little girl after a while.

"Yes." Seçkin muttered.

"Months ago… There was a solar eclipse!"

"Yes?"

"I had a dream that it would happen before it happened…"

Seçkin's eyes opened wide. He immediately sat up and stared at his sister's face.

"How was the dream? Do you remember?"

"We were on the hill next to our house. You were sitting on the grass and I was picking tulips with Defne! Later…"

As Seçil was telling, Seçkin's heartbeat was getting faster.

"Then red clouds suddenly collapsed in the sky. The light went out and everything went dark. Then a fog…"

"Okay, Seçil, shut up!" Seçkin shouted in horror.

"Abi, why are you shouting?" Seçil asked tearfully.

Seçkin took a deep breath in fear.

"I'm sorry…" the boy hugged the girl.

He was about to go crazy with fear. He had the same dream as Seçil. What did this mean? Was it a coincidence? Or would something else emerge from underneath?

No matter what, he didn't want Seçil to get involved in this predicament he was in.

While Seçkin's heart was pounding like crazy, he hugged his sister even tighter.

When he placed a kiss on Seçil's hair, the little girl had already fallen asleep...

※ ※

Prince Sapphire... The only son of the Supreme Creator and the country girl Rahme... The handsome and powerful prince of the Kingdom of the Morningstar...

These expressions could be seen as the most beautiful expressions a person could ever see, but the feeling of fatherhood was beyond everything. Becoming a father... Prince Sapphire had recently experienced this feeling and everything else seemed unimportant.

The prince stood staring at his reflection in the huge full-length mirror in his bedroom with a carved silver frame. He was a perfect father...

He had a beautiful face, pale and with high cheekbones. His deep silvery blue eyes sparkled. He had broad shoulders and a muscular body. He was just like a statue.

Then he saw it. The birthmark was two inches below his right breast. It was shaped like a star.

He looked away from his reflection in the mirror. He turned to the crib next to the bed. The cradle was wrapped in iridescent tulle that showed almost every shade of pink.

He walked slowly towards her.

When he reached the crib, the tiny silhouette under the tulle stirred. Prince Sapphire slightly lifted the tulle over the cradle.

Princess Toya…

Even though a few days had passed since the birth, she had already changed. It seemed like she was going to grow up fast.

The prince took her in his arms and put her head on his chest. She had a light, beautiful bay scent, just like her mother.

As her scent filled the prince's nostrils, the baby laughed and fluttered in his arms.

"Be quiet, princess. You don't want to wake your mother, do you?" said the Prince.

The baby turned its silvery-green eyes towards Princess Lal, who was sleeping on the luxurious bed. She raised her hand and reached out towards her.

"Do you want to sleep next to your mother?"

The little princess blinked.

"Okay. But you have to promise me you won't wake her up." replied the prince.

The baby touched her father's face and then blinked her silvery green eyes again.

The prince gently laid her down next to her mother. When Princess Lal felt her daughter near her, she wrapped her arm around her and brought her closer to herself. As soon as she laid down on the bed, the little princess's eyes slowly closed and she fell asleep with her mother.

After watching them for a while, the prince turned towards the full-length mirror and washed his face with the clear water in the silver bowl next to him. Then he put on a gold robe with high embroidered collars. He walked towards the oak door with silent steps. He slowly opened the door by pushing the iron knob. As the door opened with a slight creak, he looked at his wife and daughter once more before leaving the room. The two most precious beings in his life... They were both sleeping peacefully... Then he saw Amethyst approaching in a hurry.

"My prince…" moaned the brown haired young man.

"Amethyst… What's going on?" asked the prince.

"You need to come to the council chamber immediately. It's very important!" Amethyst said breathlessly.

"The witches are here... They are waiting for you to talk about the fate of the princess!"

The Prince's heart began to beat like crazy. Evil fate had begun to weave its webs.

-CHAPTER XVIII-
The Black Medosh Tulips of Saint Hilarion

Between wind and rain; Between stone and nature lived the Five Finger Mountains. Between day and night; Between darkness and light, Azazel was growing stronger. He had been sealed deep within this mountain for over a thousand years. And that day was a new day. A new day, while approaching the day step by step when everything will restart and come to an end...

"I ask for forgiveness, Great King of Hell…"

The boy fell to his knees. Beads of sweat were flowing from his curly hair to his swarthy face. His hands were shaking uncontrollably.

"You incompetent son of Adam!"

The voice roared so loudly that the huge cave shook for a moment. The torches went out and caught fire again on their own.

"I told you that the boy and the girl must never get together!" said Azazel's angry voice. "Because of your incompetence, the curse has been lifted!"

Korkut closed his eyes tightly. He knew. The punishment of this failure would cost dearly. For a moment he felt the urge to run away, but he couldn't. Because he didn't remember how he got to the cave. He had no idea about the way out…

He opened his eyes. He saw a pair of hooves in front of him. He raised his head and stared at the flaming figure of Hematite. His heart started beating even faster. He leaned closer to the ground. He was almost kissing the ground.

"Everything was going well, I couldn't understand how it happened, my prince!" moaned the boy bitterly.

"Shut up!" said Hematite. Then he flashed a sly smile. "I have to do it on my own."

His voice was softer than ever. In fact, it was so comforting that it was literally signalling that he was going to do something bad afterwards.

Several ravens perched within the protruding walls of the cave took wing over the boy.

"What should we do with this child now?" asked one of the crows. With a musical scream;

"Should we hang him?" said another raven.

"Should we cut him?" said another one.

Korkut stared at the crows in horror. These were the damn crows that perched on that Judas tree at school. It was the first time he heard them talking.

"Please forgive me." said the boy in a weak, trembling voice.

"The trumpet will sound very soon, son of Adam. When that day comes, I don't want anyone around me who will fail." said Azazel with his raucous voice.

A brief silence fell in the cave. Hematite walked over to the boy and gently held him by the shoulders.

Korkut shuddered as he looked in horror at the long, claw-like nails hovering over him. He jumped to his feet in fear. His body shook like crazy.

"I must admit that he actually came in handy." said Hematite in a calm, raucous voice. "So, I will reward you."

As he caressed the boy's cheeks, his eyes lit up again with a hungry expression.

"Are you ready to offer your body?" said Hematite eagerly.

The boy shook his head, not knowing what to do out of fear. He escaped from Hematite's clutches and ran for his life towards the dark corridor.

As he ran, the torches along the long corridor caught fire and illuminated the boy's path. But he couldn't get out of the cave. Because the beady-eyed ravens suddenly closed the entrance of the cave like lace.

Korkut threw himself on the ground in tears.

The red mist slowly approached the boy.

"As you see, there is no way out of here, son of Adam!" said the voice from the fog. While dancing around Korkut, it suddenly shifted in the form of Hematite again.

"Don't be afraid! Everything will happen very quickly! Just like falling asleep!" He held the boy's neck with his calloused hands and his eyes burned with fire. While Korkut was screaming in terror, a power exploded inside the boy and he lost all consciousness. "Hurry up!" said the voice in the walls of the cave.

"It's time. The boy's blood must flow on the holy land."

"It's time." said a girl miles away from Cyprus.

Two young people were waiting for their flight at Rotterdam Airport in the Netherlands. The girl with brunette hair took a sip of her coffee and frowned. The coffee vibrated like a whirlpool in the cup.

"I hear the sound of the trumpet. The blood of the Promised One will soon be shed."

The brunet young man also frowned.

"We have to find the guy before they do, Mel!" he said with a sigh.

"Oh Okalper…What if we are late?"

"I don't even want to think about it." said the young man.

"We have been traveling for this moment for thousands of years. We searched for the guy everywhere. That's why we must not be late."

"It is my only wish in this life to see the Kingdom of the Morningstar rise again." Mel said.

"Therefore, we need to reach him before anyone else." said Okalper. "He's our only chance..."

Seçkin and his friends got off the bus and started walking towards the crowd that had started to gather in front of the entrance gate of the castle. The boy was holding Defne's hand tightly as they climbed the slightly sloped road. They were no longer afraid of anyone. They were living their love to the fullest.

As they mingled in the crowd, Seçil appeared in the middle of the two. She wrapped her hands around her brother's arm, leering at Defne.

"Abi, can I walk around with you?" she asked as she played for the sympathy.

Defne smiled slightly. He turned towards Seçil and gently squeezed her pink cheeks.

"Of course, you can, princess." he replied sweetly to the little girl.

Seçil's face lit up with joy.

Everything was gradually getting better. But Seçkin wasn't feeling well.

Sahra's disappearance and the unexpected truth about Seçil caused deep wounds in the boy's soul. There was also that dream incident that Seçil told him last night. He was now completely unnerved. Seçkin wanted to tell ParuParu what happened, but the faithfuls were not around again. Wherever they went, they still hadn't returned.

Seçkin's face looked flawless as always, as if it had been made by a sculptor, but it was as if his soul had aged.

He had been feeling this more and more lately.

Ayaz with Mine and Ela with Mert broke elbowed their way through the crowd and joined Seçkin and Defne. Duru and Bora were still missing.

"Where do we start looking for room one hundred and one?" Ayaz asked immediately. With childlike enthusiasm in his voice.

"Oh, please don't start over. Do you still believe this story to be true?" Mine grumbled.

Ayaz shrugged.

"Of course, we believe it, girl!"

He looked at Seçkin and winked mischievously.

Seçkin smiled. When he looked back at what happened, he saw no reason not to believe it. The rumour that supernatural beings did not actually exist, which had been told for so long, lost its trueness when faced with what he witnessed. He had faithful jinni friends named ParuParu and BesuBesu who lived in his room... Ayaz had skinny angel wings on his back, which he concealed with a golden potion... And he had a ghost guide. He no longer had one. She had left him.

Seçkin shook his head and sighed as he cleared these thoughts. Who knows how Mine would react if she learned what he had been through recently. If she saw those angel wings coming out of the slits on her boyfriend's back, she would definitely faint right away.

The student community in front of the outer entrance gate of the castle had become more crowded. Meanwhile, a smiling woman with long, brown hair came out of the castle and addressed the crowd outside.

"Welcome, dear students. Please let's gather in groups of ten. "Each group will be guided by a staff."

Seçkin and his friends were seven. Since they wanted to leave room for Duru and Bora, they only invited Can to join them. So, they formed their group.

"Get ready Can, we are going to search for room one hundred and one." said Ayaz.

"You're doing it out of spite, aren't you?" Mine hissed.

Then he punched Ayaz hard on his shoulder.

"My strong darling!"

Ayaz attempted to kiss Mine, but Mine pulled back.

"You can whistle for it! It wouldn't be bad if I reconsidered our relationship." said the girl grumpily.

A loud laugh erupted from the group.

Ayaz did not mind this. He caressed Mine's hand and then held it tightly.

Mine softened immediately. She looked at the boy with love and smiled.

"Ok. Enough laughing, guys!" said a guide on duty who came near them. "Let the tour begin!"

Then Seçkin and his friends explored the castle behind the tour guide...

While they were roaming the castle, a stone relief caught Ela's eye. It was built on the walls of a corridor leading towards the Byzantine Church. Two figures in profile with curly hair, reminiscent of the figures drawn by Seçkin, were holding a baby in their arms.

"Seçkin!" called Ela. "Look here, how similar they look to the figures you drew!"

Seçkin stared at the stone relief in astonishment.

"They really do. Unbelievable."

"Do you have any information about who made this stone relief?" Ela immediately asked the tour guide.

The man nodded.

"It is said that it was made by a prince who lived here thousands of years ago."

Ela immediately took her camera out of her bag, took a photo of the relief and continued on her way, following the tour guide.

When they arrived at the Byzantine Church, they were greeted by the beautiful tulips covering the hillside. There were hundreds of them. And they were black.

"Black medosh tulips!" Ela sighed with admiration.

"I've read so much about them."

"How beautiful they are." said Seçkin.

"This is the first time I've seen black medosh tulip in my life!" said Mine.

"According to the research, nothing like it has been found in Cyprus or even anywhere else in the world! Black medosh tulips live only in St. Hilarion Castle." Ela said immediately.

"The walking encyclopaedia has begun again." Ayaz grumbled.

Ela ignored him.

"The kings who lived here thought for centuries that this was the result of a powerful magic."

For a moment, Seçkin thought he saw a dragonfly shining red on the beautiful tulips, but when he turned his head and looked again, it was not there. He thought of Laverna, the Queen of Fairies. Didn't she mention that fairies also turned into tulips?

While Seçkin was lost in thought, someone called out from behind.

"We're here, just wait!"

It was Duru. She was holding hands with Bora and approaching with excitement with a picnic basket in her other hand.

"Duru!" smiled Ela. "For God's sake, where have you been?"

Duru looked at Bora and smiled.

"We came with my boyfriend's Vespa!"

"Vespa?" Mine's eyes suddenly widened.

"Promise me you'll give me a ride too." he said immediately with excitement.

Duru and Bora smiled.

"Ok. Promise!"

Ela shook her head.

"This passion for motorcycles will get you in trouble one day!" he said disapprovingly.

Mine rolled her eyes.

Duru excitedly lifted up the picnic basket she was holding.

"Take a break from the tour! I made you chicken sandwiches with my own hands. "I also bought some hot pilavunas[42]"

As she said this, a loud rumble rose from her stomach...

Seçkin and Defne left behind their friends who were still eating and drinking gathered around the picnic basket. They advanced towards the western wing of the castle in the valley between two hills. They passed under an empty arch that had once served as the main gate to the royal palace and emerged onto the stone floor.

---

[42] *Pilavuna: It is a pastry specific to Cypriot cuisine. It is usually made with halloumi. It is consumed especially at breakfasts and gatherings. It is frequently homemade. It is consumed both hot or cold.*

"Silence!" said Defne. She let go of Seçkin's hands and walked to the clearing overlooking the cliff surrounded by iron railings. She stretched out against the edge of the cliff, spreading her arms to the sides. A light breeze came up and blew her brunette hair back.

Defne closed her eyes and took a deep breath. Then she opened her eyes and looked at the boy and smiled sweetly.

"I miss being alone with you."

Seçkin approached him. He wrapped his arms around her waist. They watched this fascinating sight under the bright sky for a while.

"It may seem strange to you, but while I'm here, I'm filled with more peace than I've ever been before. "These ruins make me feel like I belong here." said Defne.

She sighed.

Then she escaped from Seçkin's arms with a sudden move and held the boy's hand giggling.

She moved towards the second floor. Seçkin followed him.

"Queen's window. I want to see there." said Defne as she glided forward.

When they reached the second floor, Defne stopped in front of a large window that only had its stone skeleton remained. She folded her arms and looked wailfully at the window.

The window resembled the rose windows of the Gothic period.

Golden sun rays were reaching through the clouds on the mountain top towards the window.

Defne let go of Seçkin's hand. She approached the window and watched the view of Karmi Village standing below the castle.

"Once upon a time…" said the girl while looking at Seçkin. "This window you see witnessed a great tragedy."

Seçkin watched her with admiration as she sat on the window steps. She was as elegant as a princess.

"This window had a queen. Even though the queen lived in luxury, she was unhappy and lonely. She spent most of her day sitting here, combing her golden hair. From time to time, she would take walks in the forest."

She pointed Seçkin to sit next to her.

Seçkin sat next to his one and only love. Defne continued to explain, leaning her head on the boy's shoulder.

"There was also a goatherd living in these mountains and he played the pipe very beautifully. The goatherd was ugly and there were very few people who saw him."

Defne was startled and wrapped her arms tightly around Seçkin's arm.

"Some people say that the goatherd was the Devil himself."

Seçkin caressed the girl's hair.

"Time after time, while the queen was walking in the forest, she fell in love with this beautiful pipe sound and found the goatherd. And let alone finding him, she also fell in love with him. So they started to meet and be together frequently. The queen, who spent most of her nights secretly with this goatherd, gave birth to a daughter after a while. Her hair was also golden and her eyes were sky blue. When the girl grew up, she became more beautiful than her mother. The young girl used to go to the forest to pick flowers. One day, she heard the sound of a pipe coming from far away. She followed the sound and suffered the same fate as her mother. The girl started having a relationship with the goatherd like her mother."

Defne paused for a moment. It was obvious on her face that she was disgusted by the incident she described.

"As time passed, the queen noticed a change in her daughter and asked her why. Upon receiving the answer from her daughter, she dropped the comb she was holding here and threw herself off the rocks."

The tears flowing from Defne's eyes dropped onto Seçkin's hand.

Seçkin held Defne's chin and lifted her head from his shoulder to see her face.

"Are you crying?" he asked in surprise. His eyebrows were furrowed.

Defne stood up, hesitant to look at Seçkin, and turned around. Seçkin saw her rubbing her eyes with her delicate hands.

"No, I'm not crying." she replied in her muffled voice. Then she pointed to a sharp beam of light falling from the sky onto the ruins of the royal palace.

"Every time this golden light you see hits here, they sigh as *The Queen's hair is visible*. It is also believed that the poppies blooming around the castle are a symbol of the queen's blood."

Seçkin jumped to his feet. He moved towards Defne. He stroked her soft hair and turned her face towards him to see her eyes. As Defne looked with her green, clear eyes, tears trembled in her eyes and she sobbed silently, pressing her face to Seçkin's chest.

"My love! What's going on." Seçkin said with fear. His arms wrapped around Defne's body tightly.

"I'm so sorry for what I put you through. I'm so sorry for making you think that love is hopeless and painful. While I love you with all my heart, I am very sorry for being with someone else and causing you pain that you did not deserve."

Defne lifted her head from Seçkin's chest. Their gaze met. Her green eyes turned bloodshot.

"I don't regret anything I went through for you. Yes, maybe I felt great pain when I saw you with Korkut. Every time you passed me by in his arms, the poisonous dagger of this love stabbed into my heart. But having you in my arms right now made me forget all the pain I suffered."

Seçkin took out a ring from his pocket. He made it for Defne from the seeds of the Judas tree.

"This is for you…" said Seçkin while putting the ring on the girl's thin, delicate finger.

"Will you marry me, Defne Üzümcüoğlu?

Tears appeared in Defne's eyes and wet her cheeks once again. "Oh yes!" sobbed the girl.

"My eyes will never look at anyone else but you all my life."

Their eyes met once again. While Seçkin looked at the girl with love, he grabbed her from her temples, pulled her towards him and slowly approached to her lips.

Defne wrapped her arms around Seçkin's neck. When her sweet breath tickled Seçkin's insides, he started to kiss those delicious lips.

While Seçkin was kissing those perfect lips, he heard someone applauding passionately.

Then suddenly there was a thunderclap.

They both stepped back.

Korkut walked towards them with a malicious smile on his face.

"For a while, I felt like I was watching Shakespeare's magnificent tragedy again. An extraordinary show, huh, Romeo?" he said while looking at Seçkin with that mad bull look.

His voice was raspy and malicious, as always. Then he fixed his eyes on Defne. Seçkin's eyebrows furrowed. He pushed Defne towards the empty window frame at the back and stood in front of her.

"What do you want?" Seçkin asked angrily.

Korkut took a few more steps towards him.

"Oh… You look ambitious. Calm down, Romeo. Calm down."

This time his gravelly voice sounded unnervingly soothing and sly. He moved his sickly gaze over the boy. Those pitch-black eyes seemed like a reflection of the evil in his heart.

"What do you want?" said Seçkin again. The emphasis in his voice had increased.

Korkut got closer. Now he and Seçkin were looking at each other with anger, nose to nose.

"Go away, asshole!" Seçkin shouted. He seemed to lose the last fragment of self-control he had.

Korkut smiled slyly. When he looked into those deep, black eyes, Seçkin saw something in those eyes. A red flame flashed inside Korkut's pupils.

Thunder was heard again.

"You!" said Seçkin, squinting his eyes.

These eyes were not Korkut's eyes. Then everything happened suddenly. Seçkin felt a sharp pain in his abdomen. Defne's scream echoed in the sky as Korkut pulled the amethyst stone dagger back from the boy's stomach. Korkut ran away...

Seçkin put his hand to his stomach and stood there for a while.

He was trying to comprehend what was happening. While his body was trying to reject the pain, the warm blood flowing from his stomach and onto his hand was real.

Those red eyes, he remembered them.

He had encountered them centuries ago. Those eyes belonged to the son of the Devil. To Hematite…

Seçkin dipped his bloody hand into his pocket for a moment. He pulled out the silver pocket watch and brought it to light. The clock was stained with the boy's blood.

While Defne was screaming, the boy's feet could not resist the pain any longer and he collapsed where he was. The pain was beyond anything.

The pocket watch fell to the ground. The dragonfly relief on it flapped its wings. The minute hand began to tremble slowly.

While Seçkin was struggling with the pain, he heard someone running towards them.

"Run, Okalper! We are late!"

"Okalper…" Seçkin repeated. This name seemed very familiar to him.

"The boy was stabbed!" said the same voice again. "Okalper, we need to take the boy away from here."

The bells rang...

"We can't, Mel!" cried a young man. "It's too late now!"

"Who are these people? They heard Defne's screams," he thought to himself.

Everything was starting to get blurry.

There were voices. He couldn't immediately tell who they were coming from.

"Something happened to Seçkin!" said someone. I think this was Ayaz.

There were shouting. There was panic and anger everywhere. Defne was screaming.

"It was Korkut. It was Korkut!"

Seçkin was starting to get short of breath. He forced himself to breathe with difficulty.

Then he heard that voice.

"Seçkin! What happened to him?"

This was Burak. As soon as Seçkin heard his voice, a feeling of warmth filled him.

"It's because of you!" Burak shouted as he grabbed Defne's shoulders and pushed her back angrily.

"You finally got him into trouble!"

While Ayaz and Mert were holding Burak and trying to calm him down, Defne collapsed on the ground. She held Seçkin's head in his lap. She burst into sobs.

Sobs... It was as if the darkness in Seçkin's mind was being illuminated.

It was Defne who was sobbing... Yes, it was her...

"Do not die. Do not leave me."

Seçkin saw Defne's beautiful face, even though it was blurry. She looked so sad... This had happened before...

The minute hand of the blood-soaked silver pocket watch vibrated again.

The sobs were getting louder and the images in his mind were starting to come to life.

These sobs... He remembered them.

"Sapphire!" sobbed Princess Lal's voice. "Sapphire!"

Thunder clapped once again, splitting the sky.

"Sapphire...That was my name...I remember! I was reborn here as Seçkin Saral. To find you… Lal...My darling..."

The pocket watch started working. Click, click, click…

His mind was rapidly going back... The painful past was rapidly reliving. Lost memories were awakening as the engraved text on the back of the pocket watch appeared out of thin air...

"Old time, even if you do the most atrocious evil, my lover shall ever live young in our love."

Don't you see? True love knows no bounds

It is the only feeling worth the pain one endures

But the fate would weave its webs just as the happiness is in sight

Quick now! Open the third book,

The horn will blow!

The story will end with an epic war…

Kemal B. Caymaz

—Book Three—

SAPPHIRE

Kingdom Of The Morningstar

Coming Soon

Available at
amazon

Printed in Great Britain
by Amazon